A RHYTHMS OF REDEMPTION ROMANCE

To Believe in You

EMILY CONRAD

For those who have been betrayed,
May you find hope in the Trustworthy One.

1

*L*ina didn't have a good track record for trusting the
right people, but she did have some idea of who *not* to
trust. Matt Visser hovered near the top of that list, but
a lack of time and alternatives had dispatched Lina to Visser
Landscaping. She had no choice but to offer him a job.

She twisted the ring on her right hand. Grandma, who'd
passed the heirloom to her, had dealt wisely with Dad, a relationship far more complex than Lina would ever have with
Matt. She could cope. She *would* cope.

Beyond her windshield, stores of wood chips and gravel
flanked the lane that extended from her parking space to the
two men who worked on the far side of the yard. Both wore
matching green T-shirts and khaki shorts. From the distance,
tattoos appeared to cover one guy's arms.

That had to be Matt.

Awestruck's former bass guitar player.

Two years ago, when she'd learned he had been fired from
the rock band, relief flooded her. He and his addictions had
been nothing but trouble, and she was struggling to believe
he'd changed as much as Awestruck's manager, Tim, now

insisted. Tim claimed that, because of all Matt had overcome, he might be the right person for the position in more ways than one.

Matt's story did make quite the cautionary tale.

If he'd changed his behavior, he could be a real asset.

But that seemed like a big if. How often did people completely transform?

God could do anything.

Theoretically.

But what had He done in Matt's case? Only time would tell.

Ten-foot-tall concrete partitions separated each landscaping material from the next. Stray wood chips and gravel dotted the asphalt lane. A few steps from her car, a stone bruised her heel through her flats.

The tattooed man hoisted himself onto one of the partitions and pulled a sapling from a crack. He tossed it down to his partner—a teenager, she realized as she covered some of the distance.

Matt leapt from the wall onto the pile of finely ground gravel. He scrambled to the top of the cone-shaped mound. From there, he engaged in an animated conversation with the teen. By their hand motions, they appeared to be planning a stunt.

Pushed by a sticky August breeze, the cap sleeves of her top rippled against her arm, and one of her curls swung across her forehead.

The pair hadn't seen her yet, and if she waited for the situation to play out, she might spare herself the trouble of asking for this favor. Laid up in a body cast, Matt would be useless to her. She crossed her arms over the high waist of her jeans and stopped to observe.

A third man in a company T-shirt stepped into view at the far end of the drive. His path angled toward Matt.

The stunt planning was hard to decipher until the simple, common cadence of the words, "Okay. Here we go."

Matt lifted his arms over his head, lowered them, lifted them again, all in slow motion.

The latest bystander rushed closer with a shout, as if to intervene.

Undeterred, Matt whipped his arms forward and around. His body tucked and circled mid-air.

A front flip.

During his time with Awestruck, Matt had once fallen off a lift during a show. If that man had attempted a flip on such unforgiving terrain, he would have killed himself.

Now, though the partition blocked her view of his feet, he appeared to land upright before he slid out of sight.

Lina resumed her course toward the men.

Half a second later, to the teenager's guffaws, Matt stumbled away from the bottom of the gravel, shouted, and lifted his arms in victory.

"That was awesome!" The kid met him with a high five. "Where did you learn to do a flip? Can you teach me?"

"Matt!" Panting from the exertion of jogging up, the other man tossed his hands in exasperation.

Matt ignored him as he clapped the teen on the shoulder. "Cheerleading."

"What? No." The kid drew the syllable out with equal parts disbelief and horror.

Matt shrugged a shoulder that, as she drew near, appeared muscular.

That was different.

He had also rid himself of his sallow complexion and learned how to wash his hair since she'd last seen him, a month or two before his dismissal from Awestruck.

Maybe God really had done a transforming work in his life.

3

Matt tossed the kid a grin. "Going out for cheer is a good way to meet girls."

Or maybe not.

Gravel dust lightened the green of Matt's company T-shirt. Beneath his knee-length shorts, blood darkened a three-inch-wide section of his shin. He must've skinned it in his descent.

"You are a walking liability nightmare." A widow's peak accented the other man's tall forehead. He'd snuggly tucked his Visser Landscaping shirt into a pair of dressy khakis. Worked mostly in the office, probably.

"Relax, Pete. I'm fine." As the kid laughed some more, Matt's attention shifted to her.

Blue eyes?

Huh. She'd remembered them as brown.

Mischief lingered in his smile. "Welcome to Visser Landscaping, where we specialize in flips, flowers, and ..." His eyes narrowed in concentration, then his face lit. "Flandscaping."

The teen snickered.

"Sorry about him." Pete edged his shoulder in front of Matt's and planted his leather boat shoes as if staking a claim. "How can I help you?"

Matt rolled his eyes and stepped back to let Pete have his way.

"Actually, I'm here to talk to him." She motioned to Matt, who paused his retreat.

Pete didn't budge. "Who are you?"

She considered returning the question, because this guy obviously thought he was somebody. Visser Landscaping was a family-owned business. Did Matt have an older brother?

"He's working." Pete lifted his chin. "Unless this is about a job, I'm going to have to ask you to find him later on someone else's dime."

As if she were some teenage delinquent he had to run off the property.

Lina met his gaze with a level look. "It *is* about a job."

Although probably not of the variety Pete had in mind.

Pete cut a glance at Matt, then stalked off toward the greenhouse.

Meanwhile, the blood running down Matt's leg soaked into the barely visible upper edge of his white sock. The royal blue lip of his sneakers would be next. A large stone must've cut into his shin to cause such a thick trickle.

As Pete's footsteps faded into the distance, the teen chuckled.

Matt focused again on Lina. "So. What'd you need?"

"You're bleeding." She pointed.

He tipped his leg. "Sure enough."

"That was a spectacularly bad idea." She looked to the teen, hoping to drive the warning home.

The kid stuck his fingers in his hair and pulled them forward, blocking eye contact under the pretext of combing his bangs.

Smooth.

Matt's blue eyes cut to her car, a run-of-the-mill sedan, then refocused on her. "I know you from somewhere."

Shaving, showering, and sobriety had unburied features she hadn't known he possessed. Save for several scars, his square face had captivating symmetry. His nose was straight, his eyebrows broad but on the sparse side, and his jaw strong and clean.

His new lifestyle hadn't erased the tattoos, though. A couple of dark lines peeked past the neckline of his shirt. Familiar designs covered his arms. A rose. A skull. A lit match on his thumb, with flames sparking up his forearm. The words *love* and *hate* across the backs of his fingers. The panther was new— and especially tacky, even on a muscled arm.

She crossed her arms. "I'll give you one guess who I am."

He flinched, and his Adam's apple bobbed. He looked at his

sidekick, then back at her, as if deciding whether to hazard his guess in front of his audience. Then, he put his head down and passed her, on course for the main office building. "Come on, kid."

The teen loped by and fell into step beside him. "Is she famous?"

"Ask for her autograph." Matt kept walking.

She followed at a distance. Apparently curious, the boy kept shooting looks at her until he ran into the doorframe of the building. He jerked to attention and scampered inside on his hero's heels.

Lina was not famous and never cared to be. The only reasons Matt would've encouraged an autograph were to mess with the boy or to learn her name. Or both.

Still thirty feet from the log-cabin-style building, she checked her phone.

No one had emailed or called about the open position. If she didn't find someone to fill it, Key of Hope would have to turn kids away.

Like it or not, she needed Matt.

She heaved a breath and headed for the office. At the entrance, the teenager stepped past her on his way back out. The interior of the building had wide-plank pine floors, painted walls, and windows at the back overlooking a field of sunflowers. Much less like a dank hunting cabin than she'd expected. No movement or sound emanated from the doors that appeared to open into offices or the restroom, so they were alone.

Matt sat behind the front counter, bent sideways, presumably tending his wound. When he spotted her, he shifted, and a crank and swish sounded, a garbage can opening and closing. He watched her advance as though monitoring a wild animal that might just as soon tear him limb from limb as trot off harmlessly.

Was he afraid of her? Interesting.

All right, Lord. If he's one of Yours now, too, I'll give him a break.

A little one. In the form of a hint. "I used to wear my hair straight." She scrunched a handful of her curls. "You're not the only person to not recognize me now."

Which had been the point of accepting her natural curls.

Matt half-frowned.

Still stumped, then.

"Lina. Galina Abbey."

Matt's eyes narrowed, and concentration replaced the fear.

"You still don't remember?" She lifted a brow but managed to suppress an eye roll. "I'm Awestruck's social media manager."

Matt's mouth opened with realization. They'd worked together for about a decade as Lina supported the band by posting pictures, writing captions, managing fan groups, and replying to comments.

Of course, during his later years with the band, she'd involved Matt as little as possible, and no one—not one single member of Awestruck or the team behind them—had complained.

But if he was ashamed of his lurid behavior involving women, drugs, and inappropriate advances on Lina herself, it didn't show. As his mouth closed, his posture straightened with self-assurance.

"Who did you think I was?" she asked.

"Not important since you are who you are." He folded his hands on the counter. The movement interwove the words spelled on the backs of his fingers. Love and hate. As if the jury were still out on how he felt about her. "What can I do for Awestruck's social media manager?"

"I'm not here for Awestruck. That role's part-time. I also accepted a position with the non-profit Adeline Green is setting up—In the Key of Hope Music Lessons." The music studio, funded by the band and directed by the lead singer's fiancée,

Adeline, would offer kids from low-income families the opportunity to learn an instrument once it was up and running. "You're familiar with it?"

Matt nodded. "Didn't you live out east or something? You moved to Lakeshore?"

"All the cool kids were doing it."

Matt would know she meant Awestruck. Gannon had talked his bandmates into moving to small-town Wisconsin so he could live near Adeline. Matt *wouldn't* know that, while Gannon had moved toward love, Lina had relocated to escape it. Or, rather, to escape the wreckage of her own love story.

She had yet to find the fresh start she longed for. *Insteads* haunted her life in Wisconsin, as they had in New York. Instead of married, she remained single. Instead of cooking for two, she cooked for one. Instead of eagerly awaiting her own turn to have a baby, she stayed busy lining up instructors to teach music to other people's kids.

If those students were the only children she could look out for, she'd ensure they got the very best from Key of Hope. She would supervise Matt closely if he took the position. And she wouldn't let his silence fluster her into spilling personal details. She focused on business. "Adeline wants the freedom to travel with Awestruck after she and Gannon get married. So, she hired me to work on-site, managing the day-to-day at Key of Hope."

"Quite a change."

"You're one to talk."

This time he didn't flinch. When he wasn't strung out on drugs, he was actually good-looking. Somehow, both mischievous and dashing at the same time. He'd look killer in a tux.

But the pictures and clips she could recall of him dressed for awards shows or benefit galas involved stumbling, slurring, or worse.

Tim was convinced Matt would stick to the twelve-step program.

Lina would believe it when she saw it.

Maybe.

People could be awfully good at hiding dark secrets.

Another *instead*: Instead of her naïve, trusting nature, she'd become a skeptic.

"What brings you here?" he asked.

She drew a deep breath. Not every man was Shane, and because she wasn't as naïve as she used to be, she would take the necessary precautions to ensure Matt did no harm to any of the kids enrolled at Key of Hope. She could do this. She had to do this.

"It turns out when a famous band moves to an area, a lot of kids discover a new interest in music—especially guitar, bass, and drums. If we don't get more teachers, we're going to have to turn some students away."

His cheek twitched, and the corners of his mouth rose. "You want me to teach?"

MATT'S SHIN STUNG, and the moisture cooling his ankle had to be from blood seeping into his sock. He resisted checking. Watching Lina squirm was infinitely more fun than giving her another reason to look down her pert little nose.

From her milky skin—she either used a lot of sunscreen or didn't get out much—to her flouncy sky blue top to her pointy-toed shoes, she had *high maintenance* written all over her. She wore subdued makeup, her lips only a shade too dark and glossy to be natural.

Her curls were what mesmerized him, though. He'd seen tight curls and loose waves, but not Lina's texture of ... big curls? Frizz-free and soft-looking, her hair fell in thick swoops to her collarbone.

"Our program got a lot of applicants." Indents around her fingertips showed how hard she gripped her arm.

This one was wound up tighter than all those blond curls.

"You want me to teach." He'd like to hear her say it, since she'd been shedding judgmental vibes since she'd waltzed across the lot.

She smiled—he didn't buy it—and nodded. "It's part-time, but Tim said if you'd come, he'd work out housing for you—"

"Can't."

His interruption earned him the death stare.

"I offered you a free place to live."

"Compliments of Tim?" The manager had spent a fair amount of time running interference for Matt back when he'd been an addict. Tim operated by a different code than the band, willing to bend rules in his dogged pursuit to maintain Awestruck's success. "Nothing with him is ever free. You should know that by now."

Lina's eyebrows appeared combed. Did women do that? He watched as they pulled together, forming a crease over her nose. "What do you think he's going to make you do?"

She left the reasons for her skeptical tone unspoken. What awful thing could Tim require that Matt hadn't already done to himself?

Yeah, nothing.

"I'm just saying, if he's the reason you're here, he's got an angle, and it's not to help a charity."

"Maybe it's to help you get out of landscaping and back into music."

Music. The word resonated, as deep and powerful as a beat from a subwoofer. How placing his fingers on some strings and playing a few notes gave him as much of a rush as sky diving, he'd never understand. But for him, sky diving would be safer, no matter his love of music. "What if landscaping is where I belong?"

Her gaze combed his tattoos, and he knew exactly what she saw. He'd been seeing it himself since he'd gotten sober.

Other people's tattoos carried significant meaning. The best merged meaning and art. But his own? Some, he didn't remember getting. Two, he'd started and never finished. He'd chosen none of them—or their artists—carefully and didn't like any of them now.

Though he'd cleaned up his life to avoid going the same route his friend Auggie had, he couldn't rid himself of the evidence of who he'd been. A man bent on self-destruction.

Lina interpreted the evidence to mean he couldn't take an interest in mulch and arborvitae. He didn't. But he did take an interest in the machinery and leaving things better than he found them—and annoying Pete. Besides, he had a debt to pay.

Behind Lina, Krissy entered, brown hair straightened and makeup unapologetically heavy—unlike someone else's. His sister adjusted the strap of her huge purse as she peered toward his visitor, who hadn't turned from Matt.

Krissy must've judged Lina's profile as attractive, because she gave him a freakish wide-eyed look. He loved his sister more than pretty much any other human on earth. Only she'd want to set him up with the beautiful stranger and forget the reasons happily-ever-after wasn't in his future.

If any of his other family members happened in to overhear this conversation with Lina, they wouldn't be so tickled. His brother, Pete, would blow a gasket if he knew Matt's old life had come to lure him back in.

Or maybe Pete would bid him good riddance.

"I can't move to Lakeshore, no matter what the cool kids are doing." He smiled. After wronging as many people as he had, he didn't need to add continued rudeness to his list of offenses. "I made a commitment here."

Lina curled her lips inward and stepped back as if to leave. But then her chest rose with a massive breath. "What are your objections?"

"My objections?" Hadn't he heard Tim ask that same question a few times over the years? The guy must've been spending a lot of time at Key of Hope. Matt doubted Adeline paid him a salary, so what was in it for him? Pride?

Tim wouldn't help launch an entire business only to get Matt to move to Lakeshore, would he?

Lina swept a curl from her temple, seeming to gather resolve. "To teaching at Key of Hope."

Admiration sparked in Krissy's eyes. Whether Lina had learned these persuasion tactics from Tim or not, they were all her own now.

"I told you. Prior commitment." Beyond that, he wouldn't explain the debt he owed. Lina would tumble right back into righteous judgment if she knew. "Besides, I need full-time work."

She assessed him, the hard line of her shoulders softening. "They say you've changed."

"Trying to."

She gave a minuscule nod. With another step backward, she brought Krissy into her view. She offered his sister a polite smile before focusing on Matt again. "I'm glad for you. Take care."

Matt watched her go. His past kept showing up, and not just on his skin or in the form of Lina, come to offer him a job. Krissy had sobbed, explaining how hurt she'd been by his choices. Pete treated him like a convict sentenced to community service, though Matt had somehow managed to avoid a formal record. Awestruck produced hit after hit, and each song reminded him of how he'd failed men who'd once been his closest friends. He'd hurt a lot of people. Each time he planned a way to make amends with one, another showed up.

Maybe this run-in with Lina marked a turning point, though. She hadn't revealed some offense he'd long forgotten that he now had to atone for. Hadn't left his conscience burning, regret ready to engulf him.

She'd come, they'd had a conversation, and she'd left.

And at the thought of Awestruck, he felt only goodwill.

They worked at their craft with uncommon discipline, and Matt had only pulled them down. Without him, they owned their share of the market like few bands could dream of, especially after so many years. He wished them and, by extension, Adeline with her music studio, all the best.

They were all truly better off without him.

Krissy rounded the counter and slung her purse beneath it. "Matt!"

With a jerk, he quit staring after Lina to find Krissy gawking at his leg.

"Oh. Yeah." The bleeding had stopped, but his cleanup effort left a pretty grotesque smear. He stepped toward the restroom.

"What was it this time?" Humor lightened Krissy's voice. "Find a helicopter to jump out of? A cave to explore? A bear to tame?"

"My life isn't nearly as interesting as you think it is." He flipped on the light in the small restroom and yanked a few paper towels from the dispenser.

"It's more interesting than mine."

Interesting wasn't synonymous with good. If he'd kept his life boring, he would've hurt far fewer people. From here on out, boring ranked as his number one aspiration.

2

*M*att knew no one besides his father who considered the speed limit a maximum. Using the passenger side mirror, Matt eyed the luxury sedan hovering near the tailgate of their company truck. At the first opportunity, the car passed. He caught a glimpse of a dress shirt and tie before the sedan sped toward town.

If Matt had any real-world skills to speak of, he wouldn't tolerate his father's way of doing things either. But his employment options had been an unskilled factory job or the family business. He was opposed to hair nets and appreciated sunshine, so here he was.

Dad kept a steady hand on the wheel as the speeding sedan faded into the distance. Matt's old man had spent his whole life in one city, building the business that now supported generations of their family. He had good relationships with all three of his kids and hundreds—thousands?—of satisfied customers. Any risk he'd taken had been a calculated choice, never an impulse, never careless.

Make me like him, God.

Patient. Content. Hard-working. Dedicated.

Matt couldn't picture himself as the steady one with gray creeping into his brown hair and weathered smile lines around his eyes, the one who'd built a lasting positive legacy.

Matt could hardly repay his debts, let alone build something new.

Dad slowed as he passed the sunflower field, where morning sun illuminated yellow crowns. The blinker ticked for the turn into Visser Landscaping. "This is the day the Lord has made."

Matt couldn't bring himself to quote the rest of the Bible verse the way Mom always did.

Stray gravel crunched beneath the tires in the parking lot as Dad spared him a pointed look. "We will rejoice and be glad in it."

"Yes, sir."

Dad chuckled. "It's not an order. It's a privilege."

Saving him from having to voice his doubts, Pete stormed out of the building and toward their truck. An expression that dark, aimed this direction, meant he'd found another fault with Matt.

"He's at it early." Dad took the keys from the ignition, and they both climbed out.

"You're fired!" Pete's shout sliced through the still morning.

This, rather than privileges, was what Matt expected from his life. He followed his dad toward the office building.

Pete fell in step and shoved his phone toward Dad. "Jason Baxter isn't happy."

Matt glanced over, but his brother blocked his view of the screen. Jason Baxter owned a dozen apartment complexes around town. Visser Landscaping mowed for him in summer and plowed in winter. Matt had spent the majority of last week at one of his new builds, adjusting the slope so run-off would drain properly. He hadn't had a run-in with Baxter, his employees, or even his renters, but the new building did stand next to an existing one that had about three dozen windows pointed toward the work area.

Someone might've seen Matt's non-traditional method of keeping the skid steer from digging into the grass at the bottom of the drainage ditch.

He craned his neck and caught a glimpse of the phone. Definitely a video of a piece of yellow machinery. "I had it under control, and I saved us the hassle of having to fix ruts in the ditch."

"By doing wheelies?"

"The backend would've dragged otherwise. People do it all the time."

"Only in your world—in your mind—is a dangerous idea like that a viable option." Pete motioned at the phone screen, but the display had gone dark. "This never should've occurred to you."

"You can't tell me what I'm allowed to think."

"Boys." Dad passed the phone back to Pete and pulled open the main entrance.

Pete caught Matt's shoulder, keeping him from entering the building. "Jason called to pull his contracts with us. The only way I could save the account was by telling him you wouldn't be working here anymore."

The news stopped Dad in his tracks.

Matt clenched his teeth. "Yeah, I'm sure you tried everything else."

Pete couldn't expect to get away with this.

Dad let go of the door and turned to face them, surrendering to having this conversation on the front walk. "There must be another solution." He worked his fists into his jacket pockets and let them hang heavily, as if he were suddenly exhausted.

Matt expected conflicts as a natural consequence of

working with Pete, but Dad didn't deserve this. Couldn't Pete see what his grudge against Matt was doing?

"I tried." Pete lifted helpless hands. "I said we'd reassign Matt, but he knows he's family and said if our family would do this on his property, he doesn't want any of us there. Says he lost a brother to a farming accident."

Oh. A weight settled over Matt. If his actions had stirred up such a significant loss, Pete may really have had no choice.

Pete's grim expression turned to Matt. "I had to show him we were serious about safety, and the only way to convince him was to promise to let you go."

Dad grunted. "Call him back." He worked his hands from his pockets with more effort than it should've taken, then grabbed the door again. "We're not trading family for anyone's business."

Neither Matt nor Pete followed him in.

The door closed with a heavy thump.

Matt braced his hands on his hips and studied the moss growing between the front step and the building.

Pete huffed. "He said I might be saving your life by taking it seriously. I didn't tell him you'd just move on and do your stunts somewhere else."

Where? At one of the factories? In a construction job? If he displayed his personality in a place like that, he'd be fired on the spot. In fact, if they knew about the skid steer, even those willing to overlook his history of drug abuse might balk at hiring him.

"You are going to move on, right?" Pete sounded half sorry, half worried. "You can't let Dad throw away our biggest customer. Without Baxter—"

"I know."

Through the window in the door, he watched Dad flick on the lights in the office and close himself in, movements slow and halting instead of steady.

Allowing Dad to lose a major account would add years of lost income to what Matt already owed. Besides, living off Mom and Dad ... well, he'd seen it as his only option, but he'd never felt good about imposing on them.

Maybe this was God's way of telling him he had to do better, to strike out on his own so he could make amends for his past and move into the kind of future he could live with. And maybe God had paved the way by sending Lina with that job offer a couple of days ago.

She had said the role at the non-profit would come with a place to stay. Teaching music lessons part-time wouldn't pay what he made here—which hadn't been impressive to start with—but he did miss music. And he liked the idea of making a difference.

He also missed being valued for his talents. Despite Lina's reservations, she and Tim must've seen something in him, or she wouldn't have come. Even the begrudging vote of confidence had an undeniable draw.

While the teaching job had to be tame, he could end up in trouble if he got too involved with Tim and Awestruck. Not that any of them used, but Tim drank, and plenty of people the band worked with regularly did that and more.

He'd need boundaries.

He'd have to find recovery meetings up in Lakeshore, steer clear of the band, pick up side jobs to pay his debts on schedule, and build a safe, boring life for himself.

"You need a ride somewhere?" Pete shifted his feet like he didn't know what to do with his victory.

"I'd better talk to Dad first."

Pete nodded, studying him with an unreadable expression. After a moment, he turned, leaving Matt to go inside and disappoint his dad one more time.

LINA HAD OVERDONE IT AGAIN. The jars of chicken and dumpling soup in the passenger seat clinked against each other as she pulled into the lot behind Key of Hope. If she weren't alone in the world, her love of cooking and baking wouldn't be so problematic.

But here in the Land of Instead, where she didn't even have the prospect of a family? Her kitchen hobbies resulted in so much food that she had trouble finding enough people to share it with. Hopefully, as Key of Hope geared up for lessons, she'd get to know more families who would be grateful for a break from cooking.

She collected her purse and the shoebox packed with four jars and headed toward the building. Inside the back door, stairs leading to the second floor ascended to her right. The bathroom waited on the left. Thanks to the building's age and wooden floors, the place smelled like the elementary school she'd attended, but the furnishings were more inviting.

She continued forward into the corridor between the small classrooms. Soundproof glass separated the three rooms. Sandwiched between an optometrist office and a used bookstore on Main Street, Key of Hope had no windows on the side walls, but thanks to the open interior, the ample windows up front allowed in plenty of natural light.

Past the classrooms, at the front of the building, the space opened into a waiting room and an office area, separated from each other by the arrangement of furniture. For students and parents, sleek leather couches and chairs sat on an area rug. Lina's desk marked the edge of the office space. Plants added a touch of greenery, and the walls displayed a mix of art, old instruments, and lyrics that spoke of the power of music. Antique tin ceiling tiles hung over it all.

Adeline sat at the table that ran along the exposed brick wall, her glossy brown hair glinting in the Monday morning light. She waved hello without looking away from her laptop, then held up one finger, signaling she'd give a better greeting soon.

Lina set down her load to power on her laptop.

Adeline had set up the space and, with Tim's help, much of the behind-the-scenes paperwork before Lina's arrival in Wisconsin. Together, she and Adeline had been vetting and hiring teachers, and the first lessons were to begin next week. Lina still couldn't piece together how a place associated with so much star power struggled to interest enough qualified bass guitar instructors. She'd have thought anyone with the skill to play would've put their name in the hat for the chance to rub shoulders with the band.

Yet, as she checked her email, she found no new applicants.

Adeline, a bass player herself, could fill the gap until she married Gannon mid-September. That would buy Lina a few more weeks to find an instructor. She'd broach the subject as soon as Adeline finished whatever she was typing.

She minimized her email program. Her desktop background featured a photo of her grandma's summer home in Maine, dubbed The Captain's Vista because it had originally belonged to a sea captain in the 1800s. Throughout her childhood, Lina had spent relaxing months there with her grandparents, exploring the harbor town, eating lobster, and finding herself loved, appreciated, and accepted for something other than her grades or extracurricular performance.

If only her life's upheaval hadn't kept her from visiting the place for two summers now.

With a sigh, she carried the soup to the corner, where they'd set up a coffee station on top of a mini-fridge. She was finagling space to stash the soup when the front door sounded its familiar complaint as it scraped open.

Tim stepped in, his hair windblown. He wore dress pants and a button-down—no tie, but still, he was pulled together enough for her to believe that he'd probably combed his hair before leaving the house.

He'd been divorced longer than his fourteen-year-old daughter had been alive. Did he, too, feel like he was living an unfortunate alternate life? And how did his daughter, Isabella, feel? The few times the fourteen-year-old had stopped by, she hadn't seemed to enjoy the day camp he'd been sending her to while he worked this summer, but she did rave about the boarding school where she stayed the rest of the year. A nice meal could do them good.

She lifted a jar for Tim to see. "Chicken and dumpling?"

"Sure. Thanks." He pulled up a chair by her desk.

Great. He must be planning an interrogation about her trip to see Matt.

She dawdled putting the soup in the fridge, then brewed a cup of coffee. As the machine gurgled, she glanced again at Tim, who worked on his phone while he waited. Dark smudges underscored his eyes. Could he have drunk enough at John's wedding two days before to still show the effects?

Lina hadn't been invited to the drummer's tiny, beach-side ceremony, so she'd taken the day to drive down and see Matt instead. John's photographer had, however, forwarded her two pictures for her to share on social media, one for John's own account and one for Awestruck's. The event looked fit for a storybook, the couple appearing as happy as Lina had been the day she'd gotten engaged.

She swallowed a serving of jealousy as plentiful as the batch of soup she'd made.

With a prayer for the newlyweds' future, Lina swept her now-full coffee mug from below the spout, delivered a jar of soup to Tim, and settled at her desk. "How was the wedding?"

"Philip quit." Tim *thunk*ed the soup on the corner of her desk.

He liked to keep people guessing, and that suited her as

long as his games delayed the conversation about her failure to recruit Matt.

She adjusted her ring. Along with The Captain's Vista and funds that could finance a truly lavish lifestyle, she'd inherited her grandma's jewelry. Lina left most of the fortune untouched, choosing to live off her salary from Awestruck and Key of Hope, but picking one of Grandma's rings to wear each day had become an important part of her routine.

Centering today's emerald on her finger helped to settle her resolve about Matt. She could've tried harder to recruit him, but she respected his decision to stand by a prior commitment.

Tim wouldn't understand, so the longer they talked about Awestruck's current bassist, Philip, instead of its former bassist, the better.

"Philip quit what?" She sipped her coffee.

"Awestruck."

Her throat closed, blocking her swallow. She gulped, got the liquid down, and coughed. "What? Why?"

Tim took a breath, but Adeline's voice cut in first. "Personal reasons."

The firm tone, so different from her norm, must've carried extra weight with Tim because he clearly had more to add but kept his mouth shut.

Lina swiveled to face Adeline. "Has this been brewing for a while?" She'd seen Matt's dismissal coming from a mile away, but she'd never suspected trouble that would inspire Philip to leave. He'd only been with the band two years.

Adeline paused and tilted her head. "Maybe on his side, but we found out about the possibility last week."

Last week. Tim had been hounding Lina to recruit Matt for the teaching position since long before that, but the man was sharp. Had he foreseen Philip's departure sooner than anyone else? If so, he might have wanted Matt back in the band's orbit in case they ended up needing a bassist down the line. Or had he simply wanted to stockpile resources?

Either way, with Philip leaving, Tim would be even more motivated to move Matt closer, first as an instructor at Key of Hope where he could prove himself, then as the band's next bassist.

As if Gannon and John, who'd founded the band and made up the other two members, would rehire him. Though Awestruck was a secular group, its founding members were both outspoken Christians who liked the band to model a better way to a hurting world. Matt certainly hadn't helped that cause.

Yet Tim watched her with an intensity that seemed to promise he'd get his way.

Didn't he know it was a lost cause? Even Matt was against the plan.

What in the world could've inspired Philip to quit now? The band had just landed a lucrative new contract. Philip might not want to be away from his kids as much as Awestruck's schedule demanded, but if the children motivated the choice, Adeline and Tim would say so.

Would Lina ever learn the whole story? A press release was probably already in the works, but it was sure to be vague. Using that as her model, she'd likely have to craft equally vague social media posts about the change.

She glanced at the calendar on the wall. "You have to find a new bassist before they go to the studio? In two weeks?"

While John was gone on his honeymoon?

"Philip's going to record this album, then he's out."

"Then you have a couple of months."

Tim's phone sounded before he could confirm. "Word travels fast. I've been fielding calls since yesterday." He rose, leaving the chair next to her desk, and claimed the jar of soup. He lifted it in silent thanks. "I'll catch up with you later."

And he was gone again.

Adeline shook her head as if she didn't understand Tim's reason for stopping by Key of Hope, but Lina knew. He wasn't giving up on bringing Matt in. First as a teacher, then as a band member.

But if the teaching position was the stepping-stone Tim seemed to think, applications ought to pour in now that the band needed a bassist.

She refreshed her inbox. A few companies had emailed to offer services.

Only one individual had sent a message: Matt Visser.

So much for standing by his commitment to the family business.

3

"*I* tried everything else to feel happy, and none of it worked." Matt rested a hand on the podium next to the notes he wasn't using and looked out at the kids. "The good always faded, and it left consequences I'm still paying for. Some will literally show on my body the rest of my life. I mean, right?" He pointed at the panther on his arm.

The kids chuckled uncomfortably.

Thanks to his past with Awestruck, he'd filled the community theater. If he were a more polished speaker, he could leverage his resume to fill bigger spaces. But even before modest crowds, he felt like a fraud. His testimony was only powerful because of how badly he'd messed up. Normally, he found comfort in using his failures to showcase God's transforming goodness, but how much had he really transformed? He'd just been fired again, this time from the family business. What right did he have to stand on this stage and tell kids how to live?

None. But the God who starred in this talk wasn't done with him, and if these kids turned to the Lord now, they could avoid years of regret later.

As he gathered his thoughts for his closing, he noticed a familiar man standing at the back of the small theater.

Tim.

Lina hadn't replied to Matt's joke of a résumé, presumably because the video of him in the skid steer had gone viral with the caption, "Look what Awestruck's former bassist Matt Visser is up to now."

Most of the commenters had appreciated his talent and ingenuity, but Lina? He suspected she'd take as dark of a view of that as Baxter had.

Anyway. He had a job to do here and now.

He stepped away from the podium and made purposeful eye contact with some of the teens as he continued. "The day I found my best friend, August Peltier, dead of an overdose, I realized the things I was using to make myself feel better would eventually kill me. The Bible says sin leads to death—not only the physical kind, but eternal separation from God. Thankfully, God offers an alternative through Jesus Christ. Eternal life. A life that can start right now, today. A life that leads to the peace, meaning, and joy I was desperate for."

With another few lines, he wrapped up his talk, then circled back to grab his notes—why did he even bother bringing them anymore?—before taking a seat off to the side.

As the youth pastor who'd recruited him for this talk took the podium for closing remarks, Tim dropped into the neighboring seat. He tilted his head, checking out the panther tattoo. Must not have passed muster because Tim smirked as he focused forward.

～

AN HOUR LATER, Matt and Tim settled in a booth at a twenty-four-hour pancake restaurant.

Matt glanced at the menu, noted the French toast, and

placed the laminated booklet on the edge of the table. "What'd you think?"

Tim flipped his menu closed and focused on Matt. "How much do you make off a gig like that?"

Of course the guy went right for the bottom line, dashing Matt's hopes that Tim had found him at the theater out of curiosity about Christ. Or maybe he was hiding behind a conversation about money.

Last spring, Tim had enrolled his daughter in a Christian boarding school, and when Tim and Matt had reconnected this summer, the manager had asked some questions about faith.

But Gannon and John had been witnessing to Tim for years. Listening to Matt's weak testimony wouldn't break through after everything else had failed.

"I always speak for free," he admitted.

"Free?" Tim scoffed. "You should get an agent. Book speaking engagements. You could make a mint."

"I'm trying to pay for my mistakes, not profit off them."

"Yeah? How's that going?" Tim's gray-blue eyes flashed with amusement.

He probably knew Matt had been fired because of Baxter, since he kept tabs on his clients to head off scandals and road-blocks. Not that Matt was a client, but when Matt had reached out to make amends with Awestruck this summer, Tim had become his biggest fan. He'd been pushing Matt to write and sell other songs. Those aspirations must've led the manager to start keeping tabs.

"Don't worry about it." Tim chuckled. "You don't need that job."

The one for Visser Landscaping or as a professional speaker? Before he could ask, Tim continued.

"The fact that you're a fanatic now will work in our favor. You'll fit in better with Gannon and John."

Did he mean a religious fanatic? Gannon and John had

once seemed fanatical about their beliefs to him, too, but Matt's still-young faith didn't compare with the battle-tested beliefs of his former friends.

"I gave them the song, and I'm grateful you helped make that possible, but my story with Awestruck ends there." The lyrics and melody of "Whirlwinds" had fallen in his lap one day, not long after he'd started praying for a way to make things right with the bandmates he'd failed. He'd fleshed it out into a full song and gifted it to Awestruck.

Since, he'd thought of a few bars here and there, but nothing came of them.

A waiter stopped by for their orders. Once the menus were cleared, Tim gave his rattling silverware a pointed look.

Matt froze the foot he'd been jiggling, and the utensils stilled. "They don't want anything else from me, and I'm not looking to get back into that world."

Too easy to let himself and everyone else down.

Tim braced his palms against the edge of the table and leaned against the seat back. "Philip's out."

Of Awestruck?

A memory of a seething Gannon surfaced—the night Matt himself had been fired.

Matt had gone out, gotten drunk, and brought a party back to the house where the band was staying. Unbeknownst to him, a minor had found her way into the group. She'd been drinking, and one of the men was hitting on her when Gannon discovered their gathering. The lead singer had rightfully taken extra offense at the minor's presence, but high on who remembered what, Matt had tried to defend the situation.

Maybe that night explained Matt's burden to speak to teens when he was asked.

If roles had been reversed, Matt might've punched Gannon, but the lead singer had shown restraint even as he broke up the party. And then he'd fired Matt and sent him packing.

Had the situation with Philip gotten equally out of hand? Maybe. Addiction could take people to some ugly places.

"He all right?" Matt asked.

"He's getting help." Tim assessed him. "You're not surprised."

Matt shrugged. He'd seen enough to suspect Philip's addiction this summer.

"Takes one to know one, huh?" Tim said. "Well, maybe you'll be happy he sounds like the rest of you now."

"The rest of us?"

"You, Gannon, and John. God saves, drugs are bad, money's not everything."

Good for Philip. Faith and right priorities would help immensely on the long journey to come.

"What would you say about those things?" Matt asked. "God, drugs, and money?"

"You don't want to know."

Matt tipped his head. Whatever Tim thought, he'd heard worse. He'd *believed* worse. "Let's hear it."

"God is more trouble than He's worth, drugs can be bad, and money sure is helpful."

The changes Matt had picked up on hadn't sunk very deep. Yet. If God could reach Matt, He could reach anyone.

"Anyway." Tim planted his forearms on the table. "You've got to come teach. Awestruck will see you've gotten your act together. I can talk them into working with you."

"Lina hasn't responded to my email."

"I'll handle Lina. The job's yours if you want it, but I can't hold off your competition forever."

Wait. What?

Tim shook his head, cutting off questions. "It's a job. You need a job. Say thank you."

"I'm interested in the teaching job, but nothing more."

"This is Awestruck. Your chance to redeem yourself."

29

Or to utterly fail. Again.

"I'll teach. That's it."

Tim narrowed his eyes and sighed. "Fine. You'll teach."

Matt nodded once. "Thank you."

~

WHO, besides Lina's parents, would hire someone to serve as the voice on their answering machine? No one. She could imagine how it had gone, though. Mom disliked recordings of her voice. Dad, never one to suffer similar self-consciousness, must've thought having staff record the greeting made him seem more successful.

Lina flipped on her blinker to pull into the lot of Key of Hope as she listened to an unfamiliar female voice say, "You have reached the Abbey residence. Please state your name, phone number, and reason for calling so the appropriate party may return your call."

Eight o'clock in Wisconsin made it nine in New York. On a Thursday morning like this, Dad had probably been at the office for hours, and Mom would be off on some charitable crusade, but Lina hadn't tried either of their cell phones.

This game of tag was all that remained of their relationship, and a conversation wouldn't bring them closer unless someone had changed their mind regarding Grandma's estate—which Dad felt should've gone to him—or Shane—who Dad believed was good for the money he'd stolen.

Since Lina couldn't concede either point, here she was, calling to leave her dutiful weekly message when neither would answer.

"Hi, Mom and Dad, it's Galina." She hated her full first name, but her parents had refused to honor her requests to call her by the shortened version, and she'd given up convincing them long ago—why let one more thing come between them?

"I'm pulling into Key of Hope. We're still looking to hire our last instructor, but other than that, the staff is in place, and we're on track to start lessons on Monday. Running social media for Awestruck is even easier with the band close by. Anyway, let me know how things are going for you both. Love you. Bye."

She shifted into park, hit the button to disconnect, and grabbed the phone from the magnetic dash mount. Most likely, it would be a few days before one of her parents deigned to return the message, listing off a few facts about their own work on her voicemail.

Back in the day, she used to report about her schoolwork and extracurricular activities, and they'd drone on about their efforts to better—or take over—the world.

Only when she'd been with Shane had she seen a glimmer of her parents' interest and approval. Her ex came from a prestigious family, and he'd made Dad a tidy profit from real estate investments before Dad introduced them. Lina and Shane had hit it off, and during their relationship, they'd attended galas and dinners with her parents. Once they'd gotten engaged, Mom had been all too happy to croon about Lina's wedding plans.

Looking back, Dad had boasted about Shane, not Lina, when he'd paraded them around to his business associates. Mom had liked the status boost of the association with Shane's family. The spell had broken when her engagement did, and Grandma's decision to leave the family fortune to Lina had furthered the rupture.

Now, their so-called relationship hung on by the thread of weekly voicemails.

Sunlight streamed over the roofs of the two-story buildings in the downtown business area, gracing even the parking lot, despite its trash cans and the abandoned car in the corner, with a warm and safe glow.

Inside, Adeline sat at the sun-soaked workspace along the

brick wall, perched cross-legged on the chair. "Samantha stopped in. She took the last two jars of soup and wanted me to tell you you're an angel."

Some of Lina's disappointment lifted. Samantha, one of the first instructors they'd hired, had young kids, including the adorable eight-year-old Bailey, whom Lina had met about a week before. At least the soup tsunami would benefit someone.

"Anyway." Adeline fixed a wary gaze on her computer. "I figured out our mystery." With a lifted hand, she invited Lina to look at her screen.

Lina dropped her purse on her chair and crossed the office. Cocking her head, she recognized the job search site where they'd posted their open positions. Notification settings cluttered the screen.

Each position had a field where they could specify which email address should be notified of new applicants. Most were grayed out, indicating resumes would route to the default contact, Lina. But for the bass guitar teacher, black type indicated a manually entered email address.

Tim's email address.

"When did he do that?" Since posting the bass position, she'd received four or five applications, none viable. "He must've found a way to have the system forward ones he hand-picked? Ones he knew we wouldn't take?"

Adeline tipped her head. "There are about thirty apps here."

Thirty. Meaning twenty-plus applicants had threatened Tim's plans for Matt. "Why is he so enamored with Matt, anyway?"

Someone sucked in a breath behind her. "Don't make this awkward."

Lina stiffened and spotted Tim near the entry, Matt at his elbow, shutting the front door behind them. Of all the occasions for her to miss hearing the ill-fitting door push open.

"You're kidding." She hadn't meant to let her frustration slip out.

Tim responded with a self-satisfied smile.

Matt stepped into the waiting area, one hand steadying the strap of a ratty guitar case over his shoulder. He surveyed the couches and wall art as if his opinion mattered. Finally, his line of sight landed on her, and he gave a nod of greeting. "You did come all the way down to Fox Valley to offer me the job."

"And then ignored his email, he says." Tim lifted his eyebrows.

Lina crossed her arms. "You don't get to play like *I* did something wrong."

"You overlooked a qualified applicant."

"Thanks to your stunt, we overlooked thirty of them."

Tim grunted a laugh.

Matt seemed to note Adeline, and his expression turned apologetic.

Adeline might be sweet, but Key of Hope was her pet project, and she knew how to stand up to Tim when it was important. Knowing the staff would influence the kids, Adeline would never allow an unreliable and immature teacher. Or so Lina thought until her boss interlaced her fingers and remained seated, apparently content to observe.

Lina drew a breath and squared off with Tim. "He was fired from not one but two jobs." Awestruck and Visser Landscaping —and who knew how many others?

She'd seen the video that had cost Matt the position at his family's landscaping business—and according to the count on the footage, so had millions of other people. His coordination apparently extended beyond the control of his own body to machines he operated. Though he made it look easy to balance the little tractor thing on two wheels using the bucket as a counterbalance, she doubted that was the case.

As Pete had said, Matt was a walking liability.

"Technically, I quit Visser Landscaping." Challenge deepened Matt's irises to rival the blue of Lake Superior.

"I thought you'd made a commitment there." The inconsistency—his firm no when she'd gone to Fox Valley and his interest in the job such a short time later—irked her. Shane had taught her that the weaknesses people showed were often signs of deeper flaws. As an addict, Matt must've mastered hiding the worst about himself.

"I'll make good on my commitment another way." He scanned the classrooms. "Working here will do."

Will do? He didn't even *want* the position?

Adeline's desk chair rattled, and she took up station next to Lina. "What happened to working for your dad?"

Matt's expression once again softened for Adeline. Probably had something to do with her kind tone. "You saw the video?"

Adeline nodded.

"The property owner's brother died in a farming accident, and he reacted strongly to my method of saving him some money."

Adeline lifted an eyebrow. "How did that stunt save money?"

"Skid steers are clunky. The backend would've dragged at the bottom of the ditch, tearing up the grass. We would've had to fix it, which would've taken more hours, which would've increased the customer's bill."

Adeline nodded slowly, as if coming to terms with the explanation.

Not her too.

"Would this be a stop-gap for you until you found something else?" Adeline asked.

"Would it matter if it were? Look." Tim lifted his hands. "He can literally start right now. You've found the other applications. The first time he steps out of line, send him packing and call someone else in."

Matt shot him a look that was less than grateful.

Tim motioned him to settle down. "You're not going to mess up, but she'll only believe it when she sees it." He tipped his head toward Lina.

She scoffed.

"What? It's true, right?" A smile snuck onto Tim's face. "Come on. Give the guy a chance. What's the worst that could happen?"

"I'm sure I can't even imagine." Her parents had been letting her down her whole life, but it was Shane who'd gone and shown her how much worse a person could do.

Adeline must not have had similar experiences, because she stuck out her hand to Matt. "Welcome to Key of Hope."

4

*M*att felt like a gorilla on display in the zoo. The classrooms at the back of Key of Hope were made of glass, and from her desk in the front area, Lina kept shooting him looks clearly intended to tell him he was a monster.

The one kind of privacy the room seemed to afford was sound. As Lina worked and fielded phone calls out in the office area, he hadn't heard a thing. Which meant he could say what he needed to say without judgmental ears overhearing.

He focused on Adeline.

Their paths had crossed two years before, when the band had set up shop in Lakeshore. Matt had been deep in his addictions. Their stay in the small town had ended with him getting fired.

How must he have seemed through Adeline's soft brown eyes that summer? She dressed casually, and her long brunette hair was the shiniest thing about her appearance. She had *wholesome* written all over her, but she wasn't foolish.

She must've thought of a dozen ways he could ruin this place by now—he certainly had—but she gave no sign of worry. She'd given him this opportunity at her non-profit and had taken it upon herself to train him on the material and techniques he'd need to know in order to teach ten- to seventeen-year-olds bass guitar.

It was grace, pure and undeserved.

"Thank you for this opportunity, Adeline."

She nodded, assessing him as if she could see the regret that had him by the neck.

The night he'd gotten fired from Awestruck, before his final confrontation with Gannon, he'd come across her attempting to pick up bass guitar after setting it aside for years. He'd seen her as an enemy then. The competition. A threat to his job. After all, if the woman Gannon loved could play bass, what would stop him from firing Matt and putting her in his place?

Back then, everything except the truly dangerous things had seemed like a threat.

Turned out, Gannon fired Matt without a backup plan, and rightfully so.

"Last time I saw you," he said, "when you were the one who needed a few pointers, I wasn't so kind."

The corner of her mouth quirked, showing agreement without resentment.

"I'd like to make amends for that somehow."

"It's forgiven, Matt." She sealed the statement with a smile that was more in her eyes than on her lips.

"Thank you, but I'd still like to do something." He scanned the space. Looked recently updated. "Is there some project I can do to help you out?"

Her bottom lip pushed up as she thought, then she shook her head. "All I ask is that you do a good job for the kids."

"Helping them is important to me too. I'll do my best."

"Oh." Her eyes brightened, and she thumped the table between them. "And come to the wedding."

Matt's jaw went slack. She wanted him at her wedding?

Her wedding to Gannon? Did Gannon want him there?

Thanks to tabloids and entertainment shows, Matt knew the event was coming up next month. Invites must've gone out at least a month before, and he hadn't received one. Hadn't expected one, given how he'd exited the band.

Making amends with the gift of a song this summer didn't mean he expected a pass back into their inner circle. He waved the idea off. "You don't want me there."

"Of course." She gave a smile and a nod. "You'll know lots of people, and we're working together now. Why shouldn't you be there?"

"Does Gannon know you're inviting me?"

"Gannon was impressed by 'Whirlwinds.' And he believes in forgiveness."

Meaning what? He'd begrudgingly tolerate Matt's presence? Matt had already caused the guy enough trouble without lurking at the wedding.

"You asked what you could do for me," Adeline said.

Matt suppressed a groan.

"You can show you trust me—and the fact that you're forgiven—by attending the wedding." She tipped her chin down and leveled a look at him. "And having a good time."

Matt rubbed his forehead. Attending the wedding would be better than disappointing Adeline. Besides, the heartfelt invitation oozed redemption. "Okay."

"Great. I'll put you on the list." She tapped the tablet screen, skipping to another section of the electronic lesson book. With all the video tutorials they had access to through the online portal, the kids could probably teach themselves to play, but Adeline had assured him individual attention would help the students progress faster—and would impact their lives in larger ways.

Matt prayed he'd get that last part right.

While she searched for the next area to coach him on, he

noted another glare from Lina. "I don't know how to make amends with someone I never wronged in the first place."

Adeline followed his gaze. Thankfully, instead of staring, she returned her attention to the screen. "Are you sure you never wronged her?"

A pit opened in Matt's stomach. He'd lost years' worth of memories to the haze of drugs and alcohol. Had he done something to Lina during that time?

Probably.

He'd used a lot of women over the years. How many considered him their worst regret? Had he introduced any of them to drugs that had taken over their lives? Or what if he had a child he didn't know about running around?

"You look worried," Adeline said.

Matt rubbed his face. Lina didn't have kids and wasn't a drug addict, so whatever she had against him probably wasn't a worst-case scenario. As for other women, most likely, anyone who could've claimed having a kid of his would've come after him for money because of his income with Awestruck. None had, and he had enough mistakes to make up for without peopling his imagination with non-existent children.

Lina seared him with another glare.

He averted his eyes. "What's her story?"

"She's worked for Awestruck since graduating college."

"Does she have a family?" She wore a ring, but not on her left hand. During his Awestruck days, he'd gotten the impression she'd been taken. Married.

"She's here alone."

"That's evasive wording."

Her shoulder lifted. "You'll have to ask her for details."

Did Adeline's side-stepping mean Lina was divorced and Adeline didn't want to gossip?

He didn't remember all the women he'd been with, but he'd

recall making a move on Awestruck's married social media manager. Wouldn't he?

But what if he didn't? What if he had something to do with why Lina was single?

∼

LINA SLATED Matt into the bass guitar lessons scheduled for the following week. Each time she deleted Adeline's name and typed his in its place, she felt like she was volunteering the poor student to be a lab rat.

But Adeline was the boss, and already she'd spent an hour in a practice room with Matt, preparing him. To ensure all went smoothly with his lessons, Lina would adjust her own schedule to overlap with his starting next week. Coming in around eleven would give her a few hours of quiet in the office to keep up with her Awestruck role before lessons started after school. Then, she'd work on Key of Hope responsibilities until around seven, when the latest of Matt's lessons wrapped up.

After one final adjustment, the deed was done, and she needed some air.

She set off on foot for the coffee shop around the corner. Though Lakeshore was a small town with a tiny year-round population, the sidewalks currently bustled with tourists who would split their time between the cute Main Street shops and exploring nature.

Lighthouse tours cruised out into Lake Superior, rivers and waterfalls awaited the adventurous in the woods, and state parks offered well-groomed trails to pretty rock formations. In a few weeks, even more people would arrive in search of fall color.

For now, an occasional tree waved a yellow leaf or two as a sign of things to come, but only someone watching for it would notice.

Once she had her vanilla latte, she continued down the street. The visitor's bureau kept a wildflower garden. Since people rarely took advantage of the benches there, the spot would make the perfect place to relax away from Matt and thoughts of all the havoc he'd wreak on Key of Hope.

She settled on a wooden bench beneath the spotty shade of a crab apple tree. As she took her first sip of coffee, her phone chimed over the twitter of birds.

Dad was calling her from his cell phone? Had he even been home to hear her message yet?

She hesitated with her thumb over the icon to answer. Did he hope to reach her voicemail? Or maybe something had gone wrong. Happened to Mom.

She hit the green icon to answer. "Dad? Is everything okay?"

"Galina. How're you?" His bright tone disproved her theory about an emergency. Usually, he only turned this chipper after closing some big deal. But the good mood didn't usually turn his interest toward Lina. Even now, he didn't wait for her to overcome her surprise before plowing ahead. "Listen, we got a fantastic offer on the land in Maine."

"Oh." The deal wasn't a business negotiation, but a personal matter. She felt as though a car she'd been traveling in had been slammed into reverse. She cleared her throat. "I know you wanted to sell."

She bit the corner of her mouth, trying to imagine a new structure going up on the lot next to The Captain's Vista. The one thing Grandma had left Dad was the vacant plot next to the beloved property. Grandma had hoped he might build a vacation home there so he and Mom could stay near Lina and her family.

That hope rested on enough unlikely contingencies to make it as risky as any business venture Dad had ever concocted. Dad didn't take vacations or prioritize his relationship with Lina, and Lina had no prospects for a family of her own.

"The land is just sitting there," Dad said. "It's taking up oceanfront views, waiting for someone with a vision to bring it up to date. There's a void in the vacation rental market, but the demand is there."

She massaged her forehead. Because Shane had introduced Dad to the world of real estate investments, Dad's sales pitch conjured a picture of her ex, eyes glittering as he layered one grand promise on another. She'd bought Shane's lies until he'd betrayed her in ways no lie could cover.

At least, not with her. Mom and Dad had believed Shane when he claimed to have invested the missing funds in a spur-of-the-moment opportunity that would pay him back three-fold in a couple of months. Despite Shane's failure to return so much as a dime, Dad still associated with him. Probably because Shane's advice had made him a tidy profit.

"What are they going to build? Condos?" She nearly let out a groan at the thought of tourists on the formerly secluded beach. "What about zoning? Can they build a commercial property there?"

"The community and the county are amenable to rezoning, and you don't want to miss this opportunity."

"Me?"

"The investor wants both properties. We'll get exponentially more if we sell together than if we piece it out."

She gave her ring a twist. "I'm not selling The Captain's Vista, Dad."

"The place is a money pit, and you haven't been out there in years."

Because her life had been in upheaval. First, she'd ended her engagement. Then, Grandma's sudden illness had taken her far too soon, leaving Lina to wade through the maze of assuming control of the sizable inheritance.

"I'm going to fix it up and spend time there." He didn't need to know she had her doubts about how long it would be before she could manage a visit, let alone a renovation.

"That would be a sentimental waste of money."

A topic Dad knew inside and out, since he'd gained and lost two fortunes, once shortly before she was born, once when she was twelve. But his current company had restored his life of luxury, so neither she nor her parents needed funds from the sale of the land in Maine.

She straightened her fingers and watched light catch the emerald ring. Enjoying her grandparents' keepsakes by wearing Grandma's rings and occasionally paging through Grandpa's stamp book meant more to her than all the funds. Though she couldn't keep it equally close, The Captain's Vista held similar value. "I can't agree to sell."

"I thought you might be hung up on the place." She could practically hear him shaking his head. "Think about it and get back to me. I have clients waiting." He disconnected.

Lowering the phone, she stared blankly at the wildflowers in the raised bed before her. Next time, she was letting his call go to voicemail. If something awful had happened, she would deal with the news a minute later when she listened to the message.

She sipped her coffee, but the brew seemed to have lost its flavor. Maybe she ought to stop checking in with them altogether, but did Mom deserve silence because of Dad?

A young couple strolled down the walk, framed by the pink, blue, and orange flowers below and the low tree branches above. The woman's ponytail swept the guy's shoulder as she eyed the shops across the street, and the man tilted his head in as if to catch the scent of her shampoo. When the woman turned back, he caught her with a kiss that left her grinning.

Living the fairytale.

Once upon a time, she and Shane hadn't looked much different.

Handsome, attentive, and successful, he'd made quick work of Lina's heart.

Now, here she sat, alone.

The slats of the seat back jostled, and a dark shape dropped to the space beside her. She jumped, and milky coffee splattered her thumb.

Matt grinned.

He'd hurdled the bench?

"You couldn't walk around and sit like a normal person?" Her knee-jerk reaction zapped out before she could stop it. Mostly, she was angry with Dad and Shane, but Matt must've known he would startle her.

Unruffled, he crossed his arms. His face was tan, save for his scars. The straight, thin line on his jaw and the one shaped like a greater-than sign near his temple remained pale. The jagged half-inch mark on his cheek was pink, newer. "It's come to my attention that I should ask what I've done to upset you."

Her ribs sank as her breath left her. She shouldn't have shown her disapproval because she didn't want to explain. She took the napkin she'd held around her coffee cup and cleaned up her hand.

"Was it something specific?" he asked.

She peered at the street, but the fairytale couple had moved on. "No."

Just his ongoing disregard for safety, propriety, and family. She'd followed all the rules her whole life, and yet everything had fallen apart. Meanwhile, Matt had been reckless. He didn't deserve the success or second chances he'd enjoyed.

He stayed still and quiet for a few beats. "We got lost in Paris. Remember?"

While on tour with the band, she'd heard of a place to get the best macarons in France. Though she suspected Matt had agreed to go along more to hit on her than to try the confections, she'd tolerated his company. Figured being with him was better than being alone as night fell in the city. They'd made it to the bakery without incident, but on the way back, her phone's GPS had misled her.

"That must've been six years ago," she said.

"It was fun, watching you try to speak French to get us some directions, clutching your pink bag of cookies like you were protecting nuclear launch codes. And we accidentally found ... that thing." He made an upside-down U with his hand.

"The Arc de Triomphe?"

"That's the one." He chuckled. "You kept blaming your phone, but I'm pretty sure it was the operator."

She scoffed. "This is a pretty awful apology, if you're trying to make things right."

He surveyed her, his smile pulling harder and harder at the corner of his mouth until he grinned. "All I'm saying is, my phone consistently pointed the opposite direction of where you led us."

"You never said anything."

"It was Paris, and we never got to see the sights on tour. Like I said, I had fun."

"I didn't."

"I know." His expression turned serious. When she'd succumbed to tears, he'd hailed a taxi—an idea that had somehow not occurred to her. Though the whole excursion had been her idea, he paid the fare. "You might've enjoyed the adventure if you'd relaxed."

"We were going to miss our flight."

"Could've caught the next one."

"Easy for you to say. You were used to missing things. Letting people down. Everyone knew not to count on you."

Matt laughed ruefully. "Meanwhile, you still have to have it all together."

"Responsibility and reliability make me who I am." In the chaos after Dad lost his second fortune, her parents had sent her to stay with her grandparents. She'd slipped from bed and overheard Grandpa, whose health had been failing, calling Dad irresponsible and unfit to inherit the family estate. Grandma asked what he suggested they do with it instead. Lina had learned then, at the age of twelve and years before her parents heard a peep about it, that the inheritance would pass to her. To avoid similar disqualification, she'd known all along that she needed to be everything Dad wasn't—teachable, loyal, responsible.

After that, any money that came her way had gone into a savings account. She'd also stockpiled good behavior, mostly to impress her grandparents, whose approval was far warmer and more comforting than her parents' notice.

The only time she'd made a big withdrawal from the bank of good choices had been when she'd fallen for Shane—over Grandma's protests. Thank God she'd built up enough positive experiences with Grandma before that, because only Grandma had been there for her after Lina discovered Shane's true colors.

For the two months they'd had, anyway, between then and Grandma's sudden illness.

Now, Lina was Grandma's legacy, and she would do her proud by being a good steward of the inheritance. By extension, guarding her heart was paramount to avoid another disaster with a man who might leverage her longing for a family to con his way into her bank account.

Matt rubbed his thumb against the center of his opposite palm. "I'm not the guy I used to be."

"Then explain again why your own family just fired you."

He gave her a flat look. Instead of repeating his weak defense that he'd "technically" quit, he stood. "It's going to be Paris all over again, isn't it?"

"Lakeshore is nothing like Paris." The architecture was quaint, not magnificent, the art scene more preoccupied with lighthouses and lakes than the masters of old, and the bear claws at the local bakery wouldn't stand a chance against those macarons.

Matt smirked. "You're going to be stressed, and I'm going to have fun."

Oh. She crossed her arms and tried to let the words bounce off, but his promise to have fun stuck like a briar.

"You've got a choice. Relax or"—he waved his fingers toward her—"keep your shoulders hunched up and give yourself tension headaches."

She dropped her shoulders, correcting her posture before realizing the motion confirmed she'd been as tense as he'd suggested.

He angled one foot for the sidewalk, but he focused on her again. "Another similarity. Are you sure you're not lost?"

"I know exactly where I am." Literally and figuratively.

He shrugged one shoulder, as if the answer didn't matter to him, then shoved his hands into his pockets and set off down the sidewalk.

5

*M*att had watched a full array of emotions play across Lina's face today.

A full array of the negative ones anyway.

As he rode home with Tim following his first day of training at Key of Hope, he replayed the different expressions. She'd shown no signs of joy, relief, or contentedness. About the only time her forehead hadn't been marked with a line signaling frustration or sadness had been for the split second after he'd hurdled the back of the bench.

Not all of the negativity had been his fault. He'd walked by her, sitting there among the flowers and caught up in a tense phone call. He hadn't paused to listen in, but he had heard the word *dad*.

Hard to believe such a rule follower was on poor terms with her parents, but all families had problems. After allowing a few minutes for them to work out their differences, he'd circled back to talk to her. Waiting for a better moment, like when she hadn't just had a fight with her father, might've brought a better result.

Why did he care so much what Lina thought of him?

Saving him from analyzing the question too closely, Tim pulled into a parking lot. The architect who'd paired the modern siding and windows with exposed cedar columns probably intended to lend a northwoods-luxury-vacation feel to the condominium complex. Instead, the result was pretentious.

Matt got out and retrieved his oversized duffle from the trunk. He had meant to contribute to rent, but whatever he could afford would be laughable in comparison to the full bill for a new build on lakefront property. "How long are you staying in Lakeshore?"

Tim locked the vehicle and started for the door. "I'll go back to California when the band goes to the studio so I can get Issy settled at boarding school."

Tim would leave in a week or so? Matt couldn't begrudge him the time with his daughter, but he hadn't planned to be on his own for lodging so soon.

As he followed Tim inside, he stepped onto a ceramic floor made to imitate hardwood. A counter separated the kitchen from the living room, which was furnished with neutral-colored couches and chairs. Steps led to a loft. The bathroom and the other two bedrooms must've been down the hall. Matt wasn't made of money, but this place was.

"How much is rent?"

"I'm not charging you."

"But when you leave—"

"I'm coming back. My lease goes through the end of the year, so I'm paying for it either way."

Matt surveyed the space again. Tim had already assigned him the loft. Maybe, since the room only had three walls, he didn't have to feel indebted. Besides, Tim was the one who'd wanted him there. He started for the stairs. "You're not going to

49

change your mind when I won't reconsider Awestruck, are you? Because I owe enough people money without you coming after me for half the rent."

"Who do you owe money to?"

Matt thudded up the stairs and away from answering. Aside from the missing wall, the loft was homey. The bed took up a third of the space, and a room divider lent more privacy in the far corner. He stowed his bag between the dresser and desk. Over the railing and about fifty feet beyond the rear-facing windows of the condo, Lake Superior rippled and waved, a piece of ever-changing art.

His phone beeped. A couple of foamy wave crests rose and faded in the water as he drew the device from his pocket.

Krissy had texted. *How was your first day?*

Lina wasn't happy to see me. Since he had told his sister about the job offer and the woman who'd come to extend it, Krissy ought to remember the name.

Apparently she did, because a moment later, she sent back a laughing emoji. *She'd better look out. I know how you like a challenge.*

His sister knew him well, but his impulse to defy the supposedly impossible often ended badly. He didn't need the disappointment, and Lina would be livid—rightfully so—if she sensed she was a game to him. He needed to spend his energy on maintaining his healthy relationships, not creating problems, so instead of letting Krissy focus on Lina, he asked how things were going in Fox Valley.

When he returned downstairs, Tim was washing his hands in the kitchen sink, an apron layered over his dress pants and button-down. He'd cooked something here and there on tour, but he'd never seemed this dedicated to the pursuit.

Matt slid onto a stool at the counter. "Did that getup come with the place, or did you bring it with you?"

Tim swatted the faucet handle, cutting off the water. "Do you know how much these clothes cost?"

About as much as Matt's first car? "Seems like a shame to spend so much and look so domestic."

Tim rolled his eyes and retrieved a sack of potatoes from the pantry. He laid the bag and some paper towels on the counter, then retrieved a peeler and a bowl. He set the final item in front of Matt with a pointed look.

Fine. Matt picked up the first potato, and muscle memory from his childhood kicked in. How many times had Mom enlisted his help with this chore? Fifty? More?

Tim pulled three heads of broccoli from the refrigerator and took them to the sink. "Who do you owe money to?"

Matt's hand slipped, and the peeler skimmed the knuckle of his thumb. He should've known not to mention his debt. "My parents."

"And?" Tim paused across the counter from him, probably expecting eye contact.

Matt focused on the potato instead. "That's it."

"That's not bad." The sink gushed as Tim rinsed the broccoli. "The way you said it, I thought it was someone who'd break your kneecaps."

"It's bad enough."

"How much are we talking?"

Matt turned the potato, his fingers tracking dirt from the skin to the creamy part he'd peeled. "A hundred grand."

Distracted, Tim lowered the broccoli, and water splashed off the new angle onto the apron. The stream beaded off the thick canvas and onto the floor before Tim hit the handle to stop the flow. "They had that much to lend you?"

"It wasn't a loan."

"Ah." Tim moved to the cutting board.

The front door swished open, and a moment later, Tim's

daughter appeared. Issy scanned the potatoes, expression hopeful until she scrunched her nose at the broccoli. She glanced back to Matt. "Hey."

"Hey." He'd met her first this summer, when he'd accompanied Tim to a community event at a bookstore in Lakeshore.

She seemed like a good kid. Even if she didn't like broccoli.

"What's for dinner?" she asked.

"Steak." Tim produced a knife from the drawer and started chopping the broccoli. "You have fun at camp?"

Issy shrugged as though to say no. "The play's tomorrow night. You'll come?"

"Sure."

The girl focused on Matt. "I get to be Cinderella because I love acting and I'm the oldest girl, but the boy who plays the prince is, like, this tall." She flattened her hand under her chin. Matt winced sympathetically, then she turned toward her dad. "Because no other fourteen-year-olds have dads who think they need constant supervision all summer."

Tim ignored her long-suffering glare. "What time again?"

"Seven."

"Okay." He snagged a pot from a cabinet, then stooped again and rose a moment later with a steamer basket. "We'll be there."

"Good." Issy trooped off to her room.

Matt plunked a finished potato in the bowl. "We?"

"As long as you're living under my roof, you get tortured when I do."

"I knew rent wasn't free."

Tim chuckled and stashed the broccoli in the steamer basket before rinsing and quartering potatoes. "One hundred thousand dollars for what?"

"Doesn't matter. I owe them the money, and I'll pay it. End of story."

Tim's eyebrows quirked as if to ridicule him for being touchy. "You know how you could get that kind of money pretty quick."

Matt set the last potato, peeled, in the bowl, then stood. "Convincing Gannon to rehire me would be anything but quick."

"A lot quicker than earning what you need by teaching music lessons."

Since teaching was only part-time, Matt would have to find other jobs, too, but as soon as he said as much, Tim would suggest Awestruck again. Matt tried to head it off. "I'm not throwing my life away again."

"Awestruck isn't to blame for the choices you made. It could be different this time."

"Maybe. Maybe not. I'm not risking it."

AT LEAST LAKESHORE knew to keep its expectations low. Only a few dozen chairs waited for the audience of the day camp's performance of Cinderella. Matt followed Tim toward the meager rows, and the manager chose a spot on the aisle, leaving Matt to step over his knees to get a seat.

Settled, he opened the program. As promised, Isabella had the lead role. He would've expected her to feel the pressure last night and beg help practicing the script, but instead of showing nerves, she'd rhapsodized about her school's acting program. Some Broadway stars had started there, and Issy intended to be the next. "She have a lot of lines?"

Tim glanced at the program. "We'll see. She learned it all here."

"Mind if we squeeze in?" Adeline stood at the end of the row, flanked by Gannon and Lina.

53

Matt's lungs turned to stone. He'd thought Tim had invited him because he didn't want to come alone. Since he had plenty of company, either Tim had meant what he'd said about torturing Matt, or the manager hoped to get Matt and Gannon talking.

As if that would get them anywhere.

The lead singer's focus on Matt was intent, like when Krissy's cat spotted a toy and had yet to decide whether to let it be or hunt to kill.

Tim got to his feet to let the group pass.

Matt rose and bumped Tim's shoulder, but the guy didn't take the hint and step into the aisle. Adeline passed with a sweet smile, her shoulder brushing Matt's chest. Gannon kicked Matt's toe on his way by and muttered an apology.

As Lina slipped by, she carefully angled her body away, but the clean scent of her perfume invited him to shift closer, see if her flowy T-shirt or curls were as soft as they looked. He could easily brush her sleeve and blame it on the close quarters.

But what would he gain?

She could wear the softest cashmere and still be hardened to Matt in every way that mattered, as the down-turned corners of her mouth suggested. Developing feelings for someone who automatically frowned whenever he was near would be a self-destructive indulgence. He'd learned to deal with his other unhealthy cravings. This one, he'd stop indulging here and now, before temptation led to disaster. He retook his seat, but from there, he had way too good a view of the way Lina's jeans hugged her hips as she turned to sit. He lifted his hand to block his line of sight before realizing how obvious the movement was.

If he'd known what Tim was up to, he never would've come.

Clumsily, he scratched his neck until he heard her settle. When he lowered his arm again, she eyed the narrow space between them like a princess wishing for an alligator-infested moat.

Might be too late to act natural, but he tried a smile anyway. "Here for Issy?" As he shifted, his heel caught on something. He leaned to check.

Lina's purse.

She shoved the bag farther under her chair and acknowledged his apology with a begrudging smile. "Isabella and Bailey, the daughter of another Key of Hope instructor."

"Ah." What had happened to his ability to engage in small talk? To act like a grown man? He used to do press interviews and be the life of the party. Talking to women had been a specialty. Of course, he'd usually been drunk or high, and he never would've tried with a woman as pulled together as Lina.

Out of his league. She was out of his league.

From her other side, Gannon silently observed him.

Great. Had Gannon seen the one-sided bout of attraction? Because the last thing Matt needed was to give either Gannon or Lina another reason to judge him.

God, help me.

He'd leave, but how classless would abandoning Issy's play appear to everyone else?

Matt gulped and pretended to be engrossed in the opening announcements.

He'd see this through. And then never accept another invite Tim extended.

LINA'S back ached from the awkward angle of sitting between Gannon's and Matt's broad shoulders without touching either. At least Gannon kept his far arm around Adeline and leaned more into her space than into Lina's. She couldn't blame Matt for not wanting to crowd Tim, but she had to constantly monitor her arm to keep from nudging him.

Distracted by one of Isabella's big scenes, she shifted. The whisper of fabric touching registered louder than anything happening on stage as her shoulder brushed his. She jerked back into her own airspace. Matt leaned far enough that he could, if he wanted, move his arm up and over the back of the seat. If he tried making more room by resting that arm along the back of her chair ...

The threat fizzled as he resettled, his hands folded in his lap, an extra inch between them.

She pressed her palms together, arms glued to her sides. Beside her, Gannon kept his arm around his fiancée, Adeline's head on his shoulder. The couple occasionally whispered to each other, and their comfortable connection only accented Lina's discomfort. She sure missed the days when she had someone other than her own elbows to cuddle with.

Twenty minutes later, little Bailey-the-mouse scurried across the stage, sporting a painted button nose and a head-band with ears. To follow her movement, Lina leaned.

Her knuckles brushed something firm, the warmth and texture registering as skin. Matt's forearm. Startled embarrass-ment blazed all the way up her arm and onto her cheeks. If only he'd worn long sleeves, the contact wouldn't have felt so personal. Flustered, she blinked toward the stage.

Bailey was already gone again.

Matt remained still.

Too still?

She didn't dare cut a glance at his face to see if he'd noticed —how could he have missed it?—but her line of sight did wander to the skin she'd grazed.

The panther tattoo ogled her in return.

When the play finally ended, she and Matt rushed to their

feet. He shooed Tim out of the end of the aisle and navigated through the crowd to the exit.

Tim frowned after him. "I wonder where he thinks he's going."

Gannon's hazel eyes tracked his former bandmate, then focused on Lina. "How's it going with him?"

Lina shrugged. Her purse, tucked under her arm, vibrated. Good thing she'd silenced her phone for the performance, or it would interrupt now. And for what? So Dad could try to talk her into selling again? She lowered her purse by the straps, distancing herself from the distraction. She couldn't risk voicing her frustrations about Matt when she didn't know how Gannon felt about him. Especially since Adeline had been the one to extend the opportunity. "Adeline's worked with him more than I have so far."

Adeline threaded her fingers with her fiancé's, and the way the two looked at each other seemed to be its own conversation. If Lina understood correctly, Adeline told him to stop worrying, and he told her to stop being so trusting.

When Lina and Shane had disagreed, he'd always withdrawn. Memories of the times he'd stepped away somehow stung less than the times he'd stayed, ignoring her and leaving her hanging onto a limp hand.

Gannon's fingers, still firmly clasped around Adeline's hand, served as a reminder that not all relationships were the same. Not all men were bound to break hearts.

Did God have someone she could trust her heart to?

As they made their way into the aisle, Lina pulled her purse back onto her shoulder. Her phone vibrated again, a short beat to signal a message from whoever had called. She slipped the device from her purse. At the sight of the number on the screen, fear squeezed her so tightly, she couldn't move. She'd deleted the contact from her phone, but the digits were burned in her mind.

Shane.

Shane had called and left a message. Since she'd gotten a new number, Dad must've shared her contact information with him, but why? Was he involved in the sale of the land in Maine?

Shane and Dad ought to have known better than to send Shane to talk her into anything. On the other hand, he might have called for another purpose. Wondering about his reasons would distract her to the point of uselessness. She excused herself to find a quiet corner to listen to the message.

6

---

*T*he gymnasium door push-bar clanked as Lina exited. The window-lined hall greeted her with cooler air. She stepped from the main thoroughfare, leaned against the wall, and unlocked her phone. As she typed her voicemail passcode, a boy's taunting voice sounded down the hall to her right. To her other side, another family left into the night.

Why wasn't the message playing yet? Was it too loud in the school? She pressed the phone against her ear.

"Lina, it's Shane."

Her eardrum stung—more from surprise than the volume—and she jolted. He might've paused at the start of his message for dramatic effect, but he may also have been at a loss for words. Remorseful.

A girl could dream.

"I know you've got every reason to hate me." His low tone conveyed some of the sincerity she'd hoped to hear, but he spoke too quickly for her to read extra meaning into the words. "But would you consider calling me back?"

For what purpose? So he could apologize? So he could con her into selling The Captain's Vista?

A shriek diverted her attention toward the area where, a moment ago, she'd heard a boy.

But it wasn't just one. Three boys circled Bailey down the hall, their body language reminiscent of dogs barking at a trespasser. They alternated between clapping at her and trying to stomp on her tail.

How dare they. Lina disconnected the call, jammed her phone into her pocket, and made a beeline for the group. "Hey!"

Deaf to her call, the biggest of the boys, possibly a middle schooler, sneered at Bailey. "My dad caught one in a trap."

A trap? The taunting and clapping fit into a terrible explanation. The boys were mimicking mouse traps.

Bailey had her eyes jammed shut, tears rolling down her red cheeks.

"Stop!" Lina's most commanding tone didn't earn a glance from Bailey's tormentors.

The ringleader lunged, and for one awful moment, he seemed poised to slam into the little girl. Instead, he pinned her tail underfoot. Bailey lurched in her attempt to scamper off as the costume held. Then the tail popped loose, and the boys launched into a fresh round of jeers.

Lina reached for Bailey, but the terrorized girl fled from her touch, probably mistaking her for a bully.

"The brain guts were everywhere!" the boy shouted as Bailey escaped the circle.

"Bailey, wait." Lina bumped past the bullies, her desire to lend comfort more urgent than her searing anger toward the boys. She'd heard kids could be awful, but the continued insults—

"Scram!"

At the man's voice, the boys fell silent.

Lina reached Bailey and wrapped an arm around the girl's shoulders. She was so little. So cute and fragile. How could anyone have seen her as a target?

"I mean it. Git!" A stomp accentuated the last word.

"Come on." The panicked tone varied so greatly from the jeers that Lina couldn't tell by the sound whether the comment came from the ringleader or one of the others. Pounding footfalls signaled the group's retreat.

Bailey shuddered and clutched Lina's hand. Lina checked to make sure the girl's pants hadn't torn when the tail had ripped away. Thankfully not.

She smoothed her hair and straightened her headband. "Are you all right, sweetheart?"

Bailey shook her head, more tears spilling, and Lina pulled her into a hug. As the child clung to her, Lina looked to their rescuer.

Intense blue eyes met hers. The broad shoulders and tattooed arms that had caused her so much trouble during the play had come in handy after all.

Matt's forehead furrowed as his expression asked if Bailey was okay.

Lina brushed the girl's hair from the tear tracks on her face. "Did they hurt you?"

She sniffled. "They were mean."

Without waiting for more information, Matt stalked off in the direction the boys had gone.

What kind of scene would he make?

And would his involvement make things better or worse for Bailey? Summer camp ended with tonight's play, but she would likely attend the same elementary school with them soon.

She bent to see into the girl's face again. "Have they been bullying you all summer?"

Bailey shook her head to the negative, but tears continued to seep. The tail lay a few feet away, limp and tattered.

Lina drew a breath in hopes of dousing her anger. This sense of helplessness. She was an adult. One who hoped to one day have children of her own. How could she manage her own kids when those boys had acted like she hadn't even existed?

She hated being rescued by a man. Especially under those circumstances. Especially by that man.

And yet, she found herself hoping that, if Matt caught up to the boys, his immaturity would surface and he'd let them have it.

Then, maybe, she could turn him on Shane and her father.

Or not. She needed to learn to fight her own battles. Protect her own heart.

She refocused on Bailey. "Let's go find your family."

LINA WAS NOT WATCHING the time. Not at all conscious that Matt's first lesson would start in eighteen minutes ... Or at least, she wished she weren't.

As planned, she'd started her workday at eleven and would wrap up around the time his last lesson ended. The unplanned part was her anticipation. Or could she label it curiosity? Curiosity sounded more reasonable.

Since she'd never known him to be punctual, he probably wouldn't arrive before his student. Except, she'd also never known him to take care of himself or stand up for the defenseless, and yet these days, those actions seemed to be part of his MO.

She'd seen neither Matt nor Bailey's mom, Samantha, since the play on Friday night and had no idea if parents or teachers had taken disciplinary action against the bullies. But more than an update about that situation drew her interest toward Matt.

After all, Lina could call Samantha for the scoop on Bailey.

Samantha could not, however, satisfy her curiosity about Matt's transformation.

He'd gone from being a reckless addict to a defender of terrorized little girls, a strung-out deadbeat with glassy eyes to a fit musician with clear focus. How the new Matt had handled the situation at the play could reveal a lot about how thoroughly he'd changed.

Her phone dinged, distracting her from the vigil she shouldn't be keeping anyway.

By the time she slipped the device from the drawer where she'd stowed it, the light in the corner of the screen flashed, but the information about the texter had already faded. She unlocked the phone and tapped on the text icon.

Shane had messaged.

She hadn't returned his Friday night call. What could he want but The Captain's Vista? If he'd wanted to apologize, he could've done so in the message. She'd listened to the brief recording five times, but the words *I'm sorry* had never materialized.

And now he was texting?

Steeling herself, she opened the message, and words filled her screen. Flustered, she couldn't seem to read. The man she'd known had never been so verbose. Even his recent voicemail had been quick. Why reach out now, after a year? And why had she tensed up, as if he could force her to talk to him? She could block his number. He had no hold on her.

Her eyes stung as she blinked—they'd gotten dry in her frozen moments of panic. She redoubled her concentration.

I'd hoped to talk, but I don't blame you for not returning my call. I wanted to finally say what I should've said a year ago. I'm sorry.

Her lids slid shut over her suddenly moist eyes. He was sorry. Or he was claiming to be. It was too good to be true. Or too little too late. Something. Her jaw tightened as though that could suppress her emotions as she continued reading.

I was a fool to deny that I needed to change. When I lost you, my life lost meaning. I hit rock bottom and have been rebuilding ever since. Is there any way I can make things right between us? Can you ever forgive me?

He'd said all the right things. Every sentiment she'd hoped he'd express back when she'd confronted him about the money. But what good would a more sincere apology have done? Trust had been shattered between them, and even if she'd believed his remorse in the moment, she wouldn't have had the confidence to marry him. She might've gotten closure sooner, though.

What did he want now? His hope of making things right was vague. He might want anything from a final, grace-filled conversation to another shot at a relationship to ... to The Captain's Vista.

He had the connections to find a developer for Dad, and for facilitating the sale of the valuable property, Shane would receive a hefty commission.

"Who died?" Matt—where had he materialized from?— stood beside her desk, arms crossed.

She closed her eyes and shook her head, not realizing she swayed with the movement until the corner of her desk stabbed into her arm. She blinked a few times, flipped the phone face down, and pasted on a smile. "No one. Nothing. It's fine."

He motioned as if to circle her fake composure. "That's creepy." Without waiting for her response, he turned away to hang his sweatshirt on a hook.

Lina took the moment away from his assessing gaze to gulp and gather her wits. "Your lesson isn't here yet." If only her voice would've cooperated with her attempt to act natural. Instead, the scratchiness was a dead giveaway for excess emotion.

Matt glanced at the waiting room again, expression still

dubious. He studied her once more, then continued to the coffee maker in the corner.

Why had she been eager for him to arrive? Oh, right. Bailey.

After Matt scared off the boys on Friday, Lina had delivered the little girl to Samantha. She'd then found Isabella by Tim and congratulated her on a job well done. Matt walked up around the same time, expression grim, but he gave no indication of what had happened before they all parted ways.

Hopefully the boys had faced consequences. If they learned they could get away with bullying, they'd rack up years' worth of victims.

Had Shane been a bully as a kid?

And what was he now?

She focused on Matt. "Did you find the boys at the play?"

He stabbed the button to brew a large cup of coffee. "Cowering behind their parents."

"And?"

As if he'd recognized the hope in her voice, he glanced at her before he turned his attention to the pan of millionaire's shortbread she'd left beside the coffee maker. "Their sons would never do such a thing."

Lina scoffed, her indignation nearly choking her. "I bet there was a footprint on the tail to prove otherwise."

He took a big bite of one of the dessert bars. The caramel-and-chocolate topping must've been stickier than he'd expected because he took a minute to swallow before continuing. "Whole thing makes me glad I don't have kids. How do you defend a kid when you're supposed to be a civil adult and the parents are in denial?"

"I was sort of hoping you hadn't been a civil adult."

He cut her a longer glance, his eyes crinkling with the start of a smile. The coffee machine beeped, and he finished off the bar in one more oversized bite. He tried speaking, took a sip of coffee, then started again. "Who brought those?"

Lina lifted two fingers, indicating herself. She'd reduced the size of the meals she'd been making and hadn't needed to bring in leftovers since the soup, but she'd needed to focus her energy on something besides Shane, the bullies, and Matt, so she'd baked the dessert. What should she have done? Made one-twelfth of the recipe?

"They're really good." He reached for another, but the door opened and in stepped a twelve-year-old, no adult in tow. Abandoning the sweets, he took his coffee and met the new arrival. "Hey, man. I'm Matt. Are you Chris?"

Nodding, the kid scanned him from arms to face, clearly in awe.

He extended his free hand. When Chris tentatively reached back, he walked the boy through a complicated handshake. Matt ended with a motion and a noise to mimic an explosion, which Chris imitated a second later.

This friendly, good-with-kids instructor was another version of the man she'd never seen before. How much could a person change in two years? It actually seemed like a shame he didn't want kids.

Laughing good-naturedly at the clumsy handshake, Matt motioned for Chris to follow him. "You'll get it."

They settled in one of the practice rooms, and Lina watched as Matt listened intently to the first words his student uttered. He nodded as if Chris had told him something important, then turned to grab one of the bass guitars already set up in the classroom. As he did, his line of sight caught on Lina.

Heat rushed her cheeks, and she zipped her gaze away. Had she really been admiring Matt Visser?

As Matt wrapped up his final lesson of the day, Tim entered through the front door of Key of Hope. A weight settled on

Matt's back. Work with the kids was straightforward. No games, no complicated relationships. But work with Tim?

If only avoiding Awestruck and all the accompanying temptations were as simple as telling the manager he had no interest in the role of bassist.

When Tim had first brought him here, he'd overheard Lina's question—why was Tim *so enamored* with Matt?

He had no idea, but Tim *had* latched on to him. Why had he been willing to help Matt approach Awestruck this summer? Why bother getting him the job at Key of Hope? Why—out of all the bassists in the world—was he convinced Matt ought to rejoin Awestruck?

Matt's student met his dad in the waiting area, and they left.

Tim had been talking to Lina, but as soon as Matt sat at the computer to enter a few notes on the lesson, Tim switched his attention. "What are you doing Saturday night? Anything?"

He resisted a look toward Lina. Having her as an audience raised the stakes. She wasn't easily impressed, but grateful vulnerability had flashed in her eyes when he'd chased away the boys at the play, and curiosity swam in her glances when he'd started his lesson with Chris. He had achieved his goal of eliciting positive emotions from her, and perhaps he'd have the opportunity to gain even more ground if he agreed to whatever Tim was cooking up. After all, she'd been at the last event Tim had roped him into.

But he'd vowed to decline Tim's invites, and this little infatuation of his wasn't cause to go back on his commitment since the interest was doomed to go unreciprocated. A little gratitude did not equate to affection or even mutual regard. "I'm going back to Fox Valley."

Tim recoiled as if a bug had flown into his eye. "Why?"

Matt typed a line. Was one sentence enough detail about the material he'd covered? He added the name of the song he'd introduced the kid to, then closed the program. The tray of caramel bars Lina had brought beckoned him, but in order to escape poor decisions brought on by some fool's errand to win over Lina, he collected his sweatshirt from the hook instead.

"How're you going to get there? You don't have a car."

Matt pulled on the sweatshirt. "I found one this morning."

"You bought a car?"

"Yup." The satisfaction of surprising Tim would be short-lived. When he saw the clunker Matt had purchased for nine hundred dollars, Tim would have the last laugh. And Lina would laugh with him.

Tim shook his head as if to clear a ridiculous notion. "You can't go home this weekend."

"Watch me."

"On Saturday night, there's a bonfire at John's. You need to be there. Awestruck leaves Monday, so this will be your last chance to—"

"I'm going home." He'd found recovery meetings to attend in Lakeshore, but his sponsor and family were back in Fox Valley, about two hours away.

Tim crossed his arms and widened his stance, blocking the walkway.

Matt indulged in a glance at Lina. She had her long legs crossed in an easy posture. Amusement dusted her features as she watched the exchange and mindlessly toyed with one of her curls. Amusement. Another positive emotion. Time to set a harder goal.

Affectionate touch? Or was that too lofty an aspiration?

"You're not going to make one hundred thousand dollars here."

Shame gusted Matt's face like a cloud of steam. Tim should've known Matt didn't want that coming up in front of anyone, let alone in front of someone who already held a low opinion of him. Then again, Tim didn't seem real in touch with emotion—his own or anyone else's.

Meanwhile, thanks to sobriety, Matt now got to feel every little jab of unworthiness and twinge of shame. "No kidding? At a job where I only get fifteen hours a week?"

Tim slanted a look to Lina, apparently not willing to stop the guilting with Matt. "Fifteen hours? You couldn't manage more?"

She looked back and forth between them as if she weren't sure whether she should apologize. "That's all the bass guitar lessons. It was on the job posting."

No apology. Good for her.

Before Tim could pester her further, Matt bumped around him, since the guy had given him no choice. "I put in applications at three other places this morning. I'll do what I need to do." He gripped the key to the car parked out back. A car almost as old and world-weary as Matt.

"It's going to take a long time to make that kind of cash."

Matt kept walking toward the exit. "I've got the rest of my life."

Quieter now, Tim asked, "You'll talk sense into him?"

"And lose an employee?" Lina's teasing tone drew a smile to Matt's face. At least Tim's tactics hadn't beaten her down.

He continued into the parking lot, though he didn't relish the idea of getting in the car. The paint matched the rust-brown of the rotting areas by the wheel wells, camouflaging the decay, but based on the color alone, he could imagine a whole list of names Tim might dub the vehicle. The inside was worse. Dog hair covered the seats, a crayon or two had melted into the carpet, and a sticky substance Matt hoped was evaporated soda covered the hard surfaces.

But the car, as brown and sticky as it was, represented freedom he needed to make life work up here. Hard bought freedom, since the nine hundred dollars had set him back from his goal of repaying his parents.

What am I doing here, Lord?

69

Why piece together a whole string of part-time jobs in Lakeshore? He could've done the same back home.

He drew to a stop beside the car and stared down at the driver's seat. He'd come for music and to make a difference in kids' lives. He'd also come because Tim's mission to push him back to the pinnacle of success—misguided as it was—did something for his ego.

The age-dulled brown paint in front of him grounded him in reality.

Tim wanted him back in Awestruck. Back in the fast, exotic sports cars he used to drive, in the fast lane literally and figuratively.

This car, this life, was a far, far cry from that. And rightfully so. God and sobriety were all the luxuries he needed.

He yanked open the door, dropped to the seat, and put a hand on the wheel.

The leather gripped his fingers, and he lifted his hand away from the tacky surface.

A far cry indeed.

---

*L*ina had spent too much of her evening waiting for the opportunity to talk to Matt to waste the chance now that she had it. But with only the two of them left in Key of Hope at the end of Friday, any attempt to speak would blare like something out of a megaphone. While he shut down the equipment in his classroom, she grabbed her pen and clicked it, as if that made the silence less intimidating.

If only Adeline didn't leave at four thirty or five every day—and even earlier that afternoon to spend time with Gannon before the band left on Monday. She'd invited Lina to Saturday's bonfire at John's and had tried to talk her into taking the rest of Friday off too.

Lina accepted the bonfire invite—she needed to get out of the house more—but she'd opted to stay in the office, citing her Awestruck social media responsibilities. She managed the band's official accounts and helped with all three of the guys' personal accounts to varying levels. Gannon and Philip both posted their own content, and she moderated comments and DM's. John had failed to follow through on posts despite her help with topic ideas and filters. She'd resorted to having him

His vision flicked to her.

Oh. Had that sounded like she wanted him to occupy his time with her? Her cheeks burned. "Awestruck." Hurried, the word sounded like a cough. "Tim wants to try to help you get in with the band."

"Ah." He treated her to a view of his back as he rolled the chair into place. In his scalp, an inch-long white line showed through his short, brown hair. Another scar. Did he even remember how he'd gotten them all?

"What was ...? Can I ask ...? What was Tim talking about?"

His back stiffened, and his profile came into view as he frowned out at Main Street. "The money?"

Lina nodded, but he wasn't looking. "Yeah."

"I owe my parents. That's the commitment I was talking about when you first came down to Fox Valley."

"Money can certainly complicate relationships." Hence the reason she'd never mentioned her net worth to anyone in Lakeshore. And, come to think of it, the reason she didn't trust Shane's apology. She hadn't returned either of his messages.

"They're not asking for it, so I guess it's not complicated on their end." Matt rubbed his thumb against his pointer finger. When he turned in her direction, he didn't quite make eye contact. "But one of the steps is to make amends for what I've done."

As if he'd given her chair a good spin, her perspective shifted. He was paying back family when they hadn't even asked him to? There must be more to the story that wouldn't paint him as favorably. "What did you do?" She swallowed, hoping to subdue the accusatory edge in her voice. "I mean, how'd you accumulate so much debt?"

She suspected she knew. His old lifestyle must've been expensive, and by all accounts, he hadn't stopped living extravagantly when he'd been fired from Awestruck. The band he'd joined afterward couldn't have paid nearly as much—

73

Awestruck was one of the top-earning bands in the country. The world, even. Most musicians made only a modest income —if that—and even if the band Matt had ended up with had done all right financially, their run had been short-lived.

Literally. The lead singer, August Peltier, had died of an overdose, bringing the band to a screeching halt.

Anywhere in there, Matt could've run low on funds and resorted to getting them from his family. Judging by the family business, the Vissers got by, and probably comfortably, but she doubted they could afford to part with such a sizable amount. Had he stolen it? Talked his parents into parting with some of their retirement to get him out of trouble?

Matt sighed, ending his long silence. "A few years ago, before I got clean, I was home in Fox Valley. The lake had frozen over, and the first fishing shanties were up. Pickups were out on the ice." Vulnerability softened his eyes.

This was not the story she'd expected at all.

"One night, I took Visser Landscaping's biggest dump truck out to do a donut."

Her mouth dropped open.

"The ice couldn't handle the weight."

As a teen, she'd watched a movie where an accident forced a car off a bridge. Ever since, the horrible scene haunted her whenever she drove near water. How much worse to break through ice and have to fight both the cold and the water?

"What did you ...? How did you get out?"

"It didn't go through all at once. I got away, but the truck was a total loss, and the powers that be were not at all happy about polluting the lake. The money will pay back my parents for the fines and recovery and get them another used dump truck. They've been limping by, using their smaller one, ever since."

"They didn't have insurance on the one that sank?"

"Insurance refused to cover the loss. I was just lucky to have not gone down with it. Pretty sure my brother, Pete, would rather I had. I deserved to, that's for sure. I was drunk. High. The whole thing." He scratched the panther tattoo. "Another bad decision in a long line of them."

She agreed, of course. He'd made a lot of poor decisions. But compassion warmed her. He'd owned his mistake without blaming others or sugarcoating his choices or their consequences.

If the old Shane had done all the same things Matt had for all the same reasons, he would have found a way to blame everyone else. Anyone but himself. Had Shane changed to be more like this? Honest, vulnerable, committed to a better life?

It didn't matter. Shane was her past.

And what's Matt, Lord?

Dreaming of a future that involved the musician could too easily result in more lofty dreams shattered. But a buoyant swirl of attraction and respect circled in her core. Shane was her past, and Matt may never be part of her future, but she no longer minded having him as part of her present. In fact, she rather preferred it this way.

THE NIGHT he'd stolen the dump truck, Matt hadn't heard the ice break, but the front right of the vehicle had dropped, and he'd scrambled out. Given the state he'd been in, he couldn't explain how he'd processed the information and escaped. When he turned back, the truck had been gone, hunks of ice bobbing in the jagged black hole where the vehicle had been.

God could've let him go down then and there.

Keeping him around, rescuing him from that situation and the life he'd made for himself, had been a lot more trouble. Especially since Matt had gotten himself in plenty of other scrapes where he should've died too.

At least these days, he could tell when he was on thin ice and veering toward trouble.

Like now, with Lina.

He'd been falling for her, a little piece at a time. The first crack in the ice had been shallow—she was pretty. Then, he'd seen her concern for the bullied girl after the play. She stayed on top of things at Key of Hope, and she wrote clever captions and comments for Awestruck on social media. Not that he was following, reading her work, and hearing it in his head in her voice.

He'd been feeding this infatuation with her and, maybe if he were honest, with Awestruck. In either case, if he made a move for more, let his hopes rise any higher, he'd fall through the ice into the cold waters of rejection. He'd been clean for a year now, supposedly long enough that he could handle the ups and downs of a new relationship, but a time frame wouldn't safeguard his sobriety—that would depend on his choices, and he didn't have a history of making good ones.

He had been talking to his sponsor and attending meetings. No one had said he couldn't handle what he'd taken on—with God's help, of course—but they did say to take things easy. One step at a time.

If only Matt were a one-step-at-a-time kind of guy instead of a dump-truck-donut-on-thin-ice stuntman.

Telling her the story of the dump truck had been a weak attempt to scramble from the sinking vehicle. He'd wanted her face to harden with her familiar little frown. A cold reaction would've reminded him of her station and his own, shoring up his fracturing reserves.

But instead of the judgment he'd needed, she peered at him with something almost like ... admiration?

Still, sticking with him through one story was far different from sticking with him when he messed up in real time.

This would end badly.

Her interest and understanding would reach their limits, and her rejection would plunge him into waters as icy and dangerous as those that swallowed the truck.

He lingered in the office anyway.

On her desktop, her phone vibrated with a call.

Lina jolted then snatched the phone with the same speed she might need to catch a trout with her bare hands. Instead of answering, she watched the screen.

Intrigue formed another shackle around his ankle, holding him in place.

The frown he'd wished for surfaced as she tossed the phone back on the desk.

Finding her displeasure aimed at someone else, Matt drew a step closer. "Bad news?"

"Oh." She cringed. Her brown eyes, tinged with hints of green, first looked toward the door, then the window, then his arm, his neck, his eyes. Her confidence had been replaced with the guilt of a kid who'd been caught skipping school.

"I told you about the dump truck." He waited. He was a glutton for punishment. Despite all the reasons she'd never think twice about him, never trust him, he had to back her into a corner and make her fight her way out.

Maybe then, he'd learn his lesson and have an easier time keeping his distance.

She's your boss.

When pursuing her went south, he'd be both alone and unemployed.

"It ..." She shook her head, and her forehead smoothed as the doubt and uncertainty cleared away. "It's my ex."

Ex-husband? Fiancé? Boyfriend? He didn't ask.

"And what?" he said. "He doesn't want to be an ex?"

She averted her eyes.

Time to cash in. Lina had no reason to talk to him, and if he pressed, she'd call his bluff and he'd lose the little progress he'd made in this interaction. Besides, if he had progressed toward anything, it was disappointment. "See you Monday."

"I'm not sure what Shane's goal is, except that he wants to talk." The statement raced after him, clad in frustration. "He's called twice now. He also texted once, the day you asked who died. I haven't answered."

She trusted him enough to discuss this? A thrill coursed through his veins. He'd made it to the mouth of the hallway leading to the back door, but he pivoted back and leaned his shoulder into the corner. "It ended badly?"

"And then some." Her perfectly sculpted eyebrows drew closer together, and her line of sight rested on the phone. "We both contributed thousands to a joint account to fund our wedding. His withdrawals were reasonable at first. He said he was making down payments for the venue, the band, everything. I believed him." Her mouth puckered as though she felt ill. "One day, the bank sent notice that the account had been drained and closed. He hadn't made a single deposit for the wedding."

Matt sucked a breath through his teeth. "Where'd it go?"

"Gambling. He got nasty when I confronted him." Her delicate throat marked a hard swallow, and she rubbed her shoulder as though remembering an injury.

Fire rose from Matt's belly and blazed in his chest, his arms. Her movements could've been coincidental, but more likely, the guy had gotten rough with her.

"You're supposed to tell me you're sorry, and he's a jerk and you can't imagine why he'd betray me."

Matt crossed his arms. The problem was, he could imagine. The allure of sin, egged on by selfishness and pride, had powered his own decisions for years. Gambling could be an addiction like drugs, he'd heard.

Only God's work in his life had transformed him into a different man now.

"Anyway, he messaged to say he's sorry for everything and wants to make things right, but the timing is a little coincidental. Shane's in real estate, and my dad and I own some property in Maine. Dad wants to sell, and I wonder if he put Shane up to this."

That explained the tense conversation he'd overheard between her and her father. What sort of dad would send a scumbag after his daughter? "That sounds like a mess. I'm sorry."

Her lips twisted as though she'd hoped for more insight.

"Have you asked your dad about it?"

"We don't see eye-to-eye about Shane. He and Mom believed him when he said he put the money toward a short-term investment. He said he could replace the money in a couple of months and played it off like I was unreasonable for not being willing to wait. Talking to Dad about him would only invite judgment." She shook her head. "Also ... Maybe it's foolish, but I do wonder ... What if Shane is actually sorry?"

Steps in gambling recovery had to be similar to those in drug and alcohol addiction treatment. The protocol might encourage making amends, but only in cases where reaching out wouldn't cause more harm. If Shane had gotten violent with Lina, the man ought to be proceeding with the utmost caution. "Regardless, you're allowed to have boundaries. If you think he's dangerous, don't invite him back into your life."

"He isn't dangerous. He ..." She twisted the ring on her right hand. The stone in this one was big and blue. Other days, he'd seen her wear different colors. Four so far. The rings, gaudy in their size, contrasted with her classy, neutral-colored clothes, her careful but subdued makeup.

But today wouldn't be the day he attempted to uncover the secret behind that anomaly.

He focused on the problem at hand. "If he calls again, I'll be happy to answer."

A laugh burst through her frown. "Oh, he'd love that."

"So? I ..." Realization dawned. "You didn't marry him, did you?"

"Oh." She shook her head quickly. "I broke it off. Not even *I* am that desperate to start a family."

Relief caught Matt like a parachute. A loser fiancé had to be easier to recover from than a lying, gambling, abusive husband, right? As if her romantic past were any of his business. As if they had any kind of future. She wanted a family. Did he? His abs tightened. Why was he even going down that path? "You have a right to move on. It's none of his business if a man answers your phone."

"Oh, I know." Her voice grew quiet. "I know." She blinked, refocused. "It's just, what's the point? I don't care enough to want to make him jealous, either."

Matt took that as a good sign. "The point would be letting him know you're not alone in the world. Not defenseless."

A touch of humor turned up her lips. "You'd defend me?"

He would. The idea of someone hurting her bothered him far more than those boys harassing Bailey. But the tension in his muscles demanding an enemy to confront would do him no good here, alone with Lina in the studio.

He matched her lighter tone. "If you ask nicely, I might not even be a civil adult about it."

"How gallant of you."

Matt's laugh sounded harsh to his own ears. Forced. He pushed away from the wall, straining to keep up the levity. "And you didn't even want to hire me."

8

$\mathcal{M}$att's family resembled a team of ants spread out over the stretching grounds of Visser Landscaping. Dad drove the mower. Mom pulled weeds in a flowerbed by the office. Pete operated a string trimmer. Krissy and her daughter, Jade, weren't visible from the lot, but on his way in, Matt had spotted them in the massive flowerbed at the corner of the property. Krissy hacked at shrubs using Dad's preferred tool—a hand-operated pruner—while her daughter scooped up twigs and leaves.

Cleanup days like these had been the bane of Matt's childhood. He'd hated the seemingly endless chores required to keep up the property, but as a landscaping company, fastidious care of the grounds was good for business.

He parked, gave Dad a wave, returned his mother's hug, and made his way to Krissy and Jade.

When Krissy spotted him, she arched and twisted her back in a way that showed she was sore already, five shrubs into a grouping of twenty or thirty of them. "Didn't expect you to show up."

"I said I was coming this weekend."

"Yeah, but you don't work here anymore. Who'd volunteer for this?"

"Someone who wants to see his family." He motioned her to hand over the trimmer and went to work.

Krissy helped five-year-old Jade load the small trailer behind the lawn tractor, but she must've decided cleanup was more of a one-person job because she soon dismissed Jade to play on the swing set. Lucky kid.

Krissy appraised him. "How are you doing?"

Oh. So she'd had an ulterior motive for letting Jade go.

"I'm good." He still couldn't fight the sense of satisfaction over how Lina had talked with him about something important. She'd cared about what he thought.

"Did you find a group?" Krissy scooped up a bundle of brush.

"I did. And I'm staying in touch with my sponsor. We're doing lunch tomorrow." He circled the shrub, hearing his dad's voice in his head, coaching him on how to get the right shape. "You don't need to worry."

Krissy stayed back when he moved on to a new shrub, and he glanced to check on her.

She studied him, worried.

"How are things here?" he asked. "Is Baxter happy at least?"

"He must be." Krissy's tone lifted. "Put in a great big order, and Dad spent all day going back and forth to deliver wood chips." She chuckled, as though the payday from the task more than justified the work, but the math on that would've worked out a lot better—fewer hours and less fuel—if the order had required half as many trips.

Which it would've before Matt had sunk the larger of the dump trucks.

He needed to repay them.

Krissy leaned over and bumped his shoulder. "How's working with Lina?"

"Her ex-fiancé is bothering her."

"Oh." Krissy swept a gloved hand over the old mulch, clearing the larger sticks. With her face angled away, she gave no hints of her disapproval other than her tone. She yanked a thistle and threw it on the pile with the other debris. "Is she a believer?"

"She was at church on Sunday morning." That didn't answer the question, but it was the best he could do.

Krissy's mouth settled into a frown, and she returned to work.

"Out with it."

"Huh?" She straightened, resting the backs of her wrists against her hips, her fingers sticking out behind her.

"Whatever you're worried about." He moved to a new shrub, clipped a little too deep on one side, and winced. Hopefully Dad wouldn't notice.

"You've been through a lot, Matt."

His back knotted, but he continued the task. If only unwanted parts of his life were as easy to clip away as unwieldy plant growth.

"I'm worried about you. I'm your sister. It's what we do."

He brushed the blades of the pruners against the shrub, looking for longer branches that otherwise wouldn't stick out until Dad or Pete inspected his work.

Krissy found another weed to pull. "You're living up there, away from everybody, and working for a pretty woman who has an ex who's bothering her. Are you sure you need to get in the middle of their drama?"

"I'm hardly in the middle."

"Tell me you don't want to be." She leveled a look at him.

She had him there.

Krissy resumed cleaning up the flowerbed. "Whatever you do, don't jeopardize your sobriety."

He stilled the pruners. "I won't. I promise."

She spared him another frown.

"I won't." He'd spent the last year learning his triggers and weaknesses. He'd learned to talk regularly with his sponsor and others who would hold him accountable. He knew the warning signs and the consequences of giving in. He'd experienced the natural high of looking back—even just hours later —on a good choice.

Whether she believed him or not, Krissy worked in silence.

To break the strain, Matt tossed a handful of leaves at her.

She huffed, rolled her eyes, and fluffed her shirt until the leaves fluttered to the mulch. Then a smile crept onto her lips.

"Want to hear some good news?" Matt asked.

"Sure."

"I had some interviews this morning. You're looking at Lakeshore's newest pizza delivery guy."

She squinted at him in the sunlight, and for one perilous moment, he couldn't tell if she'd veer toward pity or pride. "Have they seen your car?" A smirk stole across her face.

"Hey now." He looked toward the lot, but the building blocked his view of the Brownmobile.

"I saw you drive in." Krissy motioned to the street, then stooped to gather more brush.

Matt started a new shrub. "I figured I should visit while I can, before I start working weekends."

"Couldn't get them to only schedule you during the week?"

"I might've been able to, but Saturdays are their busiest day. Besides, I'll be juggling a few jobs when it's all said and done. Working weekends is inevitable."

Krissy carried a load over to the trailer and returned with heavy steps. "Sorry it's come to this, working so many entry-level jobs to get by. I wish I could make it easier for you."

The pity had won after all.

"I've had it easy. That's how I ruined my life. Remember?"

The corner of Krissy's mouth bit into her cheek. "I guess. But ... still."

"Everything is exactly the way it should be. Easy isn't the answer. The answer is in the struggle."

"The answer is in the Bible," Krissy countered.

"And the Bible is full of struggles."

"A little short on pizza delivery guys, though."

Matt coughed on laughter. Maybe she did pity him some, but this felt good. Working with his hands, here with family. He'd keep struggling until everyone who cared about him could stop worrying. Until he could right his wrongs and move into his future with fewer regrets.

"WHY DON'T YOU HAVE A BOYFRIEND?"

Lina stood at the edge of the bonfire with Isabella, roasting marshmallows and struggling with insecurity, and the question the girl posed in front of the group had to be about her love life?

In all her years working for the band, she hadn't socialized much with Gannon, John, Philip, or Tim. She and Adeline worked well together, but they weren't friends, and she'd only just met John's new bride, Erin, tonight.

She ought to jump at the offer of friendship and community, but counting on these people for more than a paycheck felt ... complicated. Much like her feelings regarding dating.

Shane had duped her. Her parents were interested in her for all the wrong reasons—Mom wanted her to boost her social standing, Dad his bank accounts. Grandma had been taken from her all too soon.

What relationship would fail next?

She didn't have a boyfriend because fear had doused her

courage to date, despite how much she wanted a family. Similar anxiety had kept her quiet at the bonfire.

Unfortunately, a lull in conversation meant everyone had likely heard Isabella's question.

"Boyfriends aren't everything." This declaration came from Erin.

Thank you, Lord. The rescue meant Lina might not have to muster an answer herself.

John held Erin's hand, apparently unthreatened, because her comment brought a smile. "How about husbands?"

"I love you." She paused to grin, and Lina could hear the "but" coming before she continued. "But before you came along—and for a while after—I planned to live a full, happy life with or without a husband, so no, you're not everything either."

Over the chuckles and the crackling campfire, Lina almost didn't hear Philip's quiet offering. "Only God's everything."

He'd been as quiet as Lina tonight. His choice to break his silence with those words stoked her curiosity.

She glanced back to Isabella, who pouted next to her, probably disappointed at the way her question had been shot down.

Okay. Lina wanted to be a good role model. She also needed friends. Both required a certain amount of openness. A certain amount of trust that God had placed her here, with these people, for a purpose. She took the plunge. "Boyfriends really aren't everything. Find the wrong one, and you're better off without, but sometimes it takes a while to see the flaw in a relationship."

Isabella's expression turned thoughtful. Was she thinking about the underlying warning in what Lina had said, or was she about to fire off another personal question? The latter seemed more likely, and Lina's feet shifted as though she were standing her ground in front of a firing squad.

Tim interjected before his daughter had the chance to take

86

aim. "Which is why you're not allowed to date until you're thirty."

Isabella moaned, and the adults laughed.

"Practical solution," Gannon quipped.

As Lina and Isabella continued roasting marshmallows, the others dove into the dating rules they planned to set for their daughters—though only Philip and Tim had kids so far. The men around the fire vowed to be protective.

Unlike Lina's father, who must've given Shane her phone number.

Yesterday's message from her ex had been another apology. The softness in his voice as he'd asked her to get in touch brought back memories of their early dates. Their first kiss. A picnic dinner. An evening at the ballet. The way he'd calmed her down after a spat with her parents. All the promise of happily ever after.

All the hopes he'd dashed.

And then there was Matt. Shane's opposite. Rough around the edges instead of suave, but oddly good with kids. Protective. Willing to share about his life in meaningful ways.

A squeal from Isabella pulled Lina from her thoughts. The girl swung her stick, the treat on the end an orange, glowing blur.

Tim called out a warning, and Lina touched her arm to still her.

Together, they blew out the flaming marshmallow and went to the snack table. Lina helped Isabella pull off the burnt outer shell of the marshmallow and left the girl to make a s'more before returning to her seat between Isabella's empty one and Philip.

She'd much rather focus on Philip and his decision to leave Awestruck than Shane or Matt. Since he stared into the fire, largely ignoring the conversation around them, this made as good of an opportunity as she'd get.

She shifted toward him. "It's on to bigger and better things for you?"

Philip scratched his short beard. "I don't know about bigger, but better? I hope so."

She'd need more hints to solve the riddle.

At the snack table, John's dogs moved in to try to slip some food from Isabella. John went over, motioned his dogs off, then rolled up his sleeves to help the young teen.

Meanwhile, Erin used both hands as she laughed her way through a story directed at Gannon and Adeline. The lead singer held his fiancée's hand with both of his. Their goodbye when the band left for California on Monday would be hard.

Lina's twinge of envy prompted her to wonder what it might be like for Philip to spend even more time than she did around the happy couples. Other than a rumored relationship with pop star Michaela Vandehey, who had been around a chunk of the summer for a collaboration with Awestruck, Philip had been single since before joining the band. A widower, actually.

She studied his profile in the firelight. "Are the kids going with you to California?"

"They'd miss the start of school, so they're staying here with Ruthann, their nanny."

Isabella's guffaw by the snack table pulled Lina's attention from the bassist.

Smirking, John retook his seat next to Erin.

Isabella held a s'more so thick her thumb and pointer finger looked to be extended about as far as possible. In the flickering light, the stack seemed to include a graham cracker, a marshmallow, one of the raspberry bars Lina had brought, another marshmallow, and a final graham cracker.

Playfully disapproving, Erin bumped John's shoulder. The other conversations quieted as the group watched the girl struggle to take her first bite.

"Give it to Gannon," Tim suggested. "He's got a big mouth."

Isabella squished the creation until marshmallow squeezed out the sides and finally managed to take a bite. As she continued to work on the treat, she returned to her seat. "Want me to make you one?"

Lina laughed and declined, then shot a glance at Philip. How could he leave the easy camaraderie of the band—not to mention the money? Why would he? She took a deep breath, hoping she wasn't overstepping. "What will you do after the album is done?"

"I'm thinking we'll move to Iowa by my dad, where I grew up." He kept his face toward the light of the fire, the orange glow highlighting a quiet determination. "I want to finish my degree, live a simpler life."

That sounded a lot like her own desire for a fresh start. But had moving made things simpler for Lina? Or only added a handsome complication named Matt Visser?

9

*M*att used to be the young punk who ruled the world. Now, he was the thirty-something being interviewed by kids for minimum wage jobs. He shifted in the plastic chair in the stark office of the home improvement store. He must have ten years on the manager, but that didn't make the guy as young as it used to be. Russ was likely in his twenties. He might even hold a college degree.

The service award pins on his name tag caught the light as he studied Matt's application. In the prior employment section, Matt had listed Visser Landscaping and Key of Hope. He'd left off his longest running job. A nearly empty page looked significantly less ridiculous than if he'd scrawled the word Awestruck in one of those little boxes.

Despite the omission, Russ had recognized him.

"Well, I'm a big fan." The manager glanced up, bashful and excited like he didn't know what a blow Matt's pride had taken when he'd applied. "Couldn't believe it when they said Matt Visser turned in an app."

"Just trying to make an honest living."

Russ nodded and chewed his lip. "Corporate would have my head if I let you use a forklift."

The kid must've seen the video.

Matt stayed still. Seemed like the best way to look like he wouldn't cause trouble.

Russ swiped his fingers over cheeks that didn't appear to need a razor very often. "You know anything about windows and doors?"

"When I stood in front of the TV as a kid, my family always said people make better doors than windows."

The attempt at humor bellyflopped onto the concrete floor of the interview room. The service award pins glinted again.

"It was a joke." A bad one, because Matt couldn't compensate for it by spouting off some useful knowledge about the products. Some models were probably better at energy retention or security than others, but which ones? He couldn't even name three brands. "I know some basics."

Like, windows and doors opened and closed.

Oh, and they locked.

Probably better not to list those helpful factoids.

In the silence, Russ's mouth twisted.

"I'm a quick study." That, at least, was true.

Russ cringed in what appeared to be another moment of internal debate, then he extended his hand to Matt. "Welcome to the team."

As Matt shook, Russ's smile grew more genuine. Having a former rock star work for him must've seemed worth whatever fallout he would face from other members of the management team.

After settling training details, Russ led the way from the office. "Is it true what they say?"

Matt slowed, braced for a question about some stunt he'd foolishly pulled years ago. "What who says?"

"Awestruck is thinking of making a change, swapping Philip

out and hiring you. It must not be, though, right? Why would you want to work here if Awestruck wanted you?"

Matt crossed his arms. What was he supposed to say? He'd applied for lack of better options?

"There are as many theories the other way, too, I guess," Russ offered.

"That *I'm* the one who doesn't want *Awestruck*?" That'd be new.

"Kind of. Some people think Philip's quitting because no one wants to work with Gannon. Big personality, judgmental."

Back in the day, Matt would've agreed. Now righteous indignation—something he was rarely in a position to feel—led him to take a conspiratorial step toward Russ. "The truth about working with Gannon?"

"Yeah?" Russ looked eager enough to pull out a pen and take notes.

"Takes an awfully big flamethrower to burn a bridge with him. Believe me. I know."

Russ nodded, uncertainty tinging his hopefulness.

Right. Russ had just hired him, and now Matt was bragging about being good at burning bridges.

Off to a great start.

Matt slugged his arm. "But I've changed a lot since then. I'm looking forward to contributing to the team."

He hung around long enough to watch Russ rally another smile, then got out before he could incriminate himself further.

THE BOUQUET of orchids resembled a pink-and-white firework, dominating Lina's desk at Key of Hope and continually drawing her gaze from her laptop screen. The large arrangement must've cost a fortune. Lakeshore didn't even have a florist, and hiring one to drive the bouquet from the city two towns over must've added to the expense.

The exquisite blooms marked the first apology where Shane had put his money where his mouth was. She tapped a nail on her desk. If she kept the flowers, she ought to thank him for them ... Right?

The front door swung open, and Lina rolled her chair back, distancing herself from the flowers. As if Adeline would believe their existence on her desk were coincidence.

The arrival was a student, though, who immediately went to a practice room for her flute lesson.

Lina scooted closer again and lifted the card from the desk.

Thinking of you on what should've been our six-month anniversary. I'm sorry I stole that from us.

"Stole" certainly fit the situation.

Perhaps he really was sincere. Matt had changed. Why couldn't Shane? If he had, would talking to him provide them both with closure? Then he could stop with the apologies, and she could release some of the hurt and anger.

The front door opened again, and Matt burst in.

Lina slapped the card face-down on her desk before he could look toward the office area. She stared at the little rectangle, mortification wiggling in her chest. Her self-conscious reaction revealed whose questions she'd hoped to avoid. Not Adeline's, but Matt's.

Why had she shared details about Shane with him? And why did his presence leave her feeling foolish for appreciating the flowers?

Matt huffed as though he'd heard her questions and didn't like the answers any more than she did, but when she lifted her gaze, his head was just turning from the waiting room. The sigh must not have been about her.

She sat back in her seat and checked the time. His lesson

EMILY CONRAD

with Chris should start in one minute, but the boy hadn't
arrived yet.

As Matt turned into the office area, his gaze hitched on the
orchids, then he crossed to the secondary desk to log into the
computer. "How was your weekend?"

She inhaled, preparing to volunteer the story of the flowers,
but she would only owe him that explanation if they were
romantically involved. Which they weren't. Even if he was good
with kids, loyal to family, and roguishly handsome.

She stuck to the question—how was her weekend?

"Quiet." She'd baked the raspberry bars, read, and gone to
church. But only one of her weekend activities seemed worth
mentioning. "I went to the bonfire."

"Oh yeah? How was that?"

"Seems like a shame Philip's quitting." She'd expected
Philip to share a powerful epiphany that would leave her
cheering for his success. Instead, he'd been introspective and
quiet.

"I don't know." Matt punched a couple of keys, docu-
menting his start time. "It takes guts to recognize what it'll take
to get clean and to go for it, despite the cost."

Get clean? Philip was another addict? Tingling tension drew
her back straight. Philip, whom she'd respected and sympa-
thized with, had hidden a detrimental secret? Was no man on
earth what he seemed?

Maybe she'd misheard.

"Get clean?" she asked.

Matt swiveled from the keyboard. "You didn't think he quit
over Gannon, did you?"

"Why would I think that?" Did Gannon have some awful
secret too?

Matt shrugged. "Rumor is Gannon's hard to get along
with."

Though Gannon had asked how it had been working with

94

Matt, he hadn't criticized the choice to employ him. Considering Matt's past, that seemed gracious.

Maybe not all men were leading double lives, but to learn Philip wasn't as upright as she'd thought ...

Lord, am I ever going to learn to spot the bad ones?

If she could have a superpower, she'd choose that one, hands down.

"What is it then?" Her voice sounded scratchy with disapproval. She swallowed again, focused on the flowers, and wondered what they'd look like if she lit them on fire. "Alcohol? Drugs?"

"It's not my story to tell. I'm sorry. I thought you knew."

Right. Because the men who'd made disasters of their lives had to stick together, respect each other's privacy. Otherwise all their secrets would be out, and what power would they have then?

"To think I dared to hope there were some men left in the world not leading double lives."

For all his apologies, Shane was probably only working with Dad to get The Captain's Vista. A conversation with him would never lead to closure. He didn't even deserve a thank-you for the costly bouquet. She envisioned dropping the entire arrangement, vase and all, into the trash.

But the flowers hadn't betrayed her. Quite the opposite—at least one nice thing had come out of all the subterfuge and lies she'd encountered.

"Women don't fail?" Matt's incredulous question prodded her.

She turned to glare.

He took a step backward, bumping the far desk. As he lifted his hands again, she glimpsed his tattoos. Love and hate. The lit match.

The door scraped open, and Chris stepped in with a cheerful hello.

EMILY CONRAD

Matt skirted her like he might a rattlesnake. He greeted Chris but missed a step in their handshake. With a triumphant grin, Chris called him on it and headed toward the classroom.

Matt cast a wary glance at Lina, as if on the verge of apologizing, but her expression must've warned him off. Women weren't perfect either, but in her experience, men were far more likely to deceive, use, and discard people they claimed to love.

10

*M*att ought to know better than to poke a bear, but from the moment he left Lina fuming in the office, he knew he wouldn't be able to leave well enough alone.

On the other side of the glass walls of the classroom, Lina spent Chris's lesson—and the ones after—scowling at her computer. Wheels were likely turning under her blond curls. Arguments and comebacks in the making.

Matt's mind churned out the same. As much as he tried to focus on his lessons, he dissected what she'd said. *All* men led double lives?

Sure, a lot of men—and, to his point, women—justified addictions and a slew of other sins, but by blindly lumping all males together and assuming a general untrustworthiness, Lina wasn't leaving room for God's work in a person's life.

Matt had heard plenty of relapse stories. He'd lived that story a few times. But he'd also heard stories of redemption, and he was determined to claim one for himself. From the little he'd heard, Philip seemed dedicated to the same.

To be fair, Lina's reaction likely hadn't been about him or Philip. To have turned so potent, the venom must've been storing up for quite some time. She'd been saving it for Shane, and Matt and Philip wandered into striking zone.

If Lina realized the same, she didn't want to talk about it, because when Matt's last student was five minutes from finishing, she exited through the back door of Key of Hope.

Cute. She didn't usually cut out this early.

It said a lot about the men she was used to that she thought leaving the disagreement between them was a better solution than having a conversation and reaching an understanding, if not a full resolution.

Matt saw his student off, caught up on his notes about the day's lessons, and punched out. As he swiveled from the computer, a tan lump under Lina's desk caught his eye. Her purse. She hadn't left for the night.

Maybe she wasn't dead set on avoiding him, and a little effort could give them the chance to end the day on a better note.

He headed for the back door, angling as he passed Samantha in the hall between the classrooms. "How's Bailey doing?"

"Fully recovered, and she knows if those boys bully her again, they're going to be the ones with problems."

"You have my number." The instructors had exchanged contact information in case anyone needed a lesson covered, but defending an innocent first-grader was a much higher calling.

"I meant they'd have problems with the principal." Already behind him, Samantha laughed ruefully. "But I might take you up on your offer."

"Do that." Matt passed into the alcove at the back. The stairs to the second floor and its storage closets and meeting room ascended to his left. Ahead, the door to the parking lot looked like something out of an old-school detective's office, wooden with frosted glass. The lettering affixed to the outside showed as a shadow in the dim foyer. Matt turned the antique doorknob, and the sticky evening met him.

The weather in Lakeshore constantly surprised him—how cool the mornings could be, and yet, how even this far north, on the shore of Lake Superior, August could still pull a few punches that left him eager for air conditioning.

August.

Sobered, his step slowed on the concrete stairs leading down to the cracked asphalt.

For too short of a time, he'd had a friend named August.

Matt had sped after Lina without a plan for what to say or how to say it. He'd only known he'd wanted to prove her underlying assumption—once leading a double life, always leading a double life—wrong. He'd wanted to convince her change was possible.

He'd have likely offended her worse rather than convince her of anything.

August was the key to fostering understanding instead. If he shared his story, maybe she'd see that not all men were leading double lives. Some succeeded in their commitment to change.

Now, he just had to find her.

The parking area was large enough for about twenty cars, and few spots were taken, so he easily located her sedan. He nearly laughed. She'd only run as far as her driver's seat and hadn't even bothered to close herself in. She rested one foot on the pavement, one on the doorjamb as she scrolled on her phone.

He rested his forearms on the top of her door. "You must know not all men are leading double lives."

She lowered her phone and huffed. "Sure, but considering how hard it is to spot the ones who are, it's safer to assume they all are."

"Safe, but I'd guess it's lonely."

Lina frowned, gaze now on her steering wheel. Whatever her thoughts, she didn't appear ready to share.

"I found one of my friends dead." He swallowed, allowing the mental image of Auggie's body for only a moment. He had Lina's full attention now. As he'd known he would. "The reality of finding a body is worse than TV shows make it out to be."

Lina stilled, then seemed to recoil from some thought. Perhaps her imagination had painted too vivid a scene. Or maybe she'd watched some pretty gruesome TV shows. "Was it a good friend?"

"Depends what you call good. After Awestruck, I joined another band. The lead singer and I were probably the worst possible people to be in each other's lives, but we were close. I found him dead of an overdose. After that, I started having nightmares where I was the corpse. I grabbed onto God like a drowning man and checked myself into rehab."

She peered through her windshield, either intently listening or wishing him away.

"I can't promise to always make the right choices in the future, but I live every day knowing the consequences of a relapse. Auggie is Exhibit A for why I changed. Combine all the therapy, the meetings, and the change I know you can see in me, and you have proof I'm doing everything I can to avoid a double life."

She drew a long breath as if to see what would happen if she over-inflated her lungs.

"Philip's decision to quit Awestruck is pretty strong evidence he's dedicated to a new path." Hearing no rebuttal, Matt continued. "But it's not either of us you're really upset about, right? It's Shane?"

Her head tipped forward, but Matt couldn't tell if she'd meant to nod or simply to make rubbing her forehead easier.

"Have you asked your dad about him?"

"No, but I'm not sure I have to. Shane sent the flowers with another apology."

Matt rubbed his hand over his mouth. He'd hoped she'd bought them for herself.

Lina continued. "He said they were because today should've been our six-month anniversary."

Most guys couldn't keep up with real birthdays and anniversaries, but Shane was commemorating the six-month anniversary of an event that had never happened? "Has he offered to repay the money he blew?"

She jerked as though he'd poked her. "I gave up on that idea a long time ago."

"But he shouldn't have." Matt gulped and tried his motives. Was he trying to keep Lina away from Shane for his own sake? Or did Shane have an obligation to Lina? Addiction recovery programs usually recommended making direct amends when possible. If Shane skipped that step, he might be skipping the sincerity too. "I guess it's up to you to determine if the evidence means he's changed. If he's still gambling ..."

She twisted the ring on her right hand, silent.

Matt followed the logic. If Shane was still in the thick of his addiction, he'd seek an open door into Lina's life only if she could feed his gambling. For instance, if he thought he could get more money from her. Maybe she had it. She'd said he'd spent thousands in her money, and she'd never mentioned the loss causing a financial burden.

"I take it you're loaded." The words slipped out before he stopped to consider their propriety.

Her focus zinged to him. After holding for an intense second, she blinked and looked away. "What makes you think that?"

Now who led the double life? But she'd answered with a question, not a denial. Besides, his parents had raised him not to ask nosy questions about people's finances.

"Just be careful with Shane. Since his calls upset you, ask him to stop."

"But I don't want to throw out the flowers."

He wished she had, but he didn't even have to put that thought on trial to recognize it as motivated by jealousy. "Then keep them."

"If I forgive him, shouldn't I say something?"

"Say it or not. If you do, also set whatever boundaries you need to feel safe in your relationships. A man who's dedicated to honoring you during his recovery will support your needs."

She eyed him, almost as if she could tell he'd left out names on purpose. Shane might not support healthy boundaries, but Matt wished Lina would lay some out for himself, if only because that would mean they had a definable relationship. Something beyond co-workers.

But who did he think he was to deserve a deeper connection with her?

"Anyway." He stepped back, allowing his arms to slip from the top of her car door. "I've got to go make sure Lakeshore gets its pizzas."

Ducking any reaction to his lame closing, he cut across the lot to the Brownmobile. As he'd said, he couldn't promise to never relapse, and he still owed a steep financial debt to his parents from last time. A relationship where he was trusted enough to observe boundaries was still a long way off.

LESSONS STRETCHED into the evening at Key of Hope. After her trip to the parking lot failed to prevent a talk with Matt, Lina returned to her desk. As sunset painted the scene out the windows in pastel pinks and purples, she caught up on her social media duties for Awestruck.

The announcements about Philip's departure still garnered

the most attention, though they'd been live for two weeks already. She'd stopped trying to find new ways to word the same sentiment—that they would miss him but respected his choice to prioritize his family—in response to comments and instead simply kept an eye out for trolls or controversy.

None surfaced, and even the resentment she'd felt when she'd learned the rest of the reason for Philip's choice had ebbed.

Thanks to Matt.

Hadn't she been shocked by his transformation? He was proof people could change.

A reminder she shouldn't have needed that God could work miracles.

Shane had claimed to believe in that same God, but she'd seen little evidence of faith in how he spent his time or how he spoke. Had that changed? He hadn't mentioned God in any of his attempts to reconnect. And a couple of calls, a text, and a bouquet did little to repair the damage he'd inflicted. Had he made more extreme changes that she couldn't see because she'd moved away?

How much did his transformation—or lack thereof —matter?

She could no longer pull up mental imaginings of what their kids might look like, or what trips they might take as a family, or how they'd make meals together a priority. She no longer wanted her parents' approval enough to overlook her misgivings about him.

She'd made the right choice to leave, and she needed to follow Matt's advice and set boundaries, doing what she wished her dad had done: taken her side in the breakup and asked Shane to stay away.

What a striking idea. She hadn't needed someone else to protect her. She could've stood up for herself directly with

Shane instead of ignoring him and hoping the problem would disappear.

On a surge of empowerment, she picked up her phone, but her ability to craft replies vanished. Responses to fans on social media came naturally, but she had woefully little experience setting boundaries like this.

She started with the things he'd be glad to hear, and from there, the rest came.

I forgive you, and you didn't need to send flowers, but thank you. I wish you all the best, however, I'm not comfortable resuming a relationship. Please stop reaching out.

Without sending, she reread the message, questioning every sentiment. Did she really forgive him? She was comfortable surrendering him to God and not pursuing the debt—financial or emotional. If he was truly a believer, Christ had paid for his betrayal on the cross. If not ...

Lord, You know where Shane stands with You. Please work on his heart in whatever way he needs. Work on mine too.

Returning to the text, she kept the part about forgiveness and deleted the phrase wishing him all the best—her healing had a ways to go before that would become true—and went on to consider the merits of using the word *please.*

The nicety softened the hard line she'd taken, but she'd clearly laid out her expectations. Using manners didn't make her a pushover. She hoped.

Her finger hovered over the send button while an ache dug deep into her stomach.

If only she had Matt's courage. He wouldn't hesitate over such a thing.

With a cringe, Lina tapped to send the text.

As soon as she did, her resolve wavered. What if Shane sent a nasty reply? What if, in the spirit of forgiveness, she shouldn't have shut down all further contact?

Throat threatening to close, she opened her message thread

enough of her to use her money at the cost of their relationship.

Instead, he'd hung up.

Foolishness.

She huffed, then drew more air in. Her heart seemed to beat extra fast, as if to make up for lost time. "Okay."

Matt focused on her as if he could see the adrenaline racing through her veins. "You sure?"

"Of course." But if Shane lacked remorse and had overstepped her ban by calling once, what would stop him from calling again, this time to berate her?

She'd told Matt she didn't want to aggravate Shane by allowing another man to answer her phone, and he'd done so anyway. In that way, both had disregarded her boundaries. Matt had done so as a favor to her, but how often had Shane trampled her wishes because he thought he knew better too?

Matt continued to wait.

She smoothed the hem of her shirt, floundering. Should she thank him?

Bailey poked her hand forward, the ring pinched between her finger and thumb. "Ta da!"

"Thank you, darling." Lina accepted the ring and slid the band over her knuckle and into place.

Bailey scampered back to her babysitter. Matt watched her go before eyeing Lina again. Whether he'd noticed her lack of gratitude, or he could see deeper conflict warring in her, he returned to the practice room, though his next student hadn't arrived yet.

Lina dropped into her desk chair. She kept her feet anchored to the floor, but her mind circled. Matt and Shane were different, right?

Right.

She'd only discouraged the idea of Matt answering her phone, whereas she'd firmly told Shane to stop calling. Matt knew about the boundary she'd set for Shane and had stepped forward to help her enforce it. Also, though Shane would've happily told off another man, he wouldn't have cared if his actions left her to deal with the fallout, like when the guy called back to berate her, and he wouldn't have cared what Lina thought about any of it.

Matt, on the other hand, would care if Shane called again, and her hesitance to thank him for stepping in seemed to have hurt him.

$\sim$

IF LINA'S ex lived within driving distance, Matt would visit the guy. Shane clearly wasn't going to ride off into the sunset unless he convinced Lina to ride with him. A twisted sense of courtesy might inspire a rule-follower like her to give in.

If only Matt could recall more than a few digits of the number he'd seen on Lina's phone.

He ruffled his hand through his hair. He'd much rather numb helplessness and frustration with drugs or alcohol than feel either emotion, but he knew the devastation that followed surrendering to temptation.

Give me a way out, Lord.

His next student would arrive momentarily. He just needed to bridge the gap.

Two bass guitars waited on stands for his next lesson. One of them was his instrument of choice, exactly like the one he'd sold to help cover rehab. It hadn't been here the first day he'd come, and its appearance afterward suggested Adeline had learned his preference from Gannon and purposely brought it in.

He settled the guitar across his body.

First, he attempted a bass line he'd heard on the radio while delivering pizzas earlier. In the process of piecing it together, he stumbled across a sound he liked better and experimented from there, his attention narrowing to consider only the work.

"You can go."

At the surprise of Lina's voice from the door of the practice room, Matt's hands froze. He hadn't seen her rise from her desk or come up the hall, despite the view the glass afforded and the fact that he'd left the door open because he'd expected his next student. At some point, Bailey, Samantha, and the babysitter had left, and the waiting room sat empty. The lesson across the hall continued, though, so less than half an hour had passed.

Twenty minutes, maybe?

The time must've felt like an eternity to Lina as she'd listened to him playing.

"Sorry. Am I bothering you?"

"Your student's a no-show. I emailed her dad. You don't need to stay."

Right. Of course. He rested his hand on the body of the bass. The one he had at Tim's, he'd scored at a garage sale. He'd been driving back from a landscaping job when he spotted the electric bass propped up against an old dresser in the driveway. For the instrument and an amp that crackled worse than a bowl of cereal, he'd paid all the cash in his wallet—which hadn't been much. Before he'd moved to Lakeshore, he'd also had access to the old keyboard in his parents' basement. Nothing fancy, but enough to write "Whirlwinds" with.

He'd called the song a fluke, but his poor setup might've been at least partly to blame for his inability to create more, because inspiration flowed here.

Having someone to bounce ideas off of would almost guarantee another song.

He eyed Lina. "Do you play anything besides, like, flute?"

"No."

"So you don't want to jam with me."

Her dry expression glimmered with a hint of humor. "Paxton's lesson wraps up in ten minutes. We could see if he's interested."

"Funny." The soundproofing prevented him from hearing, but the look on Fred's face suggested little Paxton had some work to do. Fred, the guitar instructor, seemed like a nice enough guy who might be game, but the front door opened, and in walked the next guitar student. With a sigh, Matt set the bass on its stand. "All right. I'll get out of your hair."

She half-frowned but didn't object as she stepped back from the doorway.

"You ought to change your number or block his calls."

She winced. "I told you I'm not out to make him jealous."

"And he has no reason to be. For all he knows, I'm some guy you grabbed off the street to answer for you because he crossed the boundary you set."

"I wish you'd let me stand up for myself, then. I ought to be able to fight my own battles."

Guilty as charged. But ... "Would you have?"

"Not answering is an answer in itself, isn't it?" She sighed. "Besides, there's no harm in him apologizing on my voicemail."

"There is harm. His calls upset you." Matt also suspected Shane had hurt her physically at least once.

With an unconvincing nod, she stepped back as though to leave, then braced a hand on the doorframe. "Thanks, though. For trying to help."

Trying, indeed. Why didn't she treat Shane like the scum he was? Why hedge and push away help? She wouldn't receive Matt's frustration kindly. Or, if she did, it'd be just another example of her bowing to someone else's will instead of standing up for her convictions. Instead of pushing, he said, "You're welcome."

She returned to her desk.

Matt scratched his cheek and peered over at the bass guitar. For a while there, music had helped him escape his frustration about Shane. He'd only played around with the bass today, but the classroom stocked all the instruments he could want to write music—the bass, two guitars, and a keyboard. Tim's idea of making money selling songs might have the added benefit of keeping him sane and sober.

Music, which had been part of his demise, could also be part of his redemption.

Provided he could stick with it long enough to write something worth hearing.

Thankfully, Shane's pursuit of Lina and Matt's own unrequited crush on her ought to provide plenty of angst to keep driving him back to one of the few healthy outlets he had.

12

*L*ina had worked with Awestruck for years, but her stomach did a nervous flip when Gannon and John came through the front door of Key of Hope. They must've come from the airport, fresh off a plane from California. Gannon seemed on the verge of greeting her when he spotted Adeline, and his warm smile broadened.

His fiancée flew into his arms.

John shut the front door and nodded a greeting to Lina.

"You guys just got in?" she asked.

He nodded and hiked a thumb toward the happy couple's reunion kiss. "What gave it away?"

"The time in the studio went well?"

"Bittersweet, but it was a good last hoorah with Philip." His focus landed on one of the practice rooms.

Chris wouldn't arrive for half an hour, and Matt had closed himself in the unused space. Since the day he'd entertained himself during a student's missed lesson, he had made a habit of using the room when it was available, even if it meant stopping by Key of Hope for twenty- or thirty-minute stretches. Judging by the various outfits he showed up in—khakis and a blue polo, as required by the home improvement store, jeans and a tacky shirt with a pizza maker caricature, or old black work pants and a T-shirt labeled with the name of a janitorial company—finding open slots at Key of Hope around his other jobs was a scheduling feat.

But he kept showing up, closing himself in a room, and focusing on music as if he didn't have an audience in whoever happened to be in the waiting area.

Currently, he stood with his back to the glass, oblivious as usual. His head and shoulders moved with a beat that only faintly carried into the office area.

Lina leaned her elbows on her desk and focused on John. "Don't you have a bride to get home to?"

"She spent last week with us." He lifted his chin, pointing her attention back to Matt. "How's he been?"

That was a loaded question. He'd been handsome. Even-keeled. Willing to stand up for her. At the thought of mentioning any of his attractive qualities, flutters went off in her stomach. Was she blushing? She really hoped not.

"He's been working hard." Adeline's voice came soft and thoughtful from behind Lina.

She glanced back to see Lakeshore's favorite couple standing arm-in-arm, apparently ready to acknowledge the existence of others.

"On what?" John asked.

"I meant teaching, but I think he might also be songwriting. He's been using the guitar quite a bit."

The rooms each held a selection of instruments. Not a musician herself, Lina hadn't noticed Matt working with the electric guitar instead of the electric bass until now, when Adeline pointed it out.

"Have you heard it?" Gannon kept an arm around Adeline, but he studied Matt.

What would Matt think if he turned around and found this

gallery of spectators?

Probably keep doing what he was doing—or leave, since he never seemed to act like a normal person.

"I haven't," Adeline answered.

Lina had heard him once, but a year of choir marked her only musical training. She hadn't even noticed him switch instruments. Her opinion wouldn't add to the conversation. Yet, she caught Gannon's questioning glance and took a stab at it. "I heard something early on. It sounded catchy, but I'm no expert."

John shifted a foot forward, as though his interest in his former bandmate was growing. "He's spent a lot of time working like this?"

"Twenty or thirty minutes a day." Not that Lina was tracking.

"That we see," Adeline added. "I gave him a key. He's been coming in during off-hours too."

Oh. She hadn't known. Matt must've been keeping odd hours for her not to have seen him. He might've been avoiding her, but she suspected the more likely explanation was that he had to sacrifice sleep to find time around his jobs.

In his own world, Matt half-turned to the table in the practice room and made a note before again focusing on the guitar.

The heavy front door pushed open, and Chris stepped in. Without noting who stood in his way, he leaned to see around John for a clear view of Matt's practice room. Spotting his idol, he smiled. Next he cast a wave toward the desk. "Hi, Miss Lina."

"Hi, Chris."

He gave no sign of hearing her as his eyes sparked and his mouth fell open. Must've focused long enough to recognize the person who'd blocked his view.

"Chris, have you met my friends?" Lina asked.

Still gaping, Chris shook his head.

John introduced himself. "You take lessons here?"

The boy started to shake his head to the negative, then caught himself and nodded.

John sat on the arm of one of the waiting room couches, putting himself at eye level. "You look like a drummer."

Gannon moved in. "My money's on guitar."

The willingness to take time with fans was one more thing she appreciated about Awestruck. People mattered.

The boy peered from one to the other, but a glance at Matt, still oblivious in his practice room, seemed to solidify his allegiances. "Electric bass."

"You're learning from that guy?" John hiked his thumb toward Matt.

Chris nodded.

"He any good?" Gannon crossed his arms, focused as if Chris's opinion was make or break for Matt.

"The best." Chris's head bobbed again. "Taught me everything I know."

John appeared to barely restrain his laughter. He shot Gannon a look and pushed away from the chair. "In that case, we have some business with him. When's your lesson start?"

"Four."

Gannon patted Chris's shoulder as he stepped past him. "We'll make sure we don't make him late."

"Nice meeting you, Chris." John shook his hand, then followed Gannon toward the practice room.

Chris stood in the space between Lina's desk and the waiting room, holding his fingers open near his torso, as if touching anything would undo the effect of shaking John's hand. He shuffled to a place on one of the couches, attention riveted on the practice room.

～

"WHAT'RE YOU WORKING ON?"

117

In a glass room, Matt's expectations of privacy hadn't been high, but he hadn't anticipated hearing that unmistakable voice. He turned toward the question to find Gannon studying his notes and John easing the door shut again.

Matt had been hopeful about this song, but he braced for Gannon's critique.

Instead, the lead singer focused on him with interest. "New song?"

"New ideas. Not all the way to song status yet."

Gannon refocused on the notes, his fingers moving against his thigh as he ran through the piece. "Might be easier to write with a band."

Nice of him to rub it in. "It's hard enough to fit this in when I've only got my own schedule to worry about."

Gannon tapped the paper thoughtfully. "Adeline says you're coming to the wedding."

"I appreciate the invite." He might even let Tim introduce him around, but maybe Gannon wouldn't appreciate him using the wedding to network and launch himself as a songwriter.

John eyed the drum kit in the next room. "You like teaching here?"

"Most days, yeah. A lot." Maybe he ought to be upfront about his career plans. Word about conversations had at the wedding could spread. "I'm also thinking of getting into song-writing."

"I'd be interested to hear what you come up with." Gannon's focus dipped to the guitar like he might want to hear now. That, or he and John were one invitation away from claiming instruments for an impromptu jam session.

"I don't know if you guys can afford me."

Gannon crossed his arms and cocked his head.

When would he learn not to crack jokes at inappropriate times?

But Gannon shifted his feet. He wasn't annoyed. Uncomfortable? Sheepish? "You know we're looking for a bassist."

There was only one reason Gannon would've brought up the opening in Awestruck. In some capacity, they wanted him to fill it, whether temporarily or long-term. Matt's hope soared. Or was it his pride?

Even if, for the sake of his sanity and sobriety, he'd have to decline, he wanted the offer to rejoin Awestruck so badly, he held his breath.

"We jammed with some guys in California, but ..." Gannon shook his head.

John finally stepped forward. "We want you to audition."

"Audition." The word came out on his exhale. They weren't looking for a temporary fix if they wanted an audition. They were leaning toward offering him his old job back. He'd known Tim wanted this, but he hadn't believed Gannon and John would consider it at all, let alone consider it seriously enough to offer an audition.

Would they still work well together?

Not much made him nervous, but the thought turned his palms clammy against the guitar. A step back into the world of Awestruck was a step toward danger. He could not repeat his mistakes, as much as his ego loved every moment of this conversation.

"Do you have any time this week?" Gannon asked.

He fumbled for words. His planner was in the Brownmobile. He could only remember his complex schedule one day at a time. Today, he had lessons here, then a shift at the pizza place, then after-hours cleaning for the janitorial company.

And tomorrow ...

Did it matter?

"If not this week, then early October?" Furrows marked Gannon's forehead, as if he could tell Matt had hesitations but was afraid to ask what they were.

"You guys don't really want me back." Matt's fingers slipped on the guitar strings, and the amp broadcast the shriek.

John kept his gaze even. "Why not?"

"Last time didn't end well."

"You're not the same person you were."

"Says who? Tim?"

"Mostly, you." Gannon's expression remained serious. "We saw it when you came to us with 'Whirlwinds' this summer. Adeline says you're different. Your student out there is more proof."

For the first time since he'd entered the practice room, he looked to the waiting area. Chris peered at him as if Matt had invented music or something.

Admiration he didn't deserve.

He could turn any success into failure. The bigger the success, the more easily he worked his magic. "Every time we encounter temptation, God gives us a way out."

John's eyes narrowed with concentration, waiting for a twist.

"I'm not good at saying no to temptation when I'm looking it in the eye. I think my way out is to say no now, before I get myself into a tight spot."

Gannon's jaw pulsed, but he sighed as he looked again toward Matt's notes. He rapped a knuckle on the tabletop next to the sheet. "I'd like to see this when it's ready."

"Sure." His throat had gone dry, reducing his voice to a rasp.

The lead singer didn't usually take rejection without a fight. His willingness to let this go meant he agreed with Matt, even if it was begrudgingly. He didn't seem to know how to leave on the disappointing note, though, because he cast an uncertain look to Matt. "See you around. Keep up the good work with the kids."

Matt nodded.

The pure enthrallment on Chris's face out in the waiting room ... He couldn't put himself in a position to jeopardize the innocent adoration, which he'd do if he rejoined Awestruck.

As Gannon opened the door to the practice room, John lingered to shake Matt's hand.

An unexpected sign of respect.

"Pray about it." John held an extra beat and tilted his head as if to emphasize the importance of his order, then followed Gannon out.

~

GANNON AND JOHN didn't linger in the office, so Lina could only guess what they'd wanted with Matt.

By the time Matt's lessons finished, Adeline had left for the day. The other teachers passed through the office area but thankfully settled into rooms with another set of students before Matt finished his notes on his sessions.

Lina swiveled her chair toward him, poised to ask.

"I said no." He didn't look away from the computer.

"To what?"

His eyes looked tired as he lifted them in her direction. "Awestruck."

They'd asked him back.

Wow.

"Why would you turn them down?"

"Because I know where that road leads."

As did she—she'd seen the luxurious accommodations, the adoring crowds, the lavish studios. For Matt, Awestruck would mean the chance to repay his family and an escape from all the odd jobs. He could spend his days on music. "To fame and fortune?"

"To death."

She flinched. He was usually such an optimist. "What happened to your friend resulted from other choices, not starting a band."

He rubbed his hand over his face. "I know myself. The

opportunities that come with getting back into Awestruck wouldn't serve me well."

"And you're okay with saying no?"

"It was harder than I expected, but there's a reason I've been telling Tim for months I wouldn't rejoin."

Her respect for him increased with every word. When he'd changed his mind about working at Key of Hope, she'd assumed he waffled easily, but staying true to his decision about Awestruck was quite a sacrifice. One she wasn't even sure he needed to make. Couldn't a man as committed to sobriety as Matt handle the pressures of the life?

Maybe, but if he went, she'd no longer have his company at Key of Hope. She twisted her ring, heart tugging. Nothing could come of her feelings for him. He didn't want kids. He'd said as much. But his skill with his students hinted he'd be great with children of his own.

Her ringtone yanked her from her reverie.

"Who is it?" Matt's low question came from close behind her. He must've gotten up and stepped over.

"My dad." She watched the screen. She'd set a boundary with Shane, and though she hadn't warned her father of her choice, she'd determined to let voicemail screen Dad's calls. They'd traded their weekly messages like usual ever since his initial call about selling, but Mom had already left the update for the week.

The screen switched from showing his number to reporting a missed call.

"Things are still awkward over the property?" Matt braced his hands on the side of her desktop.

"He hasn't mentioned it in weeks." The notification appeared, indicating Dad had left a message. She lifted the device. "Guess I'll find out."

Matt crossed his arms.

With him standing sentinel beside her, she dialed voicemail

touching them at all. In this upbeat mood, maybe she'd forgive him.

Cheers rose as Gannon took his turn front and center. Since few people ignored the show, Tim stood out as he skirted tables, headed toward Matt and Lina with a drink in his hand. In keeping with the formal tone of the event, he wore a suit. Probably an expensive one of his own rather than a rental like Matt's.

Isabella had met a few girls her age after dinner and lingered with them at the corner of the floor. A man in a staff uniform shadowed Tim.

Tim took his seat while the stranger bent to say something in Lina's ear. She replied quietly, and Matt missed her shouting. With a confused frown, she rose and followed the man away.

He looked to Tim. "What's that about?"

"He's on the staff. Maybe there was a mix-up at the coat check." He tipped a drink of the amber liquid, then lifted a finger from the glass to point toward the dance floor. "I suppose you don't at all regret turning them down right about now."

Gannon, John, and Philip struck their final pose as the last beat dropped, and raucous applause filled the ballroom. Panting but grinning, Gannon broke formation to join his bride. When the couple kissed, more cheers went up.

Joyful abandon. Pure celebration. Happy friends and family. Love.

Matt could see it all from where he sat. Was there any way for him to claim it for his own?

∾

SHANE COULD *NOT* BE HERE.

He must be, or security wouldn't have told her he was, but ...

Shane had traveled all the way to Wisconsin? Tried to gain

entrance to the wedding of the year by claiming to be her plus one?

The sequins of Lina's clutch bit into the thin skin inside her upper arm as she followed the staff member down the hall of the country club. As the passage opened into the foyer, her gaze skipped from person to person, dismissing each before she even focused until her vision stopped on a man standing with his back to her.

In a dark blue suit, he faced the windows overlooking the golf course. His haircut was textured by neatly combed waves. He took one hand from his pocket and tapped his pant leg before turning. As he did, his expression lifted with recognition and appreciation.

She'd raided more of Grandma's jewelry than normal for the wedding, taking a tennis bracelet, hair clips, and a necklace from the safety deposit box at the bank, where she stored the pieces she didn't wear regularly. The weight of the necklace rested on her breastbone like armor.

She smoothed a hand over her dress. She'd made a special trip to an upscale shopping center in Milwaukee to find a gown, and for a moment, she was glad she had. She wanted Shane to regret losing her, even if she'd never give him another chance.

But as Shane neared, his gaze lingering, the yards of fabric suddenly seemed like skimpy cover, and the necklace, far too small to protect her heart.

To prevent fidgeting, she tensed the muscles of her arms. She hadn't wanted to face him on the phone or in text. Was she strong enough to do this in person?

She'd better be. "What are you doing here?"

THE WEDDING GREW EXPONENTIALLY LESS interesting after Lina wandered off. Tim spotted someone he wanted to catch up with and hurried away too, leaving Matt alone at the table. He could mingle, but as soon as he'd swallowed his last bite of steak, long before the dance routine, Tim had taken him around to a dozen of his contacts. Since Matt didn't have a single completed song yet, he didn't need to find more potential customers.

Instead, he plucked a stray penny from the swirling pattern of the carpet and tried to flick it into the wax of the floating candle in the centerpiece. It *splunk*ed into the water of the vase. Nobody seemed to pay him any mind, so he lifted the candle, fished out the coin, and sat back down to try again.

He probably ought to go home before he got himself in real trouble, but what was keeping Lina? A coat mix-up would've been set right by now. A valet might've scratched her car.

Philip must've gone for a water immediately after the dance routine and then made his way to Matt's table, because the show hadn't been over five minutes when the bassist took the seat Lina had vacated. "You did me a big favor this summer."

Matt lined up another shot, using the edge of the table so he could hit the penny at a high enough angle to achieve the arc he needed.

The penny plinked against the vase and dropped into the floral wreath surrounding it. Matt folded his hands and sat back, not willing to dig out the penny with Philip there. "I did you a favor?"

Philip stood and plucked the penny from the greenery. "We're aiming for the water?"

"The wax."

"Ah." Concentration marked Philip's brow as he used one finger to hold the penny on its side. He looked from the coin to the target about a dozen times. "When you stopped by my house, what you said motivated me to start changing. I still had further to go, but you gave me my life back in a lot of ways. Everything's so different now, it's hard to believe it's only been a few months."

He let the penny fly. The coin bumped the candle and sank into the water.

Philip pulled a dime from his pocket and offered it to Matt.

He accepted it with a chuckle. "Raising the stakes."

"Going all in. In more ways than one. I really can't thank you enough for being a part of that."

"Don't give me that much credit. Only God can save a person."

In his peripheral vision as he set up the dime, Matt saw Philip nod. "But He used you."

"Helping others is one of the steps." He flicked the dime. The coin grazed the far side of the vase and disappeared.

Philip rose to retrieve it. "Gannon and John talked to me before offering you the spot."

No surprise there. "I don't see how I can take it. Awestruck comes with too many opportunities to fail." The slippery thought was hard to keep front and center.

"The band comes with a lot of opportunities to help too." Philip sat with the dime between his pointer finger and thumb and rotated the coin slowly. "Not everyone listens closely to Awestruck's lyrics, but some people do. When they recognize faith is behind the music, they ask questions that lead them— some of them—in the right direction. It took you to get through to me, and I think it takes Awestruck to get through to them."

"I agree, but not everyone should have that platform. Some of us are a little more likely than others to misuse it."

Philip set the dime on the edge of the table. "In part, I quit Awestruck to escape the environment, but ..." He paused lining up his shot to lift his hand in something like a shrug. "For all the access I had with the band, being in Awestruck meant I had to work twice as hard to hide my bad decisions."

Matt crossed his arms. "You're not changing your mind, deciding to stay after all?"

"No. My kids need me." Philip let the dime fly and groaned

when he missed the centerpiece entirely. "The guys told me what you said about temptation, and maybe that is the right choice for you, but maybe not."

The dime rolled in tightening circles and finally teetered to its side on the tablecloth. Before they picked up the game again, Philip's daughter came for him. He left the dime, but Matt didn't have the heart to try the game again.

Maybe he had been too quick to say no to the position. He'd take John's suggestion to pray about it more seriously. As long as he kept God at the center, he could go against his nature—which had such a tendency to get him in trouble—and act with caution. Take one step at a time.

And right now? As he stood, his steps only wanted to carry him one direction—to see where a certain blonde in an emerald-green dress had gone.

14

$\mathcal{I}$n an action that contradicted the panic thumping through Lina's body, Shane offered a soft smile. "I had to see you."

Unexpected longing slammed her.

She missed him.

No. The thought came with such force, she shook her head. She missed the man she'd thought him to be and the future she'd hoped they'd have. Shane had dashed those hopes as the mirages they were, leaving her stranded in the Land of Instead. Her rescue from the wasteland would have to come from another.

God, first and foremost. Perhaps He'd provide the husband and the family she'd dreamed of. Or maybe she'd build her life right in her current circumstances, and maybe she'd come to love it. Whatever the case, Shane had no right to intrude.

Lina appraised his suit. He must've flown in, and he wouldn't have packed such clothes unless he'd planned to attempt entering the reception. "Why are you here?"

"I knew you'd be here." He paused for a charming smile. "No one likes to attend a wedding alone."

She crossed her arms and kept her shoulders square, her chin up. She'd asked Matt to allow her the opportunity to stand up for herself, so she risked saying exactly what she thought. "Especially not a woman who'd hoped to have her own wedding before now."

Hurt shaded his eyes. "You said you forgave me."

"I also asked you not to contact me." The necklace pendant shivered with her rapid heartbeat.

"I went to Carter and Jen's wedding. They looked happy together, and I missed you. How could I give up without a fight? I needed to see you."

Shane's friendship with a nice guy like Carter had helped her dismiss her early concerns about his character. After the breakup, she'd shocked Jen by revealing what Shane had done. Lina had assumed the couple would cut ties.

But then again, if Matt and Philip were any indication, a reformed addict could salvage friendships. Had Shane changed? She wouldn't give him another chance in her life, but perhaps a transformation would temper her disappointment over all she'd lost. "Are you still gambling?"

"No."

How would she know if that was true? She should've asked a question with an answer she could measure. "Do you plan to repay the money you stole?"

"Stole? The money was in a joint account, and I thought you said you forgave me."

He didn't want to call what he'd done stealing and didn't consider himself obligated to repay her?

"I might not have that kind of cash, but I *have* changed, Lina." He touched her arm with warm fingertips. "So much. I've had a year to work on myself. To reevaluate what's important and who I want to be. This is a public setting. It's your turf, not mine. There's security. I thought you might feel safe enough to give me a chance here. I can't undo the past, but we could pick up again at a good place."

She swallowed and blinked, focusing on the space around them to keep Shane from blinding her, the way he tended to.

The wedding had taken over the entire club. Large flower arrangements and a galaxy of lights decorated the lobby. The staff stationed at the door wore black suits, and the few people who had stepped from the main celebration to chat or rest in the foyer glittered in gowns and jewelry or satin lapels.

A man approached the closest seating cluster, about fifteen feet from her, holding his phone in tattoo-covered hands.

Matt.

His presence emboldened her as she refocused on her ex. "I asked you not to contact me. You shouldn't have come."

"So much for forgiveness, huh?" Steel reinforced Shane's question.

If she were him, the reminder of overstepping a boundary would've brought humiliation. She would've left in shame to avoid a bigger scene, but she'd miscalculated when she'd expected Shane to behave similarly. Unless she allowed him inside or left with him, he would escalate this far beyond her ability to control.

Matt slid his phone away, and her hand pulled his direction like a paperclip pulled by a magnet. But she couldn't silently summon him to her side when he wasn't even looking her way.

"I can forgive you and still ask you to leave." The tremor in her voice seemed to feed Shane's confidence.

He stepped closer, his voice low with false calm. "You can't send me away after I came all the way here. We had something special. I'm willing to do the work to get it back. If you were ever serious about us, you should be glad to see me."

"It doesn't work like that."

He huffed, eyes narrowing—but only for a moment. "Maybe you're right." At his resigned tone, she inhaled deeply.

Perhaps he was giving up. "Maybe I don't deserve another chance. But is there any room for friendship? Anything I can do?"

She shook her head, praying desperately that he'd leave.

"Your dad said the place in Maine is a burden. I still know investors who would jump at the opportunity, and you'd get more for it than what was in that account of ours."

Her dress squeezed her ribcage, and she exhaled. He'd only come in hopes of earning a commission on The Captain's Vista. She should've spun back around the moment she'd spotted him. She shouldn't have come out at all. She stepped backward. "No, Shane. There's no room for anything."

He followed her step. "You weren't blameless, either."

"What?" She hated the word as it slipped out, but she had to know what he faulted her for.

"You were dependent on your grandma, and she never liked me. I couldn't open up to you, knowing the two of you would turn on me." He grabbed her hand. "You said you loved me, but I think I always knew it was conditional. You let your grandma have too big of a say in your life. She disinherited her own son. I never stood a chance."

Lina shook her head. Had she been too close to Grandma? Too reliant on her opinions? Should she have been more forgiving?

She found Matt watching her intently, ready to step in, but her face burned at the thought of him having heard all that.

"I don't want to do this." She pulled to free herself.

Shane's tight grip kept their hands together, despite her effort. "The past is the past. You said you forgave—"

"Let her go." Matt's command snapped through the foyer as he crossed the space.

Without taking his stare from Lina, Shane lifted his free hand in a signal to hold Matt off. "You were just a puppet, weren't you? You would've done anything to end up with all the money, including break up with me at the first hiccup to keep your grandma happy."

She yanked her hand.

His grip held with bruising force. "You're a greedy—"

Before Shane could finish the slur, Matt swatted down the hand Shane had lifted to stop him. Shane let go of her, rounded, and landed a punch.

Matt reeled backward, holding his face, Shane in pursuit.

"Shane! Stop." She reached out, but Matt found his footing.

He lowered his hands, fists formed as blood ran from his nose. He ducked Shane's next punch, then threw his shoulder into her ex's stomach.

Shane crashed backward into a table. The flower arrangement toppled away from the tiled entry and onto the blue carpeting. The table thudded onto its side, and Shane slammed down after it.

He groaned and, with halting movements, rolled off the table to a sitting position between the protruding legs—one of which was broken.

Staff rushed up as Shane wiped his mouth, starting to move with more fluidity. He'd be on his feet in seconds, and then—

Warm, gentle fingers touched her arm. "Are you okay?" Matt panted, blue eyes swimming with concern, though he was the one with blood dripping off his chin. Crimson already stained the crisp white shirt beneath his jacket.

"I'm so sorry." She opened her clutch and offered him the tissues she'd packed. They wouldn't last long, but they were something.

"Sure. Run to your new boyfriend."

Lina's shoulders tensed, and she turned on her heel.

Shane had picked himself up. Other than his flushed face, he appeared fine, but she'd seen the way he'd fallen. He'd have bruises tomorrow—and probably a desperate need for a chiropractor.

Matt faced him, edging in front of her like a shield, leaving her to look over his shoulder.

Veins corded in Shane's neck. "Look out, man. She's keeping her own father from his inheritance. He sent me to talk some sense into her, but Little Miss Perfect thinks she can sit in judgment on everyone else. If you think this is going to work out for you, it won't." He stabbed his finger through the air like a knife.

Dad had *sent* Shane? Was Shane's visit Dad's so-called gift?

As her mind spun, staff added another layer to her human shield.

Shane scoffed, waved his hand in exasperation, and stormed out.

The largest of the staff members turned toward Matt. "Can we have the valet pull up your car?"

She turned. "You were leaving?" That could explain his presence in the lobby.

Matt assessed the man. Brilliant red bloomed across the tissues under his nose. "Looks like I will be."

The staff member stood still, expression unapologetic, and understanding dawned.

"You can't kick him out. He was defending me." She lifted her wrist as proof that Shane had been hurting her when Matt stepped in, but her skin bore only faint pink markings.

"It's all right." Matt pulled a valet stub from his pocket and handed it over. "I'm not staying like this anyway."

"But you can't go outside like that either. There's press."

The corner of Matt's mouth—the side not covered in blood and tissues—lifted in a smile. "Not the worst side of me they've seen."

The staff member passed Matt's valet stub to a younger guy by the door.

"Then get mine too." She fished the slip for her own car from her purse.

As a second valet was sent into the night, Lina peered

around the foyer. There had to be restrooms out here somewhere. She snagged Matt's hand and stepped toward what
looked to be an alcove.

The employee gave her a wary look.

"We'll be back in a minute." She kept walking, Matt
following her easily. "He has to clean up to leave. We're both
invited guests. We won't go back in."

Though he didn't indicate his blessing, the guy didn't move
to stop her, either.

MATT DOUBTED Lina had put any thought into it, but she sent a
shock through his arm by threading her fingers with his. Her
hands were small and soft. For manhandling her, Shane had
deserved to have Matt take the first swing. An action Matt had
narrowly resisted.

Lina rounded a corner, and her steps slowed.

This had to be what she'd been looking for—bathrooms.

But as she continued to hold his hand, he realized her
dilemma.

She intended to help him clean up, which meant either she
was going in the men's room, or he'd be dragged into the
women's. He suppressed a chuckle and waited to see what she'd
pick.

After another moment, she pushed open the women's door,
scanned the interior, then pulled him in. She deposited him
near the sink, then propped the door open with a wastebasket.

What was that supposed to accomplish?

On returning, she plucked three paper towels from a basket
on the vanity. She moved far enough from the sink for him to
step up then motioned him forward before she froze. "What?"

If she didn't know how entertaining this was, he wasn't
going to tell her. He'd hate for her to get self-conscious now and

turn back into her normal, rule-following self. He stepped forward. "What am I doing?"

"Rinse off the blood."

Might not do much good, since he doubted it had stopped flowing, but he obeyed, rinsing and spitting out what had gotten in his mouth. When he straightened, she immediately covered his mouth with the paper towel. At least she hadn't pounded it onto his nose. He took over and pinched his nostrils shut.

"You should tilt your head back." Lina flipped the faucet back on and grabbed more towels.

"That's a myth."

"Huh?" She dampened the new paper towels.

"You're supposed to tilt it forward."

"Oh. Well, do that then."

He dipped his head and regretted mentioning it, since the angle made watching her harder.

The gush of the faucet stopped, and her heel clicked on the tile as she stepped close. Realizing she wanted to get at the stains on his shirt, he angled his head to the side, keeping his chin down.

The shirt was a lost cause, but she must've been too flustered to recognize the futility because she dabbed at the stains. She should've asked a lot more questions before exposing herself to his blood. If he hadn't been tested and declared mercifully healthy since getting sober, he'd never let her do this.

Her unchecked impulse to help said a lot about her. Despite how she'd been burned, she retained a certain innocence and a powerful passion to care for people. It fit with how she regularly made a full buffet of food for Key of Hope. Finding himself the center of all that selfless concern stunned him.

What made her think him worth ignoring the risks?

"He's never gotten violent before."

He watched her hands, searching for signs of injury. "Including the way he grabbed you?"

Her tennis bracelet caught on her wrist bone and sparkled in the dim light of the room, but he could discern no bruises. She moved too quickly for him to tell if she was shaking.

"Okay. That's not a first." Still working on his shirt, she stood close enough for him to see the individual hairs in her brows as she drew them together. Her eyes glittered like her bracelet, light catching on unshed tears.

Matt's shoulders knotted with tension. "He was your dad's big surprise?"

The corners of her mouth turned down, her lips still full and perfectly red.

Maybe helping her feel better was as much a fool's errand as cleaning up his shirt, but he had to try. "Everything he said about you came out of defensiveness. Don't believe a word."

Her eyes darted to his, then refocused on her work. If not for the bloody nose, he'd smell the aquatic notes of her perfume. And this gutsier Lina who'd shown up after the fight might not mind a kiss—again, if not for the blood.

Except, she'd just had a big fight with her ex. She was shaken and vulnerable. He shouldn't be thinking about making a move.

She lowered the paper towels from his shirt. "I'll replace it."

"Don't worry about it."

"It's the least I can do." She dropped the soiled paper towels into the trash, then returned to lean on the vanity, arms crossed, eyes on him.

"The suit's a rental, shirt and all." He tested his nose by lowering the paper towels, but blood dripped to the already-soaked towel immediately. He put it back in place.

"I'll pay for it then."

As if he would let her. "You didn't correct him."

She arched an eyebrow. "About what?"

"He called me your boyfriend."

Her short laugh felt like a compliment. "There was a lot going on."

Matt nodded, a movement that required his hand as well as his head.

With a glint in her eyes, she studied him. Finally, she shook her head as if to clear a ridiculous notion.

Whatever the thought had been, Matt missed it already.

"You're not driving in this condition," she said. "I'll take you wherever you're staying tonight."

"My parents' place, but I can drive."

"You're actively bleeding for my sake. The least I can do is drive you home."

He could argue, but where was the fun in that? After accepting the extra paper towels she doled out, he followed her outside.

The press, waiting beyond a cordon on the other side of the lane, called his name.

Unable to hide, he gave them a wave as he climbed in Lina's passenger seat. From there, he watched in the mirror as a valet jogged back to his eyesore of a car to return it to the lot. At least the media wouldn't have footage of him, beaten up and skulking off in that monstrosity.

Already, this would result in enough headlines.

Matt had no sooner pointed her in the direction of his parents' house than his phone rang. Tim. Foreboding settled over him as he answered.

"You couldn't behave for one night?"

Shame mixed with his sense of justice. "He started it."

At the lame stab at humor, Lina's lips quirked.

"That is not the rumor."

"But it *is* the truth."

Tim's grunt meant he thought the truth irrelevant. "The worst thing you could've done is get yourself thrown out of this wedding. You should've seen Gannon's face when they told him. Songwriting, Awestruck—you can forget all of that now."

He'd done the right thing, defending Lina. But the fight might've served as the flamethrower he'd told Russ it'd take to burn a bridge with Gannon. His cavalier wave as he got in the car had probably been a mistake too.

Lina slowed at a major intersection, though the light was green, a question in her eyes. About the directions or the phone call?

He waved her to continue driving. "I'll talk to him."

"What good will that do? They're talking to Wes Kane right now."

Wes Kane, another bass guitarist. One who might be unhappy in his current role in a pop star's support band. Whatever Gannon wanted with Wes, Matt couldn't do anything about it now.

"We'll talk Monday." He disconnected before Tim could argue.

Lina cast him another look.

"Tim being Tim." He rubbed the phone screen on his thigh, but wiping off the screen couldn't undo the call, the worry.

Just when he'd wanted Awestruck, he'd gone and blown it. Matt hadn't thrown the first punch or caused the first injury, but he had been the first to make contact by pushing away Shane's hand. Had there been a more peaceful way to get him to release Lina?

Maybe.

But what was done was done. He was here with Lina now, and given what he'd sacrificed for this, he was absolutely going to enjoy it.

15

"*H*ave you ever been in love?" Lina's question sounded incredibly personal now that it floated in the car. Still, Matt had learned so much about her tonight. She longed to even out the playing field by learning something about him.

Or perhaps she only wanted company in having a painful breakup.

For a few seconds, nothing but the sound of the tires on the road answered.

"You remember Nadia?"

A breath slipped past her lips. Matt had dated Nadia for a few months, way back at the beginning of Lina's time with Awestruck. He hadn't yet started partying heavily, though he and Nadia were often photographed coming and going from clubs. "I don't remember how it ended."

"She bailed without a trace a few months in. It wasn't love. That's as close as I got."

That last part could also be said of her and Shane. Or maybe it had been love—the one-sided kind.

"For a while with Shane, things were really good." Lina kept her gaze locked on the road. "He blindsided me by emptying our account. Seeing him tonight flooded me with a mix of good and bad memories. I wanted to know if he'd changed for the better. I should've kicked him out instead. I wish I had."

"He turned on you awfully fast back there." Matt's injury had turned his voice nasally, but he still managed to sound confident.

She pulled her lip between her teeth. "I should've known better."

Matt pointed toward a drive sloping up a gentle hill to the left. "That's it."

She flipped on her signal, and her headlights illuminated the gravel. She pulled to a stop on the concrete pad by the garage, and a motion light flipped on. "Are you going to be okay?"

"Not my first bloody nose."

"Has it stopped bleeding?"

He lowered the wad of towels, the stain shocking, even in the dark. "Soon, I think."

"I'll wait with you." She unfastened her seatbelt and popped open her door. Oh, wait. Did he even want her company?

He didn't so much as shoot her a sideways glance to see her worry as they walked to the door, much less respond to it, as he pulled keys from his pocket and let them in.

The dining room and kitchen extended to the right, mostly separated from the living room by a staircase leading to a dim second floor. The carpet had frayed along the edge where it met the tile of the kitchen and dining area, but the color remained creamy and clean. The pattern in the tile and the style of wood-work suggested the house was three or four decades old. But instead of dated, it looked ... settled.

Like a home rather than the impersonal mansion where she'd spent her childhood.

"Did you grow up here?"

One handed, Matt untied his shoelaces before glancing over the space. "Yeah. They built it when I was two or something." He kicked off his shoes and motioned to the kitchen table. "Take a seat. I'm going to grab a real towel." He disappeared up the stairs.

Lina slid out of her heels and crossed to the table, the tile cold beneath her feet. She rolled one of the wheeled chairs out. The cushions had been worn flat, but once, they'd probably been an investment.

She sat and smoothed a hand over her skirt.

From somewhere upstairs she heard an exclamation of surprise. "What happened?" The female voice must belong to his mother.

A low murmur marked his reply, and when his mom spoke again, she did so too quietly for Lina to understand from this distance.

Matt appeared a minute later, a rag piled over the paper towels. He'd shed the suit jacket and dress shirt. She'd once imagined he would look dashing in a tux—and he had. But in the dress pants and the close-fitting tank he must've worn under the shirt?

Funny how holding the rag near his face flexed his bicep.

Their eyes locked, and he froze as if he knew exactly what had captured her attention.

Cheeks burning, she focused on her hands.

"Mom thinks she can get the stain out." His continued hesitation seemed to wordlessly ask if he needed to go put on more clothes, but when she stayed still, he pulled out the chair adjacent to hers and sat.

Lina cleared her throat. "I suppose she has a lot of experience."

He rested his elbows on his knees, and when he focused on her without moving his head, furrows marked his brow.

"Cleaning up blood." Was it too soon to tease him? Well, she'd come this far. "As your mom."

The corners of his eyes tightened with amusement, and he lowered his line of sight again.

"With so many scars, can you even remember what they're all from?"

He opened his free hand palm-up. A white line crossed his index and middle fingers between his first and second knuckles. "Lawn mower blade. I had them off the machine to sharpen them."

He straightened and rotated his arm. Another scar traced his triceps. "The corner of a shed we used to have." He rubbed a finger near the greater-than-shaped mark on his temple. "Snowboarding."

"And this?" She touched a finger to where another sharp line cut his scalp. His short hair was surprisingly soft, and her other fingers twitched with jealousy, but she withdrew. She shouldn't have invaded his space in the first place. It wouldn't do to run her hands through his hair.

Matt's palm covered the spot, and his finger traced the mark as he lowered his hand again. "You've got me there. I woke up one morning with blood caking my hair and the couch I'd passed out on." The muscles in his arms shifted as he leaned more heavily on his elbows, head still tipped down into the rag. The skin around his eyes creased again, loaded with regret this time.

"You're not that man anymore."

He cast her a wary look.

"You're not. I see how much you've changed. You've given me a better grasp on what the Bible means about becoming a new creation."

They'd never talked about faith much. How would he take the allusion to it now? And when had sharing the same beliefs become vital to her?

"This new creation still finds himself at war with the old one a lot more than he'd like."

How much had her judgmental statements about double lives and disappointing men discouraged him along the way? She'd make up for the negativity now. "That's being human, but we don't war alone. Christ fights for you."

He nodded gently as he lowered the rag. When no new blood fell, he exhaled deeply. "How about you? Any scars?" He rose and deposited the soiled cloth in the garbage. He disappeared around a corner, and a faucet ran.

Compared with his collection, her two or three scars were nothing. He'd done enough for her tonight. She owed him more than stories about surface marks from minor experiences like petting a stray cat.

The water shut off.

In the quiet, she said, "You met my worst scar tonight."

Matt remained silent as he returned to the table. Clean and dry now, a red patch on his cheek marked where Shane's fist had connected, and his nose looked tender. A little swollen.

"In fact, if it were healed enough to call it a scar, I wouldn't have talked to him. Maybe the wound is still fresh, even after a year."

"Or maybe you were willing to talk to him because you're not as scarred as you think. Maybe it shows you're still willing to hope for the best in people."

How could he deliver the vote of confidence with such a straight face when she'd been keeping him at arm's length? She'd expected the worst from him since the day she'd gone to offer him the teaching position. Since before that, actually.

When they'd both worked for Awestruck, she'd considered him a lost cause. She'd never even tried to break through to him. Instead, she'd waited impatiently for Gannon and John to let him go. She'd never once considered that God would reach him and bring him back into her life as a force for good.

"I haven't hoped for the best where you were concerned."

The ease of his shrug saddened her. He wasn't offended by her disbelief in him because he didn't believe in himself, either, despite how far he'd come.

"Thank you for getting involved tonight."

A smirk stole across his lips. "You would've done the same for me."

She snorted. "We both know that's not true."

"Good. I wouldn't want you to." His expression sobered, and he studied her evenly.

He was still out to prove himself, as if he hadn't already. Tonight, he'd once again made good on his promise to stand up for her. Her attraction toward him was based on that, rather than on the definition of his arms, the symmetry of his face, the depth of his eyes.

But his looks didn't hurt, either.

Yet, Matt was complicated. He was a risk-taker. Unpredictable. Still reeling from the surprises Shane had doled out, could she trust Matt for more than the occasional intervention?

She fingered the pendent of Grandma's necklace and blinked. "I should go."

MATT STOOD ONLY after Lina did. Her gown rustled over the tile, and her bare feet peeked out as she stepped toward the door. He liked having her here. Liked that she'd invited herself in. What might she have done if she'd been able to resist whatever sense of obligation had sent her toward the exit?

With a swallow, she met his eyes again. "I should've taken your advice." Her lips pressed shut, but only for a moment. "I need to have a direct conversation with my dad about Shane. And about The Captain's Vista."

Matt shook his head, not following. Sounded like something from a treasure hunt movie.

"My grandma's summer home. The one Dad and Shane want me to sell. I have years of good memories there, but I've always wanted ..." She blinked and cleared her throat with a delicate cough. Choking up. "I've always hated disappointing my father."

"He's the disappointment here, got it?" If only Lina's Dad had come along with Shane and been part of the fight so Matt could've throttled the man. "He has no right to even ask you to sell, let alone to send your violent, abusive, gambling ex here to get it for him."

Her frustration escaped in a sigh. She reached for the door with one hand and touched his arm with the other. The parting gesture undermined its own purpose because once she'd touched him, he wasn't about to let her go uncontested.

He caught her hand lightly. If she pulled away, he wouldn't fight her. She didn't. Instead, she fit her fingers between his.

When she shifted closer, her skirt pressed against his pant leg. "If my own father would be so reckless over a piece of land, what does that do to me? To my ... my ability to trust people?"

"You'll have to fight for it, but if I've learned anything in recovery, it's that some things are worth fighting for."

She touched his uninjured cheek. Her lips parted, and she took a breath to speak. Or so he thought until she focused on his mouth.

Indecision seemed to battle in her eyes. He'd risk his own heart all day long, but Lina's? He didn't trust himself enough to decide for her. Especially not considering the way she'd been hurt.

Let her lead.

He repeated the three words over and over as the ache to take over grew.

Her chin tipped up, and she pressed a soft, brief kiss to his lips.

Incongruent with the most chaste kiss of his life, desire pummeled his restraint. His mantra to let her lead crumbled, and he snatched the next closest objection. If he kissed her the way he wanted, he'd bump his nose and turn a sweet moment into an awkward one. Better to illustrate his trustworthiness by showing her she was safe to express how she felt without him taking liberties.

But when she stepped back, her gaze flicked to his face and away again, uncertain. "I'm sorry." Her throat tightened with a gulp.

Had he played it too safe? "Don't apologize."

She cringed. "I'm your boss."

"*That's* your hang-up?" He brushed the backs of his fingers along her jaw. "It must be exhausting to live by so many rules." As he rested his palms on either side of her face, her curls lay like silk over his knuckles. "I'll quit Monday."

He paused long enough to see a whisper of a smile on her lips, trust in her brown eyes.

Then, he kissed her back. Where she'd been soft and quick, he chose slow and intentional. Her arms, bare in her dress, circled his neck, soft and warm against his shoulders. His hand on her back glided over satin and skin, and judging by the noise she made in the back of her throat, she enjoyed the kiss at least as much as she'd enjoyed the chicken at the wedding. Fighting a chuckle, he tipped his head back. Her idea of an appropriate first kiss was probably tamer than his, and anyway, if they kept this up, he really would bump his nose. He brushed his thumbs over her cheeks one last time and stepped away.

She ran her fingers over her lips—over a smile.

He moved his head, allowing light from the kitchen to fall over her face. "You've got a little something." He touched the skin above his own lip.

She lifted her hand again and checked her finger after attempting to rub off the mark. "Better?"

The smudge of lipstick remained. Still, he smiled. "Beautiful."

Her expression flickered with disbelief. This time, when she grasped the door handle, she didn't reach back to him. Even so, her mouth bowed into a sweet smile as she said goodnight and slipped out.

He waited until she'd pulled out of the driveway before abandoning his post at the window.

After that, he wouldn't sleep for hours. He could reach out to try to do damage control, but Gannon had other things on his mind tonight, and by now, who knew how many drinks Tim had downed.

Instead, he descended to the basement and plugged in the old keyboard. Once upon a time, Mom had forced him into piano lessons, and the skill served him well when he was composing music. Since he wouldn't be sleeping soon, he'd see if he could make progress on some songs—whether or not he'd ever perform them with Awestruck.

THE NEXT MORNING, Lina sat in her hotel room, her phone in her hands, her bags packed for the two-hour drive back to Lakeshore. Until Matt said she could choose to trust, she hadn't realized she had a choice in the matter. Instead of letting experience ingrain isolating beliefs, she could fight for the connections she wanted.

She could choose to trust. She'd put the knowledge into immediate use by kissing Matt.

That experiment had gone deliciously well.

Shane had kissed her on their first date, and they hadn't known each other long beforehand. She'd been the one to break off the moment when he'd gotten too intense. Her connection with Matt had differed entirely—he'd waited for her to start, and he'd been the one to break it off. But not in cold disinterest. Quite the opposite. She'd felt safe. Valued.

In comparison, perhaps the difference in those first kisses meant Shane had been carelessly gambling with her affections this whole time.

Her phone illuminated and buzzed in her hands. Matt had texted. *Any sign of him?*

No, but I haven't checked out of the hotel yet.

She had, however, seen signs of how the press was treating the fight. The photos of Matt leaving the reception, shirt stained crimson, landed in several online slideshows about the wedding. The captions included just enough detail to paint Matt badly.

What would an Awestruck event be without former bass guitarist Matt Visser brawling with another guest?

Rocker Matt Visser is up to his old tricks.

The Vaughns may be regretting extending an olive branch to former bandmate Matt Visser, captured here after a fist fight.

What kind of problems would the implications that he'd acted alone and without sufficient reason cause him?

Another incoming text lit up her phone. *Look into a restraining order. And let me know the second you see him if he shows up again.*

She'd planned to question her dad—that chore had been her whole reason for pausing before checking out and heading for home—but legal action against Shane? She ran an internet search on restraining orders. The articles seemed in agreement; a court wouldn't instate one for her because Shane hadn't made any threats or left any marks—on her, anyway.

She tapped back into her text thread with Matt. *I doubt it'll come to that, but if he shows up, you'll be my second call. Police first.*

I guess that'll have to be good enough. Stay safe.

She read and reread the message, expecting him to send more at any moment, but the phone went dark. No allusions to their kiss. No questions about when he'd see her next.

Hm.

What had she hoped he'd say? When did she want to see him next? She'd kissed him first, and she'd enjoyed the time they'd spent together, but would it last? Was she really right to trust Matt so much?

She wouldn't be able to sort out her tangle of emotions in the next couple of minutes, but she could follow through on calling her dad.

With a prayer for help, for truth to win out, she dialed his cell.

And got voicemail.

"Hi, Dad. Give me a call back when you have some time to talk."

16

On Monday, an envelope stuck from beneath Lina's laptop at Key of Hope. She was alone in here, wasn't she? She checked over her shoulder, but she'd locked the door she'd entered through. The windows and front entrance didn't appear to have been disturbed. Dim and still, the practice rooms sheltered no intruders. The only discernible movement in the whole place was steam curling from the slow cooker she'd set up on the office area table.

After arriving back in Lakeshore yesterday, she'd swung by the grocery store for supplies, then baked cookies, made coleslaw, and cooked a batch of pulled pork. One less thing for the staff to worry about, if their weekend had been as frazzling as hers.

She took a seat and cast another look around. There had been no lessons this weekend. Who had been in here to drop off this envelope? The caution and worry linked straight back to Shane's surprise appearance at the wedding. If he'd also found a way into Key of Hope, she might never feel safe again.

She slipped her finger under the flap, tore open the envelope, and read the short, typed letter inside.

To whom it may concern:
I'm resigning my position as bass guitar instructor for Key of Hope, effective 10:35 PM last Saturday. Though I'm sorry to leave, I couldn't pass up a new opportunity.
Good luck breaking the news to Chris.
The signature was sloppy to the point of illegibility.

She laughed, once.

Matt wasn't serious, was he?

The kiss had been memorable, but it didn't warrant anyone quitting a job. Especially since, aside from their connection to Key of Hope, neither of them had reason to live in Lakeshore.

But what were they going to do? Return to the status quo? Ask Adeline if it was okay for them to date? She pressed her hand to her flaming cheek. The relationship wasn't serious enough to warrant that, and Adeline was on her honeymoon anyway. By the time her boss returned, perhaps she'd have this figured out.

In the meantime, no sudden moves.

She slid the envelope in her desk drawer and sent Matt a text. *Don't quit just yet.*

MATT PARKED on the crumbling asphalt behind Key of Hope. He'd put some extra miles on the Brownmobile this weekend. First, he'd driven down for the wedding. Then, once he'd gotten back to Lakeshore, he'd looked up Lina's address. The rarity of her name made the search easy, meaning Shane could find it in seconds too—if the man hadn't already gotten her location from her dad. It was a long shot that Matt might see something and be able to help, but he'd driven by a few times anyway.

The drive, fifteen minutes out and fifteen back to Lakeshore, had given him time to pray about Lina, Shane, and the things Philip had said at the wedding. He couldn't shake the idea that they hadn't seen the last of her ex, but in the areas of Awestruck and Lina, he didn't sense the Lord telling him to hold back.

Lina had been coming in late morning and working into the evening, so around ten thirty a.m., he'd stopped by Key of Hope to check that the place was undisturbed and to leave his resignation.

The thought of his letter brought a smile as he pulled open the back door of the studio.

He'd hoped for more of a reaction when she found it, but at least she'd told him not to quit.

Other teachers and their students occupied the practice rooms as he advanced down the hall. Lina sat at her desk, her brown eyes focused on her laptop. If she'd worn any lipstick today, it had faded, but that was probably for the best. Her lush lips didn't need the added allure of attention-grabbing colors. Especially when a kid sat in the waiting area.

Instead of lighting up on noticing him, she tilted her head with a guarded smile. "Hey."

So they wouldn't be picking up where they'd left off. Nothing good was ever easy, was it?

"Hey yourself." He continued to the second computer and eyed the buffet next to it. "The weekend wasn't busy enough for you?"

Lina shrugged. "I like to cook."

She'd brought food in often enough to prove the claim, but her decision to take the time for her hobby yesterday made him wonder if there wasn't more to her cooking than enjoyment. Maybe taking care of others distracted her from her own problems.

"Still no sign of Shane?"

"None." She kept studying him as if ... as if he were a sweater she'd purchased, and she had a case of buyer's remorse.

He dropped into the seat at the second desk and woke the computer.

The screen sighed to life.

"We should talk about the other night," Lina said.

"Yeah." He swiveled away from the desk. If the jury was out on him, he'd do what he could to keep it from coming back. "What'd your dad say?"

"Oh." Her throat shifted with a swallow. "He didn't call me back. I'm going to try again tonight, after work."

The front door bumped open, and Matt half-hoped the newcomer would turn out to be Shane. The red-and-yellow bruise on his cheek and alongside his nose must not be striking enough to earn her sympathy, but another run-in might show her the benefit of keeping him around.

But the new arrival was Tim, not Shane. With his crossed arms and glare, the manager appeared equally willing to launch an attack.

Matt swiveled back toward the desk and opened the app to punch in. The night before, Tim hadn't returned to Lakeshore before Matt left the condo to drive by Lina's once and report to the office building he cleaned. Normally, he wouldn't need to put in a shift on a Sunday night, but he'd taken off Friday so he could head to Fox Valley for the wedding. The extra excuse to avoid Tim was a bonus.

The manager could say whatever he wanted about Gannon's reaction to the fight. Only Gannon, or possibly John, could tell Matt how much of a setback the altercation had really been.

"I hope it was worth it." Tired amusement carried Tim's voice as he focused on Lina.

"What?" No doubt, the note of guilt in her voice traced back to their kiss.

As if Matt would've told Tim about it. As if the kiss were something to feel guilty about.

EMILY CONRAD

Matt hit the key to punch in harder than necessary.

"Introducing Matt to your ex. How'd you really expect that to go?"

Lina already harbored enough reservations about Matt without Tim implying he couldn't control himself.

Matt jerked to his feet. "She didn't introduce us, and don't act like I'm some gorilla who can't be trusted in polite company."

"You got in a fight. At Gannon's wedding. To anyone there who believed you'd changed, you looked like the same old clown up to the same old tricks."

As if he needed a dressing down in front of Lina. But the rise of his own embarrassment gave him insight into Tim. "I embarrassed *you*. Is that it?" And now Tim was out to return the favor.

"You embarrassed yourself. Who wants to work with you now?"

The lesson in Matt's normal room finished up, and the instructor and child made their way toward the front.

Unable to let his question go unanswered, Tim supplied his own reply. "Not even Awestruck."

"I didn't want it anyway." The lie hit harder than Shane's fist had, but denying his interest in the band was easier than admitting the truth—he'd wanted the spot and jeopardized it by not finding a peaceful solution.

Like so many other things he'd jeopardized.

The Lord had been gracious to protect and restore so much for him already. Matt might not sense the Lord cautioning him against Awestruck because God had already closed that door. If so, nothing Matt could do would reopen it.

Chris tromped in off the street, and his grin brought a smile even to Matt's face. Matt played up the handshake, since the ritual might be the day's highlight for both him and the kid, and they proceeded to the practice room.

~

PRESSURE BUILT in Lina's chest and throat. Explanations waiting to be shared.

Why hadn't Matt stood up for himself? Even if he didn't want to work with Awestruck again, why let them think badly of him when the fight hadn't been his fault?

"This smells amazing." The lid of the slow cooker rattled behind her as Tim perused the mini buffet. "You mind?"

"Have at it. And take some home." Normally, she'd get up to make sure he filled one of the to-go containers she'd brought, but today, she let him fend for himself.

In the practice room, Chris dropped his book bag and jacket, talking the whole time. Matt shut the door and sat across from him, listening. When Matt did speak, Chris's grin got even wider. The boy picked up his tale again, his hand motions more exuberant.

Matt really had a way with his students.

He wore jeans and a simple gray shirt that cozied up to the fit shape of his shoulders. Shoulders that seemed broader than before the weekend. His scars, more intriguing.

A figment of her imagination, spurred on by the way he'd used those shoulders and earned an injury to protect her. He'd been attractive before. She'd simply been better at ignoring it.

"He doesn't know how hard he makes it to do my job." Tim took up station next to her desk, hunched over his plate, and tried the sandwich before continuing.

Lina crossed her legs, still peering at Matt. Either he really didn't care about songwriting for Awestruck, or he was protecting her privacy by allowing her to choose how much to share about Shane. His willingness to take the fall—something Shane never would've done—again proved his consideration for her.

She had to return the favor—hoping that he *would* consider

it a favor. "Shane—the man he fought with—was hurting me, and Matt didn't throw the first punch. They didn't get that in the pictures I saw."

Tim's brow drew low. "Are you all right?"

She slipped a finger beneath the cuff of her light sweater and moved the sleeve back from her wrist to check again that no bruise had surfaced. She found only her pale skin, a freckle or two, and the usual map of bluish veins. Unbelievable, considering how Shane's grip had burned. "Thanks to Matt, I'm fine. But if any rumors are painting Shane as anything other than a gambler with a temper, they've got it wrong."

Tim put his plate down and crossed his arms. "Why didn't I know you had an ex like that?"

"Because I didn't know he'd follow me here, and I certainly never expected him to crash the wedding." She pushed her sleeve back into place. "Besides, I'm only telling you so you don't blame Matt. Shane's not your problem."

Tim lifted his eyebrows, silently telling her to reconsider that statement.

Shane had affected Matt and to a lesser extent, Gannon. Tim would go to any lengths to defend his assets.

She sighed. "Right. What was I thinking?"

"Is he going to keep showing up?" Tim managed a group of men. They probably responded better to his bossy and gruff manner than she wanted to.

"Hard to say." An image of Shane slithered to mind. The tension in his face as he'd grown more desperate. "I didn't expect any of this."

"You live alone in the country." He waited, but if he expected her to disagree, she couldn't. "You shouldn't come and go by yourself. Here or there."

Lina lifted an eyebrow. "Are you volunteering to escort me?"

His expression soured. "Do you have any kind of security system?"

"A couple of motion-activated doorbell cameras." To date, they had only captured images of Lina and woodland creatures. She'd stopped paying much attention to the notifications until returning home on Sunday. Since turning up the app's sound, she'd jumped each time it went off. A family of raccoons seemed to enjoy waddling across her driveway.

"What time do you go home?"

"I don't have a firm plan for tonight." But Matt's last lesson ended at six thirty, and if she stayed, she could probably snag a couple of minutes with him before he rushed off to wherever he needed to be next. "Six thirty or seven?"

"Make it six, and you've got yourself a deal."

"A deal?"

"I'll meet you here and make sure you get home safe. I can probably swing following you into town most days too. You don't come in most of the time until almost lunch, right?"

She blinked at him. If she hadn't already said she didn't have a firm plan, she'd decline tonight's offer for the chance of talking with Matt. But given Matt's loaded schedule, he probably wouldn't be able to accompany her home, and maybe Tim had a point. Maybe she shouldn't be alone. Just in case.

Of course, she would be alone when she was in her house, but maybe arrivals and departures were when trouble was most likely. Especially the routine trips, like driving to and from work. Hopefully random outings to run errands didn't require the same precautions, because she didn't want to lose the independence to leave when she wanted. Besides, she'd hate to ask anyone to go so far out of their way for her.

Even the offer to follow her to and from work seemed extravagant. "You're sure?"

"I'm not a gorilla either."

He'd prove that claim more easily by sitting instead of wolfing down his meal while pacing the office, but Lina held her peace. He finished eating and left her to complete her work day.

She mindlessly checked off tasks as she told herself over and over again to appreciate the space from Matt. After her bad decisions with Shane, she needed to be cautious. So, as six neared, she shut down her computer. No sooner had that screen darkened than her phone lit up.

The sight of Dad's number twisted her stomach. She'd much prefer another false alarm involving raccoons. She would let his call go to voicemail, but she hadn't left enough information in her own message for Dad to know why she'd called. They needed to have a conversation.

In the sitting area, Matt's next lesson waited while he finished with thirteen-year-old Luke. Carrie worked with a young violinist in another practice room. For privacy, Lina would have to step outside or into the back hall. Since it was a cool September evening, she opted for the hall, swiping to answer.

Pleasantries with Dad were short, as always.

As they petered out, the front door opened, and Tim blustered in. When he spotted her in the back, he lifted his eyebrows.

Lifting a finger, she stepped out of sight and sat on the staircase. The back hall was one of the only dim places in Key of Hope. Since she hadn't flicked on the light in the stairwell, the only illumination came through the frosted glass window in the door leading outside.

She leaned her shoulder on the wall, her head tipped against the railing. "Shane has been reaching out to me. He showed up at Gannon's wedding and caused quite a scene."

"Oh?" Dad's tone embodied false innocence.

"He said you sent him."

"Why would I do that?"

Really? He wouldn't own his actions, even after his accomplice had implicated him? Maybe the consequences of what he'd done would coax him to take some ownership. "I have to imagine it's because you didn't believe me that he's untrustworthy. It's been over a year, and he still hasn't returned a dime of what he gambled away. He's also violent. He started a fist fight in the lobby."

"I certainly would have no part in violence."

"Then why, when all else failed, did he try to talk me into selling The Captain's Vista?"

"He must want the commission."

"He's representing you in the sale?" Lina picked at her thumbnail with tense fingers. "You both stand to earn more if I give up The Captain's Vista."

Dad scoffed. "Lina, please."

Anger simmered in her chest. "You said you were sending a gift, and not long after, Shane showed up, claiming you sent him."

"It *was* a gift." His voice snapped with accusation. "I happen to have the utmost respect for the man, and he's convinced he wants to win you back. You could do much worse, so I decided to help him show you reason, but I obviously can't make up your mind for you. If you're bent on rejecting him, you will."

Lina's disappointment settled in like a mangy cat. "He started a fist fight at Gannon Vaughn's wedding."

"That was not my doing."

She could mention the way Shane had grabbed her, but he wouldn't believe her without the same kind of proof required to obtain a restraining order. She focused instead on her dad's side of the situation. "What *was* your doing? The idea? The airplane ticket?" Her arm felt too weak to keep holding the phone to her ear. She adjusted to rest her elbow on her knee. "All of it?"

"People make mistakes, Lina. You're alone in this world because you wrote off the man you intended to marry over one perceived lapse in judgment. He's offered to pay you back repeatedly, but you won't return his calls, so what's he supposed to do?"

"That's not true."

He continued over her. "Without a family, who will you leave your fortune to? Or do you intend to spend it all?"

She was still plenty young to start a family, if the Lord chose to provide the right man. If not, she'd handpicked charities as her beneficiaries. But the part about spending it all didn't deserve a reply.

Dad wasn't in the listening mood anyway. "I suppose you'll squander it through mismanagement, not spending."

"You're the one who's lost fortunes, Dad, not me."

"This conversation has run its course. I'll let you go." He disconnected.

Lina's arm slumped away from her ear. She'd thought she and her father would someday mend their rift, but his involvement in Shane's return to her life seemed to suggest the chasm between them, dug by his disregard for her, was too great. Matt had been right to suggest she set boundaries with Shane, and she ought to establish some with her father as well.

If only boundaries would heal her aching heart.

17

*M*att stopped talking to his student mid-sentence when Lina disappeared into the back hall with her phone to her ear.

Shane? Or her parents?

Either way, he hurried through some final instructions and wrapped up his lesson a few minutes early. He saw his student out, but Lina hadn't returned to the office area.

Tim paced near the front window, working on his phone when he wasn't glaring toward the rear hall.

Matt would much rather have Tim's gruff manners pointed at him than at her. He stopped where he could obscure Tim's view of the back entrance. "You need something?"

"She told me what happened. I'm following her home, if she ever decides to leave."

"She ask you to follow her?" A flare of jealousy fired the question. If she needed an escort home, why hadn't she asked?

"I offered."

Matt should've more wisely used the few seconds he had before Tim and Chris showed up. But then, he hadn't been sure of where he and Lina stood and hadn't wanted to do anything to inspire her to reject him outright.

Besides, she may have had practical reasons for not asking Matt for help. He'd come from a shift at the home improvement store and was due at the pizza place twenty minutes after his last lesson here.

Already, his next student sat in the waiting area, kicking his feet. Still three minutes until the scheduled start time, though.

Matt peered toward the back hall. What would he encounter if he approached her? Upset, she might send him away. Worse, she might turn to him and find he had nothing helpful to say. "Have you checked on her?"

"She's in the building and I assume Shane isn't, so she's fine."

"It ever occur to you there's more than one way to hurt a person?"

Tim muttered a reply, but Matt was already on his way to the back, praying as he went that God would give him the right words for whatever he found.

Lina sat on the stairs, slumped against the wall. Her hand drooped between her knees, her phone in what looked like a precarious grip. Her closed eyes didn't even flutter.

Matt sat beside her in the dim space, slid his hand across her back, and guided her to lean on him instead of the wall. She came easily, her cheek fitting the curve of his collarbone, her forehead against his neck. So gentle as she settled against him, she deserved protection, not heartache.

"Who do I need to go pick a fight with?"

"My dad." A quiet, rueful laugh puffed across his skin. "If it's not too much trouble."

"Not at all." He wanted to kiss the top of her head but settled for rubbing her shoulder. "I take it Shane was his surprise?"

Her body seemed to rest against him more heavily. "Yeah."

Footsteps neared. Heavy ones. Tim poked his head around the corner.

With a jerk of his head, Matt ordered him away. Whatever Lina needed, he would make sure she got, even if he had to cancel his next lesson and call in to the pizza place.

Tim rolled his eyes, but he went.

If only taking care of his next student would be so easy. He heard Carrie saying goodbye to a student. Was she done for the night? He hadn't seen anyone but his lesson in the waiting room. He gave Lina's shoulders a gentle squeeze. "I'll be right back."

She straightened. Her bottom lip pushed her mouth into a frown, but she appeared to be dry-eyed. More composed than he had expected.

He caught up with Carrie in the office, bribed her to cover his lesson by promising to deliver pizzas for her family on Friday, and returned to the hall.

Lina opened her mouth, then tilted her head, sighed, and stayed silent, her vision trained somewhere near his feet.

"You want to talk about it?"

The corners of her lips dug downward.

"Let's get you home and make you a cup of tea or something."

The frown remained, but her irises lifted. "A cup of tea?"

He'd happened upon Krissy crying into a mug as she discussed her problems with Mom more than once, but he was out of his depth. "Hot chocolate?"

She gave a sad laugh and used the railing to hoist herself to her feet. "Tim's waiting for me."

"Nah, he's gone already."

"Oh." She checked her phone screen, then her mouth scrunched with her next objection. "You have a lesson. You're late."

"Carrie's covering."

"You have an answer for everything, don't you?"

"In the name of honesty, I'll admit I'm tempted to say yes."

She slanted a long look at him. "Promise me something?"

"Sure."

"Don't lie to me or pretend to be something you're not."

He'd done a multitude of things he'd rather never admit to her. She already knew the gist of his past, but his face stung with embarrassment as details flashed to mind. Praying she'd never ask for specifics, he nodded. "I won't."

"You know what's funny?" She leaned against the wall, appearing close to relaxed.

Maybe they were pulling through this. Maybe he'd helped in some way, even without a tea kettle. "What?"

"Whether you were lying or telling the truth, your answer would've been the same." She pushed off from the wall.

Frustration and disappointment made a halfhearted attempt to harden him, but they couldn't overtake the melancholy. She'd been deceived enough times to justify the skepticism.

"I don't know how to prove I'm different than I was, different than the people who've hurt you before, but I'll find a way."

"You know a broken promise won't help."

"I'll keep my promise."

But something told him fulfilling his vow wouldn't be easy.

LINA PARKED in her garage and let the overhead door rumble shut as she climbed from the vehicle. The descending door hid Matt's monstrosity of a car, parked in her driveway, from view. She probably should've let the guy join her in the garage and enter with her, but she'd hit the button on the garage door remote without thinking about it. This way had bought her a few more seconds to consider what she was doing with Matt and why. With a sigh, she let herself into her house.

The faint aromas of vanilla and lavender welcomed her. She'd accented the gray kitchen and sand dining and living rooms with sage, eggplant, and rose. The color palette spoke of peace, the soft fabrics of comfort. Her haven.

And now she was about to open the door and let Matt into it.

Her head said she'd been fooled before and could be fooled again. But her heart? Her heart was tired of fighting. Of guarding itself.

She slipped off her flats and crossed the tile to the front door. As Matt stepped inside, the blue of his eyes struck her again.

She'd known him for years and had thought his eyes brown the whole time. Mistakenly.

Maybe the problem wasn't deceitful people but rather her failure to recognize what was staring her right in the eye. Shane was a gambler. Her dad was a businessman with no heart.

And Matt? How should she summarize him? What did she know of his character when she dropped her desires and expectations and considered the facts?

He'd protected her repeatedly. He'd also gotten involved on Bailey's behalf at the play. He worked well with his students. The evidence suggested he was a good man.

She retreated to the kitchen, praying as she went that if she was wrong and needed to be protected from Matt in some way, the Lord would do it for her. "You didn't have dinner, did you?"

"I picked up a burger on the way here." Humor glinted in his eyes.

He'd stayed close behind her during the drive from Key of Hope, and he'd chosen a bad time for a complete lie, even if he'd meant to be funny.

"Sorry." His amusement dimmed to the faintest glimmer, then extinguished. "No. I didn't. But you don't have to feed me."

"I'm hungry, and I'm always cooking for an army anyway." An army or a non-existent family.

He pushed up the sleeves of his waffle knit shirt as he stepped around the island and into the workspace. "Then put me to work."

She brought out ingredients, a sauté pan, a cutting board, and a knife. After he sliced the chicken to be sautéed, he took the cutting board and knife to the sink. Without being asked, he washed the utensils and gathered the vegetables. Cooking with Shane had never been effortless. Her ex had retreated to his phone each time he finished a step instead of taking the initiative.

When Matt finished prepping the vegetables, he slid the cutting board onto the counter next to the stove where she worked. Asparagus, tomatoes, and roasted red peppers waited in colorful piles.

Maybe he fit in here pretty well, bruises, tattoos, and all.

He collected the ends he'd removed from the asparagus. The letters of the word *love* on his right hand showed as he brushed the cuttings into the trash can. She'd hardly been noticing his tattoos these last couple of days, even when his arms had been fully exposed after the wedding. The neck on his tank had revealed a glimpse of a pattern on his chest too, hanging close below his collarbone. Yet she hadn't wondered what it was or how much of his skin it covered.

All the designs remained, but it was the play of veins and tendons in his forearms that captured her eye. The shape of his fingers suggested strength and agility. He was a musician, after all, and a good one.

Perhaps he could best be summarized as a loyal musician. Someone she could trust.

"Grandma knew." Blurting out the admission felt as impulsive as kissing him had.

He let the lid of the garbage fall, studied her for a beat, then went back for the rest of the discarded cuttings. She had yet to throw him a curve ball that seemed to ruffle him, and his calm manner of listening without watching made it easier to continue.

"She knew both Dad's and Shane's character. She limited Dad's inheritance to that single plot of land because she and Grandpa didn't trust his judgment. She also talked to me about having Shane sign a prenup. When I refused, she changed the setup of her estate so he wouldn't be able to get his hands on it in the event of a divorce. Meanwhile, I refused to admit there was any possibility we wouldn't work out. And then we didn't even make it to the altar."

Matt frowned as he rinsed a dishcloth. Instead of commenting, he turned for his workspace and wiped it down.

She lifted the cutting board with one hand and slid the vegetables into the pan. Stray asparagus and halved cherry tomatoes bounced to the stove. "How did she foresee trouble I completely missed?"

"Here." Matt came close, and the clean scent of his soap infused the air. His arm brushed hers as he took over the cutting board, and her fingers grazed his as she released the load.

As a single woman, living alone, few people touched her. Maybe that explained why an accidental graze of the hand shot fire through her nerve endings.

"You have better judgment than you think." His voice came low and steady as he held the cutting board for her. "I knew not to trust Shane or your dad, but only because of what you'd said."

She tightened her grip on the spoon and focused on transferring vegetables to the sauté pan. "You came along after

Shane made his character obvious. By then, there was overwhelming evidence. Grandma saw a lot earlier than I did."

When his reply didn't come immediately, she wanted to look at his face, but if she turned, only inches would separate them. Too close. Too personal.

"Tell me about your grandma."

Grateful for the unexpected reprieve from her self-doubt, she spent the rest of their time in the kitchen telling him about summers at The Captain's Vista, the holidays they'd celebrated together, the trips the two of them had taken after Grandpa's death.

Matt prayed over their meal, and she picked up her fork. She'd gone on too long, sounded ridiculously spoiled. She shouldn't have gone into detail about her grandmother's imposing house, European vacations, and The Captain's Vista. In the process, she'd also tipped her hand about the inheritance, hadn't she?

No wonder his expression looked serious. He stabbed his fork into his food with what could be annoyance.

She cleared her throat. "Sorry."

His focus lifted. "For what?"

"Complaining. Feeling sorry for myself. I've had it good."

He shook his head. "What about friends? Other family?"

"I had friends. Sleepovers, school dances, volleyball, the whole bit." Just not much attention from her parents.

"Not you. Your grandma."

"Huh?"

"Who was she close with?"

Grandma? Dad had been her only child. Grandma's brother and his kids had been around some, but they weren't close. "She had friends." Lina had never been introduced, though. She'd gotten the feeling the connections had been casual, not deep. "Maybe not a best friend, but she got along with people."

"How long before she died did she lose your grandpa?"

"I was thirteen, so quite some time before, but she talked about him often right up until the end—showed me 'Howard's little stamp collection' lots of times. He spent hours poring over that book. We loved looking at it together and remembering him." He'd been soft-spoken and gentle, more likely to walk with Lina to the park than sit and discuss business with his son. Grandpa had believed in building things slowly to stand the test of time while Dad threw strategies at the wall to see what would stick. No wonder the two hadn't gotten along. "Grandma wore his wedding band on a necklace the rest of her life."

"She loved and lost."

Maybe experiencing that heartbreak had made Grandma a positive force in Lina's life as she reeled after the demise of her relationship with Shane. Grandma knew how good a marriage could be and wanted Lina to hold out for the best. She'd believed in Lina's worth.

Matt set his fork down, covered his mouth a moment, then slid his fingers under hers, loosely holding her hand. The touch rendered her breath shallow, even before his eyes locked on hers. "Is it possible your grandma had trouble trusting people?"

Lina opened her mouth. Closed it. A breath fluttered in her lungs, stretching wings of mismatched emotions. A desire to defend Grandma. A softening over Matt's gentleness with her, in voice and touch. And a hope that whatever he said next would shift her perspective and relieve the burden she carried.

"She lost her husband, and that could've left a mark." Matt released her hand to cross his arms on the edge of the table, ignoring his food. "Or maybe, she had trouble believing anyone could live up to the standard your grandpa set, especially when her own son didn't."

Lina searched her memories. Grandma had never acted bitter or exacting. "I don't think that's fair. And she was right about both Dad and Shane."

Matt shifted his arms off the table. "If she only got close

with you, she held a whole world of people at arm's length. Being right twice isn't a good average."

A whole world of people.

Had Grandma been lonely?

"Don't get me wrong. She sounds amazing. I'm glad you had her in your life." Matt picked up his fork. "But don't judge everyone by Shane's example. Or by your dad's."

If only she could claim she hadn't, but if he judged her by the same measure he'd used with Grandma, she'd be hard-pressed to prove she let anyone in.

Maybe she should stop using professionalism as an excuse to refuse Adeline's invitations to friendship. She could also make more of an effort with the acquaintances she'd made at church.

She glanced at their still half-full plates and offered Matt a sheepish smile. "You have a knack for counseling."

"I've spent a lot of time in therapists' and pastors' offices this last year."

He must've.

His transformation since getting clean and sober had been so complete, she wouldn't have recognized him if not for the tattoos when she'd first gone to Visser Landscaping to recruit him. He'd gotten fit, yes, but he'd also changed his attitudes, his priorities, his beliefs.

"The result is pretty impressive."

Surprise registered on his handsome face, but as the compliment sank in, he gave a smile. "Only by God's power and grace."

The same God she knew and followed. Which meant she, too, had hope of transformation.

18

 $\mathcal{M}$ att left Lina's shortly after dinner because the coworker he'd asked to fill in for him at the pizza place could only cover the first part of his shift. He spent the night wishing he could've accepted when Lina had invited him to stay for a movie.

At 11:15, he let himself into the condo, ready to go to bed so he could do it all again tomorrow. Dim light reached the entryway.

Tim sat on the couch. When Matt stepped into the living room on his way to the loft, Tim set aside his tablet and slid off his reading glasses. "What was that about?"

"Her parents."

"This related to the scene at the wedding?"

Unfortunately it was, which meant Tim wouldn't stop digging until he had the story, likely stepping on Lina's toes to get it. Better for Matt to tell him.

Tim's upper lip lifted with distaste as Matt relayed the story. "Okay. Well, she told me how he instigated the fight. I talked with Ray Brandt, and he still wants to hear what you come up with."

EMILY CONRAD

Work with Ray Brandt, an up-and-coming musician, didn't interest Matt as much as other opportunities. "What about Gannon?" His throat had gone dry, his voice slipping up a couple notches.

"We haven't talked." Tim's focus flicked toward the ceiling. "He said if I call him on his honeymoon, he'll announce Awestruck's going country and won't rescind until he gets back, which will be a week later for every interruption."

"And that worked?"

Tim's mouth shrank into an unamused line. "He'd tank tour ticket sales. Anyway, I did talk to John. If you have a song ready, he'll consider it, but I'll warn you now, he won't decide on his own. You'll also have to talk Gannon into it."

Matt hadn't been wondering about who might buy the song, but once he told Tim about his change of heart regarding Awestruck, there would be no taking it back. Still, he hadn't been able to get his conversation with Philip out of his mind. He wanted to audition.

More than that, he wanted back in.

As he'd prayed about it, he'd been struck by how far he'd come this year. Before losing Auggie and finding Christ, he never would've prayed over a decision. A new man, relying on Christ, he could make better choices if he stuck with the program and took advantage of the accountability built into the band.

Of course, God might have closed and locked the door on the opportunity, but Matt refused to be the guy waiting in the hall without bothering to try turning the knob. "What about the Awestruck audition?"

Tim's eyes lit. "I thought you weren't interested."

Matt shrugged. He was, but he also didn't want Tim going overboard to make something happen that wasn't meant to be.

Tim shook his head. "Gannon gets back on the third, and Awestruck business is on hold until the fourth. He was pretty ...

I won't say angry, because he kept his cool, but he was disappointed about the fight. The only way I've been able to pitch you to them is by saying you've changed."

Fresh evidence to the contrary would prove hard to dispel. Back in the day, he'd been a pro at making everything sound like anyone's fault but his own. Even if Matt took ownership for his part in the fight, the truth of Shane's actions might come across like deflection and blame.

"I guess it's a good thing I have a week to craft an apology." Matt ran his hand over his hair. After marinating with pizza grease and cheese in the Brownmobile for a few hours, he needed a shower. Halfway up the stairs, he paused and looked over the railing. "Leave Lina alone about the whole thing with Shane and her family, okay?"

"I'm planning to make sure she gets to and from work okay for a week or two."

If only, between jobs and recovery meetings, Matt's schedule weren't already maxed out most days, he'd take the responsibility himself. As soon as Awestruck was a sure thing, he'd quit everything but Key of Hope. And meetings, of course. "Just don't pry. You'll upset her."

Tim mumbled something that sounded like agreement, and Matt continued to the loft, collected clothes to wear to bed, and plodded back downstairs for the bathroom. "Seems pretty cold, doesn't it?"

Tim slid the glasses off again. "What does?"

"Lina's dad. I thought fathers were supposed to look out for their kids. Care about them. His priority is getting his hands on a property she owns, but aren't kids supposed to be, like, the biggest blessing? That's how my parents are always talking."

Krissy was pretty enamored with Jade too.

Tim gave a non-committal nod, but then why would he agree? Tim had spent the majority of Issy's life far, far away from her. Not that Matt had meant to criticize the choice. He thought of apologizing, but if Tim hadn't interpreted the remark as a rebuke, Matt didn't want to point it out. He continued toward the shower.

Tim's voice followed him down the hall. "Sometimes, the kid's better off."

How many times had Matt heard Gannon engage Tim on topics like this? Somehow, those two still got along. If only, during the years he had spent in the band, Matt had been in a state to notice Gannon's approach so he could mimic it now. Instead, Matt had been in equal need of the same kind of perspective as Tim.

In both cases, all Gannon's attempts had fallen on deaf ears.

But Matt wasn't Gannon. Maybe he could get through where the golden boy had failed. He returned to the mouth of the hall and leaned against the corner. "Maybe, but broken families are evidence of a broken world. It's not supposed to be like this. Families are supposed to be about commitment and unconditional love."

"What's the difference? A traditional family is no guarantee of a happy future or kids who grow up to contribute to society. You'd call your family committed, wouldn't you? But you still went pretty far down the rabbit hole."

Touché. "Another example of how broken a person can be. I thought I knew how to be happy. I was so wrong that I almost killed myself. A good family isn't everything. It's just helpful. But we all still need a savior. I found Him in Jesus."

"All roads lead to God now, huh?"

"He's the answer." Matt waited a beat. When Tim didn't reply, he started down the hall.

A belated response chased him. "I suppose you think you'd do better."

"At what?" Leery, Matt returned to the doorway.

Tim glared from the couch. "Family. Raising a kid."

This was what he got for the pride of thinking he could

succeed where Gannon had failed. "It's not about doing better than anybody else. If I ever have a family, I'll do my best. I'm sure I'll botch it up in countless ways, but if nothing else, I hope I can teach my kid what I told you—the world's broken, and Jesus is the answer. I wouldn't want any kid of mine trying to navigate life without having that down."

Tim let out a heavy breath, still glowering.

Matt didn't want to quit there. He wanted to add that his own father had modeled how much bigger of a role a man could play in his children's lives. He wanted to be a similar force in the lives of his own kids. Someday. If he had any.

But he was miles from parenthood, and he suspected Tim would hear all of Matt's hopes as direct attacks, so he kept them to himself.

~

As LINA PARKED NEXT to Matt's car behind Key of Hope, Tim pulled away. Usually, the manager had lingered in the lot to make sure she got in okay, but with Matt around, he must have decided the precaution wasn't necessary.

The day's lessons wouldn't start for a few hours, and as usual, she'd planned to use the quiet office to manage Awestruck's social media. Talking to Matt would be more fun, though. Had he come to see her?

Apparently not. He occupied one of the practice rooms, working on a song.

She didn't want to interrupt his limited free time, so she continued to her desk with only a wave of greeting. The guitar went silent, though, and he joined her before she'd shed her coat.

"I've got some news."

"Yeah?" Warmth saturated her chest as she slipped out of the light trench coat that had held off the September chill.

"First, a confession."

Oh. She rubbed the center of her chest. Maybe talking to Matt wouldn't be as fun as she'd hoped. She crossed the office to put her jacket on the coat rack. As if a few feet would lessen the impact of whatever he was about to confess. She hadn't meant to give him so much power to hurt her.

"Tim asked what was going on last night, and I told him."

"Okay." She retraced her steps toward her desk, but Matt leaned against the corner of it, staking claim to the space.

With his arms crossed and shoulders raised slightly, he looked as on guard as she'd felt when he'd said he had a confession. Maybe he wasn't the only one who had the power to hurt some feelings here.

But his worry only stirred more of the same in her. She threaded her own arms together and waited.

"Philip and I talked at the wedding. He gave me a new perspective on some things, and I've been praying about it." He watched her carefully. "When I told Tim yesterday that I'm not interested in Awestruck, I lied. I wanted to tell you because you asked me to be honest with you."

She eyed her desk chair longingly. She had respected Matt's decision to avoid Awestruck. What did the change mean? "What did he say to change your mind?"

"He talked about the accountability in the band and about the difference Awestruck makes in fans' lives."

The band's impact showed up all the time in the form of posts to Awestruck's social media accounts. Long private messages. Handwritten letters. Some of it came from the music, people who encountered the right lyrics on the right day. Others put the more ambiguous songs together with Gannon's and John's interviews and came to believe in Christ.

God worked through the band. But ...

"How would joining now be different from last time?"

"Any time I got clean in the past, I did it on my own

strength. This time, I have God. And last time, the account-ability was optional. This time, it'll be required. And probably enforced with drug testing."

Lina nodded slowly. Matt had been set against rejoining Awestruck. His one-eighty after voicing such a serious objection stirred uneasiness. Perhaps he wouldn't get his way. Not if Gannon and John were as upset as Tim made them sound. "Did the fight burn a bridge?"

Matt winced. "I'm not sure. John wants to talk, and I'll apologize to Gannon too. I've got to try."

She wanted to question him about why he hadn't told her sooner, but her problems had dominated both nights since the wedding, and she could only credit him for waiting. Appreciating his timing, however, didn't mean she could easily support his new aspiration. "A drug test could be too late when it only takes one overdose. You said yourself that lifestyle leads to death."

"Give me half an hour, and I could score in Lakeshore too. It's not that much safer here." An unsettling claim, but his steady eye contact asked for her support.

"Have you been tempted to start using again?"

"The thought's crossed my mind, but I'm not a slave to it like I used to be." He offered a sad smile. "I remind myself of the consequences and pray and go find a better way to cope with whatever sent me down the destructive line of thinking to begin with."

She dragged the toe of her sneaker across the floor, a desire she didn't understand suggesting she close the space and take his hand. She resisted. "What helps?"

"I call someone, go to a meeting, or work on music for a while. Work out. Do the next thing and remind myself how far I've come. I get that my jobs are nothing impressive, but a year ago, I couldn't have kept one of them, let alone four. I get to send my parents a deposit every week. Sometimes, on a bad day, I send an extra payment. That always feels pretty good."

He didn't say it, but with Awestruck, those payments could be much larger.

Would the band still consider him, despite the scene at the wedding?

She massaged her hand. "How are your parents?"

"Switching gears. They do snow removal, so they're prepping all the equipment for winter."

She nodded, though mostly she'd asked to remind Matt of the people she suspected he most wanted to spare from pain. With them in mind, he had to be more likely to make good decisions.

He lowered his arms, and she realized she'd moved closer. The openness of his stance promised a warm welcome if she closed the distance. "I set up a time to talk with John next week."

"It's decided already?"

"The conversation is. Nothing else."

Her hand lifted toward him, and he met her halfway, intertwining their fingers and drawing her closer so she stood with one foot on either side of one of his. With the way he half-sat on her desk, their bodies were still eight inches apart.

She spanned the distance by resting her free hand on his chest. "But you want it."

"I do." This close, his eyes were a study in shades of blue, flecks as varied as waves in Lake Superior. "Until recently, I thought I'd seen everything God would do for me. Already, it's more than I deserve. Jesus came to destroy Satan's strongholds, and when I did business with Him after Auggie's death, that's exactly what He did in my life. But you know the verse about how God can do more than we ask or think? Or the mention of Him restoring the years the locusts have eaten? I didn't expect Him to go that far for me, but if He gave Awestruck back ..."

Beneath her hand, his chest rose with a deep breath.

She smoothed her fingers over the knit of his shirt, a soft black Henley today. "The opportunity means a lot to you."

And he would be crushed if Awestruck wouldn't even consider him.

"It would also mean a lot to have your support."

He wasn't demanding it, but he'd fare better with her on his side. She could explain the fight to Gannon and John. They'd give him a chance then, wouldn't they?

And if they did and Matt rejoined Awestruck ...

"What if you fall again?" She hadn't meant to whisper.

"There's always a risk, Lina, but God has a hold of me, and where I'm weak, He's strong. Whatever happens, He'll be strong for you too." With gentle fingers, he slipped her curls behind her ear then let his hand rest against the side of her neck. "He's brought you this far."

Oh. Had that been her concern? Her own well-being and what might happen to her if she experienced another heartbreak? Maybe, but only in part.

She bit her lip and noticed his eyes dip, drawn by the movement. When he lifted his attention again, mischief had seeped into his expression.

Her heart stuttered. "What?"

"Just wondering how much longer I have to let you lead before you believe I have willpower." His gaze brushed her lips again.

A flurry of desire rushed her, but she couldn't let him change the subject. What they'd been discussing had been serious. It had serious consequences. "I'm not nearly as addicting or tempting as a drug."

He lifted an eyebrow, and a slow smile crept across his mouth. He rose, moving into her space, and her breath caught. Maybe she'd been wrong, if this felt the same for him as for her. She'd never tried illicit drugs, but being close to Matt? Could something be more addicting than this? She ached for him to go ahead and kiss her. His thumb caressed her neck. She closed her eyes.

"A little longer then." Matt's voice was husky, but he shifted until her hand fell away from his chest.

By the time she opened her eyes, he was on his way back to the practice room.

She laughed and rubbed her forehead. Fine. He deserved her trust.

What he didn't deserve? To have to fight to overcome problems Shane had brought into his life.

She pulled up her message thread with John, the one normally only used for coordinating social media posts, then stole another glance at Matt. He looked healthy, so ... alive, even as he moved about the practice room. A new man compared to who he'd once been. What if, by getting back into Awestruck, he turned back into the husk of a human she'd known before?

A counter-argument rose. What if, when he got back into Awestruck, all the good changes she'd seen in him remained, multiplying the positive effect both he and the band had?

She hesitated only a moment longer, then typed John a message. *Can we talk about Matt?*

19

*L*ina stood at the back of the sanctuary on Sunday, debating where to sit. John and Erin alternated between attending church in Lakeshore and attending Erin's home church a town or two over. Today, they sat beside Tim. Lina regularly joined that group on Adeline's invitation, but the newest newlyweds were still off on their honeymoon.

Meanwhile, Matt sat alone toward the back. She'd dressed up for church in slacks and a blouse, but if anything, he'd dressed down in jeans and a hoodie. Could they be any more opposite? At least none of his clothes had holes. And there was something honest about the lack of pretense. Joining him would be a public display of a connection between them when she wasn't exactly sure what that connection ought to be.

He caught her looking his way and waved a greeting.

Who was she kidding? Matt had also publicly displayed their connection by defending her from Shane, and she was invested in him no matter where she sat. She'd already made that much obvious by talking to John on Matt's behalf. As usual with the drummer, the conversation had been short, but she'd explained that Matt had been protecting her.

To be sure the events at the wedding wouldn't hurt Matt's chances with Awestruck, she'd also talk to Gannon and Adeline. Besides, she ought to offer to pay for any damage to the broken table and toppled vase that might've been billed to them.

As she closed the distance, Matt scooted over to allow her space beside him. Throughout the service, he seemed more focused than she'd expected, and she chided herself for harboring such a low opinion of his ability to sit still.

They rose with the rest of the congregation for the closing song.

Ahead, Erin stepped into the aisle. Tim and John passed her, and as Erin retook her place, the men left the sanctuary.

Lina leaned close to Matt's shoulder. "What's that about?"

Matt's voice cut out of the song as he seemed to track the early exit. "Tim's been off all week."

"What started it?"

Matt seemed to have an answer, but instead of offering it, he picked the song back up and focused on the service until the pastor finished the benediction. Their first time sitting together for a service, and she was the one distracting him. Who would have thought?

The service ended, and a pianist played as the congregation broke into movement and conversation. Lina turned toward Matt.

He motioned her to pick up her purse from the pew. Once they were on their way out, he rested his hand lightly against the small of her back. "We got to talking about family values on Monday. Considering his situation, I might not have been as tactful as I should've been." His voice emanated from just over her shoulder.

His feathery touch marked their first contact since Tuesday, when he'd said he was letting her lead. All week, she'd been thinking about it. He might have to wait forever if he left it up to her, but if he instigated another kiss, she'd happily go along with it. If this was premature and ill-conceived, at least he'd be the one who started it.

The one to blame.

That wasn't fair to him, though. If she did make the next move and this didn't work out, she doubted he'd blame her. He'd chalk it up to experience, be glad they'd enjoyed it while they had it, and move on to the next thing.

If only she were equally resilient.

Anyway. He stayed near now simply to avoid losing her in the crowd.

She glanced back at him. "What exactly did you say to him?"

"Broken families are signs of a broken world. Evidence that we all need Jesus. I was not trying to say I'd be a better dad than he's been, but I think he took it that way."

Her step slowed as her imagination sprinted toward the idea of Matt as a father. Boy or girl, his child would be a dare-devil who'd put him through his paces.

Matt's sheepish look beside her pulled her back to the present. Back to Tim. "Ever since, when he hasn't been avoiding me, he's been eyeing me like he might kill me in my sleep."

Lina laughed and stepped outside. "He's feeling convicted?"

Matt shrugged, the autumn sun playing on his shoulders. He scanned the parking area. Both John's sports car and Tim's luxury sedan waited in stalls, neither man in sight.

A family with young children made their way to a minivan parked nearby.

"Are you sure you don't want kids?"

"Um." Matt's surprise settled into an exaggerated frown. "Did I say I didn't?"

"After Bailey was bullied, you said you were glad you didn't have any."

He scratched his scalp. Had she finally managed to fluster him? "I think being a father would be the hardest thing I've ever done." He fit his hands into his pockets. "And the most worthwhile thing. If that day ever comes." He seemed to have regained his composure, and he studied her now as though he'd asked her a probing question in return.

She fiddled with her purse strap. "I like that perspective."

"But?"

"Hard isn't the first description I think of. Fulfilling, maybe."

"I'm sure it's that too." Matt's focus dipped to the keys in her hand. "What are you up to now?"

If she was to take the lead as he'd said, she ought to invite him to lunch. After all, he wasn't as opposed to kids as she'd thought. They had a chance, didn't they? Instead, she found herself telling him she was going to run errands and then reward herself for it with an apple crisp latte.

"You want me to hang around in case Shane shows up?"

She shook her head. "It's been a week. If Shane were going to resurface, he would've done so days ago. Considering he's broke enough to need Dad to fund his ticket, he wouldn't have paid for a hotel this whole time. At some point, life needs to go back to normal."

"Normal's boring."

"And yet, it's what I do best."

"I can learn a lot from you." His eyes sparkled with kind amusement. "But, okay. Call me if you need me."

There he went again, putting the ball in her court. One of these days, she'd work up the nerve to return it.

～

MATT STRAIGHTENED AWAY from the fridge when he heard the condo's front door open. A moment later, Tim tossed his keys on the counter, sighed, and spotted him.

Lunch would have to wait.

Matt shut the appliance. "Everything all right?"

Tim's jaw shifted as he shook his head. "You might not agree with me sending Issy to boarding school, but it's best for her."

He nodded. Since when did Tim ever explain himself? The guy usually made up his mind, acted, and let people think what they wanted.

Splotches formed on Tim's cheeks as he rambled on. "My ex is married again. We're on as decent of terms as possible. But this other thing I hadn't even thought about in years suddenly came back up." He dipped his chin and, with it, his attention. "This time, I don't know if it's something I can right."

"I've been there." Matt could still recall the roaring despair he'd experienced, standing beside August Peltier's casket. "We can never truly right our wrongs. That's why Christ paid for them. When we believe, He cancels our debt."

"But He doesn't undo the past. You—there are people who wouldn't be so happy to call it all even, and I don't know how to fix that."

How much time and energy had Matt spent on making amends with the people he'd wronged? He still wasn't done paying back his parents. Yet making amends wasn't the first step. "Getting right with God is the main thing, and He'll help you from there."

"Get your head out of the sky. This isn't about God."

If Matt kept pushing, Tim would get angrier. Time to meet him where he was and trust God to connect the dots. "Okay. What's eating away at you?"

Tim pulled out one of the seats at the peninsula, sank onto it, then dropped his head into his hands.

Cold, gnarled fingers squeezed Matt's gut. "Was it illegal?"

"No."

The dread-filled pressure didn't let up. "It has to do with Awestruck?"

"Yes."

He rubbed his stomach, the ache there lessening. "I'm sure they'll forgive you, whatever it is." It couldn't be worse than the years of offenses Matt had racked up.

"It's not up to them."

"Who's it up to?"

"You." Tim still held his head in his hands, preventing Matt from seeing his mouth move.

He thought he'd heard the word clearly, but what had Tim done to him? The worst Matt could accuse him of was enabling him during his run with Awestruck. He'd done so much good for Matt since then, building bridges when the time came to make amends. He'd gotten him the job at Key of Hope, was letting him live at his place rent-free.

"You don't owe me anything."

Tim lowered his hands and lifted his bloodshot eyes.

Matt's abs hardened against the coming blow. "What did you do?"

"Nadia." His voice was hoarse.

Her image sprang to life in Matt's mind. She'd been petite and energetic and always up for an adventure. Until one day, she'd changed her number, deleted her social media profiles, and disappeared.

Awestruck had been new to fame back then. They'd traveled almost constantly, met by bigger and bigger crowds, more and more enthusiasm. The hurry helped treat the heartbreak, but in quiet moments, Matt had been miserable, trying to figure out what he'd done to cause her to leave so abruptly.

Growing up, he'd often felt like he didn't measure up to the standard Pete set. Nadia's rejection had confirmed his shortcomings once again. Since the wound had been there all along, it had probably only been a matter of time until he turned to all the wrong things to treat it. In fact, the things he'd done with Nadia—heavy drinking, sex—had been the start of self-medicating.

Self-destructing.

Matt pulled himself back to the present. "You scared her off?"

Tim nodded.

Made enough sense. Before her, Matt had behaved pretty much like Gannon and John. If Tim saw Matt starting to lose his moral compass, he might've assumed Matt would clean up without his partner in crime.

Though losing Nadia had hurt incredibly, it was part of his story now. A story God had worked for good. "That was a long time ago. I don't hold it against you."

"Gannon was a lot rasher back then. He would've had your head, and I couldn't have everything we worked so hard for disintegrate."

"I understand. I forgive you." Now if only Matt's absolution would leave Tim hungry for reconciliation with God too.

"No." Tim shook his head, a small, ongoing movement. "I haven't told you yet."

"Whatever it is, Tim—"

He held up a silencing hand, face skewed as though he'd just as soon double over with nausea as speak. "She was pregnant."

EARLIER IN SEPTEMBER, the Lakeshore coffee shop had released an apple crisp latte, and Lina was hooked. Unfortunately, with fall color in full swing, so was the autumn tourist season. She waited for two middle-aged couples and a family with tween children to order before taking her own turn at the register.

The drink would be a while. She settled by the cream and sugar station. Though she generally didn't work on Sundays, checking notifications in social media apps passed a few minutes until the people in front of her had been served. Shouldn't be much longer now. She glanced toward the windows, where sunshine highlighted the passing pedestrians. A man wearing sunglasses paused outside the coffee shop window. He sure looked like—

The barista called her name, and her attention flitted toward the counter before returning to the man outside. He'd resumed his course, weaving around others so Lina didn't get a clear view of his face before he was gone from the window entirely.

He'd resembled Shane, but she was imagining things.

Right?

After collecting her drink, she cast another look toward the windows. No sign of the man.

Reminding herself of the things she'd said to reassure Matt about her safety, she stepped up to the glass and peered down the street. Not only did she not see the man, but she'd parked a quarter block in the opposite direction from the way he had been walking. In the unlikely scenario Shane was out there, at least there were lots of witnesses. She could get to her car, drive home, pull straight into the garage, shut the door behind her, then go into the locked house.

That'd be safe enough.

She hoped.

Uneasy, she called Matt as she left the shop. He didn't answer, and she hung up without leaving a message.

Dad had purchased Shane's ticket. He might know when Shane's return flight had been. Or the two may have met in person since the wedding, which would lend even more peace of mind that he was in New York and not Wisconsin.

After she got Dad's voicemail, she tried her parents' home number. Mom answered—and claimed to know nothing about Shane coming to Wisconsin or about Dad's campaign to sell The Captain's Vista. Instead, she started up on the latest about her various projects for clubs and charities.

Lina considered cutting her off and calling Tim for an escort home, but her glimpse of the man had been brief and obscured by sunglasses. He could've been anyone. If Shane were in town, why would he lurk without talking to her? It wasn't as if he could get The Captain's Vista by following her from a distance.

So instead, she let Mom talk as she drove away from Lakeshore. They didn't chat often, and on the slight chance Shane *was* in town, surely her mother would call 911 if Lina screamed and the call disconnected.

When she got to her own road, she made sure no other vehicles were in sight before she zipped up her driveway and into the garage.

"Cheryl informed me of the company *you're* keeping," Mom said.

She'd been listening just closely enough to remember the last few words Mom had said each time she paused, but even having a sentence's worth of context didn't help this time.

Lina collected her purse, got out of the car, and scanned the garage as she locked the vehicle. Unless Shane was hiding in a garbage can, he wasn't here. Besides, her doorbell cam covered the driveway and hadn't alerted her to anyone's arrival.

"What company?" She let herself into the house.

"Washed up rock stars."

"Awestruck is hardly washed up, Mom." Now inside the house, she locked the door to the garage behind herself. "They're one of the top-grossing bands in the country."

"I'm not talking about Awestruck. I'm talking about Matt Visser."

Mom's friend Cheryl, whoever she was, must've seen the photos of them leaving the wedding together. Lina checked the deadbolt on the front entrance. In place. "Matt is a teacher at Key of Hope and a pretty decent guy."

"But is he going to marry you and provide any kind of life for you?"

"I don't want him to marry me." At least, she didn't want that yet. She reached the sliding patio door that allowed access to the backyard. Cattails swayed in the marsh. No ominous shapes. She checked the lock and pulled the blinds. "Also, I have a life. I don't need a man to provide one."

The claim didn't sit well. Financially, she didn't need provision, but a husband played an important role in her dream of a family. Also, she wouldn't mind having a man—a particular man with a knack for fending off bullies—around right now in case Shane showed up.

"Daisy Wentworth landed one of the Carson brothers. You should see the ring." Mom described the wedding plans in detail.

The tactic to make Lina jealous might've worked, but the Carson brothers were no prize. While handsome, little mattered to them aside from appearances. Much like her own parents.

Mom paused—possibly for only a breath—and Lina cut in. "I'll let you go, but have Dad call me, okay?"

"I'll relay the message. But, dear, the clock *is* ticking."

"I'm sure it is, but I know how much you want me to be happy." If only they didn't have such different convictions about how to achieve that.

"Every parent wants only the best for their child."

Before Mom could spoil the positive note by pointing out

the discrepancies between their goals for Lina's life, Lina bade her a cheerful goodbye and hung up.

Alone in the quiet of her living room, Lina could almost hear said ticking clock. This house wouldn't be large enough for the two or three kids she'd always hoped to have, but it was comfortably furnished and in the countryside. She could see living here with a husband and perhaps a baby.

But could she see Matt as that husband? His openness and patience highlighted how closed off and demanding Shane had been. But the flip side of his courage was a disregard for consequences. He wouldn't purposely bring trouble on his family, but accidentally? Her careful nature might not be strong enough to curb Matt's risky impulsivity, and where would that leave their family?

Their non-existent family.

She prayed God would help her see Matt for who he really was. And for God to help her to act on what He revealed. After all, she had dismissed hints about Shane, and her heart couldn't afford another such fallout.

20

*C*haos woke Matt from a dead sleep. A weight slammed into his gut, and a staccato voice hammered his barely-computing mind. He opened his eyes to a closeup of a little girl's face as the jabs of small elbows and hands marked his niece's scramble to get off of him.

"You said I could wake him up." Jade's knee skewered his thigh, and then, mercifully, she was on her own two feet beside the couch.

"I didn't mean like that." The disapproval in Krissy's voice was probably enough to correct her daughter, but a note of amusement lifted her tone. She probably considered this payback for all the dolls he'd dismantled and otherwise endangered during their childhood. "Why don't you go make him some coffee?"

Matt forced himself to sit up, rubbing his face. Krissy and her husband had a guest room, but he hadn't felt capable of sleep last night. After everyone else turned in, he'd sunk hours into an online search for Nadia and the child. He'd found no leads.

Sleep must've caught up with him.

"Sorry. Kids."

Right. Kids.

He'd done the math a million times. Given the short window of his relationship with Nadia, his own child would be older than five-year-old Jade.

Tim had had very little information to offer. He said he'd intercepted Nadia, upset, the day she disappeared from Matt's life. She'd been looking for Matt, but he'd left the hotel for a sound check. Tim got her to tell him her news. Convinced paying Nadia to make a quick exit from Matt's life would be best for everyone involved, Tim had written her a check on the spot. Even she hadn't known at the time if she was carrying a boy or a girl.

Worse, Tim couldn't say if she'd gone through with the pregnancy.

But he'd stared at Matt with such desperation, desperation Matt himself had felt often enough in life. As one who'd been forgiven much, he'd formed the words he'd known he owed: *You're forgiven.*

He should've mustered the strength to watch the statement land and field Tim's response, but instead, he'd retreated straight to his car and started driving. He prayed God would undo any damage he'd inflicted in the hasty departure.

He'd been a couple miles from Lakeshore when Lina called. He'd promised her honesty, but how could he tell her this? Either he would be one more man she distanced herself from because of his failures, or she'd accept him as he was because she didn't know how much better she deserved.

He'd let it go to voicemail.

He rubbed his face again, but the pressure in his head and the grit in his eyes didn't clear. His stomach churned, too, and not because Jade had used it as a trampoline. "What time is it?"

"Eight thirty."

He'd cleaned up his language when he'd turned his life

over to Christ, but the word that ripped through his mind was anything but holy. He'd told Lina his ability to keep four jobs served as a sign of how far he'd come, and now he was an hour and a half overdue at the home improvement store two hours away.

He felt his pocket but didn't find his phone. "I've got to call in."

"It's charging on the counter." Krissy rubbed his shoulder as he passed and fell in step behind him. "Jade and I will take good care of you. We can go explore the state park, make a day of it."

"I've got Key of Hope this afternoon." And a delivery shift afterward, followed by a couple of hours of emptying trash cans and mopping floors.

He stepped into the kitchen as Jade pressed a button on the six-cup coffee maker. After hopping off the stool, she bounced to another cabinet, where she stretched to reach a coffee mug. He glanced to Krissy to ask about teaching a kid to make coffee, but his sister watched him with such sad eyes, he didn't have the heart.

He dialed the store and, when Russ came on the line, started making his apologies.

"If you come in for part of your shift, it's better than nothing. If you miss the whole thing, it's the same as if you didn't even call, since it's well into your shift."

"Meaning what?" He rubbed the bridge of his nose. Life had been a lot easier when he didn't care about things like this.

"It would stay on your record for a year, and if anything like this happened again, you'd lose the job. But if you show up, it counts like a normal attendance issue. You get more of those, and the record drops off after sixty days."

Outside the kitchen window, a tree waved red leaves. Near Lakeshore, some sections of the forest had already begun to look sparse.

If he left now, he could cover the last hour of his shift, but he couldn't muster the energy to race back. "I've got a personal situation. I won't be in."

A few seconds of silence ticked by. "You've done a good job, but you know I can't do you extra favors."

Matt's throat burned to complain, but he held his peace. "I wouldn't expect you to."

"Okay. Just make sure this is a one-time thing. I really don't want to fire you, but they don't give me much leeway here. The attendance policies are strict."

He hated failing at something as basic as showing up for work. Hated feeling like he'd fallen short and had to scramble to catch back up. "You got it."

"Okay." Russ's voice lifted, apparently easily reassured. "See you tomorrow."

He disconnected and accepted a mug from Jade. Her pour had left something to be desired, but the drips on the outside of the mug could evaporate. He took a long drink to counteract the lost sleep.

Now all he needed was a way to undo all the rest of it.

Or something stronger to drink.

Probably ought to call his sponsor.

Definitely ought to.

"You'll stay for a little while?" Krissy patted her daughter's head when the girl delivered a mug.

"Through lunch. Then I have to get back." For better or for worse, he wanted to be near Lina. He'd missed her call yesterday and hadn't reached out because he didn't know what to tell her about Nadia. Hopefully, in the bustle of students, she wouldn't have time to question him.

"I saw the picture of you leaving Gannon's wedding."

He downed the rest of the coffee and set the mug on the counter. "And?"

She licked her lips, scanning the room like she hoped to

find a script printed on the backsplash. "You've got a lot going on."

Jade trotted up, slid his mug off the counter, peeked inside, and mounted the stool to refill his cup.

"You've got her trained."

"Mama likes her coffee." Krissy shot him a furtive glance. "But Matt ... there's a rumor you're getting involved with Awestruck again."

One of the few bright spots in his life right now, the hope of a second chance. *If* he could talk them into overlooking the wedding fiasco.

Krissy moved closer and tapped a fake nail on the counter. "I'm disappointed there's so much you didn't tell me yourself. For years, I got my only news about you through the tabloids, and it feels like it's come back to that."

"I'm not interesting enough for the tabloids anymore." A lame excuse, but she ought to give him credit for coming here with news of what Tim had confessed. He'd told no one but her.

She lifted a carefully penciled eyebrow. "You and Lina are getting close, aren't you?"

"They wrote about us?"

"They didn't have to. You fought with her ex after you said you weren't going to get in the middle."

"He was hurting her."

"And who are you hurting?"

Judging by the sadness in her voice, he had hurt Krissy. He should've had the same discussion with her that he'd had with Lina to explain his choice to try Awestruck again. But did he really need to keep his sister posted about Lina?

If he subjected their relationship to too much scrutiny, the impossibility of it would become undeniable. Lina had it all together. Always had. Matt was a train wreck. Always had been. He was hurting Krissy, and he would hurt Lina and would probably disappoint Awestruck, too, since failure seemed to be his MO.

"You, Matt. You're hurting yourself. With the news you learned yesterday, Lina and her ex, all these jobs, Awestruck, living away from your support network ... I'm afraid it's too much all at once. You need to simplify before you get over-whelmed."

Simplifying sounded as undoable as hurrying back to Lakeshore for a shift at the home improvement store. He couldn't force quick solutions. The complications would have to work themselves out—and they would, because the items on Krissy's list were at odds with each other. He might lose Lina over the news he'd learned yesterday. If Awestruck worked out, he could quit the part-time jobs and would gain a stronger support network. If the band didn't take him back, Awestruck would be gone. As for Nadia and the baby, much remained to be seen there. Had she had the baby? What should his role be? Would she give him a choice?

All the challenges and opportunities would battle it out, and he'd be left with whatever remained. He just had to hang on to his sobriety long enough to see what the outcome would be.

CHRIS HAD CHOSEN the perfect day to be late. Lina offered Matt a smile of greeting as he rounded her desk to enter the office area.

"Hi." Instead of going to the other computer to sign in, he first crossed to the coffee maker in the corner. "How was the latte?"

"I got it, but then I thought I saw Shane, and I hardly tasted the drink."

He turned from the coffee maker. The machine gurgled as

his jaw ticked. "Where?" The question came out in a low rumble.

If the bruise from Shane hadn't disappeared a few days ago, she would've guessed the shadows under his eyes resulted from the bruise's progression. With the rest of his face pale, the culprit had to be fatigue. Was he stressed about Awestruck? She should've told him she'd talked to John to pave the way for him, but at the moment, he wouldn't care about that.

"I was waiting for my coffee when I saw someone who looked like him through the window. I figured it wasn't actually him, but I tried calling my dad to see if he knew Shane's whereabouts."

Matt's expression remained dark.

"He hasn't called me back."

"Your safety's at risk, and he can't return a phone call?"

"Neither did you." The reply shot out, unchecked, and she immediately regretted it. She hadn't left a message or texted, both things she could've done. Why hadn't she?

Matt's lips all but disappeared with the way he jammed them together. He took his mug from the coffee maker. With it in hand, he dropped into the other desk chair. "I'm sorry."

"No, I am. Sorry for lobbing that at you. The guy I saw must not have been him because nothing came of it." Lina fiddled with today's ring, which featured a black onyx gemstone. His failure to call back stung, but she shouldn't have resorted to an accusation. "What did you end up doing? How are you?"

He turned his back and woke the computer. "I don't like the idea of you out in that remote house while he still might be around."

"He probably isn't. I imagine Dad bought a roundtrip ticket, and if Shane *did* scrape together a couple hundred dollars, I'm sure he would rather gamble it away than spend it on the fee to change a plane ticket."

"Unless he got your dad to shell out for those flowers, too, he's willing to invest something in getting close to you. And he *is* trouble." Matt punched in and rose, posture and expression tense.

"I'll give you that last one, but the sighting was a false alarm. Everything's okay." Hoping to keep her audience, she scooted her chair an inch closer to the walkway. "Anyway, what were you up to?"

"I'd rather not get into it."

Her jaw and shoulders slackened. "What? Why?"

He eyed her and rubbed his chest. "Leave a message when you actually need something. I would've called you back."

"When I 'actually need something'?" As though talking to her under normal circumstances wasted his time? "What were you doing?"

"I made a trip to Fox Valley."

"Oh. That's a long drive for one afternoon." She held her breath because if she released it, questions would escape with it. Why was he being so secretive and defensive?

He didn't take the awkward, lengthening silence as an opportunity to explain.

The front door opened extra-wide, and Chris appeared with his characteristic grin for Matt.

Her heart beat a warning to leave it for now. She'd recently prayed that God would show her Matt's true character, and his sudden refusal to talk—especially delivered in that tone—waved like a red flag.

What was going on with him?

What if he'd relapsed? Was it unlikely? Or with all the stress, was confronting him a matter of life and death?

Matt greeted Chris, his voice enthusiastic, but not even a ghost of a smile on his face as they completed their handshake. The student moved ahead toward the practice room.

Lina waited until Matt was even with her desk to ask her question. "Is it already too late for that test?"

His confusion was his least negative expression since the start of this conversation, but once he decoded her meaning— he'd mentioned drug testing being a part of his return to Awestruck—his features and his fist tightened. "No."

He worked with one student after another, yet as he ushered them in and out right past Lina's desk, he failed to acknowledge her.

She'd completed no work before his last student arrived with Tim close behind.

The manager's hair lifted and swooped in more disarray than usual, and tired creases feathered beneath his eyes. He studied Matt before he straightened the lapels of his coat and asked if she was ready.

Both Matt and Tim were out of sorts. That couldn't be a coincidence.

Her hands hovered over her keyboard, hesitating to shut down the computer. Each second she delayed bought her more time to question Tim. "Is everything okay?"

He shifted his arm as if to work a kink out of his shoulder. "Why?"

"Because you and Matt both aren't yourselves today." A new possibility occurred to her. "Awestruck didn't call off the audition, did they? I talked to John, and I'm planning to talk to Gannon too. He hasn't already decided against Matt, has he?"

"Gannon's just getting back today. All Awestruck business is on hold until tomorrow, at the earliest."

"Then what's bothering Matt?"

Tim swept his fingers down his face. "He'll have to tell you himself."

Since when did Tim believe he'd meddled enough in the affairs of others?

She turned her back to the practice room in case Matt could read lips. "He's all right, though, isn't he?"

Tim glanced toward their subject. The longer he waited to answer, the harder Lina had to struggle to avoid following suit.

She stepped close enough to smell the spice of Tim's cologne and dropped her voice so the student on the couch across the room couldn't hear. "You would know if he started using again, right?"

Tim's gaze snapped back to her. "Why do you ask?"

"He's so different today. He ..." She moved back to a more normal distance. "I don't know what else would explain it."

"I do." Tim bumped his fists together. "I'll keep an eye on him."

"Something happened. You're worried."

"It didn't occur to me that he might ... It's fine." His hands loosened. "It'll be fine. He's been clean over a year. I'll keep tabs on him and make sure he keeps going to meetings."

If only Matt hadn't told her how easily he could buy drugs. Her concern drew her attention back to the practice room.

But he wasn't there. He'd wrapped up the lesson and was only a few feet behind her, coming for his next student. The square set of his shoulders suggested he was as on guard now as when she'd asked about the drug test over an hour ago. He met her eyes with the intensity of a silent rebuke.

She shouldn't have asked about his sobriety the way she had. Gentle kindness would've been more effective, and a second try could only go better.

"I'd like to work a little longer." She forced hopefulness she didn't feel into her expression. "I can stay until Matt finishes his lessons, and he can follow me home."

Matt barely bothered to shake his head. "I've got delivery after this. Go with Tim." He waved goodbye to one student, then motioned the next to the room. As he closed the door, the glass walls of the classroom were the least of the barriers between them.

21

*L*onging and dread deadlocked in Matt's chest when he spotted Lina waiting for him on the couch in the condo's living room. He'd known he couldn't delay their conversation forever, but he hadn't expected to have to face her tonight when he returned from his janitorial shift. It was one thirty in the morning. Tim must've let her in and failed to give Matt a heads up.

A lamp crowned her curls with glowing light in the otherwise dim space. She held her phone, as if she might've entertained herself with it until she'd heard the door, but as he stepped into the room, her eyes focused on him—dark, but not hard to read.

She'd come for answers, but he couldn't step into the room knowing where the conversation would lead. Exhausted and with few answers, he'd never manage to tell her about Nadia and the baby in a way that would soothe instead of upset her. If only she weren't in such a rush for this explanation.

"What are you doing here?" he asked.

Why now? would've been a more fitting question.

"When Shane got distant with me, I excused it and didn't

206

push, and look where that got me." She pulled her feet onto the couch and crossed her legs like an anchor to hold her in place against his objections.

"I've got to be at the store in six hours." The more nights he racked up with poor sleep, the worse he would function. And he'd already done pretty poorly today. Rest. That had been one thing his sponsor had reminded him to prioritize when he'd called him earlier.

She laid her hand on the back of the couch. "If I leave, you'll be able to sleep? Because I won't."

Well, no. Especially not if he knew Lina was tossing and turning because of him.

He approached the end of the couch and tucked his hands into his pockets. "You asked me not to pretend to be something I'm not. I don't think I'm ready to lay everything out tonight."

"Honesty isn't always convenient, but it is necessary."

The air in the room seemed to press on him, weighing down his head, his shoulders, even his ability to make eye contact. "I haven't lied to you."

"But you haven't told the truth either. Since when are you afraid of anything?"

He'd miss how she believed the best in him. He already missed what he'd thought about himself—that he'd survived the worst consequences of his choices, had made amends with everyone but his parents, and could move forward without guilt.

And now to find out he'd failed Nadia. He'd been an absent father for eight years. Nine, if the pregnancy counted, too, and to Nadia, he suspected it did.

To him, it did.

He should've tried harder to find her when she disappeared. He might've uncovered Tim's involvement, located her and, from one or the other, learned the truth. Instead, he'd numbed out by partying.

Nadia had deserved better.

Lina did too.

"Once I tell you what happened, it'll change everything. I don't want to risk that."

"I thought you were a risk-taker."

He was a coward who preferred drugs to honesty. But if he turned back to his addictions, he'd lose Lina, Awestruck, all hope of making things right with Nadia and the child. He'd lose everything.

Her eyes, pleading, belied the stillness of her expression.

He'd stepped closer, or he wouldn't see such details.

When she stood, only a couple of feet separated them. "There are very few things you could've done on Sunday that you would refuse to tell me." She crossed her arms unevenly, and they angled askew from her shoulders. Her face tipped down and away, yet another unparallel line. "Is there someone else?"

"No." Only after he spoke the word did he recognize it as a lie. Or, at best, a half-truth. There'd been someone else. And now there was someone else—a child. He hoped.

Nadia would've had the child, right?

"Are you using again?"

"No." Though at moments today, the thoughts had buzzed around his head like wasps.

Being even more tired tomorrow would not help matters. He'd attend a meeting in the evening, even if he had to call in to the pizza job. He'd have to check his planner.

Lina advanced another stride and let her arms down. "Then I don't understand what you'd be afraid to tell me." One more step, and an assessing glance. "You've been trying to earn my trust. Maybe I haven't been working hard enough to earn yours." She linked their fingers with kindness he didn't deserve and couldn't refuse.

"Lina." His voice had roughened from the long day, the

yearning to let her do whatever she had in mind clashing against the obligation to do what was right.

Moving closer still, she slid her arms around his waist and joined her hands behind his back.

He put his hands on her shoulders, looked her in the eyes. "You don't want this."

"You said you wanted me to lead." She tipped up to kiss his cheek. "I'm leading."

"This isn't some ploy to move you along."

"No. It's a ploy to move *you* along." She kissed the corner of his mouth, and his eyes sank closed.

Her breath traced across his lips until her mouth met his.

He lost himself in the moment, and when he pulled back, his hands cupped her face. He tried to make eye contact, but she never lifted her focus. Her next exhale swept cool across the moisture on his lips.

When he kissed her again, he only meant to linger another second. But she smelled so good. She tasted even better. Her sweater, her curls, the skin of her neck were all velvet soft. When he deepened the kiss, she moaned quietly. If he opened his eyes again, she'd have him completely, all five senses.

Intoxicating. She was intoxicating.

The word sobered him. Reminded him of what was happening and why. The stakes were too high for this. When she learned his secret, she'd feel used that he'd let it happen.

His biceps shook as he pulled back, smoothing his hands down her arms so he could keep her from advancing again. "This has to stop."

Pain flashed in her eyes. "You can trust me."

He almost blurted out the reason she shouldn't trust him, but this was too intimate a position. She'd want space as she processed his announcement, and when she left him, it would hurt less if she didn't have to escape from his arms to do it. He motioned for her to sit on the couch. He sat only after she did, leaving an empty cushion between them.

No. Too close. Watching her eyes shutter against him from here would be nearly as bad as feeling her slip from his reach. He paced to the other side of the coffee table.

Lina sat with her feet close together on the floor, her knees angled to one side, her hands clasped. Her shoulders had gone rigid, and her focus seemed flighty, like she was watching for danger.

Not knowing was clearly its own kind of torture.

"All these years, Tim knew where Nadia went. Or, why anyway."

"The girl you almost loved."

He shouldn't have mentioned her when Lina had asked about his romantic history. His time with Nadia had been a tug-of-war of wills, each of them behaving poorly to get what they wanted from the other. Without knowing it, they'd both missed the key ingredient of love—sacrifice. A willingness to put the other person first.

In his long history with women, Lina marked the first whose needs he wanted to honor above his own desires. He didn't want anything to leave her questioning her unique importance in his life.

If only his old ways weren't still haunting him. If only he deserved her.

"Tim paid her to go." The words scratched out. He cleared his throat and pushed on. "She was pregnant, and Tim thought Gannon would fire me. He didn't want the band to fall apart. We'd already lost Fitz, our second guitarist, early on, and maybe Tim's right that another dispute of that magnitude would've ..." He ground to a stop. Safeguarding the band's success didn't justify what Tim had done.

"She was pregnant." Lina took agonizing time with the sentence. Her face lowered, and he could see her tracing the fact to a more complete understanding of his relationship with Nadia. She'd known before—she had to have known he'd slept around, but maybe she'd glossed over it. And now, his history—one chapter of it, anyway—was real. Now, his choices impacted her.

A pit of shame opened in his gut. "I'm sorry. I just found out yesterday, and I ..."

She brushed the knee of her jeans as if to wipe off dust. "You don't owe me an apology."

Her tone contradicted her statement, and though he didn't relish causing her pain, at least it meant she cared about him, their relationship, and their future.

"I lived in the moment, not realizing the only lasting part of my pursuit of happiness would be the consequences, which would hurt people I hadn't even come to care about yet."

She ran her fingers over her curls, moving them back from her face. Her eyes were as glossy and deep as a winter pond with a thin layer of ice. "What now?"

Now, you say you forgive me. He swallowed his desperation. He couldn't voice his plea. It was too much to ask. "I don't know."

LINA HAD ENVISIONED Matt making a great father, given how well he related to the kids at Key of Hope. Her own father had never chatted with her about things she cared about or taken the time to teach her a skill. He hadn't even bothered to show up for her recitals, concerts, and games.

She'd been attracted to Matt because he was different.

Yet now, he didn't know what to do about his own child. He studied his hands, fingers straightened, as if considering which of the words tattooed there he would choose to live by. Love or hate?

"There are only a couple of options," she said. "Either you go find them or you leave them be."

He lifted his line of sight, as if startled. As if neither option had occurred to him. "I meant between us. I don't know how this affects us."

"Oh." She shook her head, looked away. She'd asked God to show Matt's true colors, and his next move with Nadia and her child would be a window into his character.

He lowered himself into an armchair perpendicular to the lamp, the light washing his left side as his right lingered in shadow. "I've been looking online, even tried reaching out to some people we knew back then, but nothing's panned out. I'll keep searching. I'll hire someone to find them if I have to."

She blinked. Nodded. Of course he would. She'd known he would.

"Or Nadia, anyway. I don't even know if she had the baby."

The possibility hadn't occurred to her, but now another potential situation came to mind. "I suppose you also don't know if the baby is yours."

He didn't waver with surprise or offense, as though he'd already considered the same. "There are a lot of unknowns."

"Will you try for partial custody? If the child is yours?"

He flinched and his mouth opened, but he said nothing.

"Fathers have rights. She shouldn't have taken off without telling you."

His index finger traced the lit match on his hand. "I was a different person back then."

"You don't think you deserved to know?"

"If I had known ..." He tilted his head and sucked a breath through his teeth. "Part of me wonders if it might've scared me straight. But if I would've hit rock bottom either way, I'm glad they were spared that journey." He turned pensive. "I hope they were spared that."

She followed the thought. "Nadia might not be a good mother."

His tight frown confirmed the worry as a possibility.

"What then?"

He inhaled sharply, rose, and paced away. "This is the never-ending conversation I've been having with myself since yesterday." At the fireplace, he turned and ran both hands forward over his hair. "But I can't cross any of these bridges until I come to them."

"It's good to have a plan. Being a dad is a big responsibility."

"I know." He balled his fists and crossed his arms.

"You're offended." She had meant to apologize, but she was only trying to be helpful.

"I'm worried enough. I know you like your neat and tidy plans and rules to follow, but you were never going to get those with me."

"I thought we were making plans together."

"I'm not writing up a book of all the contingencies. My plan is to find Nadia and talk to her."

"But what will you say? She might not want you in the child's life, so you need to go into it knowing what kind of involvement you're asking for. And what about child support? A lawyer could help navigate it all."

He sank into a seat and gripped his head with his hands.

"I know it's a lot to consider, but I also know what it's like to grow up with parents who could take or leave me, and how you go into this might make all the difference to your child."

He lowered his hands and glared at the dark fireplace. "Whatever kind of parent yours were, I'm worse. Didn't even know my kid existed. If you can't forgive your parents, how are you going to forgive me? And how will my son or daughter manage it?"

"You're different than my parents. You didn't even know. That's not your fault."

Tendons in his jaw shifted.

"There's nothing for me to forgive here. I knew you had previous relationships, and I know you've changed since then. But if you need to hear it, yes, Matt, I forgive you."

His frown cut deeper.

She didn't understand. Wasn't forgiveness exactly what he'd asked for? Maybe he didn't even know what he wanted. Wouldn't know it until he heard it. A vote of confidence couldn't hurt. "The child will forgive you, too, because now that you know about him or her, I know you'll do the right thing—"

"Do you?" His eyes had turned cold.

Where had she gone so wrong? She hadn't experienced this level of misunderstanding since ... since Shane. Her stomach clenched against the blow of the realization.

"Matt." She rose to approach him.

He lifted his arm, and she stopped. His left hand, the one that bore the word hate, pointed toward the door. "I don't have the energy for this now. You got what you came for. Let's call it a night."

Her breath turned ragged. "I thought you were worried about losing me over this."

His jaw pulsed again. "I was always going to lose you over something."

"I want to be supportive."

He walked ahead of her to the door, opened it, and went to his car.

He must intend to follow her home.

Sunday's possible sighting of Shane had made her grateful for Tim's escort to and from work, and when she had asked the manager if she could come meet Matt after his shift, Tim had insisted he would come out and follow her into Lakeshore.

The precautions might be overkill—had she seen Shane, or had paranoia gotten the better of her?—but she appreciated not having to navigate the shadowy parking area alone. She got in her car and set off, and Matt tailed her. His car idled at the end of the drive until she waved to him from the living room window. At the signal she'd made it in, he disappeared into the night.

When she'd chosen to meet him tonight, she'd expected the truth to bring them closer together. Instead, it might just break them.

22

*M*att didn't remember hitting snooze, but he must have. Twice. When he'd finally become conscious enough to note the time, he only had one minute before his scheduled shift at the home improvement store. He jumped into action but was already four minutes late before he entered the kitchen. The aroma of coffee promised he could grab a cup to go. He glanced to where Tim sat at the peninsula with a mug and his tablet.

Each time Matt had seen Tim yesterday, the man had shrunk back like a dog afraid of being kicked. His morning routine involved catching up on the news, but at Matt's entrance, he pushed the device away, a cringe haunting his features.

Matt slowed his step. Arriving fifteen minutes late couldn't be much worse than ten. Either way, Tim's peace of mind was worth Russ's disapproval. "I'm not mad at you."

Tim's frown deepened, and he seemed to search for something to say.

Matt took his travel mug from the drying rack and poured

some coffee. As he twisted the lid on, he turned toward the snack bar. "I forgive you. I said it, and I meant it."

"Yeah, but at the time, you looked like I'd just skewered you with a butcher knife." Tim's upper lip lifted. "Still kind of do."

"I'm angry with myself, not you."

Tim crossed his arms on the counter and leaned against his elbows. "Holding Issy when she was born? Highlight of my life." His worried eyes flicked to Matt, then away. "You missed that."

"You don't know that I would've been there, even if I'd known." The band had traveled constantly back then, and nine months after Nadia left, he hadn't been sober often.

Tim reclaimed his coffee and drew himself up straighter on the stool. "You and Lina have a nice chat?"

More of Matt's shock had worn off since yesterday, but in its place, his fatigue had multiplied. Maybe he should call in to Key of Hope. A nap would do him far more good than digging a deeper hole with Lina.

"She's angry?" Tim asked.

She was something all right. Maybe not angry. Determined was more like it. Determined to fix Matt's mess, as though a plan could erase all the pain. "I didn't want to hash out every possible scenario with her."

"Ah."

"It's not worth theorizing until I talk to Nadia."

Tim nodded. "And you know how to reach her?"

"I've looked at hundreds of online profiles, and none are her."

"She may have a different last name now."

Matt nodded.

"You know where she's from? Where she grew up?"

"Yeah. We used to make fun of it. It was a food ... Sounded like a food ... Hamburg."

"State?"

217

Matt cringed. His relationship with Nadia had been one of the most notable of his life, yet he knew little about her. "Must not have been as easy to make fun of."

Amusement trickled across Tim's face. "And her maiden name was Holmes."

That much, Matt had remembered, and he'd used the surname in his searches to no avail. Tim's memory surprised him, though. Perhaps writing the name on a check had seared it into his brain, or he might've refreshed his memory.

Either way, Tim finished his coffee and stood. "I'll find her info for you."

"You don't owe me that."

"You make amends your way, I'll make them my way."

Matt nodded. At least, for once, Tim would be using his knack for learning the details of other people's business for good. But the mention of amends didn't sit right. "Maybe there's another reason you don't feel better."

Tim waited.

"You don't need to make amends with me as much as you need to get right with God."

"And you need to get to work."

Right. Twelve minutes late and counting.

LINA'S sleepless night gave her plenty of time to brainstorm ways to turn things around with Matt. Advocating for the audition he wanted seemed like a decent first step. Besides, she owed him for defending her the way he had.

Hoping her boss had her phone silenced if eight a.m. was too early—and one day after her honeymoon, it probably was—Lina texted Adeline. *Welcome back, Mrs. Vaughn! It doesn't have to be today, but eventually I'd like to talk to you two about the altercation at the wedding.*

She set her phone on the counter to clean up her breakfast dishes, but a ding drew her right back to read Adeline's reply.

You can drop by the house this morning if you have time. We're both here. I'm testing our new espresso machine, but Gannon's not a coffee drinker.

Easier than expected. Lina hurried through her morning routine, then plundered her kitchen for gifts. If only she'd had some warning, she would've baked a coffee cake or something, but without, the best she could do was collect a bottle of unopened coffee syrup and a box of tea she'd meant to keep for herself. Then, with Grandma's blue diamond sparkling on her finger, she drove to the Vaughn's gated property near Lakeshore, along Lake Superior.

Beyond the wrought iron gate, maples, aspens, and pines splashed the landscape with red, yellow, and green, blocking the view of the brick house beyond. She loosened her grip on the wheel, tempted to grab her phone and reread Adeline's message. Had she understood the invitation correctly? Or over-looked a passcode to enter on the keypad next to the drive?

But before she'd woken her phone, the gate jerked into motion. She had a lot on the line here. A new friendship, her connection with Matt to preserve, his opportunity with Awestruck. Her foot twitched on the accelerator, but she corrected in time to ease up and keep the car from bursting down the lane. She could do this, advocate for Matt. It wouldn't be awkward. Adeline was a friend. And her boss. But a friend.

She parked by the front door, and with a deep breath and a prayer for favor, she grabbed the grocery bag. Adeline opened the door before she'd rung the bell. Dressed even more casu-ally than her usual jeans, Adeline wore leggings, a loose T-shirt, and a soft gray cardigan.

This visit really was an intrusion.

Lina lifted a shaky smile and the coffee syrup. "Before I

moved, I bought a couple bottles of salted caramel syrup from my favorite shop back in New York. It's amazing."

Adeline accepted the offering with both hands. "Are you sure you want to part with it?"

"Of course. Lakeshore's coffee shop has some good flavors, and I haven't needed it as much as I was afraid I would." Besides, the coffee syrup was the only bribe she could think of to smooth over the fiasco at the wedding.

She followed her host to the kitchen. Between the stretching ceiling, the views of the lake, and the gleaming counters and appliances, the room belonged in a magazine.

Adeline took milk from the refrigerator and poured it into a small metal pitcher. While she steamed it, Lina unpacked the second item from the grocery bag, set it on the counter, then opened the coffee syrup.

Gannon ambled in wearing sweatpants and a hoodie. At best, he'd finger-combed his hair.

Lina dropped her gaze and froze. What if Adeline hadn't warned him she'd invited company?

"Consider yourself lucky." The laughter in his voice told Lina to relax. She looked up as he motioned toward his wife with his mug. "Instead of winging it, she actually looked up directions and practiced."

"The guy in the video said I had no chance of doing it right the first time." Adeline seemed to test the temperature of the milk by tapping the outside of the froth cup. "According to the recipe and the instructions, those"—she tipped her head toward two shots of espresso waiting on the machine—"should be pretty good, but we'll see."

Gannon picked up the box of tea Lina brought. "Lemon cake, huh?"

Winning him over was even more important than Adeline, considering Lina's reason for coming. "I know you're more of a tea guy, and that's the best there is."

And she was betting Matt's career on it. Poor guy.

Lord, grant me success.

"That's quite a vote of confidence." Gannon swirled his mug, then lifted it and drank the last of whatever he'd had in there.

Adeline glanced at Lina's second offering. "You know you didn't have to bring us anything."

"I had it on hand, and I feel bad encroaching on you guys right after you got back like this."

"Friends are never an intrusion." Adeline shot her a smile, then grabbed a mug and began assembling the first latte.

Friends. Why did Lina have such a hard time accepting the role when they kept offering?

Gannon didn't suffer similar reservations with accepting gifts because he plunked the lever to turn on the electric kettle, opened the box, and dropped a tea bag in his mug. "I hear you have a story to tell us."

Now that they'd been thoroughly bribed was as good a time as any. "The fight at the wedding wasn't Matt's fault. My ex grabbed my arm. Matt was trying to get him to back off."

"Who's your ex?"

"Yeah." Adeline slid the first latte toward Lina. "We wouldn't have invited him if we'd known."

"He wasn't invited. Showed up and didn't make it past the lobby, which I'm glad for. The last thing I wanted was my drama to intrude on your reception. If you were billed for the broken table or anything else, I want to pay for it."

Gannon waved the offer away and poured steaming water into his mug. "The important thing is that everyone's all right." He eyed her, assessing.

"I think we are." She hesitated, but they kept insisting she was a friend. With a deep breath, she took them at their word. "As long as Matt can still audition for Awestruck. I don't want him to lose his chance because he was defending me."

Gannon had lifted his tea, but he lowered it at her statement. "He turned us down."

"A conversation with Philip changed his mind." And hopefully everything Matt had come to believe about the accountability within the band and the opportunity to make a difference was all true, or this favor would end up being a death sentence. Forcing her mind back on hope, she lifted a smile. "Tim didn't tell you?"

Smirking, Gannon checked his phone. "Not yet, but my ultimatum on not contacting me ends in about an hour. Either my phone will blow up then, or he'll be on my doorstep."

"With Matt, probably." Adeline chuckled as she steamed milk for the second latte.

"Wouldn't do any good without John, and he's not headed over until tomorrow."

Lina sipped her coffee and found Adeline watching for her reaction. "It's at least as good as the ones from the coffee shop."

With a quick laugh of triumph, Adeline assembled the second latte.

Lina shot a glance at Gannon. Even with John available as early as tomorrow, Matt might appreciate time to prepare for an audition. "How about he auditions Monday?"

"Matt?" He frowned thoughtfully. "The audition will take more than a day, but we could get started."

Nineteen minutes late to work, Matt was in sight of the home improvement store when the car hit a pothole. An ominous bang sounded from under the front end. He hit the gas, but the car wouldn't accelerate. He rolled as close to the curb as he could, jabbed the hazards, and scanned his options.

Lakeshore was small, but this was one of the most traveled roads. Two lanes led each direction, connecting the town to a larger city about thirty minutes away. Lakeshore residents commuted to work there, making now a bad time to stop in a lane, but this last shopping district before the countryside had no shoulder, just lanes of traffic, a curb, and lawns that stretched like football fields. The large businesses here, like the home improvement store, were spaced out, and none of the parking lots had an entrance close enough for Matt to push the car out of traffic.

A horn blared as a sedan swerved around him.

"Yeah, I'm not happy about it either." He checked his mirrors.

Any inattentive driver would rear-end him. The bills for a tow and mechanical repair would be bad enough. If the car got hit, the liability insurance he'd purchased wouldn't cover the damage to his own ride. He couldn't add a possibility of whiplash to all that. He unbuckled, slid across the front seat, and exited out the passenger side.

Even with the grass beneath his feet, a band across his chest left his heart straining as though he remained strapped in a vehicle careening into danger.

Only this time, the vehicle he couldn't escape was his life.

If only he could walk away as easily as he'd slid out of the car. Instead, his movements felt nightmarishly sluggish.

He knew ways to escape this feeling, of course.

Jesus, help.

He puffed out a breath and forced himself to take the next logical action. Once he'd arranged a tow, he turned toward the store, about a quarter of a mile away, and called Russ.

"Matt. Where are you?"

"I was on my way, but my car broke down in the middle of the road. The tow company said it could be an hour. I'll call a friend to wait with the car, and I can walk over—I'm literally looking at the store right now—but it'll probably take him a bit to get here."

"That's the best you can do?"

Today wasn't the first time he'd been in the driver's seat of a precariously positioned vehicle. Unlike the time he'd driven the dump truck onto the lake, this situation wasn't life or death, yet Russ's question sounded like thick ice cracking.

"I admit I was late. I had a personal situation, and it's ..." He rubbed his forehead. The specifics didn't matter, and he couldn't risk the rumor getting out. "Anyway, I'll get there as soon as I can. It counts as a late then, right?"

"Yes, but if you have three of those in six months, that's it."

"I thought you said the policy was more lenient if I showed up."

"This *is* more lenient. Look, Matt, at the rate you're going—"

A screech of tires and crashing metal whirled him back toward the road.

An SUV had swiped the back left of the Brownmobile. Matt's trunk lid bobbed open. The SUV's hood bowed, glass littered the pavement, and the white of airbags filled the cabin.

"There's been an accident. I have to go." Matt hung up and jogged forward, only then spotting the other sedan with its nose pressed into the driver's side of the Brownmobile.

In the attempt to avoid Matt's car, the SUV must've hit the sedan. The driver of the sedan appeared to be moving, no airbags deployed, no visible blood. Matt hurried around the rear of the SUV to check the last driver.

The SUV's door creaked open, and a man swayed to his feet, gripping the armrest for balance. His sluggish focus lifted to Matt. "That your car?"

"Yeah, it broke down." He put a steadying hand on the man's arm and scanned his balding head, looking for a lump. "Are you all—"

A blur in Matt's peripheral vision coincided with a shift in the man's stance. Pain flared in Matt's face, and he jolted backwards, only then registering what happened.

The man had punched him.

Anger scalded Matt's throat. The man had punched him? How ... Who jumped out of a wrecked car and hauled off and punched someone?

Did it matter? He'd deserved it. If he hadn't made such a royal mess of his life, he would've had a nicer car. His vehicle wouldn't have broken down in the middle of a lane because of a pothole.

The driver pushed past him, shaking out his fist, and stalked toward the grass.

As shock wore off, the heat of pain in his temple sharpened. Matt pressed the heel of his hand to the area, and it came away red. Was the guy wearing a ring?

The driver of the sedan blinked at him, stunned, a phone to her ear.

At least someone had responded to the wreck by calling the police.

Matt would need to stay to talk to them—about the car, not the punch. Could he hurry through this and still arrive in time for his shift at the home improvement store? Maybe, maybe not, and the tension of the unknown was one more stressor in a long list of them.

He touched his palm to his cheek again and came away with another smear of blood.

He couldn't do this. Couldn't keep fighting to make things work. He was exhausted. Tired of fighting. Mentally. Physically. All of it.

He got Russ back on the line. "Someone hit my car. I'm not going to make it in."

Russ missed a beat. "You know what this means."

Sirens cut through the morning, police responding to the accident. If only the tow had been so quick. Then again, the accident had happened in under five minutes, an impossible time frame.

"You have to let me go."

"Come in and sign the papers when you're done there." Russ sounded an awful lot like Dad had after Matt had put the dump truck through the ice.

To think he was supposed to be a better man these days. Instead, he was clean and sober and still making a mess of his life. But go in and sign to make it official? "No offense, but no thanks."

"You'll be leaving on bad terms," Russ said.

Seemed pretty unavoidable at this point. "Sorry it worked out this way."

"All right. Lesson learned."

Which lesson? Not to hire former rock stars? Don't take a chance on drug addicts? On applicants who'd been fired from their previous job? On employees who knew nothing about doors and windows?

There had been a host of reasons to not hire him, and Russ had given him a chance anyway. Russ's optimism was probably gone now, one more casualty in a long list of people Matt had disappointed.

He disconnected and lowered himself to the grass away from the others.

After his deductible, insurance would cover the damage to the other cars if this was deemed his fault, but it wouldn't replace the Brownmobile. Tim might let him borrow his rental occasionally, but he couldn't drive that indefinitely for the pizza delivery job, which meant that source of income was out the window too.

Down a car and two jobs in one day, on top of everything else.

All the losses would be okay if he could land the Awestruck gig.

But was that ever how life worked out for him?

No, no it was not.

23

"*W*ho'd you pick a fight with this time?"

Lina's fingers stilled over her keyboard as Samantha's question rose from the back hall of Key of Hope.

Only one person could elicit such a question. Lina rose but caught herself before she leaned over her desk to see all the way down the hall to the back entrance. Moments later, Samantha stepped into the walkway between the classrooms, followed by Matt.

Once he stepped past the glass wall of the classroom, Lina spotted the purple-and-red gash next to his eye and along his cheekbone.

Samantha cast him an uncertain look.

His gaze locked on Lina, however, as he finally answered the question. "I don't want to talk about it."

Lina dropped back to her chair, stung. Pressuring him to open up last time he'd refused to share hadn't gone well. What option did that leave for connecting with him? She could explain about the Awestruck audition, but depending on what had happened to him, this might not be a good time.

Matt continued to the other computer to sign in, and Lina didn't dare swivel to stare.

She didn't know his elaborate work schedule, but she could usually tell what job he'd come from by his clothing. Today, he wore jeans and a light gray sweatshirt rather than one of his uniforms. If he hadn't been working, a coworker hadn't injured him.

He and Tim wouldn't have come to blows over something.

What if Shane had shown up, and he'd once again injured himself defending her?

She checked over her shoulder.

Matt had finished clocking in and stood to allow Samantha her turn. As he stepped away from the workspace, his line of sight fell on her. She couldn't pull her eyes away. In addition to the gash, his temple looked red.

Maybe he'd fallen and didn't want to talk about it because he was embarrassed.

Lord, please help him choose to trust me.

Instead of asking, she could do as she'd planned—apologize for being overbearing last night and try to cheer him up with news of the audition. Unfortunately, those ought to be private conversations, and Samantha still occupied the other workspace.

Lina mustered a smile. Matt hesitated, and when he returned the expression, he did so with a sad wince. Wordlessly, he retreated to a classroom to wait for his first student.

"He's usually a lot more fun." Samantha's pouting tone reminded her of some of their young students.

Lina pointed her smile—now maintained by sheer willpower—toward the teacher. "I'm sure he'll tell us about it when he's ready."

Samantha smirked. "If you don't know, I doubt he'll tell me."

The instructor must have picked up on their connection. As tenuous as it was.

"What in the world?" Samantha picked at the sleeve of her shirt and held up a piece of cereal. "This is why I work here. At least the students don't stick their breakfast to me." Chuckling, she tossed the piece of cereal and launched into a good-natured story about her day.

Lina listened and responded at the right times, but as soon as she was left alone again, her mind circled back to Matt.

At least three times during his lessons that day, he caught her staring, but she never found a moment alone with him. The longer the day went on, the less she felt she could blurt out the news about the audition. If they weren't close enough to talk about basics, they weren't close enough for her to go arranging his life like she had.

Still ... She couldn't take back the meeting with the Vaughns. She had to tell him.

He saw his last student out while she was talking with a parent. She tried to wrap it up, but the woman had a litany of questions about the Christmas recital, still months away. Matt punched out and escaped. Not a single word had passed between them all day.

Tim would probably tell him about the audition. Hopefully. It would be awful for such an important opportunity to be sprung on Matt at the last moment.

She couldn't leave it to chance. She pulled out her phone and composed a text. *I didn't want my problems with Shane interfering with you and Awestruck, so I talked to them. They say you can audition Monday.*

Typed out, the whole thing looked presumptuous. She should've quit after clearing Matt's name instead of lining up a day. Especially considering Matt's crowded schedule.

She added one more line. *If the day doesn't work for you, please blame it on me acting without your blessing.*

She hit send, then monitored her phone anxiously, but he sent no reply.

No problem. She could wait. He'd come to her when he was ready.

If that moment ever came.

Tim followed her home as usual, and she fixed herself dinner. After she'd cleaned up from the meal, her book failed to hold her interest. TV, too, and it was only eight thirty—dark out, but too early to go to bed.

She could bake something. Nothing hit the spot like the tangy sweetness of warm apple pie in the fall, and peeling and chopping all the apples would take some time. Especially since she'd first have to go buy ingredients.

She glanced out the window overlooking the front lawn. Was it safe to leave alone? She kept insisting her Shane sighting hadn't been real. And she'd been running the occasional errand alone this whole time. Besides, if Shane wanted to get at her during the drive, he'd either have to run her off the road—unlikely—or do something in the well-lit, busy grocery store parking lot—also unlikely.

After consulting a recipe, she scribbled a list and headed out. As she pulled up to the end of her drive, the vehicle advancing down the road traveled far below the posted limit of fifty-five.

The SUV slowed even more, as though to turn into her driveway. Her heart pattered, fear freezing her until she recognized the vehicle. That was Tim's SUV, wasn't it?

The engine hummed as it pulled in next to her, and finally she could discern the features of an unexpected driver. Not Tim or Shane, but Matt.

Thank God he hadn't made her wait too long.

Yet now that she had his attention, did she really want to know what he'd say?

He rolled down his window and waited until she'd done the same. "Going somewhere?"

"Nowhere important." She shifted into park, though her nerves were speeding along a rollercoaster. Had he come to thank her for the audition? To talk about his child? To mend things between them? "I didn't know you were coming."

"I wasn't. I'm not." He seemed to note her expression, which confusion and worry undoubtedly clouded. "It's just that you live all the way out here, and with Shane ..." He gave his head a shake.

His concern sent warm light through her, as if the sun had suddenly taken the place of the dim moon. "Thank you for looking out for me."

"He's bad news, Lina. Why are you going somewhere alone?"

"Because normal people don't get bodyguards to protect them from their exes."

"He's not a normal ex."

True, but he also had never gotten violent with her—aside from tightly grabbing her arm. As far as abusive exes went, others had it worse. She motioned toward the house. "Go ahead and park. I'll pull back in."

"I don't think talking is a good idea. I went to a meeting and decided to swing by after. I wouldn't have stopped ..." He gave her a furtive glance.

He wouldn't have stopped if she hadn't caught him.

"But you did." And he'd attended a twelve-step meeting, another good sign. "We don't have to talk. We could watch a movie."

As though he could hear her silent prayer, pleading for him to agree, Matt glowered at his windshield. Then, his SUV advanced down the drive. She reversed all the way back into her stall in the garage. By the time she finished, Matt stood in the drive. The solar lights lining the pavement did little good against the darkness.

She stepped toward the front door, where a stronger light cast a welcoming glow. "The TV's inside."

He didn't smile or make a move for the house, so she stuffed her hands in the pockets of her open trench coat and approached him. She'd offered to not talk, but between his prediction that he'd lose her, news of Nadia and the child, and the audition, her questions could fill an Awestruck concert venue. Maybe he hadn't come inside for the movie because he wanted to clear the air.

She cautiously picked a conversation starter. "Have the night off work?"

He hung his head and rubbed his brow with the back of his hand. "Yeah. My car got wrecked earlier, so I'm down to two jobs. Key of Hope and the cleaning company."

"Oh." She could still picture his smug expression when he'd told Tim he'd bought a car, and he'd been proud to manage multiple jobs. The losses had to sting. "I'm sorry to hear that."

He continued to avoid eye contact.

"At least the Awestruck audition—"

"You shouldn't have arranged that."

"You were defending me. I had to speak up for you. You still want it, right?"

He pressed the side of his fist to his mouth. So much for her peacemaking efforts bringing him relief.

She stepped closer but didn't dare touch him, as much as she longed to lend comfort. "Are you okay? How can I help? The offer to watch a movie still stands."

Her eyes had been adjusting to the darkness, and now that she stood nearby, she could see the line between his brows and the stony set of his mouth. He looked at her long and hard, as if to memorize what he saw so he could call it to mind later. As if he was about to say goodbye.

I was always going to lose you, he'd said. Did he ... Had he meant that as a breakup?

"I shouldn't have been so overbearing last night." Her words scrambled, like hands desperately trying to grab something—anything—to stop a fall. "Finding out about Nadia must've been incredibly disorienting, and it's going to take a while to work everything out."

He deflated with a sigh.

"But you will, and I won't hammer you with unsolicited advice. I'm sorry I overstepped. Tell me what you need from me, and that's what I'll do. Listening, getting your mind off of it, whatever it takes."

His face turned toward the road. "You asked me to be honest with you. I promised to earn your trust."

"And you were honest, even when you thought it would come between us."

"A little honesty doesn't make me reliable."

Her cheeks burned, and her stomach twisted. Last night, she'd credited his attitude to the long day and the emotion of recent events. Sleep and time should've helped him begin to recover. Instead, his outlook seemed to have deteriorated further.

"What happened with the car accident? Why did that mean losing some of your jobs?"

"The car broke down in the road and got rear-ended. Because of the accident, I missed another shift at the home improvement store, and they let me go."

She scoffed. "That sounds strict."

"It is what it is. Without a car, I can't deliver pizzas, so I quit."

Couldn't he have found a way to make delivery driving work? She hated to see him looking defeated, giving up on things. Yet, if she voiced her concern, he'd take it as an accusation, not seeing how she hurt for him and wanted the best for him. "Okay. Four jobs was a lot."

Troubled lines marked his forehead. "I need to cut my losses."

"Makes sense. You have enough on your plate."

Matt swiped his fingers over his mouth, as if to rub off his frown. He failed. "I don't see a future between us."

She was one of those losses he wanted to cut? She took a staggering step backward. "Is this because of last night? Because I'm sorry if I was pushy—"

"It's not about that."

"The Awestruck audition? Are you angry I talked to Gannon and John? I—"

"You did nothing wrong, Lina." Finally, he made eye contact. But if he was telling the truth and she hadn't failed, why was he doing this? "Just steer clear of Shane. You can do better." He stepped backward toward the SUV. "With some distance, you'll see it too."

The Shane comment must be a distraction, the unrelated sentence in the word problem.

He'd said he'd been doomed to lose her from the start. He thought she could do better than him.

He pulled open the door and got behind the wheel.

As the engine came to life, Lina's breaths came fast and shallow. Did she deserve this? To be left again? Was there something about her men couldn't stand? Or was she still too trusting?

It's not about you.

The foreign thought brought calm, even as the pain rippled out. Working together at Key of Hope would become awkward at best. She wouldn't get to hear about his audition. He'd no longer lend a listening ear. Whatever happened with Shane and her dad, she was on her own. If Matt found his child, she wouldn't get to meet him or her. Wouldn't get to see Matt step into the role of father.

God had answered her prayer to see Matt's true character. He was trustworthy and courageous, but not impervious to injury—physical or emotional. Hurt by recent events, he'd concluded pushing her away would protect her. And maybe himself.

She could never convince him of how wrong he was.

Far faster than she would dare, he reversed down the drive and pulled onto the road. His headlights flickered behind dark trees as he drove off until a rise in the land stole him away.

24

*M*att sat in the passenger seat as Tim pulled up to the gate at Gannon's house. Gannon and Adeline's house now. The woman in the security booth at the gate waved as they rolled past and onto the property.

All this felt eerily similar to a few months before, when he'd come with Tim to seek forgiveness and offer "Whirlwinds" as a token of his sincerity. He'd gone into it telling himself that, as long as he apologized and offered to make amends, his mission would be a success no matter how he was received.

That was no longer the case. He'd come this time to regain a spot in Awestruck, and if he failed ... He'd trust God with what he couldn't control. After a year of sobriety, the thought ought to come more easily and do more to slow his speeding pulse.

The house came into view, a blank canvas of sky beyond it —evidence that not far from the building, the land dropped away to the lake.

Hopefully Matt's black T-shirt would hide sweat stains.

Tim shifted into park. "Don't get off on the wrong foot."

Matt unbuckled. He shouldn't have told Tim he intended to come clean about Nadia before the audition. Ever since, the manager had been moping, as if honesty wasn't hard enough. "Letting them hire me without telling them isn't the answer."

"Still doesn't have to be the first words out of your mouth. Get them to buy in first."

"You can wait out here." He might be right back out, anyway, depending on whether John and Gannon would tolerate the baggage he brought with him.

"You're sabotaging yourself."

Maybe he'd given up on a couple of things too easily recently. On a bad day, a day like the accident, he shouldn't have made knee-jerk decisions about the home improvement store or the delivery job. And what about Lina? If he'd pushed through, would he have eventually found perspective that would've allowed him to stay with her?

That hope seemed impossible and more than a little selfish. Still, the decision to walk away didn't sit right.

But he'd prayed and deliberated for days over when and how to tell the guys the truth. His body protested with tightly corded muscles and waves of queasiness, but he knew the right path.

"I'm trying to eliminate bad surprises." He hopped out of the SUV. One foot in front of the other, up the front walk. One breath at a time. He rang the bell.

Adeline answered less than a minute later. He'd been focused on Gannon and had already forgotten she lived here now too. Happily, it seemed, since she grinned as she let him in. "How are things at Key of Hope?"

"Good. The usual." Except he and Lina hadn't been talking for almost a week already. Once, he'd come across her with red eyes. It killed him that the next guy to earn her trust would have to clean up after Matt the way he had tried to clean up after the trust issues Shane had inflicted.

"They're in the studio." Adeline lifted a hand toward the hall. "You know the way?"

"Yeah, but first, I wanted to say I'm really sorry about the fight."

"We should be thanking you. I'm glad you were there for Lina. Besides, what's a wedding without a little drama?" She touched her own temple. "That's not still from him, is it?"

His bruise from Shane had disappeared over a week ago. He ran his fingers over the scab on his cheekbone, the only remaining evidence of the hit he'd taken after the accident. Tim couldn't fathom why Matt hadn't pressed charges. "You know me, always getting into scrapes."

She chuckled, and he took his leave before she could ask more questions—or notice he wasn't laughing with her. All in less than three weeks, he'd gained a child—possibly—had been in two fights and had lost two jobs, one relationship, and his car.

Was Awestruck going to be another loss on that list?

In the studio, John saw him first, and Gannon must've noticed his arrival register on his friend's face, because he turned.

"Hey, man. Glad you made it." He clapped Matt's shoulder. "Ready with those songs you've been working on?"

Matt shuffled to a stop and eyed the gleaming equipment. Tim had assured him he didn't need to bring his own bass, and three top-of-the-line instruments waited here. Doing this Tim's way by claiming one and getting to work would be easier, but as he'd told Krissy weeks ago, he'd had it easy, and look where that had gotten him. "I've got some news first."

Tim, who'd followed him in after all, dropped to a seat on one of the couches hard enough that a spring clunked.

Gannon shot him a teasing look but didn't comment.

John studied Matt. The guy had always been observant. Could he guess what Matt was about to say?

No. Because Matt himself had been blindsided.

Tim propped his elbow on the armrest and leaned his head against his hand, partially shading his eyes.

Matt drew the kind of breath he'd need at the top of a high dive and took the plunge. "It sounds like I probably have an eight-year-old kid somewhere."

The news pushed Gannon back a step.

John palmed the back of his neck.

"I didn't know it was a possibility until last week. We're still trying to find Nadia for more information, but I wanted to be upfront about it."

"An eight-year-old …" John lowered his hand, expression pained with what Matt hoped was sympathy. "How'd you find out?"

Matt restrained himself from looking to Tim. "Someone who knew us back then finally told me she was pregnant when she disappeared."

"Me. I'm *someone*." Tim's voice came out at a growl. "I paid her to go because you"—he jabbed a finger toward Gannon —"would've fired him over it."

Gannon widened his stance.

Matt tensed his arms to keep from fidgeting. "If that's still the case, now you know."

The singer inhaled, chin lowered.

John braced his hands on the back of a chair. Though he turned his face away, Matt caught the worry there.

Gannon crossed his arms. He seemed to weigh his options of who to address first, then settled his attention on Matt. "The news must've thrown you for a loop. How are you coping?"

The singer's stance remained unyielding, his voice gruff, but the words themselves? Understanding in a way Matt hadn't expected.

"It's been a rough week."

"Did you relapse?"

"No." And finally, all the little decisions that had maintained his sobriety seemed worthwhile.

Gannon gave a single nod. "Who are you talking to about all this?"

From the couch, Tim watched with an intensity that suggested he shared Gannon's questions. Wait. Was concern for his sobriety the reason Tim had been shadowing him whenever possible and pelting him with questions the rest of the time?

"I went to an extra meeting, and I've been checking in with my sponsor each day since I found out."

"Smart. Is there anything you need from us?"

"Ah." He'd been primed for disappointment. But acceptance and support? He laughed. "Just a chance, I guess."

Gannon crossed deeper into the space and picked up a guitar before tipping his head toward the waiting basses. "Pick your poison."

"You still want to go through with this? You don't have more questions?"

Gannon turned to John. "You have questions?"

John paused putting in his in-ear monitors to shake his head.

Gannon adjusted his mic. "We're concerned about your sobriety. Otherwise, assuming what you told us hasn't changed your mind about Awestruck, it hasn't changed our minds about you."

Tim hunched forward. "But it would've nine years ago."

Gannon speared him with a sharp look. "*You* might want to lie low for a while."

Scowling, Tim pulled himself off the couch and disappeared into the control room.

The basses glimmered, opportunity ripe for the picking.

He hadn't been asked to leave. Miracle of miracles. Yet as he chose an instrument, fit the strap over his shoulder, and settled the bass across his body, his stomach crawled with the suspicion that he should've been. That he hadn't earned his place here and never would.

~

LINA TWISTED HER RING, a blue sapphire. Chris had arrived early for his lesson and immediately asked after Matt.

Since their conversation in her driveway, he hadn't spent an extra minute at Key of Hope. At least, not while Lina worked, though she frequently found evidence that he'd stopped in. A coffee cup in a waste basket she'd emptied. A light left on.

Chris spent twenty-five minutes playing on his phone and shooting longing glances at the door, waiting for his hero to arrive. At his scheduled start time, the boy put his phone away and started kicking his feet.

Matt was two minutes late. He was still coming, right?

Of all his students, Chris was the most enthusiastic, and that made him the one she least wanted to disappoint.

When Matt hadn't told her she needed to find a sub for today, she'd assumed he wouldn't miss his sessions, despite the Awestruck audition. Had he expected her to find someone to fill in for him?

She reached for her phone. It was too late to ask anyone to cover for Chris's lesson, but she might be able to line up someone else for the later ones. Adeline hadn't been in much since returning from her honeymoon, but maybe she could spare a couple of hours.

A shadow moved on the glass, the front door swished open, and Matt stepped in. He wore jeans, a black T-shirt, and a light jacket, much the same as what he wore every day, now that he didn't have other jobs to dress for, but he looked different. Stronger, better.

He offered Chris a ready smile.

The first day of the audition must've gone well. A longing to hear about it, to celebrate the win with him, stirred in her chest. Unfulfilled, the desire prowled like a wounded animal looking for shelter.

As Matt and Chris began their handshake, the pressure built to somehow connect with Matt. She longed to be close to him, to hear the latest about Nadia, to update him with the one tiny piece of news Dad had given her, that Shane's ticket had been round trip. He'd had a way back home two days after the wedding. Unfortunately, Dad hadn't seen him in New York since, so he couldn't say whether he'd left.

At the end of the handshake, Matt shrugged out of his coat and followed Chris to their usual room. As he shut the door behind them, he smiled absently.

She'd known he'd move on from a breakup more easily than she would, but the gap seemed so wide. Why couldn't she will herself past this? Why did she feel so lost and alone?

The moisture in her eyes betrayed her will to retain composure. She jolted up from her desk. She didn't dare look straight at Matt, but his worn tennies paused in the middle of turning from the door.

She clenched her jaw, prayed her face wasn't red, and trained her eyes on the end of the hall as if this trip to the bathroom had nothing to do with him, as if all was right in her world.

She shut herself in to the small, dim space and braced her hands on either side of the porcelain sink. The face staring back from the mirror couldn't have fooled anyone, eyes a desperate pink, bottom lip trembling, cheeks ashen.

Matt had his reasons for breaking things off between them, but she missed him. And though she knew he had issues of his own, insidious thoughts taunted her, saying perhaps if she'd said and done the right things, he wouldn't have cut her out of his life.

By WEDNESDAY, Matt was dying to break the silence with Lina. She'd focused on her computer, students, or business calls any time he'd been in the office, a little furrow between her brows, mouth a joyless line. He rarely saw her banter with the other teachers. Superior Dogs, the local food truck, had probably experienced an uptick in business because Lina hadn't brought in food for the Key of Hope staff all week.

Since cooking comforted her and she was clearly upset, her choice to forgo the hobby worried him most.

Had he upset her this much? Or had something happened with her family?

But how could he help when he was barely keeping up with his responsibilities as it was? Awestruck—jamming with the guys and working on his own to ensure he was *ready* to jam with the guys—had packed all the time he'd freed up by quitting some of his jobs.

In the middle of his last lesson, Tim entered the waiting area. Lina gathered her purse, phone, and jacket and headed out with the manager.

Matt's student played a riff of wrong notes.

Right. He was here to do a job—for another week or two at least.

Earlier that day, Gannon had asked how quickly Lina could find a replacement for him.

Trying to read the deeper meaning—to make sure he understood correctly—Matt hadn't answered.

Tim had filled the gap. "Next week."

Gannon had clapped Matt's shoulder. "Welcome back to Awestruck."

In. He was in with Awestruck.

He'd expected to feel like he had a new lease on life.

And maybe for the two-minute phone call where he quit the janitorial job, it had.

But the high had faded quickly, leaving him feeling like he was half-way across a rotting rope bridge. He hadn't had the heart to take another step along the path by breaking the news to Lina.

By the time he finished his lesson and made his notes, Tim had followed Lina home and circled back. Matt buckled himself into the passenger seat and tipped his head against the rest as the manager pulled into traffic, headed for the condo.

If Tim had expected a lighter mood from him, given the day's developments, he didn't comment. Instead, the quiet in the vehicle stretched. No radio.

Come to think of it, Tim's mood ought to have improved with Matt's offer from Awestruck too. Instead, Tim's knuckles jutted up, his grip on the wheel tight.

He must've sensed Matt's attention on him, because he drew a breath. "I found them. Nadia's been married six years. They live in Texas with two kids, a four-year-old girl who's theirs together, and one kid she brought with her into the relationship. An eight-year-old son. His name is Axel."

25

*L*ina smirked as she typed a reply to one of Awestruck's diehard fans. The band might have a lot of those, but a few had been around long enough and commenting often so Lina knew them pretty well. She'd even met several in person, and bantering with them online was proving to be the highlight of her week so far—a sad fact for a Thursday evening.

"Can you arrange a sub for my lessons tomorrow and Monday?"

Lina startled at Matt's voice. He had ended their relationship over a week ago, and he'd stuck by the decision so doggedly, he hadn't chatted with her about how the audition went on Monday, much less whether he was still in the running for the role of bassist. Was the request related to the band? And why hadn't he approached her during his teaching shift? He'd left Key of Hope just an hour ago. When she'd heard the door, she'd assumed it was one of the other teachers.

But there he stood on the opposite side of her desk, thumbs hooked in the back pockets of his jeans, expression drawn as though he worried she wouldn't grant his request.

They did ask their teachers to plan further in advance, but

giving Matt a hard time would force interaction neither of them wanted. "I'll see if one of the others can cover for you." She clicked on the scheduling app and watched it load, mostly to stay occupied. Adeline had stopped by the office yesterday and had actually seemed a little disappointed not much required her attention. She might not mind picking up a couple of shifts.

Matt's shape, beyond her screen, didn't budge.

This whole week, he had looked happy and confident. Now ...

Now he was looking down at her, the picture of handsome concern.

She dropped her focus to the panther tattoo. Tendons played in his forearm, and her fingers could practically feel the texture of his skin. She diverted her focus to her computer screen. "If I can't find someone, we can reschedule your lessons. I'll let you know."

The attempt to dismiss him failed.

He, his tattoos, blue eyes, and toned arms remained in the walkway on the other side of her desk. "Any news with Shane? Or an apology from your dad?"

She could talk for ages about the nothing that had happened since he'd ended things. But this polite inquiry he thought he owed her didn't mean he missed her the way she missed him.

She gave what she hoped was the appropriate response—a shake of her head.

"I heard you called off Tim."

She'd texted the manager that morning, canceling the escort home. He and Matt must've been together. Or did they talk about her? Hope flared that he cared enough to do so. "Dad did pay for Shane's return ticket home. Presumably, he went. It's been a couple weeks since the wedding, over a week since that supposed sighting. If Shane was going to show up, he would've by now. Besides, driving to and from work isn't the only time I'm alone."

She was alone almost all the time, even here.

I don't see a future between us, he'd said.

She'd pictured having a family with him, but the vision hadn't included solutions to logistical issues. What would their professional lives have looked like long-term? They both could've kept working at Key of Hope and for Awestruck, her as social media manager, him as a songwriter. They'd have spent their free time on each other and whatever hobbies or pursuits interested them. She would've enjoyed it all, but would any of that have satisfied a thrill-seeker like Matt?

Probably not.

She ought to get back out there. Find not only a good guy, but the *right* one. The one God had for her.

Hopefully God *did* have one for her. If not, He'd have a lot of work to do on her heart to teach her to be content.

"You know I want things to work out for you." The low timbre of Matt's voice flooded her with longing.

It wasn't fair that her affection waited at his beck and call, as though a little notice amounted to the love she craved. She crossed her arms on the desk. "In what way?"

His brow knit. "I want you to be happy."

"I am." She paused to steady her voice. "I'm very happy."

He nodded slowly. "So the honesty thing is off now."

Her conscience pricked. Even if they didn't have a future, she wanted the best relationship possible with him. She wanted to ask how he was doing. But her interest in him was too intense to be healthy. Whatever friendship he offered would never fulfill her ache for more.

"We don't have a future." She cleared her throat, her composure draining like sand from an hourglass. "Right? But we do work together. You asked for time off. It's short notice, but I'll work it out."

He swallowed visibly. Nodded. Flinched.

She caught herself chewing her lip, realized he could see the movement, and stopped. But fidgeting had been one of the few things standing between her and tears. She knotted her fingers together.

His eyes narrowed with concentration. Maybe his skin was a little pale. The scab on his temple hadn't disappeared yet. "I need the time off to go talk to Nadia. She and her son live in Texas."

The words cracked her defenses in half. A son.

"Are you okay?"

He laughed ruefully. "Not by a long shot. But I'm sober and trusting God's going to be enough, whatever's in store in Texas."

He spoke of his faith so naturally and quickly. She could do so much better at trusting God in her own circumstances. "That's good. I'm glad to hear it. I mean, not the part about not being okay, but sober and with faith ..."

Matt nodded as he backed away from her desk. He paused at the mouth of the hallway, as though on the verge of choosing to stay. Instead, he left.

"WANT TO DETOUR THROUGH THE DEALERSHIP?" Tim drummed his fingers on the wheel. "We've got a couple minutes before we have to be on the road."

At least one of them was looking on the bright side of Matt's return to Awestruck. His role had been finalized with a contract and a check and everything. Gannon, John, and Philip were meeting them for dinner to celebrate. With some time to spare before Philip could make it over from his home in Mariner, Tim had brought Matt to Key of Hope so he could quit and transition fully into his new role.

Little did Tim know Matt hadn't put in his notice. He hadn't even told Lina the band had signed him.

He'd meant to do both.

Matt studied the back entrance of Key of Hope. Despite the fresh paint and the new sign over the door, it was just another old downtown building. One that had come to mean a lot to him, mostly thanks to Lina.

Because of her, he always looked forward to his shifts. Working together eased the pain of their severed connection ... or did it only keep the pain fresh?

Signing with Awestruck meant the time had come to walk away. The longer he waited, the more likely that Tim, the guys, and even Lina would press about why he was attached to a job he didn't need.

He could blame the kids without being completely dishonest.

Chris was blitzing through the material twice as fast as Matt's other students and had already started his own band. Never mind that they'd probably never made it through a full song—and if they had, it must've been an ear-splitting racket. Chris had enough passion to take him places someday, and Matt didn't want to give up his spot on the sidelines as the boy came into his own.

After his trip to Texas, he'd broach the subject of Key of Hope with Gannon and John. If the guys really couldn't spare him a few hours a week, he'd quit, but he suspected they'd respect a decision to finish out a commitment by seeing the semester through.

"So. Dealership?"

"Not today." Matt rubbed his face. Before he spent the check on a car, he needed to clear his debts. "Maybe after I pay back my parents."

"Maybe?"

Matt nodded. Splurges on himself would depend on how

things went this weekend. In fact, whether Nadia accepted money from him or not, the trip underscored why having the check wasn't as much of a relief as it would've been just weeks before. He might be on the verge of clearing the books with his parents, but he was nine years behind with Nadia and Axel in ways money wouldn't solve.

Tim shifted into gear, and Key of Hope slid from view as the vehicle turned for the street. "You could call first. Or get lawyers involved, make sure the kid's actually yours before you go down there."

"It's not a topic I want to introduce over the phone."

"Things could get messy. She'll hear you're back in Awestruck, might figure you have money again."

Which would be true. "She'll hear whether I go or not. If he's mine, I want to contribute." Financially and otherwise.

"It's my job to look out for your best interests, something you haven't been doing for yourself lately. If I'd been at that accident scene, things would've played out differently."

"Then you know why I didn't call you." Instead, Matt had walked back to the condo. His fingers tightened around the armrest. "Is that the problem? I'm taking Krissy with me to Texas instead of you?"

"I'm not some jealous ex-girlfriend."

Matt snorted. "Kinda acting like one."

"Let me ask you this. Did you want to bring your sister?"

Yes and no. She'd pointed out he could use the support on such an emotional trip, leaving her underlying concern—that he'd relapse—unspoken. "She made some good points. It's not smart to isolate myself." As much as he might want to.

"She talked you into it."

Matt didn't reply because he saw where Tim was going. If Krissy could talk him into something, Nadia could. And unlike his sister, Nadia might not be motivated by his best interests.

"You let a guy get away with punching you."

He could claim he'd been out to follow the Bible's command to turn the other cheek, but his decision to not press charges hadn't been noble. He deserved a good knock upside the head. He didn't deserve Lina or the massive check in his account.

Tim parked at the restaurant, and they met up with John in the lot. Inside, a giggling hostess showed them to a corner booth where Gannon and Philip had already been seated. Perhaps the waitstaff was equally flustered, because a manager waited on them instead of one of the normal servers. A guy at a nearby table shamelessly recorded them on his phone.

Had it always been like this with Awestruck?

He remembered crowds at shows, hotels, and events during his first stint with the band. He'd been recognized plenty of times, but he didn't remember the nonstop buzz. He'd been too full of himself to look around and see how their presence affected everyone.

He tried to enjoy the steak while allowing the others to carry the conversation. The guy who pointed his phone toward them would get nothing but footage of them eating, swapping stories, and joking with the manager who served them.

What kind of footage had people gotten of Matt before he'd gotten sober? Attempting to get through to him, Krissy and Tim had occasionally shown him clips of him making a server cry. Stumbling to his car. Getting in a bar fight. Worse.

He was a new man now. Supposedly, he could do better, but instead of feeling calm assurance, only the weight of responsibility registered.

His every action would either please or disappoint masses of people.

Maybe he'd signed the contract too soon.

Maybe he needed longer to get himself together for this.

Maybe he'd never arrive.

Too recently, he'd been the guy with the old car broken

EMILY CONRAD

down in the middle of the road, falling through on the simplest commitments.

"This is probably unprofessional." The hostess materialized at the end of the booth, clutching a napkin. "But could I get your autographs?"

"Sure." Gannon pushed his plate forward, opening up a few inches of space. "You've got a pen?"

She handed over the napkin and produced a pen from her pocket. Gannon signed, then John, who sat next to him. The hostess collected the napkin and pen and offered them to Philip, opposite the other two.

Philip lifted his hands. "If you're looking for Awestruck, it's him you want." He hiked his thumb toward Matt.

She blinked, uncertain, but extended the napkin and pen to Matt.

He hesitated, the tip of the ballpoint hovering beneath Gannon and John's familiar signatures. As soon as he did this, there would be evidence that he'd rejoined the band.

He should've given Lina a heads up, because in the small community of Lakeshore, word would spread like wildfire. Then, it would reach news outlets and beat him to Texas too.

But he'd signed the contract and deposited the check.

Ready or not, he was part of this now.

26

*T*exas wasn't all cacti and longhorns. In Nadia's neighborhood, trees provided shade for layers of landscaping. The houses boasted signs of wealth like balconies, columns, and tall windows. The address Tim had procured led Matt to a cinnamon-colored one-and-a-half story home with a massive pair of planters flanking the front walk. A shiny SUV waited in the circle drive.

Matt could've spared himself one more surprise—a mild one, but still—by looking up the address before he'd come. He'd had ample time yesterday, at the airport, but he'd also been a ball of nerves. He'd forgotten to take a water bottle out of his backpack before the security screening. The officers had picked him out of the line for a pat-down, and he suspected the reason wasn't his tattoos.

"She's done well for herself." Krissy waited a beat, then the oval of her face turned his direction in his peripheral vision.

As if fifteen seconds after parking here he'd be ready to jump into the riptide by walking up to the front door and ringing the bell. But to Krissy, maybe this seemed like a slow build up.

They'd arrived yesterday, a couple of hours before dinner. Krissy had asked if he wanted to go right away. He'd said he'd rather try on Saturday morning, so here they were.

"It's not too late to call first."

True, but he'd come all this way on the belief it would be best to ask about the pregnancy in person. To see the look on her face, to read from her body language truths she might not voice.

And if Axel was his ...

Light and shadows slid across the front door. At first, he thought it was the power of his imagination or wind in tree branches causing the illusion of movement, but a young girl ran out, followed by a woman. Nadia had curves she hadn't had before. Her hair, twisted and clipped up, appeared darker. The girl disappeared on the far side of the SUV. Nadia called back into the house.

A fist grabbed Matt's stomach and twisted.

She was talking to someone, either her husband or her son. Maybe both.

"Breathe." Krissy swept a hand up and down like an orchestra conductor counting off a single beat.

He inhaled.

"You could go talk to her."

His fingers found his seatbelt buckle, but before he clicked it, a boy joined her on the front walk. The skinny scrap of a kid had brown hair darker than Matt's, the same color as Nadia's. He held a basketball under his arm and ran to the side of the SUV closer to the street.

"He's got your energy."

The boy tugged the back door of the vehicle open with one arm, but in the process dropped the ball. He left the door ajar as he ran after it. When he retrieved his prize from the landscaping, he lifted the ball over his head and grinned.

Krissy gasped. "And your smile. Wow. Does Jade look that much like me? That's uncanny."

His smile? Really? It had been a long time since he'd grinned so freely.

The boy turned his back and scrambled into the SUV. The door shut, and window tinting hid him from view.

"You've got to talk to her."

Nadia must've finished securing her daughter, because she came around to the driver's side. Her face was still recognizable, but this life? Completely different from what they'd shared. She had permanence and maturity, a family, responsibilities. She'd grown up.

And Matt was supposed to walk up as if he had a right to infringe on what she'd built for herself and her children?

She got behind the wheel of her new, reliable SUV, and the vehicle advanced down the drive. It would take a lot more than a pothole to derail that family.

"Matt?"

He shook his head. She'd succeeded without him. She'd succeeded *because* she was without him. If they'd stayed together, he couldn't imagine all he would've put her through. Tim had spared her years of torment.

"Another time." He made the vow only because he knew he couldn't back out. Not after coming all this way, bringing Krissy along. "She's got the kids with her."

STILL BLINKING sleep from her eyes, Lina checked her phone first thing Saturday morning. Notifications crammed her screen. What in the world ...?

She'd watched a few episodes of a baking show last night, then had attempted to recreate one of the recipes featured in the competition. The misadventure had left her tired and frustrated. She hadn't even turned on her bedroom lights as she'd found her way to bed, but she had checked her phone. Bad habit.

Or not, since sometimes her vigilance meant she discovered posts that could prove problematic for Awestruck before they had the chance to go viral.

Pictures of the guys at dinner Thursday had prompted a low-level buzz as fans guessed whether Matt would replace Philip, but even as of last night, that conversation had been limited to comments on the photos. Lina had let it be. Despite the rift between her and Matt, as a team member, she'd be among the first to know when the band made an official decision.

So what had caused this tsunami of activity?

She pulled her other arm from under the covers to steady the phone as she tapped on the first notification.

A post on one of Awestruck's fan pages opened, some fan asking about Matt's return to Awestruck.

Matt's return to Awestruck? She squinted and scrolled to the next post and then the next. What had fed rumors compelling enough to prompt all of this?

She tapped back into her notifications, looking for the alerts she'd set years ago to notify her of online mentions of Awestruck.

One article after another shared news of an Awestruck press release.

Matt had officially rejoined? How could he have dared to question her honesty while sitting on a secret like this?

Someone on the Awestruck team must've gotten trigger-happy, sending out the announcement before notifying staff who would need to respond as comments came flooding in.

She came to a quote from Gannon and swiped a hand across her forehead, pushing her curls away from her face so she could read more clearly.

"We didn't want to lose Philip, but how can you fault a guy for wanting to focus on his family? In his absence, there's no better way to serve our fans than to bring back someone who knows Awestruck and has the talent to keep us moving in the right direction. Matt's done the hard work to become the best version of himself, and we're excited to start a new chapter with him."

The best version of himself.

Was Matt the best he'd ever been?

Sobriety counted for something. For a lot.

And as left-out as she felt at learning the news this way, he'd trusted her with his whereabouts this weekend, which didn't seem to be in any of the articles.

She groaned.

His personal life wasn't any of her business, but as long as they both worked for Awestruck, she'd get to curate posts about him. Today, that would mean replying to the deluge of fans interested in his return to the band.

She tossed her phone, and it plunked onto the comforter at the foot of the bed. She dragged herself to her feet and plodded to the bathroom. Bottles, cosmetics, and brushes cluttered the vanity.

She'd have to straighten up today. After brushing her teeth, she started with the easiest task by slipping the ring she'd worn yesterday from the dish by the sink. With the tip of her index finger hooked through the gold, she padded back into her bedroom.

The jewelry box she'd inherited from Grandma waited on her dresser.

Open.

Her lungs froze. She lifted the lid daily to retrieve a ring, but she rarely touched the drawers where she kept her own meager collection of necklaces, earrings, and bracelets, gifts from her parents and Shane, mostly. The last time she'd slid one open had been a couple of weeks ago, to store the extra jewelry she'd worn to Gannon's wedding, since she hadn't been to the safety deposit box yet.

Now, several of the drawers were tipped open, and one lay stacked on top of Grandpa's stamp book on the dresser, a gaping black hole where it fit into the box. The sapphire of the ring she'd worn yesterday bit into her breastbone. She'd lifted her hand without realizing it until the pain registered.

She jammed the ring in place on her finger as she rushed across the room. The drawer, which had glittered with precious cargo last time she'd opened it, now displayed only blue velvet. Despite the disarray, not one stray stud or necklace charm lay on the dresser. Nothing glinted from the creamy carpet.

Her hands raced across the fuzzy velvet, verifying what her eyes told her. Yesterday, she'd selected the blue sapphire from among a dozen others stored in the top section. Today, her fingers bumped over empty slots.

She tipped open one drawer, then another.

The bracelets, the earrings, and most importantly, the rings —all missing. Her stomach pitched.

Someone had broken in.

Someone had been in her bedroom.

Fear clutched at the nape of her neck, dug into her stomach, and crawled up the backs of her knees like spiders. She locked her arms across herself so tightly her ribs ached when she breathed. All was still and quiet, but ...

She dared turn only her head toward the closed closet door.

An intruder could lurk anywhere. Could she safely bolt to her car?

She refolded her arms, and the sapphire ring scraped the skin inside her forearm as she again walked herself through the events of the day prior.

She'd taken a ring from the jewelry box yesterday morning. The next time she'd been back to her bedroom had been late, after learning the hard way why the reality show contestants had struggled to master crème brûlée. She'd turned on the lights in the bathroom, where she'd gotten ready for bed and removed the ring. Then, she'd flipped the switch and found her way to bed in the dark.

The disturbed jewelry box could've escaped her notice. Which meant the break-in could've occurred yesterday, while she'd been at work. If so, the culprit was long gone—as were Grandma's rings.

And the other jewelry, but the rings ...

Her phone pierced the quiet, and she yelped in surprise. She lunged to grab it, as if the sound would alert the thief to her presence. But he—she?—would already know Lina was here. She'd been sleeping only minutes before.

If he'd wanted to hurt her, he'd had the chance.

Not the world's most comforting thought, but her hands steadied enough to turn the phone so she could read the screen. The notification had come from social media. Another post about Matt, probably.

She clamped her teeth on her lip.

Matt. She wanted to talk to Matt.

Foolish, since she'd told him she'd call the police before she called him in case of trouble with Shane.

Was this trouble with Shane?

She tried to imagine her ex pulling open the dainty drawers, dumping the contents into a bag. Small and valuable, the jewelry made sense to take if he was desperate for money.

Although, she may have more losses yet to discover.

But to resort to theft, Shane would have to have been desperate.

Her feet didn't want to budge from the spot they'd warmed in the carpet. She'd been safe right here so far, and moving seemed like a risk. From right where she stood, she called the police.

~

MATT LIFTED his focus from his menu at the noise Krissy made. Food had lost its appeal, but Krissy deserved lunch, and coming here bought him another hour before he'd have to crash into Nadia's life.

His sister tapped her menu. "When I suggested we try authentic Mexican, I didn't expect"—she leaned closer and switched to a whisper—"to find tripe on the menu."

Tripe? Matt scanned his choices again. The dish names and descriptions were written in Spanish, followed by an English translation. He'd taken four years of Spanish in high school— and had learned what tripe was at some point—but he'd fried a lot of brain cells since then, and whatever he had left, distraction had dumbed him down so he couldn't read either language.

"Lamb head?" Krissy cringed and flipped a page. "Grasshoppers with avocado." She laughed. "We're not in Kansas anymore. I had no idea how true it is when people say Mexican food up by us is nothing like the real thing. Or do you think they put this stuff on here for the shock value?"

Matt forced himself to decode the words in front of him. She'd been excited to come here. Normally, he'd embrace the experience, making her glad she'd suggested an adventure. "Tortilla soup or enchiladas look pretty safe."

"Enchiladas. I can do that. What are you getting?"

Enchiladas sounded good to him too, but he picked two other items. "It's between the grilled brain tacos or the beef feet tostadas."

Krissy's chin jerked, and she checked the menu as if she didn't believe the items were listed. She must've found them because she looked up again, mouth gaping. "You're kidding?"

His phone vibrated in his pocket. He put the menu at the

end of the table. "I guess you'll find out when the server gets here."

She groaned, but when she took a sip of water, she seemed to be hiding a smile.

He freed the device and answered Tim's call.

"How'd it go?"

"I haven't talked to her yet."

"Okay. When you do, be careful. Whatever she says, tell her you'll think about it. Don't agree to anything you're going to regret later."

They'd been over this plenty of times. "We're trying to have lunch here."

"Fine. If you don't want to talk to me, you probably also don't care that someone broke into Lina's place."

"What?" Matt rose and smacked his hip on the table. The ice in their glasses rattled, but nothing tipped. He started for the airlock by the front door. "Is she okay?"

"Shaken. She's not sure when it happened, if she was in the house or not. Her doorbell cams cover the front and back doors, but if the jewelry's worth as much as she said, she should've had a nicer system."

How could Tim focus on the heirlooms when Lina's safety had been jeopardized? Someone had been in her house, and an image of Shane looming over her while she slept injected him with adrenaline that had no outlet. Suppressing a growl, he yanked open the interior door and stepped into the glass alcove that led outside. "Did she tell the police about Shane?"

"Yeah. They're going to find out if he's in the area. If not, she has more problems than she knew. Either way, they say odds of recovering the pieces are poor."

Lina must be devastated. The rings meant a lot more to her than their weight in gold. She wore them all the time, but—with the exception of the wedding, when she'd gone to more trouble—

she didn't walk around glittering in jewels. Other than Shane, who might've known to raid her house? A parent from Key of Hope? Or one of their teenage students? It'd take an expert eye—or a nosy inquiry—to know the gems were real, not costume pieces.

"How did they get in?"

"Broke the laundry room window. It's on the side of the house, and the cameras are only on the front and back doors. No window sensors, which seems like a pretty big oversight."

"She would've heard a window break." Which meant she hadn't been there at the time.

"Who knows. She overlooked something. If it happened before she got home, she didn't notice the jewelry box was emptied until the next morning. Adeline swooped in and insisted she stay at her and Gannon's place until a new system can be installed."

At least Gannon and Adeline had security, but tension coursed through Matt. He was literally a thousand miles away. Helpless.

"Even with a better system, if Shane's around, she shouldn't be alone."

"Good luck. It was hard enough to scare her into taking Adeline's offer in the first place, but you can try to talk sense into her when you get back."

"She won't listen to me." Matt rubbed his neck. "We're not on good terms."

Tim stayed silent for a beat. "I imagine the thief wanted some quick cash and a fast getaway, so they're probably not hanging around, looking to cause more trouble."

An unspoken apology lurked in Tim's unusually kind tone. The manager must've guessed the news of Nadia's baby had something to do with Matt and Lina's falling out.

Tim cleared his throat. "Anyway, don't get bogged down in Texas."

If he had been looking for a way to motivate Matt to get

back to Wisconsin, he'd chosen the right button to push. They ended the call, and Matt fidgeted with the phone.

At the table, Krissy spoke to the waiter, but Matt couldn't go back in there yet. Not while he knew Lina was in trouble.

He pulled up her contact information and called. Voicemail picked up on the third ring. "Hey. I heard about the break in. I'm sorry they got your grandma's jewelry. I hope they left the stamp book alone, and maybe your grandpa's ring was somewhere else? In any case, I'm sorry." He'd said that already. He pushed ahead. "You can always call me. I still care."

As if that'd do any good when he wasn't even in the area. Even once he returned to Lakeshore, he couldn't string her along when he knew they couldn't work out.

He started back for the table. Krissy smirked as she handed the waiter their menus. She must've ordered for him, and who knew what she'd picked? Brains, probably, since he seemed a little short on those lately.

27

To think that Lina had felt awkward about visiting Adeline and Gannon for coffee, and now they were putting her up in one of their guest rooms. She parked in the drive and peered up at the house. She'd lost Grandma's rings, and now no one trusted her to even look after herself.

And why should they?

Shane's true nature had eluded her. Even after learning of the gambling, she hadn't predicted his controlling tendencies or his penchant for violence.

The security system she'd chosen wasn't nearly what it should've been—what she might've chosen if she'd foreseen the possibility of a jewelry theft.

Had it been Shane? Or someone else?

If her ex were the culprit, at least that would mean she hadn't overlooked some other enemy.

The front door opened, and Adeline waved hello from the step. Lina lifted her purse and Grandpa's stamp book from the passenger seat to head inside. The theft had exponentially increased the book's value to her—it and the only ring from Grandma she had left would live wherever she did.

With the book clutched to her chest and Gannon's and Adeline's friendly greetings to reassure her, she popped the trunk.

Gannon lifted Lina's suitcase from inside and didn't even bother acknowledging her offer to carry it herself as he motioned her toward the house.

Adeline held the front door as Lina stepped into the foyer. "I thought you'd like the first-floor guest room." Adeline passed through the kitchen, and Lina and Gannon followed. "It has its own bathroom and TV, and it is right by the kitchen."

Adeline opened the first door on the left, then stepped back to allow Lina into the room first.

The color palette of white and cream lent a clean, cozy feel. The teal lake and autumn trees out the window added color, and a window seat offered a plush spot from which to enjoy the view. As promised, a private bathroom was through a door off to the right. A bed, dresser, and armchair filled out the space.

Though comfortable, the room wouldn't be home.

Home.

The word conjured mixed feelings, a longing for safety that wouldn't be fulfilled here or in a house that had been recently violated. She hugged the stamp book closer.

"I'm sure it's been a long day." Adeline slid her arm around Gannon, who'd left the suitcase inside the room. "Don't feel like you have to hang out with us, but you're welcome to, of course."

"Hopefully this will only be for a day or two." She ran a hand over the stamp book, then placed it on the dresser, choosing to relinquish the fear that would have her clutching the keepsake forever. "I'll go back when the new system is in."

Uncertainty tinged Adeline's expression, and she shot a glance up at her husband, but he gave Lina a smile. "Until then, our house is your house."

The couple left, their voices fading as they moved away.

Lina sank to a seat on the edge of the bed and checked her phone. The phone gave a short vibration at her touch, signaling she'd missed something. A new voicemail notification topped the other updates.

In a few taps, Matt's name appeared. Someone had told him about the break in? Or he simply needed something related to Key of Hope? Oh, or Awestruck.

Regardless, she didn't have the energy for it. All her brain wanted to do was rehash the burglary. The thief had entered through the laundry room and had only stolen jewelry from Lina's bedroom. Their route would've taken them past electronics, which the police seemed to think would normally have been snatched before the intruder checked the jewelry box.

Who would target the jewelry exclusively?

She could narrow the suspect list to people who fell into one of three camps.

One, someone who wanted the jewelry for himself. Two, someone who wanted the money and knew how to unload jewelry more easily than other stolen merchandise. Or three, someone who understood the collection had special significance to Lina and wanted to hurt her.

Shane ticked more of those boxes than anyone else.

MATT DRUMMED his fingers on the laminate tabletop. Maybe he should've found a church service to attend instead of meeting with Nadia first thing on Sunday, but he wouldn't have internalized a thing he'd heard from the pulpit with this hanging over his head.

The old diner harkened back to the nineties with faded mauve and teal décor. Morning sunshine streamed through the generous windows to highlight the other patrons, mostly his parents' age or older. A round of laughter rose from his left as a waitress—also his mom's age—delivered a steaming plate of French toast to the table on his right.

Normally, the butter and maple syrup wafting on the air would tempt him, but he hadn't come for the food.

"What can I get ya, hon?" The waitress pulled an order pad from her apron pocket.

Nadia used to order pancakes with fresh strawberries and whipped cream every chance she got. But he wouldn't presume to order for her when she likely wouldn't feel any more like eating than he did.

"A glass of water"—for Nadia—"and a coffee, for now."

"One cup or a carafe?"

He didn't want to get anything wrong today. Nadia had enjoyed coffee, but only the milky, sweet kind. She'd used up all the sugar packets in his hotel room on more than one occasion. A dish on the table brimmed with packets of sugar and alternatives, and another dish held creamer.

"A carafe and two mugs, please. I'm waiting for someone."

"Comin' up." She stuffed the order pad in her pocket and started for the counter.

Another table waved, and she greeted them by name.

Seemed like everyone here was a regular but him.

Regular. Had he ever been a normal person?

He rubbed his thumb over the letters on the back of his fingers, as if he could erase the word *hate* in time for Nadia's arrival.

"Matt." The smoky tones of Nadia's voice cut through time, instantly familiar.

He dropped his hands beneath the table.

She stood at the end of the booth, a large beige purse over her shoulder. She wore her hair down today, and loosely rolled waves hovered just above her shoulders. Her face had changed in ways he couldn't quite put his finger on. Still her, yet different.

She shifted from one foot to the other. "I was surprised to hear from you. You're in town for something?"

"To talk to you." He motioned to the seat across from him.

"Excuse me, hon." The waitress dipped in with a water, the carafe of coffee, and two mugs. "You need a menu?"

"No, thanks. Coffee's fine." Nadia licked her lips and scooted into the booth.

"Holler if you need anything." The waitress disappeared again.

Nadia poured herself coffee, selected one of the natural sugar packets, and dumped in the contents. "What can I do for you?"

How could she remain calm and cool while facing the prospect that Axel's father was about to interfere in their lives? Maybe the boy wasn't his. Krissy could've been wrong about the boy's smile. He hadn't seen a strong resemblance himself.

"You look good." She looked him up and down, as far as the table allowed. "Rehab's going to stick this time?"

She'd been following news about him. He ought to pour himself coffee too—or maybe claim the water, since she didn't seem interested—but doing either would mean using his shaking hands. "I've been sober over a year now. How are you?"

"I went and found a normal life for myself. Seemed like the best thing I could do at the time, but I am sorry about not saying goodbye."

"I'm sorry about a lot of things too."

Her brown eyes held with his for a long moment, then she sipped her coffee.

"Since getting clean, I've been trying to rebuild my life. Making amends with people. That meant reaching out to Awestruck, which meant talking to Tim."

Her chin lifted, and her fingertips turned as white as the mug she held.

"A couple of weeks ago, he told me why you left. That was first I'd heard of it. It took a while to find you."

She pursed her lips in a frown and turned her head toward the center of the dining room, glaring as if her worst enemy had walked in.

"Axel ..." But he couldn't finish the thought.

She refocused on him, venom in her eyes.

"Is he my son?"

"He has a father. A good one."

The protectiveness only clarified what she'd clearly hoped to blur. "But biologically, he is my son."

"I don't regret the choices I made where he's concerned."

Matt willed her to say more, unequivocally confirming the news that had thrown him into such chaos.

Nadia's throat pulsed. "Zach's been in his life since he was a year old, loving him like a father should. Axel's happy, believing that's exactly who Zach is—his father. I can't have you upsetting him when in every practical sense, it's the truth."

Maybe in the moment, but practicalities would change if Axel ever needed a blood relative or his family's complete medical history. Besides ...

"I had ..." He stopped. Tried again. "I had a right to know."

She dipped her head and braced her arms on the seat, as if staying calm required all of her energy. "We were both young and making bad decisions back then."

The admission that she'd made a mistake took him by surprise, and the arguments he'd been brainstorming died.

She parted her tense lips. "But years have passed, and what might've been right in the moment back then isn't the right thing now. The circumstance has changed."

The waitress passed, balancing a tray crowded with entrees.

Matt had hoped to learn the truth about Axel from Nadia. Beyond that, he hadn't known what to expect. Perhaps he'd hoped she'd make demands of him. She'd ask for money or make a comment about him being a deadbeat who didn't want to see his son. Either would've been an opening for him to get involved.

But Nadia gave very little. Almost as though, what she most hoped for was ...

"He's not supposed to know about me, and I'm supposed to pretend I don't know about him. Is that it?"

A slight lift in her eyebrows confirmed.

Only then, as his hopes tumbled into a canyon, did he know he couldn't live with that. He should've reacted differently when Lina had tried to brainstorm this situation with him. What would she advise?

She might've argued for his right, as a father, to be in his son's life.

But what kind of father had he been to date? Did that kind of father have rights?

The canyon deepened into an abyss.

"He has a good life."

And, in her opinion, Matt's involvement would make that less true.

"There must be some way ... something I can do."

"The role of father is already filled. Don't take that away from him."

Shouldn't coming forward only ensure that the role of father was even more meaningfully fulfilled? Where Axel had only had one father figure before, now he had another person he could count on.

But who did Matt think he was, dreaming of becoming a father figure? He was in his thirties, and what could he say for himself? That he played in a band?

What a joke.

"Could you introduce me to him? Say I'm an old friend if you have to, but let me meet him."

Her eyes didn't soften.

"At least that. Please."

"I don't trust you. You'd say something to upset him. And how would I explain when he happens to see you on the news? I saw it already myself. You're back in Awestruck. He's a bright kid, and you're recognizable."

"I'll wear long sleeves. Gloves. Whatever it takes."

"No good would come of your meeting. You don't understand."

"Explain, then."

She shook her head, a tiny movement as if chiding herself. "If you waited to look us up until you felt like you had something to show for yourself, getting clean? Great idea. But rejoining the band? You want me to believe you're going to stay sober when you're invited back into that lifestyle?"

"It's been a year. I found God. I have accountability. Awestruck is a good job—"

"Good? Fame and money have never been *good* for you." Nadia slid to the end of the booth, pulling her purse behind her. She rose, paused to study him with worried eyes. "Axel has been loved every day of his life. He's never missed out on a single thing."

Except Matt. But maybe that hadn't been missing out at all.

"I'm not going to upset his whole life just so he can watch you crash and burn." Nadia studied him, daring him to disagree with her prediction.

Could he? He'd failed so many times.

With a nod, Nadia turned and left.

28

---

ina felt like a bobblehead doll teetering on the edge of a cliff as she nodded at her boss's instructions on Monday morning. She'd accessed Awestruck's brand management team meeting from the quiet of Key of Hope, where the first lesson wouldn't occur until after school. Normally, she enjoyed the interaction with the far-flung Awestruck team, but this time, conversation had centered around Matt.

He'd said they didn't have a future, and her already-off-kilter heart would fall—and not in a good, lovesick way—if she had to listen to him repeat the rejection. She'd hoped to avoid him.

"We need to get posts up as soon as possible." Though it was impossible to tell which person Kim looked at as she spoke, social media posts were Lina's responsibility.

She nodded again. Because the press release and photos of the guys' celebratory dinner were circulating, the band's accounts needed to reflect the new addition as well.

"The photographer will shadow them next week, so we'll have a nice library to pull from after that. In the meantime,

Lina, can you stop by the studio and take a few to start with?"

Her neck ached as she nodded again. Hanging out in the studio and writing posts to celebrate his return to the band sounded about as safe for her emotional wellbeing as swimming in Lake Superior during a windstorm, when twenty-five-foot waves could crash down on her.

But it had to be done.

Stuck at Gannon and Adeline's until the special-order cameras and sensors could be installed at her house—tomorrow, thank goodness—Lina couldn't very well object to a detour down the hall to get the photos.

Kim tapped a pen to her lips as she looked down, presumably reading notes. "While you're at it, his personal account could use your help."

A fake smile stretched Lina's lips. She helped Gannon and John, so it was only fair she'd assist Matt. Hopefully, no one would mention to him that she basically maintained John's online presence for him.

When the meeting wound down, she signed off and scrolled through the list of to-do's relating to Matt. Topics for him to post about shouldn't be hard to brainstorm. Sobriety, music, and ... tractor stunts?

Okay, the plan would need more work. And, unfortunately, a conversation with Matt.

She sighed. Outside the windows, Main Street resembled an idyllic painting. An antique truck was parked along the curb. A pair of old farmers greeted each other near the door of the café across the street. Some tourists strolled by, in the area for the small shops, apple orchards, and fall color.

When she'd moved to Lakeshore, even the doorbell cameras had seemed like overkill. Now, even after the home security company finished installing gadgets at her house, she wasn't sure she'd feel safe.

Shane hadn't been home or at the office when police tried to find him. The promise to keep looking didn't comfort. If he'd been the intruder, had he gotten what he wanted? If someone else had broken in, what was to stop another random act in the future? The cameras and sensors would only alert authorities to the problem—not protect her from an intruder or recover property they got away with.

Whoever was behind it, the theft had robbed her of her favorite reminder of Grandma and slashed the already-tattered remnants of her feelings of safety.

At the thought of safety, she recalled Matt's message.

I still care.

Warmth flushed her skin at the memory of his earnest tone, but if he cared the way she wanted him to, he would've been able to envision a future for them. He would've worked to make that future their reality.

She was on her own.

Her phone sounded, pulling her out of her reverie.

Dad was calling. Maybe he'd finally heard from Shane. She picked up, but instead of offering information, he greeted her with a question. "When were you planning to tell us you lost my mother's jewelry?"

Lina straightened her fingers to study the remaining ring. "It was stolen, not lost."

"Gone, either way, isn't it? I imagine odds of recovery aren't good. Melt it down, sell it off, and who's the wiser?"

She massaged her forehead. The police had listed each stolen piece in a database searchable by law enforcement and jewelers, but Dad was correct about the low odds of recovery. Insurance would cover replacing the items, including the rings, but they wouldn't be the same ones that had graced Grandma's hands for decades. "How did you hear about it?"

"It's in the paper."

"Which paper?" She'd known news of the theft had spread

locally. In hopes of someone recognizing the pieces, she'd granted permission for news outlets to share the photos she had of the jewelry from their insurance appraisal. An isolated incident involving a private, unsecured collection wouldn't have interested a national station or major paper.

"*The Lakeshore Happenings*." He named the local paper with mocking emphasis. "Think as little of me as you'd like, but I'm still your father, and I'm still concerned with how you're managing."

He might be concerned, but only because he wanted The Captain's Vista. How did scouring the papers help with that goal? "Reading the paper on the chance they'd include something about me isn't logical."

"You work for celebrities. You've done numerous interviews for that charity of yours. Imagine my surprise to see pictures of your grandmother's jewelry. Why weren't the pieces in a safe?"

Perhaps they should've been. She did have one, but she hadn't expected anyone to break in. "I wear the rings, and I had the necklace, bracelet, and hair clip out of the safety deposit box because of the wedding."

Dad *tsked*. "Well, I'm glad this happened with something insignificant so you could learn from it."

Insignificant? The man was heartless. "Learn what?"

"You aren't a bad person, Lina, but you are naïve and unprepared for the challenges of managing wealth. You can correct your grandmother's mistake. Let me manage everything. I'll even train you, and when you come back into it someday, you'll have a better idea of how to safeguard the family legacy."

Wow. He'd escalated a long way from wanting her to part with The Captain's Vista. Grandma had left her millions. Was he only leveraging the situation to convince her of her unworthiness, or had he orchestrated it? Her face flashed hot, then cold. She never would've suspected him of such devastating manipulation, but he'd sent Shane here. Could she put anything past him?

"Do you know where Shane is?"

If the question seemed off-topic, he didn't show his surprise. "I do not, and the police have asked me as well. I haven't seen him since he left for Wisconsin, but he was due back weeks ago. I'll remind you, he's a businessman, not a common thief."

Shane had already stolen from her once. And Dad? At best, he hadn't believed her about Shane's true nature. At worst, Dad had arranged Shane's trip, the scene at the wedding, and the theft as a means to his own ends. "And what are you doing, calling on such an awful day to manipulate me into thinking even less of myself than I already do?"

"If Shane *is* a gambler and *did* spend such a chunk of your money without your permission—without your knowledge, even—then the jewelry's disappearance isn't the first indication that you're not fit to manage the family's wealth."

A towering sense of failure overshadowed her anger. She should've seen through Shane sooner. Perhaps she also should have predicted or prevented the theft. What calamity might befall her next?

She felt as blind to danger now as she'd been as a child, on vacation with Grandma and Grandpa when a cave tour guide had extinguished the lights for a few seconds.

Jesus, please light the way.

The darkness around her didn't suddenly turn to light, but one step did present itself.

She might not foresee most threats, but she could do her best to ensure whatever pain befell her, it didn't come through her father. "Goodbye, Dad."

She hung up. Whatever her father's involvement with this scheme, the police would have to sort it out.

MATT LIFTED Krissy's carry-on into the overhead bin before shedding his backpack and stuffing it in next. The meekness of Krissy's smile of thanks served as another reminder of how awfully this trip had gone. Leaving Texas wouldn't erase what had happened here.

She took the window seat, and he dropped into the one next to her as a long line of passengers filed past, headed for coach.

Krissy wordlessly straightened her legs and wiggled her feet, then began exploring the options to recline the seat, the place to plug in earphones and a charger, the pocket with information about the flight. Watching her enjoy first-class gave him one thing to feel good about.

Or not.

Why hadn't he treated her to fun trips when he'd had money the first time around? Because he had blown his funds on destroying himself. And now, Nadia thought he'd do the same thing all over again.

Krissy stilled, and when he looked over, her eyes tracked with the passing travelers.

Matt had been avoiding eye contact with them, but he risked it now to see what interested his sister. The curious glances seemed to flit over the other first-class passengers and linger on Matt. No one whispered. No one pointed him out to friends or family, the way they might if they'd recognized him and cared about Awestruck. They just stared, probably wondering how a guy like him could afford the upgrade.

Krissy's shoulder pressed his as she leaned close. "It's not too late if you want to make a break for it. I'd be right behind you."

His surprise forced a chuckle, but he shook his head. Nadia had asked him to stay away from Axel. He couldn't stand to remain close and honor her wish, so the sooner he left, the better.

Unfortunately, returning home meant facing other challenges. Could he manage Awestruck better this time? Could he in any way come through for Lina?

Or was he doomed to keep stacking up debts until the day he died?

"I suspect there's something going on in that head of yours that I'd vehemently disagree with."

"Nadia thinks the band's a bad idea for me." He left the name Awestruck out of it, in case of eavesdroppers.

"What would she know?"

Matt gave her a sidelong look. "You said the same thing."

"I'm your sister."

"Is it less true when it comes from someone else?"

"I speak the truth in love. If you're retreating like this, whatever she said wasn't loving."

"She was thinking of her son. I'd rather have her act loving toward him than toward me."

"She could've let you meet him."

Matt hadn't told her he'd begged for the opportunity. He studied his hands and the tattoos that had been part of her reason for refusing. The other part, the band. He'd worked, hoped, and prayed to get back in. But he hadn't known that getting back in would cost the chance to meet his son. The price was steep, and what if Nadia was right, and the band would be part of his undoing?

"I was shocked the first time you joined them." Krissy had dropped her voice. "I didn't know you liked music that much. Up until then, you'd only dabbled. I figured it was more about the adventure than the music."

It had been, at first. Music had won him over though.

"I think it suited you. You got a lot out of being chosen at a time when you were feeling lost. Remember how much you didn't want to go to college? Of course, running off to California didn't seem like a good career move, but I figured when the band fell apart, you'd come back and apply yourself to school."

"Really? School?" Didn't she know him better than that?

"You do know most bands don't make it." She laughed. "I didn't start to worry about more than your career options until you mentioned Nadia."

"I told you about her?"

"In passing. I called you, but you were late to meet her and couldn't talk. You were rushed and cagey, and for the first time, I realized how much the choices you were making would impact the rest of your life. Like, from then on, it wasn't just a skip year between high school and college. With a wife or a kid to consider when you came back, you wouldn't be able to dedicate yourself to the same things. At least, not as easily. Then she was gone again, but you got cagier than ever, and I realized having a wife or a kid would've been worlds easier than some of the other stuff you could get into."

He hung his head. Last time had gone so badly. Would his life turn out better if he backed out of Awestruck now?

"But colleges have party scenes, too, and who's to say you wouldn't have gone down a similar path, regardless?"

"There's an encouraging thought."

"Your path is your path, Matt, and God knew every step of the way before you took one of them. You're stubborn as all get out. My theory is, you needed to know how much you needed Him. He let you pick a path that would get through that thick skull of yours."

"Great." Stubbornness, a thick skull, and a painful path he'd brought on himself.

Sounded about right. Discouraging, but right.

What trouble would his thick skull bring on him next?

"But He *did* get through to you. And Gannon and John didn't succumb to the same things you did. So is Awestruck an inherently bad choice? I'm your sister and I worry, but objectively, I can't blame the band. I do think you're going to have to stay vigilant and connected, but that's true no matter what. At least all of you are older and wiser now than you were."

"You think it'll be okay?"

"I'm choosing to believe it will be."

Not exactly glowing with confidence then.

The stream of passengers had ended, and a flight attendant appeared. She doled out a lemon-lime soda for Krissy and a water for Matt. Instead of drinking, he rotated the glass on his tray, his touch displacing bubbles trapped by ice cubes. They rose to the surface and disappeared into the air.

God might've intended him to do the same—rise to sobriety, then disappear into anonymity.

Krissy asked, "You ever wonder why Jade wasn't afraid of you?"

"Huh?"

"At Christmas, when you washed up at Mom and Dad's, a couple of months sober and still looking pretty rough. You stepped in the house like the prodigal son fresh from the pig pen, complete with the unhappy older brother, but Jade warmed up to you in minutes."

He shrugged. "She's not shy."

"She's not, but she doesn't sit on strangers' laps, curl up, and fall asleep either."

Matt hadn't known what to do when Jade had climbed into the armchair with him. The whole morning had been awkward—stilted conversation, gifts for him when he'd brought none, well-deserved annoyance radiating from Pete. He'd expected someone to throw a fit about Jade snuggling up to him, but Mom had smiled, and Krissy had mimed that he ought to put an arm around the girl's shoulders. Until then, he hadn't realized he'd lifted his hands away as if she carried the plague. In minutes, she'd been asleep, her head on his shoulder.

"I had pictures of you around the house. She asked about you, and I said you were my brother, but you were sick. And ..." Were those tears shimmering in Krissy's eyes? "And she asked if it was like her brother. Because, of course, she never met him, either."

Jade was an only child. As Krissy struggled to maintain composure, a sense of failure rang in Matt's ears as loudly as a jet engine. He'd heard something about her having a miscarriage, but he'd forgotten. He'd been embroiled in his own problems and couldn't recall how far along she'd been. Another failure.

Krissy dabbed her eye with the knuckle of her index finger. "I said yes, you were sick a little like her brother—to an adult, I know, the circumstances were completely different, but it was life or death. And that much, Jade could understand. So I said, yes, you were that sick, but God could still save you. So, she prayed for you every night at bedtime. When you showed up at Mom and Dad's, you weren't a stranger. You were an answer to prayer. And that's why she treated you the way she did."

Matt palmed his eyes. They were dry, but if he kept thinking about everything he'd put his family through and everything he'd missed, they wouldn't stay that way.

Krissy sniffled. "But anyway, I have a point." With concentrated effort, she blinked and forced a cheerful expression that wasn't fooling anyone. "Nadia knows Axel, and I don't. She is doing the best she can for her son, and I respect you for honoring her wishes. But I don't want you taking that situation as a representation of what you deserve on a larger scale. You may not know your son, but you are worth knowing. That's why I told Jade about you. As long as you stick close to God, I don't think you're going to relapse, but even if you do, you'll still be worth it all."

"I'm not going to relapse." Not if he remembered the stakes. Replacing the dump truck would be a nice gesture, but it would only be the start. He owed Jade an uncle, Pete and Krissy a brother, Mom and Dad a son. He owed them reliability and concern and company and relief.

But even the idea of stepping into the roles he'd failed seemed like too little, too late.

He'd never be able to repay his debts to his family, and certainly not those he owed Nadia and Axel.

29

*L*ina smoothed her sweater, her damp palm clinging to the fabric. If only she could avoid going to the studio for the photos. Unfortunately, Matt was back today.

The best way to welcome a new member to Awestruck was probably to have a shot that included all three of the guys. John and Matt might not be able to manage that in a selfie. Gannon probably could, but the band paying her to maintain a strong online presence deserved better. That left Tim, who had no eye for composition.

Lina must take the photographs herself. She rested her hand on the cover of Grandpa's stamp book. On her ring finger, the blue sapphire from Grandma winked, as if to say she could handle whatever the day threw at her.

She'd snap a couple of shots—enough to get her through until the pro's photos were at her disposal—and then work the rest of the day from Key of Hope. Perhaps the home security installer would call her away to show her how to operate her new system around the time of Matt's lessons so she could avoid him.

She pulled up the camera app on her phone, brainstorming

shots. Videos performed well. If they were practicing an old song, she'd go that route. If it was off the new album, which hadn't dropped yet, however, she'd have to stick with images.

Unless she wanted to hang around, make requests, maybe ask interview-like questions.

She sent up a prayer that Awestruck would be playing something shareable, then let herself into the control room. Tim sat at the soundboard, watching the band work through the window that looked into the main studio. He wore headphones, but speakers also piped the sound into the room. Lina hadn't heard the song before, so the piece must've been off the new album.

She dropped into the office chair beside Tim's. "Hi."

He spared her a fleeting glance of greeting, then refocused on the band. Must not have heard her, and no wonder. This wasn't one of Awestruck's quieter offerings.

By listening, she never would've guessed the three musicians beyond the glass hadn't played together in years. Though the song was new, Gannon's voice and Awestruck's sound made it feel welcoming.

She couldn't blame Matt's movement for the way her eyes tracked to him, because Gannon was equally animated. Also in constant motion, John sat behind the kit, the drumsticks occasionally sweeping within an inch of his ears. Perhaps Matt's white T-shirt drew her attention? The excuse didn't hold, because the studio was well-lit with light-colored walls and floor. The white didn't stand out.

But what did stand out? Matt's fit shoulders. The way his five o'clock shadow shaded his jaw. His confidence.

Gannon belted out the lyrics with enough force that a vein stood out on his neck. "I sow seeds bought off the street, reaping whirlwinds ripe with defeat. I came up wanting."

The mix of ideas, a Bible verse and something else, lent a dream-like quality to the lyrics.

Matt moved closer to his own mic, and they sang the next part together. "A better shot. A better life. A better high."

In sync, they stepped back from the mics, fingers flying across the strings to create the driven and angry music, though if the lyrics were any indication, the speaker's anger was directed mostly inward.

Lina found herself nodding to the beat, waiting for the signature turn-around most Awestruck songs had—some indication of hope.

Gannon returned to the mic. "Dropped in the grave, left for dead, gasping for air with lungs of lead. The wind goes where it pleases, reaping the lost, defying defeat."

Matt joined him again. "Another shot, a different life, You're the lasting high."

The lyrics came quickly, some syllables more implied than sung to fit the rhythm, yet Matt matched Gannon on each word, as if they'd sung this together a hundred times. She hadn't given him enough credit during his first run with Awestruck. He must've had talent, or he never would've been able to keep up as well as he had. Now sober, he was a force.

The result of the three men working together in the studio created an immersive experience, tugging her emotions along, drowning out most of the thoughts she'd come in here carrying.

Only when they finished and she found Matt's eyes on her did her desire to flee resurface. She should've tried to take pictures through the glass to avoid directly interacting with the man who owned a far larger share of her heart than she ought to have entrusted to anyone.

"Good, right?" Tim pushed the headphones back until they settled around his neck.

Lina rose and tested how her phone's camera did with the glass, but her reflection showed in the shot. She'd have to head in. "He's a quick study."

"Their history's helping." Tim clipped his sentence, seeming to listen to the discussion occurring on the other side of the glass regarding adjustments, piped into the control room through the same speakers that had carried the song moments ago. "Otherwise, they'd never be so in sync."

Gannon played a few notes. Matt nodded along and joined in. Abruptly, they stopped, and Gannon resumed talking.

Tim half-turned toward her, still distracted by the happenings in the studio. "Plus, Matt better know this one. He wrote it."

He had?

No wonder Tim had maintained such faith in Matt.

"You're not really planning to make him finish out two weeks, are you?"

"Huh?"

"At Key of Hope. He said he has to cut out so he can teach lessons this afternoon."

Beyond the glass, Matt spoke, gesturing with one hand while the other steadied his bass.

Lina replayed their conversation last Thursday. "He only asked for the weekend off."

Tim's chin dropped. "He was supposed to put in his notice."

"Oh." If he quit, Key of Hope would become even more of an escape from him, so why the disappointment? She chided herself. Of course this had to happen. He'd leave on tour in January. "I can try and hire someone. Maybe by next week?"

They did have all those applicants Tim had hidden from her when they'd first posted the bass instructor position. But was this how things would be now? Would she get her news about Matt through Tim, like she'd heard about Philip's resignation?

Actually, even that was wishful thinking. The only reason she'd seen Tim often this summer was because he'd helped launch Key of Hope. With the non-profit running and no longer part of his scheme to promote Matt, she'd only see him at times like this—when she was needed for Awestruck. In January, Tim and Awestruck would leave Lakeshore for the next tour, and she'd go months without seeing any of them in person.

She'd instead get updates through department meetings, press releases, and tabloids. She'd better take advantage of Tim's insider information while she could. "How did his trip go?"

He sighed heavily, finally rolling back from the soundboard. "He's not happy how it turned out, but at least he didn't sign away all his income."

"The boy is his son?"

"That seems to be the consensus. I still think a paternity test wouldn't be the worst idea in the world, but he's focused on how he didn't get to meet the kid. I reached out to N—"

"Earth to Tim." Gannon's voice broadcasted through the speakers.

Tim snapped back to attention as Gannon asked him to play back an earlier run of the song.

As Tim streamed the clip into the studio, Lina gave up on learning more about Matt and his trip. He was just another band member now, and his personal life was none of her business. She'd come to do a job, and she needed to complete that and then move on to her other responsibilities. She let herself into the main sound stage.

Gannon acknowledged her with a nod, John by raising a drumstick. Matt's short-lived smile seemed to ask if she really needed to be there. Yet, none of them voiced any questions about what had brought her.

She took candid photos of them talking. The next time their discussion led them to replay a couple of bars, she snapped more pictures, then showed herself out through the control room, where Tim promised to come find her to escort her to Key of Hope in a few minutes.

As she waited, she crafted the Awestruck post. Not her best work, but when it came to Matt, all she could think about was that he had seemed to be falling apart when he'd ended things with her. Such a short time later, he seemed solid, despite whatever had or hadn't happened in Texas. He'd said he needed to cut his losses, and perhaps he was better off without her.

She was glad for him. And honestly, a little envious, because since the jewelry theft, she didn't know how to stop her life's crazy spiral.

She could wash her hands of responsibility by signing the estate over to Dad. Awestruck and Key of Hope combined would provide a comfortable life. In the personal sphere, she could get by with a few loose friendships, quietly supporting others without allowing them close enough to hurt her or put her in a position to disappoint them. At least, not too badly.

Grandma had essentially done the same.

If only such safety didn't sound so bleak.

MATT WANTED to get to Key of Hope, but he knew better than to walk in blind. When rehearsal ended, he paused in the car he'd rented to pull up Awestruck on social media.

As soon as Lina had appeared in the studio, he'd longed to stop practice to ask about her jewelry, the progress of the security system, Shane, and her dad, and to share the little that had happened with Nadia and Axel. If she'd given him the slightest invitation, he would've.

As far as he'd seen, she'd barely even looked directly at him, except, perhaps, through the lens of her phone's camera.

Did the pictures capture his expression, revealing he'd been dying to set aside the bass and talk to her?

She'd posted a few images. First up, one of him looking down and smiling. The picture must've been snapped the moment after Gannon called one of his suggestions brilliant. The other photos showed them talking and playing. If she'd taken any while Matt had been peering her direction, she'd kept them to herself.

The caption beneath the gallery of images was short.

Like old times. Only better.

Did she believe that, or was the positive spin for the fans' sake?

He skimmed comments. People were excited to have him back. Said the next tour would be the best in ages, and Lina's replies, all from Awestruck's account, played up the hype.

But her true feelings? Those, he guessed, didn't skew positively. Down in Texas, if Nadia was watching, she likely felt the same.

What a fraud he was. Matt tossed his phone on the passenger seat and spotted Tim headed toward him, motioning him to roll down his window.

When the manager reached him, he braced his hands on the open sill. "I meant to ask. You didn't buy this, did you?"

Matt shook his head. He'd rented the sedan at the airport. It would get him by until he had the mental capacity to make a purchase.

"Good. It's ugly as all get-out."

Not uglier than a certain brown monstrosity that was probably in a scrap heap by now, but he knew Tim wanted more for him than a run-of-the-mill sedan. And finally, the reason why he had been dedicated to seeing him succeed clicked. "All this time, it was guilt, wasn't it?"

"Huh?"

"The reason you tried to keep peace between me and Gannon last time I was in the band. The reason you championed me this summer when I wanted to give them 'Whirlwinds.' The reason you found a job for me and tried to launch me as a songwriter. It was all to ease your conscience about Nadia and Axel."

Tim lifted a shoulder, averting his eyes. "Your point?"

"Did it work? Feel better?"

"I don't know why you're after me about this. You're the one putting your fortune toward a dump truck to right some old wrongs."

It wouldn't be his whole fortune, but since Awestruck had paid more than required for a used truck, he'd set up a call with a commercial vehicle dealer to obtain a new one. If he moved quickly enough, he might have the truck before the commercial driver's license he'd acquired to work at the family business expired.

Delivering the truck to his father would be one of the best moments of his life. The thought of it alone almost coaxed him into laughter.

In contrast, Tim looked miserable.

"Once that's done, my debt will be paid. When are you going to stop feeling bad?"

"I've got something in the works."

"What?"

"You'll see." Tim crossed his arms. "Tell me. When's your last day at Key of Hope?"

Matt squirmed. He'd meant to talk to the guys today about extending his time at the non-profit.

Tim seemed to read his expression. "Don't worry. I talked to Lina for you today."

"Huh?"

"She said you hadn't put in your notice, so I did it for you. She'll have someone new hired next week."

So soon? "Is that really necessary?"

"It is the plan we discussed, and you've got a to-do list a mile long in your inbox. The sooner you start checking things off, the better." He turned away as he spoke, starting for his own rental.

Last time Matt worked for Awestruck, he'd never been emailed to-do lists. Had he? He'd operated on the assumption that if he put things off long enough, someone else would do them. It had worked well enough.

This time had to be different, but did he really have to sacrifice Key of Hope?

Perhaps. As much as he hated to leave Chris hanging, he'd bet Lina had used the last couple of hours to dig up a new instructor. And he'd bet she'd been happy to do it.

He drove to the nonprofit, half expecting to find her in the middle of interviewing his replacement. If not, he might convince her to put it off. Shifting his lessons ninety minutes later would put his last session around eight or eight thirty, but his older students—and hopefully their parents—might not mind. The change would prevent him from having to leave the studio early. As long as he was present when required and completed whatever checklists Awestruck threw at him, they couldn't complain about how he spent his off-hours.

Since changing the schedule at the non-profit involved more than his and his students' lesson times, convincing Lina would take negotiation skills to rival Tim's. Good thing there was no one he'd rather spend time winning over than her.

The plan failed on arrival, though, because he found her desk empty.

30

*L*ina stood in Gannon and Adeline's foyer, her suitcase at her side and a probably lethal man in front of her.

"We'll have someone on the road within two minutes." The head of Gannon and Adeline's security team was muscular, his face a study in serious lines. His posture and manner of carrying himself suggested a military background, and coming from him, the promise to send assistance if one of her home's new sensors went off meant something.

The home security technician had done as she'd hoped—finished the work on her house and called her away from Key of Hope in time to spare her from seeing Matt. He'd shown her the window and door sensors. When movement triggered one, an alert would go off on her phone. If she didn't clear the notification, law enforcement would call. If she didn't answer, they'd check on the property.

Satisfied, Lina had packed her bags to move back home. Adeline had intercepted her before she made it out the door and roped in Gannon's security team.

With Shane still on the loose, Lina didn't protest the added precaution, but she also didn't want to unnecessarily call in the cavalry. She intended to arm her system religiously—whether she was leaving the house for a few hours or tucked away inside. At some point, she would forget to turn it off before she opened a window or took the trash out. "What if there's a false alarm?"

"We'll call you on the way." He crossed his arms, biceps flexing.

"But what if her ex is in the house, forcing her to say what he wants?" This cheery thought came from Adeline.

The guard didn't miss a beat. "If you're not at liberty to talk, tell us it's all clear. Use that wording—all clear."

Lina adjusted the strap of her laptop case on her shoulder. "All clear."

Would Shane put her in the position to need a code word? He'd grabbed her arm a couple of times and fought with Matt, but he'd never done worse. If he had stolen the jewelry, he'd avoided confronting her.

And now she needed secret ways to ask for help? What was next? A safe room?

"He can follow you home," Adeline offered.

Lina forced a smile as she accepted.

"I'll meet you at the gate." The guard set off.

Even with the precaution, uncertain lines squiggled across Adeline's forehead. "You could wait until they locate Shane. He can't hide forever."

He had managed to hide for weeks already. She wouldn't impose on her friends that long. Besides ... "We don't even know it was Shane. Whoever broke in probably did it on Friday, when they had plenty of time to take whatever they wanted. And if they did miss something, the house was empty all weekend. No smart thief would wait until now, when there's a new system, to go back. Besides, the installer and I activated the system when we left, and not even a raccoon has stepped foot near the house so far."

Adeline quirked her lips. "I guess there isn't much else to do, huh?"

"We've taken all the precautions." Lina led the way outside.

Adeline quietly followed to the car and supervised as Lina packed up and pulled out.

True to his word, the guard waited in a black SUV by the gate, and he followed closely out to her house. While he waited in the driveway as Tim had so many times before, Lina pulled directly into the garage, shut the garage door, and entered the house, rolling her suitcase behind her. She deposited her purse on a hook by the door, her luggage in the bedroom, and her laptop case on the counter. Hands free, she armed the security system from her phone app.

Had the guard left, or was he waiting for some signal?

She parted the living room curtains and waved. A moment later, his vehicle backed onto the road. Lina turned to her refrigerator.

Food hadn't been on her mind when she'd left on Saturday, and the meat she'd meant to cook had passed its expiration date. She took a couple of raw chicken breasts from the freezer and started defrosting them in the microwave.

While the appliance hummed, she took her laptop bag to the living room and powered up her computer. She had tried to pick applicants to interview for the bass instructor position before she'd been rescued by the installation tech. As she'd reviewed the resumes they'd collected last time they'd posted the job, distrust had haunted her—distrust so strong it might have qualified as anxiety. Plenty of the applicants looked fine on paper, but what were these people really like?

They might interview well and turn into problematic employees. She'd also seen the opposite—poor interview skills in people who turned out to be excellent instructors. A half-hour conversation wasn't nearly enough time to judge a person.

But what choice did she have? Given the tight deadline, she

needed to get started.

As the list of candidates loaded on her screen, she grew cold and unsteady—dizzy almost.

Abandoning her laptop on the coffee table, she returned to the front windows and pushed back the curtains to allow the evening sun in. In mid-October, only the evergreens retained their color. The other trees seemed to scratch at the sky, like their bare limbs might've been responsible for shredding the thin cloud cover into the narrow rows that stretched overhead. At the horizon, the sun did its best to add cheer by slanting golden light across the grass, but the effect didn't temper her unease.

She could call references, but most applicants would only list people who would speak highly of them. Background checks might help, but considering neither Shane nor her father had formal records, no database could prevent her from hiring a controlling or deceitful person who might be a bad influence with the kids.

So many unknowns. So many untrustworthy people, and her, a sitting duck.

She ran her fingers through her curls, and her hair sprang against her palm, frizzier than a moment before. And that was why she usually resisted touching her hair.

Beyond the dining room to her left, a counter marked off the kitchen. On the far wall, the microwave continued counting down. From this distance, she couldn't read the shifting numbers, but the fact that it was still going meant she'd managed to work herself up in under six minutes. Maybe what she needed more than dinner was comfort.

Her Bible. She hadn't spent nearly enough time in it recently.

The microwave still whirring, she padded back to her bedroom.

She'd left the blackout blinds closed when she'd departed

on Saturday, and they continued to dim the room despite the daylight outside. She flipped the light switch, but one shadow didn't disappear.

She froze.

A man stood at her bed, her suitcase open before him.

Shane.

A shock of hair fell across his forehead as he leveled his gaze on her. He offered no quick smile, no excuses or explanations.

Her breath shuddered.

How could he be here? She'd heard no alarms.

All clear. That was the code. If he'd broken in, someone would call in a minute or two and ask if she was okay. And she'd say it was all clear. Would her pounding adrenaline erase the words from memory? *All clear.*

Her muscles shook. What had he come for? If she backed away, would he take the item and leave? She retreated a step, and her shoulder hit the doorframe.

"You'd better stay where I can see you. In fact,"—he motioned with his index finger—"toss your phone here."

He must've guessed—correctly—that she had the device in her back pocket.

Okay. She could surrender the phone. If she didn't answer the calls from Gannon's security or law enforcement, both would descend on the house shortly. Gannon's team first, she suspected. The guard wouldn't have made it all the way back to Lakeshore yet, and Shane was no match for him.

All clear. She rehearsed it again as she drew her phone from her pocket. As though only an observer, she saw her hand toss her cell onto the comforter, next to the suitcase. How odd that she could still control her body when she felt so disconnected, so locked away. *All clear.*

She wouldn't be able to use the code.

She crossed her arms, but the posture felt like cowering.

She tucked her hands in her pockets, but that left her too defenseless. She settled them behind her back, gripping the doorframe, calculating whether she could run, and where she might hide for the five or ten minutes it would take for the guard to return.

Even though I walk through the valley of the shadow of death, I will fear no evil.

The snatch of Psalm 23 carried like a warm breeze into her mind. Best to wait this out in place. She'd already seen him. She could give him what he wanted and send him on his way. "What are you looking for?"

"Hands." Shane lifted both of his, and she realized it was an order, not an answer.

She obeyed. He was paranoid if he thought she had a panic button behind her back, and that concerned her. Help should have already been on the way, but if he was unstable, what would happen when it arrived?

And what if ... what if something had gone wrong and help wasn't coming?

The possibility was too horrible to dwell on.

Gaze constantly flicking from her to her luggage, Shane resumed his search, tossing aside her jeans, her makeup bag, the pouch where she'd stowed her dirty clothes.

"Whatever it is, you'll find it faster with my help."

He flung aside her now-empty suitcase. "The stamp book."

Her last great reminder of Grandpa? "Why?" There was more to the question, but the words fizzled as he headed toward her.

She *did* stand at the exit. Maybe he wanted to leave.

But as he neared, his grim focus rested on her, not the hallway. "Where is the stamp book?"

"I don't know." She'd packed the keepsake in her luggage. Or so she'd thought. If the book had been there, Shane would have it. "I must've forgotten it. Why is it important?"

"Where is it?"

Had she placed the album in her car? No, she'd only carried her suitcase, purse, and laptop out of Gannon and Adeline's. He would not be happy to learn the stamps weren't on the premises, but she'd thought them in love once. He must have a soft spot for her.

"Shane." She touched his arm.

With force like a bear trap, he caught her hand. "Don't test me."

"You don't want stamps. You're mad at me. I get that. And you probably need money, right?" Given the amount he'd blown through in their joint account, he could go through it quickly. Maybe he'd fallen in debt with the wrong people, hence the jewelry theft. "The stamps aren't here, and they aren't worth it, anyway. I'll give you cash. How much do you need? Let me—"

"A million dollars."

"What?"

"That's how much the collection is worth."

"What?" She'd carried the leather-bound book from one room to another, one place to another, dozens of times. Cumulatively, she'd spent hours paging through it, always thinking more of Grandpa than the little squares in their tiny acrylic holders.

Howard's little stamp collection, Grandma had said.

When Lina had been through the estate, had the stamps been insured? She didn't think so. They certainly weren't insured now.

"You're mistaken. I'm sorry, but they're not worth all that. The collection is sentimental." Why hadn't her phone rung yet? Had it really been under two minutes since Shane had entered the house? "They're worth something to me, though. How about ten thousand dollars?"

"You have that here, sunshine?"

"No, but—"

"Where are the stamps?" Shane's grip on her wrist cinched tighter.

"They're not here."

The microwave beeped. How could only seven minutes have passed since she'd started it? Was help on the way? Would she be okay until it arrived?

Shane yanked her arm to send her stumbling ahead of him into the hall. "Liar. I saw them right next to the jewelry case."

"Why didn't you take them then?" If only he had, her return home would've been peaceful. Except she'd be missing another important memento of her grandparents.

"I thought about it. Even paged through. Then decided to be *nice*"—he said the word with a sneer—"and leave you with something from them." A doorknob rattled behind her, and Lina turned to see him scanning her linen closet. "You always made the book sound worthless." He shut the closet, and his glare sliced into her. "Imagine my surprise when I got curious after, found out they're worth a fortune, and came back just in time to see you leaving with them clutched to your chest. You knew their value all along."

"I didn't. I swear."

Jaw pulsing and mouth a menacing line, he prodded her to move.

She ran her hand along the wall to keep her balance while walking sideways and watching Shane. "Is my dad involved in this? If he told you how much the stamps are worth, he's using you to scare me."

"Your father is a tool of mine, not the other way around. Got it?" He shoved her arm, moving her along.

They reached the kitchen, Lina trying to sort conclusions. It didn't sound as though he cared about protecting—or helping —Dad, which meant Shane only wanted money, likely to feed his gambling habit, maybe pay off some debts to people even scarier than himself. But how could she use that information to get herself out of this?

Shane scanned the counters.

How long until help arrived? She should have heard her phone, but other than their voices and the microwave's occasional reminder beeps, the house remained silent. "How did you get in?"

He prowled onward, dragging her to the dining room. "You'd think a security company employee would be better trained."

"How so?"

"Left the front door unlocked while he was installing window sensors."

Shane had been in the house for hours? Breath left her like she'd been punched in the chest. She'd put all her faith in the security system. A system he'd been past long before she had hit the activation button.

No one was coming.

She had to get out of this on her own. "The stamps must be at Gannon and Adeline's. I can get them for you."

"As if I'm going to let you out of my sight. Sit." He barked the last command and shoved her toward the closest dining room chair.

She caught herself on the table. He stalked into the living room. As he went, he pulled a gun from the back of his waistband and lifted it toward her.

All sound muted. He had a gun, and it wouldn't take long to scan the living room and see the book wasn't there.

Exit through the main entrance waited fifteen feet and one deadbolt away. Oh, and the knob. She'd locked both when she'd left after the tour of the system earlier. Could she make it there, release the locks, and get out before Shane fired? Even from the couch, he'd only be a step away from having an angle on the exit.

He advanced farther into the living room, now circling the coffee table to look at the computer screen.

The patio door was beyond him, off the back of the living room, but a hallway behind the kitchen sheltered the door to the garage. If she ran, she'd have seconds before he could turn the corner after her. He bent to pick up her laptop case.

She bolted.

Three steps in, Shane shouted.

No gunshot.

She braced a hand on the corner as she passed the kitchen and flew into the hall.

In her panic, she turned the deadbolt, only to find she'd never secured it. Right. Putting her faith in the new system, she'd left the door between the garage and interior unlocked. She ripped the door open and spilled into the garage, praying that Gannon's guard would now be executing a U-turn to check on the triggered alarm.

She slammed the button to lift the overhead door, her car useless because she hadn't grabbed her keys on the way through. Even if she had, she wouldn't have had time to get behind the wheel and back out, because as she crouched on the far side of the vehicle, waiting for the door to lumber high enough for her to escape, its ascent jerked to a stop. The four-inch gap started to close.

Shane must've hit the button again. She stuck her foot out, and the sensor that kept the door from shutting on anything activated. Once again, the door lifted, revealing the autumn evening inch by inch.

If she could make it out, she'd bolt for her closest neighbor, the one across the street. If only both of their homes weren't set so far back from the road. Could she cover their stretching front lawns before Shane caught up? Before he fired a shot?

She glanced over her shoulder to see Shane closing in on her. She'd have to roll through the small opening. She flattened, but before she could slide under the door, he hooked her around the waist and heaved her up.

Her head banged the concrete—or the car?—and her vision went black. As it returned, she couldn't catch her breath. Shane's arm around her middle suppressed her air supply. With each step he carried her, pain jolted her like a punch to the gut.

She kicked, and her legs tangled with his. The band around her stomach released, and he dropped her. The concrete caught her with a smack, stealing the half-inhale she'd managed. She scrambled away, toward the light of the now-open garage door.

Miraculously, he didn't latch onto her leg. Didn't catch her foot.

"Help!" Were any neighbors close enough to hear?

Could they help?

She reached the garage door opening. She'd make for the road, weaving through the trees along the property line. Hopefully Gannon's security team would reach her before Shane caught up.

Shane grunted behind her, more distant than she expected. She tossed a glance back into the garage, then froze.

Shane wasn't alone. A second man scuffled with him on the floor of the garage. A man who, instead of wearing a polo like Gannon's security team would, wore a white T-shirt.

Shane crouched, on his way up. Still on the ground, Matt grabbed his ankle. Shaking off the hold left Shane stumbling.

Or had he bent close to the ground for another reason? He moved quickly as he spun back toward Matt, but Shane now gripped something in his hand.

"Matt, gun! He has a gun!"

31

*M*att found his footing and lifted his eyes.

Sure enough. Shane stood about eight feet from him, panting and holding a pistol in his right hand. He gripped it at chest height. Matt didn't have much experience with guns, but he'd heard accurate aim required lifting the weapon to eye level. A cold comfort. At this range, it'd be hard to miss.

The car offered the closest cover, but ducking behind it would mean moving farther from Lina, whose good sense must've fled without her. She remained at the mouth of the garage.

Matt stood his ground. He didn't want to die today, but he couldn't both hide and protect Lina. "Run!"

She blinked. Bit her lip. And then took a step the wrong direction, hands partially raised as if Shane were already aiming at her.

Matt would have to survive this, if only to talk sense into her.

Attempting to keep Shane's interest, Matt notched his hands higher. Drawing a breath to speak ignited pain in his ribs. Shane had to be hurting, too, since landing on the guy's arm when he'd tackled him had caused Matt's injury. "You don't want to do this. Just go. Free and clear."

"I need the money."

"What money?"

"From the stamp book. Do you know where it is?"

Matt shot a glance to Lina, who mouthed, *It's not here.*

Sweat beaded at Shane's temples. "I would've settled for the commission on the property, but no. Now I'm left with scraps."

"You already got the jewelry. That's more than scraps."

Shane's gaze shifted closer to Lina.

To retain his attention, Matt spoke faster, louder. "Whatever money you think you need won't do you any good if you're rotting in jail on a murder charge."

"You think jail's the worst thing that could happen to me?"

According to Lina, Shane had a gambling problem. An addiction. That would explain this—escalating consequences and yet Shane couldn't walk away.

Matt may not have held a gun to anyone, but he also hadn't been able to stop himself in the thick of addiction. Making amends for his own disastrous actions might take the rest of his life. And then some. "No, man, I don't think jail's the worst thing that could happen to you."

Shane's chest heaved.

"The worst thing is the regret." Matt swallowed. "The worst part is knowing no matter how I live from here on, I'm the guy who went that far off the rails, hurt everyone I've ever loved, lost control of myself. You know what you don't realize until it's too late? You can never make amends. Not the kind that will give your soul peace anyway."

Matt's own words stopped him. Since when had he been depending on amends to give his soul peace? Hadn't he known from the moment he stood over Auggie's body that he would never be enough, could never fix himself or his mistakes, could never save himself? Helpless, he'd turned his life over to God, yet somewhere in the twelve steps, he'd adopted a new plan to right his own wrongs by paying back his parents, by being the man Nadia and Axel and Awestruck and even Lina needed.

How foolish. How doomed. No wonder he hadn't been at peace.

"There is hope in Jesus." And nowhere else.

Shane sneered. "Save it."

Matt kept his hands lifted. "Then, if I were you, I wouldn't rack up any more debt. Put the gun down and get out of here before the cops show up."

Shane shot a panicked glance over his shoulder toward the road.

"You did know she had a new security system installed, right? If the abandoned car I passed on the way here is yours, you'd better get a move on." Reaching the field where the car had been left at the mouth of a tractor lane would take a couple of minutes.

Shane seemed to wrestle with his options, the gun lowering. If he lost focus, Matt might be able to take him by surprise. Then again, a close-quarter struggle with a gun wouldn't end well, and he didn't want to be on either end of it going off.

Shane turned, the weapon in his grasp.

Lina still hadn't moved.

Shane started toward her, and Matt sprinted to catch up. If he laid a hand on Lina—

But Shane broke into a run as he continued out the garage door and into the sunlight.

Matt reached her, grabbed her in a hug with one arm, and held her head to his shoulder, shielding it as he pivoted to put his body between her and Shane in case the man changed his mind and doubled back.

"Inside." Concern had roughened his voice, and his ribcage protested each movement with pulses of pain.

As she ducked toward the door, he checked over his shoulder. Shane had advanced halfway down the drive, still running.

Nothing in his hands. Had he holstered the gun or discarded it?

If Shane went free, what would prevent him from showing up again, perhaps when Matt wasn't around to help? But if Matt gave chase now, would Lina wait inside, or would she keep exposing herself to danger?

He hit the button to close the garage door behind them, then ushered Lina into the house.

WHY DID she feel like she was floating? Lina held one hand to her head and lifted the other to study it. Trembling. She ought to feel more.

Matt shut the door, and the lock snapped into place.

At least she had hearing.

He rubbed a spot on his side. An itch or an injury? He eyed the security panel. "I was bluffing. Is help actually coming?"

Bluffing? He hadn't flinched when he'd seen the gun. She'd assumed such nerves of steel were based on unshakeable belief in imminent rescue.

A notification did flash on the control panel. Her phone sounded in the other room. "Should be."

Although Matt himself had been helpful enough.

Dirt from the garage floor marred his T-shirt. A hand-sized red splotch circled his neck, and the first hint of rising bruises darkened his arms. His eyebrows pulled low as he studied her in return. "Are you hurt?"

"No. Are you?"

"What ... ?" He pointed to his head, and it took her a moment to realize he'd ignored her question in favor of focusing on her.

Now that he mentioned it, the hand she held to her head covered a throb. A lump filled the hollow of her palm, but when she lowered her hand, she found no blood on her fingers. Exhaustion threaded through her muscles. Her lungs stretched with a breath. The ache in her head gained a sharp edge. She shouldn't have been so quick to wish away the numbness. But she was still standing. Thinking. "I'm okay. You?"

"Fine." If he kept peering at her with such concern, she'd fall into his arms.

The phone, still singing away in the bedroom, gave her a reason to step the opposite direction. "I need to tell them what they're looking for. You saw his car?"

"Blue sedan parked by the field next door."

She went to the bedroom, answered the call from Gannon's security guard, and gave him a summary.

Only as she hung up did the words *all clear* materialize in her mind again.

"Are you sure you're okay?" Matt stood in the doorway. His brow furrowed as he moved closer, his step soft against the carpet. "Why didn't you run?"

Her pulse notched higher. "I didn't think he'd hurt me."

He blinked with shock. "That was stupid."

She nodded and clamped her palm to her stinging goose egg.

He lifted a hand toward her but came up short of touching her arm. Still, she felt the gravitational pull to fall against him increase.

"Are you sure you're not hurt?" Low with concern, his voice wasn't helping her stand on her own two feet.

"I think I hit my head."

"Here." With careful fingers, he nudged her hand aside and felt the lump. His eyebrows twitched closer, and he parted her hair to see the injury. Her scalp tingled as he settled her curls back into place. "Let's call 911."

She stiffened. Was she more injured than she knew? But there hadn't been blood. Only a lump. And he'd spoken matter-of-factly, not with urgency. She eyed his hand, now at his side, and wished she could grab it. "Police should already be on the way."

"They'll come quicker when they know." He pulled his phone from his pocket and dialed. "With a heads up, they'll have a better chance of catching Shane, and a lump that size needs attention."

"I'm sure you've hurt yourself far worse without seeing a doctor."

Given the running blood the day she'd gone to Visser Land-scaping to hire him, he might've needed stitches. And what would he have said if she'd tried to deliver him to a doctor after his fight with Shane at the wedding? For all they knew, his nose had been broken.

"I'm your role model now?"

No. He was nothing to her now and better for it, right? Well, he was a coworker. Nothing more.

"You didn't run either." In fact, he'd done the opposite. When he'd confronted Shane, he might not have known about the gun, but once he saw it, he hadn't sought cover. "Why?"

His lips parted, but instead of replying, he shook his head.

"What were you doing out here?"

"Besides saving your skin?" A hint of a smirk in his expres-sion reassured her like little else had. If he felt secure enough to tease her, maybe the worst was behind them.

In moments, he'd connected with an operator. As he talked, he made his way through the house, and she followed him to the front window. He was still on the line with the emergency operator when a black SUV pulled up and the guard she'd met earlier stepped onto the driveway.

"I'd better go meet him." She unlocked the door.

Matt waved for her to wait, then held the phone away from his mouth. "Stay in."

Oh. Shane hadn't been caught. She looked through the decorative glass at the blurry yard. Remaining in the house should've been a given. She didn't know a thing about keeping herself safe.

Pressure built in her throat and eyes. She willed herself to stay strong as she opened the door. By the time she finished relating what had happened, distant sirens whined. Minutes later, police and paramedics descended on the house.

Emergency personnel encircled her. She ended up in the back of an ambulance. The paramedic seemed concerned about her account of losing her vision when she'd hit her head.

"Did you lose consciousness?" The man was fifteen or twenty years older than herself, and the lines in his round face spoke of kindness and experience.

"Maybe? But not for long." She couldn't have missed more than a second of what happened in the garage.

The lines beside the paramedic's mouth deepened. "In these cases, we recommend a trip to the hospital."

"In the ambulance?" The gray walls surrounding her were full of compartments and equipment, but he'd only used the most basic of it on her when checking her vitals. "Is that really necessary? I can drive. Or a friend could."

"Complications might arise on the way, and if that happens, you'll want the best care possible."

Matt would never be so cautious as to take a ride when he felt fine, would he?

But he had been the one to call 911, and he wasn't nearby to consult now.

The way he'd avoided naming his reason for coming hinted something other than business had brought him to her house. He might've wanted to smooth over not telling her about Awestruck himself. Or, who knew? Perhaps he wanted to rekindle a relationship. But she'd seen how well he was doing without her. Meanwhile, disaster seemed to follow her. Especially in her love life, if Shane was any indication.

Right now, the paramedic seemed like the best judge of what she needed. Maybe all this time she'd been longing for the wrong thing—love—when what she really needed was the guidance of a disinterested stranger.

"Okay. You're the pro." She leaned back on the gurney and let the ambulance whisk her away.

32

*H*ostage situations sure had a way of upsetting plans.

Matt had gotten off work early thanks to Adeline. She'd come to Key of Hope and offered to cover his last two lessons so he could go check on Lina. Despite the security system and having sent a guard to see Lina home safely, Adeline had worried Shane might find a way to bother her.

Matt's reasons for taking Adeline's offer weren't so noble. He had suspected Shane had what he wanted—the jewelry—and would leave Lina alone, but he couldn't pass up a chance to take back what he'd said about not having a future with Lina.

Unfortunately, Adeline had turned out to be right, and his visit ended when he and Lina were each carted off to the hospital.

If he'd earned any points for saving her life, they must not have counted for much, because when he'd texted to ask how she was doing, she hadn't opened the door to connecting. Instead, she'd reported that she'd been given a clean bill of health and would be staying at Adeline's for the night.

Meanwhile, Tim had barged into Matt's room and hovered

while Matt had answered investigators' questions and awaited the results of his chest x-ray. After diagnosing him with a bruised rib, the doctor offered a prescription. Sudden twists or breaths caused stabbing pain, but Matt opted to make do with over-the-counter meds. With that, the doctor had released him.

Now, Tim was driving Matt back to Lina's to collect his car.

If only she'd be there so Matt could try his errand again.

"The morality agreement didn't cover nearly enough situations." Tim worked his fist around the steering wheel as he accelerated down the dark highway.

Matt bounced a fist against his knee. "What about today strikes you as immoral?"

"You could've died, and then where would we be?"

"*I'd* be in heaven." The sun had set before the ambulance had taken him from Lina's, and night had deepened while they'd been in the hospital. Above the shadowy countryside, stars glittered. "You'd probably be talking Philip into coming back."

"Seriously, Matt, for once in your life, act like a sane person who would mind dying."

"The gun wasn't even loaded." A fact the police had uncovered, confirming Lina's conviction that Shane never intended to shoot anyone. He had intended to flee the country, based on the passport the police found when they picked him up a few counties to the north.

For the hundredth time, he thanked God Shane had been apprehended.

Now, Matt's biggest regret was having severed his relationship with Lina in a moment of despair. A few days of despair, actually. He pressed careful fingers over the tender spot in his ribs. Convinced he had too many wrongs to right and was too likely to make more unfixable mistakes, he'd gone and made another misstep by cutting loose the one woman he wanted a relationship with.

Except their broken relationship wasn't unfixable. As the true righter of his wrongs, God could accomplish what Matt couldn't. A man learned a lot from staring down the barrel of a gun.

The dash lights cast a faint glow over Tim's scowl. "You didn't know about the gun until hours later. It's not okay for you to act like a man with a death wish. It's bad for business."

As if Tim hadn't spent the entire wait in the ER working on a press release because of the boost the publicity would give Awestruck. Business didn't worry Tim. He'd claimed a sane person would be afraid of death. Had the close call scared him?

"My belief in heaven makes not fearing death perfectly sane."

"You can't bank everything on a fairytale."

"It's not a fairytale. Look around. This complex world didn't just happen." He peered out again at the quiet night. At the innumerable stars. Tim wanted to call faith a fairytale? Wasn't Creation more unlikely than any storybook plot? "If you lived your whole life during the day, would you ever guess there were entire galaxies waiting beyond the blue sky? People with the right tools could tell you about stars, but would you believe in them?"

"Science is different. There's proof."

"You've seen proof of God too. You know I didn't have it in me to change. I am who I am today because of God. Gannon, John, and Philip would all tell you the same thing—they wouldn't be where they are without faith."

"People change and get morals without God."

"A commitment to self-improvement also points to a soul created by God, a soul desperate to attain the life it was made for."

Tim flipped on his blinker, as if by delivering Matt to his car, he could escape this conversation.

Lina's house waited, a pale blur at the end of the drive.

Though he'd known better, he hadn't entirely convinced himself he wouldn't see her here. Maybe she'd stopped by to pack a bag or something? But no lights glinted in the windows. So much the better. Tim deserved his focus.

"It's kind of crazy to think you've watched all four of us— Gannon, John, Philip, and me—but no matter how many times a redemption story plays out right in front of you, you keep denying the evidence that it's true. God is real, and He wants a relationship with you."

Tim braked, bringing the vehicle to an abrupt stop inches from Matt's bumper. "If God is real, I've been nothing but trouble for Him."

"Same. But He hasn't given up on either of us."

Tim hit the button to unlock the doors and motioned Matt out.

Matt didn't move. "You saw the stars today, and I'm betting it wasn't the first time."

Tim rubbed his eyes, then shifted into reverse. The movement lacked commitment.

"What if next time's the last time?" Matt asked. "I know you've got some kind of plans to make yourself feel better about Nadia and who knows what else, but none of it will make you innocent before a holy God. Set your pride aside. Let Him make things right for you."

"Let Him? Like it's some kind of gift?"

"The *best* kind. He created you for a purpose, Tim. Is it so unbelievable He'd want you to live it out? He's your father. Would you want Issy wasting her life?"

"No."

No? No flippant arguments or orders to get out of the car?

Matt's pulse quickened. "You've been looking out for me. Let me return the favor. Let's pray together. I'll introduce you to Jesus."

Tim pressed his lips together, still for a moment before his chin lifted. And lowered. And again.

He was nodding. Agreeing. Finally, after all these years, ready.

~

LINA FELL ASLEEP AROUND two a.m. only to wake moments later when her head hit the concrete. The flashback felt so real, her stomach hardened against the imaginary arm that banded around her middle.

She sat up in bed, panting, eyes on a desperate hunt for light.

She found the clock on the bedside stand, the numbers blue instead of the white of her own bedroom clock. With a breath that was supposed to be calming, she shifted her focus toward the windows. A whisper of moonlight fell on the sill.

She rubbed her hand over the ache in her gut.

After all she had gone through with Shane in those minutes between discovering him in her bedroom and finding herself free in the garage, why hadn't she run?

When Matt had asked earlier, she'd cited her conviction that Shane wouldn't hurt her. Yet moments before she'd discovered Shane, she'd been drowning in distrust. She hadn't trusted Shane, her dad, or even her own judgment. And then, a few minutes later, she'd risked her life on it?

Matt was right. She'd been stupid to stay.

She was going to get herself killed one of these days.

Or blunder into some other foolish situation that shattered her heart again, lost more family heirlooms, or botched up her grandparents' legacy even more thoroughly than she had already.

Her lungs seemed to shrink, and her breath raced to provide enough air. She flipped on the bedside light and slid

Grandpa's stamp book from the nightstand, where she had indeed overlooked it when she'd packed up and left the Vaughns' house earlier. What a relief it had been to see it waiting for her, safe and sound, when she had returned.

She paged through it, running her fingers over the square edges of the acrylic holders that protected the valuables. She'd have to reach out to her insurance company to begin the process of having the collection appraised and, if Shane had been correct about its value, insured.

Focusing on the sensible course of action helped calm her. Or was it the tie to her grandparents?

What would they advise to cure this haunting anxiety?

Prayer, first and foremost. She let out a long exhale and closed her eyes. As she asked God for peace, an image of The Captain's Vista rose in her mind. The solid old house, the ocean view, and the solitude might shelter her.

She opened her eyes, and the picture evaporated, but the desire to go only grew.

Psalm 23 talked about God providing rest in green pastures and near quiet waters. The Captain's Vista had always been such a place for her. If she could find restoration anywhere, she'd find it there.

33

*W*hen Matt arrived at Gannon's, he checked his phone. Since he and Lina had texted a couple of times yesterday, he'd tried her this morning.

How are you feeling?

The message remained unanswered. Lina had probably had a late night, and he hoped she was resting. No Awestruck or Key of Hope tasks were important enough to deserve her attention the day after being held hostage in her own home.

Although, no one had bothered to check in with him to ensure he was up for work.

He was, mostly because Tim's sunny mood had rubbed off on him. Pain in his ribs and unfinished business with Lina had kept him awake on and off, but he didn't want to miss Gannon's and John's reactions when the manager shared about the decision he'd made last night. Especially not when the alternative was to sit alone and replay the events of the day before.

He entered the passcode on the pad by the Vaughns' door and let himself inside, as he'd been instructed to do when he'd rejoined the band. Movement to his right signaled someone's approach, and his hopes rose. Perhaps Lina had been waiting for him?

Instead, Adeline offered a sympathetic smile. "How are you holding up?"

Emotionally? He'd had troubled dreams, but the details had faded from memory shortly after he'd woken. The gun hadn't been loaded, no one had been seriously injured, and with Shane facing charges, hopefully the danger was behind them. "I'm fine."

Adeline wrung her hands. "Next time I'm worried about someone, I should probably send a professional out. I didn't mean to put you in danger. I was worried, but not that worried, you know? I'm really glad you're both okay."

Matt signaled her to stop. "I got there at exactly the right moment, which tells me that ultimately, God sent me, not you."

Adeline chewed her lip, looking like she might come back with another regret.

He redirected. "How's Lina?"

She sucked a breath through a cringe. "Hard to say. She requested a week off and left early this morning for her grandma's old house."

"She went to Maine?"

"Ah ..." Adeline lifted her shoulders helplessly. "She called it a retreat. I assumed it was in driving distance."

Lina didn't have local family. She'd described several of her grandparents' properties, but The Captain's Vista, which Lina had painted so fondly, would make the most likely location.

"You think she's okay?" Adeline asked. "Maybe I should've tried to talk her out of it, but she was in a hurry. Not really looking for feedback."

He could imagine. He'd seen Lina on a mission or two in the last couple of months.

She'd seemed confident—almost to the point of arrogance

—when she'd waltzed through the yard of Visser Landscaping, won the standoff with Pete, and offered Matt a job.

She'd also gone toe-to-toe with Tim when he'd first brought Matt to Key of Hope. Despite Tim's position with the band and Matt's presence, she'd articulated her objections to entrusting Matt with the teaching job.

Yet, the bluster had a soft underbelly.

Lina's tenderness had sent her running to comfort the little girl who'd been picked on at the play. Shane's calls had flustered her, and she'd shrunk with embarrassment as she related the details of his betrayal. Stories of her grandparents brought her comfort, and her parents' disregard chipped away at her self-worth.

She tried so hard to do things right, but her efforts hadn't netted her the meaningful connections she'd longed for.

Matt carried some blame in that area.

She'd been trying to help him cope with the news of Axel, but too focused on his fears of failing her, he'd shut her out. She hadn't deserved to be pushed away any more than she'd deserved the pain Shane and her parents had inflicted.

But was she assuring herself of that right now? Or did a toxic narrative play in her head?

He excused himself from Adeline and started for the studio. As he walked, he withdrew his phone. Pulling up short in the hallway, he leaned his shoulder into the wall. With a prayer for wisdom, he composed a message.

Read it about a dozen times.

Hit send.

And then set about trying to forget that he had as he joined the others just in time for Tim to start the story of their conversation the night before.

∽

FOR ALMOST TWO HUNDRED YEARS, The Captain's Vista had weathered sunshine and storms from its station on the coast of the Atlantic Ocean. White trim outlined the grayed cedar siding, and the wooded property prevented Lina from viewing the water from the drive. She shifted her rental into park.

Variations in the shade of the grass proved the landscaping company had mowed recently, though the golden-tinged vegetation suggested this had been a dry summer. Around the house, the planters and flowerbeds offered pops of fall color. The temperatures, similar to Wisconsin's, would soon dip below freezing, killing off the flowers, but for now, the effect was welcoming.

How had the sea captain who'd built this house felt upon seeing it after a long journey?

Probably not equally conflicted.

She'd moved from New York to Wisconsin on a gust of optimism that distance from Shane and her father would help her heal. Then, her problems followed her. Might they catch up to her in Maine too?

With Shane in custody, the worst she should face here would be a call or two from her father. And troubling texts from Matt.

His most recent message ran through her mind again, almost visible in front of her. What a thing to write.

She hefted her suitcase from the trunk and rolled it up the stone walk to the front door. She'd told Adeline she'd be here for a week, but she wasn't sure the time would be long enough to recapture the peace of mind she'd need to resume her life.

The motherly shushing of waves was out to do its best though. The sound continued even as she stepped into the parlor. On short notice, she hadn't been able to have the house cleaned, but the maintenance company had turned on the water, cracked open the windows for an hour, and uncovered the furniture.

She left her suitcase at the foot of the stairs and made her way through the first floor. Squares of sunlight on the medium-brown wood floors highlighted a layer of dust. Though the dining table and chairs had been covered, they too needed a dust rag.

She rested a hand on the old wood-burning stove's brick chimney, which stood between the kitchen and dining area. Grime coated the mugs and cast-iron pots hanging on the wall, as well as the glass hurricanes of the lanterns. All the rugs, from the one under the dining table to those in the bedrooms upstairs, should be vacuumed. Most of the chores could wait for tomorrow, but she'd better get to washing her bedding because already, she could collapse.

Before leaving the kitchen, she checked the refrigerator. The handful of groceries she'd requested waited for her, ready to sustain her for a day or two, until she had the house running and could venture to the store.

Grandma would've been pleased Lina came here when she'd needed an escape.

After starting a load of bedding in the wash, she made her way outside. The curved shoreline made for gentle waves. Grandma used to enjoy watching birds and the tide from the rocky outcropping by the waterfront, but Lina hauled one of the patio chairs from the shed only as far as the rear patio. The ocean view wasn't as good here, but staying close to the house provided much-needed shelter.

She'd spent far too much time exposed recently.

No more. She would play it safe the rest of her life.

Doubt about her ability to do so crept in as steadily as the tide. Her supposedly wise choices often contained disaster-sized blind spots. She'd thought her dad would let go of selling the land, but he'd sent Shane to get it. Shane and the police confirmed Dad hadn't been any more involved—he hadn't encouraged Shane to steal from her. Not aside from her heart, anyway. The truth was bad enough. She'd told him Shane had stolen from her and broken her heart, and Dad had sent him anyway.

And Shane himself? She'd been engaged to the man.

Given her penchant for trusting the wrong people and getting hurt, what would come next?

She might lose The Captain's Vista. Or the whole inheritance.

She could live without the funds, but she couldn't fathom the sense of failure that would haunt her if she lost the family legacy. Even that goal—guarding the fortune—came up short. Grandma would want her to do more, to use the funds to make the world a better place.

Why hadn't she found a cause to support yet? Another failure.

But with her luck, she'd choose a charity that turned out to be corrupt.

She waved air toward her face and huffed, struggling to catch her breath.

Even though I walk through the valley of the shadow of death, I will fear no evil.

The verse had upheld her during the struggle with Shane, but evil did roam the earth, and Lina couldn't imagine navigating the danger at all, let alone without fear.

"I DID A THING." Tim balled his fists and crossed his arms.

Matt looked to Gannon and John, but the manager had focused on him, and both of his bandmates appeared clueless.

That morning, Tim had come to the studio to tell Gannon and John he'd turned his life over to Christ. After, he'd supervised as Matt figured out he'd have to play seated, with the bass resting on his thigh to avoid feeling like a knife was stuck in his side. Everyone agreed Matt would hold off on singing backup until the pain in his ribs subsided, and they got to work. Tim had left, returning only now as they wrapped up.

Did Tim intend to retell the story of his newfound faith?

"I was there, remember?" Matt laughed, but the sound came out nervous.

"It's not that." Tim cleared his throat. "I told you I would help out with Nadia."

Matt shifted, embarrassed at his choices, their consequences. But what did he have to hide here? Everyone present knew exactly who he'd been, and now that Tim was a believer, everyone here also understood grace. Redemption. "What do you have in mind?"

"I reached out to her."

Matt's throat constricted until he could hardly get a response out. "What?"

"Yeah. Before you went and almost killed yourself. I explained how you've changed and how much good you're going to do in the world, and I asked what her objections were to your meeting the kid."

The kid. Axel.

Throat now thoroughly knotted, Matt rubbed his face. If only he could rub hard enough to remove the regret from his brain. His life. If his own pleading hadn't softened Nadia, Tim's negotiating had probably sealed her against the idea forever. Had Tim learned nothing from causing this problem in the first place?

"She said you're recognizable and Axel's smart. He'd have questions about randomly meeting a rock star. I think she's overestimating an eight-year-old's reasoning prowess, but that's what I had to work with."

"You didn't have to work with anything—"

"I said, maybe you do tell the kid he's meeting a rock star.

Tell him you won a sweepstakes for a behind-the-scenes look at how Awestruck works."

Behind-the-scenes with Awestruck? Now this involved everyone?

Gannon tipped his head, mouth skewed with skepticism.

John, seated, leaned his elbow on the edge of the sound-board and supported his head with one finger, looking poised to go either way—shoot Tim down or laugh him off.

"And here's the thing." Tim shoved his hands into his pockets. "She refused at first, but then she called back and accepted. Though she did have a condition—a few of them, actually. I paid travel, the husband came too, and under no circumstances is the kid to get any hint of any kind of relationship."

Tim *paid*, and the husband *came*.

"Past tense." At least, that was what Matt meant to say. His voice didn't kick in until the second word. He cleared his throat. "When is this happening?"

"See, the thing is ..." Tim freed his hands, splayed his fingers, then interlocked them. "You were upset when you came home from Texas. I reached out that afternoon—Monday. She said no. Then after we finished up here yesterday, she called back. Her husband's work schedule suddenly opened up for a short window, but in the chaos of last night, telling you sort of fell by the wayside."

"When are they coming?"

Tim's skin flushed such a deep red that it showed even in his scalp, through his hair. "They're in the driveway."

Gannon yanked out his phone. A moment later, he turned the screen toward Matt. The security app showed a family of four clustered in the drive, straight ahead of the main entrance as if they'd been told to wait there.

Matt's insides twisted, and his lungs burned. He drew in a breath that sounded like a gasp and caused a slicing sensation in his injured side. "This is a massive overstep."

"I ..." Tim scratched his scalp, then nodded. "Yeah. I was hoping it'd be like ripping off a bandage, but I can see how this wasn't the nicest plan."

Matt rubbed his forehead. "I have to teach in half an hour."

"I told them this afternoon would be a meet-and-greet. All you have to do is say hi. Tomorrow, we'll show them the studio, maybe take them to Superior Dogs and tour Key of Hope. Since you're the only one who works there, I figured you'd do that part. Then, they're on their way again, and you got to meet him."

Matt massaged his arm, registering the feeling, trying to ground himself in reality and work up the nerve and composure he'd need to go out and say hello to his own son.

"You want me to take the lead?" Gannon posed the question hesitantly. For any other fans, he'd already be out the door.

Matt nodded and found himself following the singer toward the door, John's hand on his shoulder, a silent assurance.

The sunlight filtered through the nearly bare branches and onto the drive. The bearded man beside Nadia wore jeans and a flannel. Looking serious, he held their four-year-old daughter. Nadia wore a long dress and a jean jacket. Axel stood in front of her, and she clutched his shoulders as if he'd float away like a balloon if she let go.

The boy wore jeans, a green T-shirt, a light jacket, and a hopeful expression. When the band stepped outside, his eyes widened, and as they descended the steps, he craned his neck to look at his mom.

She was too busy offering Matt a strangled smile.

Axel was old enough that he would remember this meeting. As an adult, would he look back and wonder why his parents had been tense? Or would he write it off as nerves surrounding meeting celebrities? Or would he know the truth by then?

Even if Nadia continued to refuse to reveal Matt's identity,

EMILY CONRAD

Matt could tell him when he turned eighteen, or with DNA tests so readily available, Axel might stumble across the truth himself.

Gannon started his greetings with the husband, and a moment later, John introduced himself as well. But instead of moving on to meet Nadia and Axel, they remained focused on the guy.

They were giving Matt, Nadia, and Axel space.

A flash of inspiration he could only credit to God moved Matt forward.

Thanks to working at Key of Hope, he'd met plenty of starstruck kids and their mothers. He'd treat Axel the same as he'd treated Chris, secret handshake and all.

He felt anxious and unworthy and vulnerable, but he also felt awe, gratitude, and joy. The last of these emotions, he pushed to the forefront. With a quick smile, he silently thanked Nadia for bringing Axel, then he set his focus on the bright-eyed kid who gawked at him.

"Hey, man." Matt extended his hand in the first movement of the handshake. He waited until his son's knuckles bumped his—on the word *love*, tattooed on Matt's fingers.

At the warm, light touch, Matt's legs weakened, threatening to drop him to his knees where he could look in the boy's eyes, find a resemblance, apologize, and ask for a place in his life. Clutch him in a hug.

The action would ruin Nadia's tenuous trust and perhaps shatter something in his own kid, as if Matt hadn't already played a big enough role in obstacles Axel would one day have to overcome.

He couldn't rush into rectifying this. Instead, with faith that God would one day do a much better job at redeeming his broken past than Matt himself ever could, he committed to navigating the situation one step at a time, one cautious interaction, one experience building on another.

Refusing reckless impulse, he opened and turned his hand, guiding Axel into the next step of the handshake. And instead of blowing his cover, when he introduced himself, he simply said, "I'm Matt."

The kid watched Matt's hand closely and mirrored his movements at the first indication of the next phase of the handshake. Distractedly, he replied. "Axel."

Matt caught his hand in a shake, even though it wasn't part of the routine, and met the boy's dark blue gaze. "It's an honor to meet you."

34

*I*ndirect morning light seeped into the kitchen, gray and lonely. As she rinsed her rag in the sink, Lina blinked to clear the grittiness left over from another sleepless night. If only her mind were as anxious for rest as her body. She'd already vacuumed, mopped the first floor, and cycled two more sets of bedding through the wash. What task could she cross off the list next? Preferably one that didn't demand much energy.

Something like dusting, but she'd already wiped the thick layer of grime from every surface in the kitchen. Carrying the rag and lemon-scented spray, she stepped into the dining area. Against one wall stood a short bookshelf stuffed with cookbooks and knickknacks. She dusted the wooden whale figurine, then lifted the old family Bible from beside the carving.

The hardcover King James translation hadn't been Grandma's primary Bible. Lina passed her rag over the cover, then set the cloth down to crack open the book.

She didn't recognize the name written in sloppy calligraphy inside. The next pages contained space to write births, deaths, and family trees, but very little had been filled in. The glossy pages for record keeping gave way to tissue-like pages of the text itself.

Lina exhaled. Whether because of the evidence of family history, the knowledge that Grandma had likely been the one to place this Bible here, or the hope Scripture described, calmness wafted over her more strongly than the scent of lemony polish.

She gathered a blanket and a fresh cup of coffee and stole out to the patio. The chilly air soaked through the thin material of her pajamas, and she wrapped the blanket around herself before snuggling into the chair.

She turned to the last place she'd found any semblance of comfort—Psalm 23. If the passage had worked while facing Shane, it would help now.

To force herself to focus on the text and not her worries, with the King James to prompt her, she muttered the modern-day translation she'd memorized aloud. "Even though I walk through the valley of the shadow of death, I will fear no evil, for you are with me."

For you are with me.

She hadn't remembered that part during the standoff with Shane, but it smoothed the waves of anxiety now, almost as though Jesus Himself had told the storm in her to be still.

The psalm didn't end at not fearing. Instead of blind optimism or rose-colored glasses, faith grounded the psalmist's confidence.

"Your rod and your staff, they comfort me."

She smoothed her finger under the words on the thin page, the paper rustling.

She didn't have to protect herself, though dangers lurked on every side. God was with her, and He would lead and protect her. Her part was to draw close to Him, ask for guidance, and wait for leading.

She'd beaten herself up for decisions she'd made, like not

running from Shane. Who better than she knew how poorly she could discern another's character? But perhaps God had allowed her to discern what was true—or at least true enough —of Shane when it counted.

Maybe the reason she hadn't run was because God hadn't told her she had to. If His plan for her life had required her to run, He would've ensured she did.

The assurance left her aching heart hungry for more. She read on, eyes next lingering on the verse that promised God would prepare a table for her in the presence of her enemies.

If she'd known her enemy was in the house two days before, she wouldn't even have been thawing chicken for dinner. And yet God promised a sense of safety so complete, she could enjoy a banquet, regardless of present dangers. The picture illustrated the epitome of feeling secure.

A gift to her as a believer.

The God who'd protected her from Shane would also prove trustworthy in whatever she faced in the future—threats to the inheritance, issues with her parents, even the risk of loving again.

She lifted her eyes to the ocean, but the view blurred with memories.

Matt's heart had pounded against her ear when he'd pulled her into that protective hold as Shane ran. Had he been afraid after all? Regardless, in his arms, she'd felt secure.

The words of his text came back to her as clearly as the Bible verses she'd just read.

I was at your house because I need you, and I didn't run because I love you. You asked and I never answered, so there it is.

She hadn't replied, and after such a message, a day constituted a significant delay. Had he managed to put it out of his mind, or was he feeling as tortured as she would've felt, were the situation reversed?

The poor guy deserved reassurance, but a conversation that

involved declaring one's love ought to happen in person. Should she go back immediately?

As a seagull swooped over the beach, she pulled the blanket tighter. She'd only just run from Lakeshore to find shelter here, yet she'd found the safety she was looking for in God, not in a location.

She was physically secure right now. Spiritually, forever.

She might have to remind herself of that a million times before she recovered from the scare with Shane, but that was okay. Truth wouldn't wear out with use.

WHY DID YOU NEED ME?

Matt looked from Lina's texted question to the control room. Headphones dwarfed Axel's little noggin, and they must've lifted his chair as high as it would go, or his shoulders wouldn't have been visible through the window. They'd given their guests a tour of the studio suite, and the plan now was to run through some songs for the upcoming tour.

Gannon was still adjusting his tuning, so Matt typed a response to Lina. His injury meant he still wouldn't be singing. This nervous, he wasn't sure he could play, either, but he did manage to hit the tiny letters on his phone screen. Maybe he had some hope of not embarrassing himself.

Advice about Axel. I wish I'd let you brainstorm with me. Now, Tim brought him and his parents here, and it's ...

Behind the control room glass, Tim pointed out something on the soundboard. Both Axel and Zach, Nadia's husband, focused on that, while Nadia seemed lost in thought as she bounced her daughter on her knee.

Matt finished typing his text. *... wonderful, terrifying, and awkward.*

If only Lina were here to help him navigate this. But God

had a hand in it, and Matt had yet to put his foot in his mouth, so hopefully they could get through the day without disaster.

But then what? Axel would eventually need to know Matt's identity. He'd feel betrayed by Nadia and Zach for lying to him, and now that he'd met Matt, he might also resent that his own father hadn't spoken up.

Matt eased a breath in and out. His rib protested, reminding him of his place in all of this. Limited in many ways, he couldn't control the future—or much of the present. That was okay. God had arranged this without Matt's help, and He didn't need assistance now.

He silenced his phone as he put it away. If Axel could only know him as Awestruck's bassist, he would be the best musician possible.

AXEL'S ATTENTION span put Matt's to shame.

Lessons for students so young normally only lasted half an hour, but because he'd wanted as much time as possible with him, Matt had pushed his luck and quoted Nadia and Zach an hour.

After consulting Nadia, Zach had taken their daughter back to the hotel. Tim had left too. Nadia sat in the waiting area, alternating between reading on her phone and watching their interaction.

Not that Matt paid her much attention. He was too busy trying to soak in every detail of his son. After the lesson concluded, Nadia would take him away. Matt had heard the family making plans for their second and final evening in Lakeshore. Nadia and Zach would let the kids swim in the hotel pool, then they'd all get dinner and catch a movie.

No one had proposed Matt have any future involvement in his son's life.

A buzzing note from the bass guitar drew his attention back. "Press closer to the fret. And see if you can straighten out your wrist." Matt modeled the correct hand placement on the neck of his own bass guitar.

Axel's mouth scrunched up as he adjusted.

"There you go. Try again."

Usually, he started his students with classic rock songs, but he'd risked introducing Axel to a worship tune. From the sounds of it, the family wasn't religious. If Matt sent Axel home with this as the only song in his repertoire, he might look up the lyrics and eventually, someday, get curious about the God they praised.

The strategy was a long shot, but what else did Matt have? The lesson was already winding down. Other students and teachers were arriving, getting ready for a normal day of lessons.

Axel was bright, outgoing, and adventurous. He didn't get frustrated with the learning process or mind when Matt corrected him. An eager learner with boundless energy, Axel could grow into a force to be reckoned with.

He could do a lot of good in the world.

No, take that back. It wasn't about the accomplishments the kid could rack up.

Axel *was* good in the world.

If Matt could change his past, he would, but if ever he'd seen God bring something truly good from Matt's failures, Axel was it.

But the excitement and the hope and the longing to connect were all tempered by the impending departure. When Axel left, taking all that promise with him, how was Matt supposed to go about his life as if the best thing he'd ever been a part of didn't exist?

Ten minutes to go, and Matt's breath turned shallow. He cleared his throat and found it scratchy.

Axel played some wrong notes, bit his lip, and focused on Matt. "Is there a bathroom here?"

"Sure thing." With a prayer of thanks for a break to get himself together, Matt showed Axel to the restroom then retreated out the back door to get some air. At the top of the steps leading down to the lot, he braced his hands on his hips and lifted his face toward the sun.

Eyes closed and the light's warmth registering despite the cool air, he silently recited the Serenity Prayer—not just the famous first part, but the whole thing. God would show him the way. And somehow, someway, God would work everything to His good and perfect will.

The noise of a car turning into the back lot prompted him to open his eyes again. The last thing he needed was some stranger taking a picture to hawk to a tabloid. He hadn't missed some aspects of fame.

He sniffed and blinked, then focused on the newcomer.

He knew that car. Or one very like it.

He descended a step toward the asphalt as it parked.

The driver did have curly blond hair. He took another step.

Lina rose from the driver's seat and started for him. "How'd it go?"

She'd come back from Maine—from The Captain's Vista— for him. Hope blazed sudden and bright. He wanted to run to her, crush her in a hug, and ask her to stay close always.

Instead, he thumbed over his shoulder. "Still in there. We're about to wrap up."

At that truth, his voice caught on his despair over Axel. Or was it his gratitude that Lina had come? Was his longing to embrace her amplified because he couldn't hug his own son? He huffed. He had to get it together and get back inside. "I'm not sure how to let him go."

She stopped at the bottom of the steps, hand on the railing across from him. "He still doesn't know?"

"He thinks his family won some kind of sweepstakes to spend time with the band."

Lina scoffed. It *was* unlikely. Adults must've asked more questions about this trip and the supposed prize than Axel. What had Nadia and Zach told their friends and bosses? And Axel's school?

She propped her arm on the railing. "You want him to know?"

"I do."

"And then what?" A notch appeared between her brows.

If he answered wrong, would she feel betrayed, projecting her father's failures on him?

It didn't matter. He'd promised her honesty, and he'd give it. "I'd like to stay in touch and visit, but the news will be upsetting enough without me taking him away from his family by fighting for any kind of custody." Axel had a good home with two parents who loved him. He'd watched Zach interact with him, and they had a solid bond. "For my visits to make sense, he'd have to know."

Lina nodded. "I've been thinking. She's worried what the truth will do to him, but he's got to find out sometime. What if you got a therapist involved and followed his or her advice for when and how to tell him? That way, you're prioritizing Axel's mental health and making sure he has the support he'll need. Offer to pay for it, of course."

He suppressed the impulse to retreat inside and run with the idea. "Other advice?"

She laughed weakly. "You should probably talk to a lawyer."

Probably. He didn't want to bully Nadia, but a lawyer could help him settle on a reasonable offer of child support—support which Nadia may or may not accept. Either way, he could store the money in an account to give to Axel when he became an adult.

If Nadia continued to insist on keeping Axel in the dark,

waiting ten years for him to grow up would be torture, but with God and with Lina by his side, he could find the next best step, no matter the scenario.

As the optimism settled, he studied Lina. Chilly autumn air filled the space between them, but she was all warmth and sunshine, hair alight with the afternoon rays.

"I should get back inside, but after ..."

"Our regular lessons are about to start. You'll have students."

He laughed, and his ribcage was quick with a complaint. "Yes, boss. And after that?"

Smiling, she stepped by him, passing close enough for him to catch the scent of her perfume. Or maybe this time she smelled like the ocean because she'd just been there. She grabbed the door and held it for him. "Then, we'll talk."

35

*A*fter resting poorly before a whirlwind of activity, Lina would sleep soundly tonight, despite the late cup of coffee she sipped—unless Matt had changed his mind about her since he'd texted.

She glanced over the rim of her mug to where he sat at the other workspace.

Or if he'd meant something other than *love* love when he'd said he loved her. Tone might've gotten lost in translation, and here she'd come all the way back over the simple message.

Well, at least this way, she'd met Axel. While Matt and Nadia talked upstairs, away from the curious eyes of the other students and teachers, she'd made the boy hot chocolate and asked him about his favorite school subjects. If Axel had thought anything of his mom stepping away with Matt, he hadn't mentioned it as he'd launched into animated tales about gym and science.

Matt and Nadia descended just in time for Matt's first student. He'd bid Axel an enthusiastic goodbye and turned his attention to his job. Between lessons, he'd found a minute to

EMILY CONRAD

tell Lina that Nadia was open to the therapy idea. Hopefully, from there, things would fall into place.

He hadn't broached the subject of the text he'd sent Lina, however. He also didn't seem to be in a rush to cover the topic, because even now that he'd finished his lessons, he was taking forever to type notes on the day's sessions.

She couldn't ask about his true feelings now, because two mothers occupied the waiting area while their children worked with instructors in the classrooms. As the keyboard continued to click behind her, Lina shut down her computer and locked her desk. Next, she straightened the items on the work surface —a pen, sticky notes, the dish where she set her rings when she put on lotion.

Finally, the wheels of Matt's chair rumbled on the hardwood, indicating he had finished.

She swiveled toward him. "Done?" Her voice squeaked.

Matt smirked. "I'm all yours."

At his earnest tone, a pang shot through her core, anticipation and longing a combustible combination. His smile broadened. The guy knew exactly what he was doing to her.

And she hoped he'd never stop.

"Walk me out?" she asked.

Matt crossed to the coatrack. As he returned with both of their jackets, his posture expressed calm confidence, but his eyes moved constantly as though he harbored real concern that she might be a figment of his imagination.

He helped her into her trench coat, then pulled on his own jacket as they started down the hall. "You were in Maine?"

"I wanted to feel safe. It took going there to realize what I should've known all along—I'm always safe with God."

Matt's low chuckle seemed incongruent with her statement. Lina glanced into the practice room they were passing. Samantha had turned from her student to wiggle her eyebrows at them and give a thumbs up.

338

Lina's face blazed. Whose idea had all the glass been? She stepped into the alcove at the back, exhaling as they finally achieved a bit of privacy. Outside would be even better, but before she gripped the knob on the exit, Matt touched her shoulder.

She turned toward him.

"You *are* always safe with God." His fingers traced to her elbow, then he let his hand fall to his side.

He may have noticed Samantha's antics, but he'd been listening, and that reassured her in a way pangs of attraction never could. After the initial fireworks came and went, this kind of real connection would light the way.

"But it's understandable you needed a reminder," he continued. "You have been through a lot."

"Not because anything got past God. He allowed what happened, carried me through, and will use it for good. Someday. Even if I don't see it now." She caught herself fidgeting and interlaced her fingers. "How about you? How are you doing?"

He leaned his shoulder into the door frame between the back foyer and the rest of the studio. "I'm good. It's funny that as soon as I surrendered my death grip on making amends myself, God brought Axel and Nadia here without my involvement. It's like He was waiting for me to stop trying to take care of everything myself."

"He does seem to expect us to treat Him like He's God." She took a step backward, meaning to lead the way outside.

Matt stayed in place as a laugh rumbled in his throat. "Along those lines, I've been talking to Him about you."

"Oh?" The one syllable was the best she could do.

Matt hooked one hand in his pocket. "You've got good reasons to not trust me. Lots of people have broken your trust, including me when I pushed you away after I learned about Axel. You were generous to come back to help me brainstorm."

"Well, you said ..."

He'd written that he loved her, but it seemed inappropriate to put the words in his mouth.

The hardwood creaked as she backed another half-step toward the exit. If this conversation headed where she wanted it to, she'd rather not finish the talk here.

Matt seemed to inventory the growing space between them. Mischief tugged at his mouth and sparkled in his eyes as he maintained his place. "Which one got you to come back, being needed or being loved?"

"Being safe." She meant to quit there, but she smiled with joy she couldn't suppress. "And needed. And loved."

"And what'll get you to stop running for the closest exit?"

She laughed. "We're at work, remember?"

"So?"

So there were students and teachers and parents nearby. Sure, the practice and waiting rooms didn't have a view of the alcove, but anyone moving around the space could catch a glimpse of them.

If only Matt had done the normal thing and waited for a romantic moment to declare his love instead of shooting it off in a text, having it hang undiscussed for days, and then ... And then she'd come back, and he'd had lessons to teach, and ... "You shouldn't have told me in a text."

He cocked an eyebrow. "Is that a rule?" Challenge smoldered in his tone, and her defenses smoked like kindling.

"Not a rule, per se, but a social norm."

"Maybe it used to be." He straightened away from the wall, and the already-small alcove seemed to shrink. "I'm pretty sure text is an official communication channel now." A step brought him nearer.

Her body buzzed to draw close, but instead, she stayed anchored in place. She hadn't felt so torn between adventure and safety since childhood, when she'd stood on the towering diving board at a friend's pool party, second-guessing the decision to jump. "I guess I'm old-fashioned. Does that change your feelings?"

He dipped his chin and focused on her with confident amusement as though she'd just double-dog-dared him to steal her heart and keep it forever. "I need you, Lina." The man might have talent with a bass guitar, but the low words packed more power than a song ever had. He caught her hand and tipped his head to secure eye contact. "I love you."

Mouth dry and heart racing, she felt as though he'd joined her on the high dive and pulled her to the edge. Daring her to jump. She opened her mouth to accept the challenge by admitting her own feelings, but they hadn't even made it outside.

Samantha's reaction moments ago had been embarrassing enough. What if a student stepped out? Or a parent might wonder what kind of environment this was for their child.

They'd be better off anywhere else. Her house, maybe. Or the parking lot, at least.

"We should take this conversation away from our workplace." She reached behind her for the handle, then stepped forward to get out of the swing of the door, expecting Matt to comply, but he didn't budge. She bumped into him and fumbled back, the meager space between them teeming with invisible currents.

"It must be exhausting to follow so many rules." He watched her expectantly, as if he could sense her muscles tiring of resisting the pull toward him.

Did he remember saying something similar before their first kiss? Probably, and the troublemaker was hoping for a similar response.

"Technically, I'm still your boss here."

"I'm quitting." His promise brushed her cheek as his hand found her waist.

"Oh. And in Awestruck, it's the opposite. You're higher up the chain than I am."

EMILY CONRAD

"Different departments." He circled one of her curls around his finger then released it. "But if it makes you uncomfortable, I'll quit the band too."

She laughed. "You wouldn't."

"Pick you over Awestruck?" Reckless allegiance flashed in his eyes. "Try me."

His resignation letter from the last time he'd promised such a thing remained in her desk drawer. He drew her closer. She kicked his feet as she found her footing. Her hands—wayward things—found their way to his chest.

Awestruck was a much bigger deal than Key of Hope, yet his expression remained sincere. "All I'd need to hear is that you love me too."

"I don't want you to quit Awestruck."

"Then what do rule followers do to make a workplace romance work?"

She realized then what kind of company he would've been on that high dive. He wouldn't push her into the deep end. He'd only keep inviting her until she made the decision for herself. And she loved him all the more for it.

"Talk to HR, I guess."

"Does Awestruck have an HR department?"

"Yes. Her name is Brittany."

Laughing, Matt traced her jaw with a fingertip. "Okay. So do I need to talk to Brittany, or do you ... are you not interested in this?" His focus dropped to her lips and stayed there. He must've seen her smile, because one ghosted his mouth.

She might be able to help him with plans and organization, but he balanced her caution with courage, spontaneity, and the occasional front flip. The least she could do was face the high dive. "I love you, too, Matt."

Where she saw barriers, he saw possibility, and she needed that in her life. Needed him.

She could tell him so—that might even be the reasonable

thing to do—but instead, she kissed him. When reason raced up to warn her about workplace rules and broken hearts and an uncertain future, she tightened her hold on him. He'd proved himself trustworthy in a multitude of ways, from his bravery with Shane to the way he cupped her chin as he kissed her now.

No one in Awestruck or Key of Hope wished them anything but happiness, and they would have it. The future, in every way that mattered, was certain in the hands of the Lord.

36

Three months later

*L*ina tilted her head, focused on the sideview mirror. Behind the vehicle where she sat with Matt, Awestruck's tour bus loomed. In the years she'd worked for the band, she'd spent a cumulative total of four weeks living in a bus. Even then, she'd never stepped foot into the band's own bus. That would change after their next stop, when she and Matt would join Gannon, John, Erin, Adeline, and Tim in the vehicle that now tailed them.

She, Adeline, and Erin were all tagging along for the first week of the tour. Then, Erin and Lina would return to their jobs in Wisconsin while Adeline continued with the band.

This year's schedule included at least a week off every month. If that didn't prove enough for Erin and John, Erin was considering a job change—the couple liked to throw around ideas about opening a custom auto shop. Like Adeline, Erin would hire someone to run the day-to-day, freeing her up to travel as she pleased. As for Lina, she and Matt weren't engaged, and she'd save any job adjustments until after the wedding.

If there was a wedding.

Matt lifted her hand from the broad center console and kissed the back of her fingers.

There would be a wedding.

She squeezed his hand. "Does your commercial license cover tour buses?"

His eyes lit. "Yeah, but it's about to expire, and I think there's a reason the bus is staying behind us until we're almost to Visser Landscaping."

Lina snorted. Both the bus behind them and the truck Matt was driving seemed to be doing fine in the thin layer of snow that had fallen overnight. "They don't trust you to not rear-end them?"

"It is a risk."

"As if those ever stopped you."

"Me? No. Them?" He tipped his head side to side.

Lina settled back into her seat. She hadn't expected the interior of a dump truck to remind her of a cockpit, but the dash angled to give the driver access to a surprising number of controls. A massive center console separated her from Matt, who drove the thing as casually as the pickup he'd purchased a couple of months before.

They'd driven this same road in the smaller truck when she'd accompanied him to spend the holidays with his family. The warmth and love of the celebration had reminded her of Christmas with her grandparents. She looked at the blue sapphire ring she wore daily.

The stolen pieces hadn't been recovered. The contacts Shane had shared with the police had evaporated like morning fog. With the insurance money, she'd commissioned a jeweler to make rings using gemstones from some of the pieces remaining in the safety deposit box. Still, it wasn't the same, and most days, she opted for the one original ring she still owned.

As for the stamps, Shane had overestimated the collection's worth, but Grandpa had acquired a few valuable enough to warrant insurance. Other than when she occasionally paged through the collection, she stored the stamp book in a case that met the appraiser's recommendations for protecting the delicate collectables from the threats of humidity, light, and thieves. Not that anyone had attempted to steal from her since Shane.

She imagined Grandma would be proud. Lina was learning not only to manage her wealth, but to use it for good. She'd set up scholarships for Key of Hope graduates to pursue music in college, and she was talking with her advisors about other opportunities.

Shane was still in custody, awaiting trial. The charges against him were serious, and the district attorney seemed confident in the case.

However the trial—or anything else—went, Lina knew who to trust. The Lord was her protector and defender. If Grandma could hear her thoughts, she'd utter a heartfelt *amen*.

And what might Grandma have thought of Matt? If she were around, he would drive the reserved woman crazy sometimes, Lina guessed, but she also imagined him taking Grandma for a spin in a golf cart, him driving a little too fast, her holding on and roaring with laughter.

Lina's reverie ended as her phone rang. She checked the display and then scanned the white countryside stretching outside her windows. "How long do I have?"

Matt glanced at her, a shadow passing over his handsome features. "Who is it?"

"Dad." She'd been meaning to talk to him. He'd been cleared in the investigation into Shane, but he wasn't innocent.

He'd sent Shane, and he still hadn't given up his campaign for her to sell The Captain's Vista.

"Ten minutes."

That would be long enough. Lina took a steadying breath and answered. "I don't appreciate you sharing my contact information with strangers, Dad."

"Jeremy isn't a stranger. He's an associate of mine and very talented at what he does."

Jeremy was in the hotel industry, and he'd emailed to convince her to part with the house in Maine. She'd copied her father on her response, explaining to both that the supposed "money pit" more than paid for itself as a vacation rental. "I already shared my answer, and I don't want to keep repeating it."

"What you're doing is no different from letting a good hotel go in. Except your way allows fewer people to enjoy the place and takes your continued involvement. If not for sentimentality, you'd have sold. Jeremy's offer is the best you're likely to get."

She'd hired a local company to oversee the property, so The Captain's Vista took little continued involvement. And she'd blocked off several weeks during the summer, one for herself, another for Adeline and Erin to join her, another yet to be planned. Dad's failure to see the difference between memories made in the old house and those created in a big hotel underscored why she wouldn't take his advice. "I've made my choice, but I'm glad you called."

Matt shot her a questioning look, as if to remind her not to sacrifice honesty—a pillar of their own relationship—even with her father.

"Oh?" Dad must've liked what he heard in her tone because his voice brightened.

"You may not like how I manage the estate, but it was Grandma's choice, and I can't have you second-guessing me at every turn." She'd lived too long hoping for his approval, and in recent counseling sessions, she'd been learning about setting boundaries. "I would like our relationship to continue, but we will no longer discuss finances, properties, or the estate. Do you think you can honor that?"

"Your grandfather—"

"—loved Grandma and me very much, and I think he'd be perfectly content to let me find my own way. Can you?"

"If your new boyfriend put you up to this, it's to get his hands on the family fortune."

"You're thinking of my old boyfriend. The new one doesn't put me up to anything."

Matt tipped his head in disagreement.

Okay, he *had* challenged her to try a difficult run on the ski slopes last week. The momentary fear had given way to exhilaration as she'd soared down the hill. Thanks to him, she'd begun to suspect she was capable of more than she'd ever known.

"Think about what I've said. We can try again in the future." She disconnected.

Matt let out a low whistle. "Did you just set a boundary? All on your own?"

"Not all on my own." She'd made the decision based on Matt's encouragement, not to mention advice from others, counseling, and prayer.

Matt shifted his hand, threading their fingers together. "I'm proud of you."

And she was proud of him. He'd changed completely from the man she'd known years before. Even since they'd reconnected over the summer, he'd grown, and she suspected he didn't see how much. He wasn't afraid of his past anymore. He didn't refuse himself a seat at the table out of a sense of unworthiness. He didn't scramble to prove himself.

He simply moved forward in faith, which was exactly what she planned to do.

MATT HAD PROMISED to show his family the tour bus. To hide the surprise—the shiny new dump truck—he parked it so the bus blocked the view of the gift from the office building. Loaded with all the bells and whistles, the truck had taken months to come in. If the dealer had taken three more weeks, he wouldn't have been able to deliver it before embarking on his first Awestruck tour since returning to the band. But God had mercifully granted this chance at closure.

Matt hopped from the driver's seat and reached Lina's door in time to help her down, then held her hand as they circled the bus and started for the building. The noise of the diesel engines—or the massive, black bus out the window—must've alerted his family to their arrival. Jade came tearing out and slammed into him with a hug around his waist.

Lina released his hand, allowing him to swing his niece in a circle as the rest of the family caught up—Mom and Dad, followed by Krissy and her husband. Pete was last.

The sky had been overcast all day, but as Matt did introductions between his family and the Awestruck entourage, the sun broke through the haze, adding a yellow glow to the otherwise white and gray landscape.

Jade, on her own feet again, tipped her head back, staring at the sleek, black behemoth.

What had Axel looked like at Jade's age? He'd missed years, and the pictures Nadia had shared filled in so little. At least the therapist had given the green light to tell Axel about him back in December. Axel hadn't wanted to talk to him for weeks, but Matt had sent a Christmas gift anyway. A few days later, Axel had called to thank him.

Since then, they'd messaged or spoken every couple of days, and Matt had given him a virtual tour of the bus. The band's schedule couldn't take him to Texas soon enough. The day he'd scheduled with his son would go far too quickly, but Matt had prayed about the situation extensively. He'd do his best by his son, and right now, the best he could do seemed to be staying in touch and occasionally visiting.

Jade tilted her head with skepticism. "That doesn't look like the bus I ride."

"That's because we stay on it a lot longer than a trip to school and back. This one's more like Grandma and Grandpa's RV."

"Doesn't look like that, either."

Chuckling, Matt led the way to the door. "I'd better just show you."

From his post in the driver's seat, Jimmy V, who'd been driving for Awestruck for years, offered a wave as they entered.

Jade chirped a hello and proceeded into the lounge. "Whoa." She stopped short, leaving Matt to edge around her. "This is nicer than Grandma and Grandpa's *house*."

Couches, a big TV, and the windows were the main features of the front area, with storage drawers beneath the seats, canister lights in the ceiling above, and strip lighting in the higher space down the center of the vehicle. In the kitchenette, Lina's spread of appetizers and baked treats waited on the table in the four-person booth.

He'd once thought Lina cooked to handle stress, but the fridge stocked even more food, evidence that she turned to the kitchen when she was happy too.

Beyond, the walkway narrowed past the bathroom, bunks, and to the master suite. John had drawn the long straw, so the drummer and his wife got the room for the first leg of the tour.

Matt had asked the guys to leave the blinds open, so the dump truck was visible from the lounge. Outside, John had accompanied Erin to examine the industrial truck. With Matt's family far enough inside, Gannon stood near the front of the lounge with his arm around Adeline, waiting for the realization. But Matt's guests were too busy inspecting their immediate surroundings. Matt answered their questions and led them deeper into the bus.

When the tour brought them back to the lounge and no one had bothered to notice the elephant just outside the room, Matt called up to the driver. "Hey, Jimmy, think we've got enough room to show them the pop-outs?"

"Room?" Pete motioned toward the window. "The lot's hu —" His expression narrowed with confusion. "What is that?"

Gannon grinned, and Adeline bit her lip, smiling.

Dad turned, hands in the pockets of his winter coat as if the furnishings were too nice to touch. "Huh. Wasn't expecting a delivery today. Were you?" He looked to his older son, who was already headed for the exit.

Lina bumped Matt's arm with happy energy as she took his hand.

Dad surveyed the lounge again and chuckled. "Far cry from the van you first left in, back when you three packed up to try your luck in California."

"Those were *not* the days." Matt scratched his neck and shot a glance at the truck.

Pete had probably noticed the absence of the driver by now, if John and Erin hadn't outright told him what the truck was doing there. If they'd held their peace, would he go to the office in search of the non-existent worker before circling back to tell Dad about the mystery?

"Maybe you ought to go see about the truck."

Gannon pressed the back of his wrist over his mouth, clearly suppressing laughter, and led Adeline outside.

Dad waved a hand. "Oh, he can handle it."

"Yeah, but ..." Matt coughed, and Lina's face pressed his shoulder, probably turned to hide a great big grin. "Go see about the truck."

Dad cocked his head, then looked to Mom. "You know anything about this?"

"I'm as bewildered as you." Happily bewildered, judging by the crinkles framing her eyes.

Krissy gave him her wide-eyed, what-did-you-do-now? look.

He shrugged in answer and followed his parents from the bus.

Tim smirked as he watched, his hair kicked up in the breeze. Next to him, Gannon and Adeline cuddled arm in arm, eyes shining with amusement. Ahead, Dad took Mom's hand as they rounded the front of the bus.

John and Erin stood near the dump truck, John motioning to make some point. When they caught sight of Matt's family, they stilled, holding hands and watching.

Dad peered up at the new truck much like Jade had the bus. He shuffled, pivoting back toward Matt with a question in his eyes.

Matt held up the key. "Now I'm not the only one with a cool ride. Except, I have to share mine with a bunch of people, and it's a rental. This is yours."

Krissy squealed behind him and jostled his shoulders.

Dad hadn't moved. Matt stepped forward, offering him the key.

Pete, speechless for once, looked from the truck to Matt and back again.

Mom nudged Dad, whose nose had turned pink. Tears glimmered in his old man's eyes. "You didn't need to do this, Matt."

"I did. I totaled your last one."

"We've gotten by with the ten-foot."

"But it hasn't been convenient."

Dad pushed his hand through his hair and then dusted his palm on his thigh. "This is a lot newer than the one that went under. A lot nicer."

"That's kind of the point, Dad. It's a replacement, and an apology, and a thank-you. All in one."

"Nothing says you're sorry like a dump truck." Pete laughed.

Dad passed his wrist over his eyes. "I'll remember that next time I'm in trouble with your mother."

Mom snickered and pressed him to take the key.

Dad looked at it in his palm. "You don't owe me this, son."

"The fact that you're still willing to call me that after everything I've put you and the family through ..." He took inventory of the faces around him.

Lina beamed at him. Krissy held her husband's hand as she aimed her gaze lovingly at Mom and Dad. Pete gave him an appreciative nod. Mom nudged Dad's arm with contented joy, and Dad cleared his throat.

"I haven't always been the easiest man to please," Dad muttered.

"I haven't always been the easiest to love."

"Well, you don't have to do this for your mother and me to love you." Dad lifted his watery focus from the key. Mom looked about to scold him for refusing, but Dad continued. "But we sure appreciate the gesture."

Mom tsked, apparently impatient with the speed of the exchange, because she rushed forward and clutched Matt in a hug. "We're so proud of you."

Dad's hug was silent, but it involved a lot more back-thumping than normal. Then, he and Pete went to inspect the truck while Krissy snagged Matt for a hug of her own.

As she stepped back, she patted his cheek twice. "Even when you didn't believe in yourself, we believed in you. Believed you were destined for great things."

"Only because of God."

"Still." Krissy winked and settled her arm around her daughter. From his spot by his family, her husband gave Matt a reassuring nod.

With the embraces over, Lina retook his hand with both of hers. She rested her head on his shoulder as his family talked and laughed about the new addition to the Visser Landscaping fleet. One of her curls glided across his neck. "I believe in you too."

It felt like too good of a gift.

Especially when he looked beyond her and saw his other family, Awestruck, waiting for him to rejoin them. They'd get on the road, and the next day, they'd perform the first show of the tour.

Maybe it was too good.

Back in the thick of his addictions, he'd imagined himself an unforgivable failure, but over the last few months, he'd heard more of Gannon, John, and Tim's stories. He'd also talked to Philip a couple of times. They'd all failed. They'd all needed redemption. Not one of them had deserved it. Yet, they served a God who could transform chaos and pain into a song of deliverance, and they'd live the rest of their lives singing to His rhythms of redemption.

Therefore, if anyone is in Christ, he is a new creation. The old has passed away; behold, the new has come. All this is from God, who through Christ reconciled us to himself and gave us the ministry of reconciliation; that is, in Christ God was reconciling the world to himself, not counting their trespasses against them, and entrusting to us the message of reconciliation.

— 2 CORINTHIANS 5:17-19

DISCUSSION GUIDE

1. Which character did you relate to most? Why?
2. People and events from the life of King David were one source of inspiration for the Rhythms of Redemption Romances. In *To Believe In You*, Lina's character has some subtle nods to Abigail. Which ones can you find?
3. Matt and Lina knew each other for years, but Lina is surprised by Matt's eye color when they reconnect. Have you ever noticed a person's behavior changing how you see them?
4. Matt and Lina have both experienced traumatic events since they knew each other last. Matt's experience with Auggie prompted him to draw closer to God, while Lina became less trusting of God and others after her breakup with Shane. What do you think contributed to their differing responses?
5. What are some of the lies Lina struggles with in the story? What might you tell her if you were her friend?

6. Matt takes a number of risks throughout the story, yet he also exercises caution in some areas. Do you think he shows good judgment overall? Is there a situation where you might've counseled him to act differently?
7. Did you play an instrument as a child? Have you kept up with it?
8. Were you surprised by Tim's confession? Do you think Matt handled it well?
9. Were you satisfied by the arrangement between Matt and Nadia at the end of the novel? If you hoped for another resolution, what was it?
10. Have you received an heirloom that is precious to you?
11. Tim has appeared in each novel in the series. What were your hopes for him? How did you feel about the way his part of the story played out?
12. If you've read the other books in the series, where do you think Gannon and Adeline, John and Erin, Philip and Michaela, and Matt and Lina will each be in five years? Ten?
13. What was your favorite moment from the book? Share about a line or a scene that has stuck with you.

ACKNOWLEDGMENTS

First, dear reader, thank *you*. Thank you for picking up this series and investing in these characters. Thank you for all the reviews and encouragement. It's truly an honor to publish stories and share them with others.

I'm grateful to my husband for all he's done to make this dream of publishing possible.

Jessica B., Janet, Amy, Carol, Katie, and Jessica J., thank you for your insightful critiques of this story. Elizabeth, thank you for fitting Matt and Lina into your crazy schedule. I don't know how you do all that you do, but I appreciate the help ensuring I'd portrayed the situation with Axel in a realistic way.

Robin, you've truly helped make this entire series what it is. I'm so grateful to have had your expert guidance on every one of these stories. Working with you has been an answer to prayer and a good, good gift.

To my professional proofreader, Judy, and my volunteers— Kendra, Jane, Sarah, Teresa, and Maria—thanks for tirelessly hunting typos and correcting my grammar. For the record, I wanted to plant a typo in that sentence, but I didn't want to make anyone's eye twitch. If there is a typo there—or anywhere else in this book—that's on me.

Lord, thank you for walking with me through each and every one of these pages. When I first skipped after joy and penned that opening scene between Adeline Green and Gannon Vaughn, starting *To Bring You Back*, I had no idea what

You were up to. You've used this series in my life in ways I never could've predicted. You've once again shown Yourself to be all-knowing and good. I'm awestruck.

Spend more time in Lakeshore with an email subscriber exclusive.

Food trailer owner Asher has seen too many tears he couldn't dry. Determined to be part of the solution, he avoids romance and all the heartbreaking drama that comes along with it.

At least, that's the plan until his heart decides it has a mind of its own. If he can't rein it in, he's destined to break not one but two women's hearts.

Subscribers to Emily's email newsletters will have the opportunity to download *Between the Two of Us*, which is a prequel novella to the Rhythms of Redemption Romances, as a welcome gift. Plus, they receive updates about sales and new releases.

Sign up at emilyconradauthor.com.

ALSO BY EMILY CONRAD

The Many Oaks Romance Series

EmilyConradAuthor.com/ManyOaks

A new series with some old friends.

Philip Miller left Awestruck to secure a quiet life in Many Oaks, Iowa. Several years later, he's running the most successful restaurant and music venue in town. But even charming small towns aren't immune to trials.

A decade before, high school basketball coach Judah Voss lost his life, and each of the twelve players who survive the tragic bus accident was impacted in a different way. Now, these former athletes are trying to make sense of life, faith, and love.

From responsible Anson, who's made it his mission to step into Judah's shoes, to military vet David, who's never met a risk he won't take, the lies reinforced by the accident obscure the truth they need to truly thrive.

Only love will bring it back into focus.

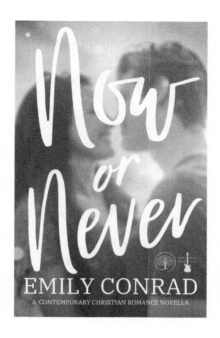

Now or Never - a prequel novella - Gabrielle Voss and Tim Bergeron are both single parents of adult daughters and determined to leave positive legacies that go beyond their successful careers. Will doing so mean kissing their own happily-ever-after goodbye?

The Rhythms of Redemption Romance Series

EmilyConradAuthor.com/RhythmsofRedemption

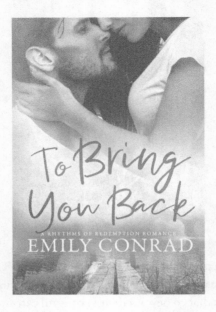

To Bring You Back - Book I - As if her biggest regret wasn't hard enough to forget, now the man she never should've loved is famous. And he's determined to win her heart.

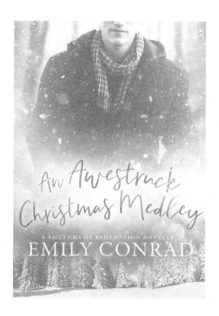

An Awestruck Christmas Medley - Book 1.5, a novella - Four hundred miles of snow-covered terrain, not to mention troubled relationships, stand between the men of Awestruck and a Christmas spent with loved ones. Gannon's made a promise he's determined to keep, and he's not about to let a blizzard stop him.

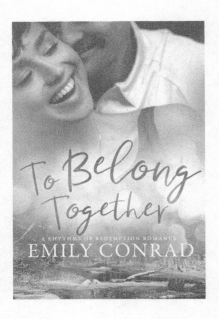

To Belong Together - Book 2 - Drummer John Kennedy can keep a beat, but he can't hold a conversation, so he relies on actions to show he cares. Unfortunately, when he's instantly intrigued by a spunky female mechanic, he can't seem to convey the sincerity of his intentions. Could God intend this pair of opposites to belong together?

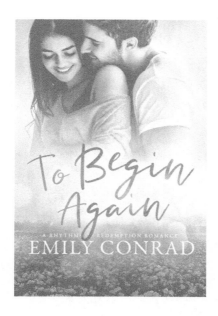

To Begin Again - Book 3 - Whatever faith Philip Miller had died with his wife. Now, "Amazing Grace" is nothing but a lullaby to sing to his children in her memory. With a dark secret threatening his family's future, he has no intention of finding love again. If only he weren't so drawn to pop star Michaela Vandehey, who is in Lakeshore to collaborate with Awestruck.

Subscribe to emails at https://www.EmilyConradAuthor.com for updates on new releases, or find all the latest on the series at https://www.EmilyConradAuthor.com/RhythmsofRedemption.

Stand-Alone Title

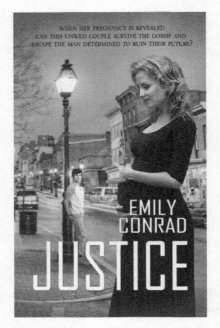

WHEN HER PREGNANCY IS REVEALED
CAN THIS UNWED COUPLE SURVIVE THE GOSSIP AND
ESCAPE THE MAN DETERMINED TO RUIN THEIR FUTURE?

EMILY CONRAD

JUSTICE

*The love of a lifetime, a quest for justice, and redemption that
can only be found by faith.*

ABOUT THE AUTHOR

Emily Conrad writes contemporary Christian romance that explores life's relevant questions. Though she likes to think some of her characters are pretty great, the ultimate hero of her stories (including the one she's living) is Jesus. She lives in Wisconsin with her husband and their energetic coonhound rescue. Learn more about her and her books at emily-conradauthor.com.

facebook.com/emilyconradauthor

twitter.com/emilyrconrad

instagram.com/emilyrconrad

DID YOU ENJOY THIS BOOK?

Help others discover it by leaving a review on Goodreads and the site you purchased from!

Made in United States
Orlando, FL
19 May 2024

47022854R00225